Praise

Ana

"With smart and snappy dialogue, spot-on Manhattan vibes, and a heroine you can't help but root for, Lissette Decos's debut is the escape we all need all year round."

—Meredith Schorr, author of *As Seen on TV*

"It's clear from the outset that veteran reality TV producer Decos knows her subject matter, and Ana is a likable, fun character who will make readers laugh and believe in finding true love."

—*Library Journal*

"Decos's snarky, yet lovably flawed, heroine possesses a searing wit that complements many daring escapades that reroute her career and lead her down a twisty road to love."

—Shelf Awareness

Also by Lissette Decos

Ana Takes Manhattan

Lissette
Decos

takes
one to
know
one

FOREVER

New York Boston

Forever
Hachette Book Group
1290 Avenue of the Americas, New York, NY 10104
read-forever.com
@readforeverpub

First Edition: April 2025

Forever is an imprint of Grand Central Publishing. The Forever name and logo are registered trademarks of Hachette Book Group, Inc.

The publisher is not responsible for websites (or their content) that are not owned by the publisher.

The Hachette Speakers Bureau provides a wide range of authors for speaking events. To find out more, go to hachettespeakersbureau.com or email HachetteSpeakers@hbgusa.com.

Forever books may be purchased in bulk for business, educational, or promotional use. For information, please contact your local bookseller or the Hachette Book Group Special Markets Department at special.markets@hbgusa.com.

Print book interior design by Amy Quinn.

Library of Congress Cataloging-in-Publication Data
Names: Decos, Lissette, author.
Title: Takes one to know one / Lissette Decos.
Description: First edition. | New York : Forever, 2025.
Identifiers: LCCN 2024049638 | ISBN 9781538706770
(trade paperback) | ISBN 9781538706787 (ebook)
Subjects: LCGFT: Romance fiction. | Novels.
Classification: LCC PS3604.E26 T35 2025 | DDC 813/.6—dc23/eng/20241101
LC record available at https://lccn.loc.gov/2024049638

ISBNs: 978-1-5387-0677-0 (trade paperback), 978-1-5387-0678-7 (ebook)

Printed in the United States of America

LSC-C

Printing 1, 2025

for gabby

takes
one to
know
one

Chapter 1

There's a bare butt shaking in my face. Correction. There's a sparkly butt in a barely there thong shaking in my face. There's a butt on the wall, a butt near the ground, and a butt bent over and balanced on one leg. Everywhere you look, there are strong, beautiful booties gyrating to the music.

A dozen or so backup dancers have decided to rehearse in the middle of the hallway in the basement of this arena. They are pure, uninhibited sexiness. And then there's me. The girl in the oversized vintage eighties silk blazer. Standing tall, but stiff. Like a gymnast that's just nailed her floor exercises.

I check my phone again, but the walls down here must be solid cement. I only have one bar and it's more of a stubbed toe than a bar.

I want to bolt for the exit, but some greater force is making me stay put. Like in one of those dreams where you can't move no matter how hard you try. A lunatic with a chainsaw is running toward you but there's a magnet holding you in place. That's how I feel at the moment. It isn't the dancers. *Though they're definitely not helping.* It's because I can't afford to lose my job and there's a very nice man standing inches away, trying his best to get me inside this door so I can interview a singer I know nothing about. I don't even know what René "El Rico" Rodriguez looks like. Is he the one with the bleached-out goatee? Or the one with the thin, twirly mustache?

Ángel, René's manager, has the imposing physique of a bouncer. "We weren't expecting anyone from the label tonight," he shouts over the music.

"Yeah, sorry about that. It was a last-minute thing."

He nods and checks his watch. "He should be ready. Give me a second." He knocks twice on the door and steps inside.

The back of my neck feels clammy, so I pull my thick, wavy hair up into a tight bun with the hair tie on my wrist and check my phone again. Nothing. Not even the stubbed toe is lit up now.

A new, faster-paced song kicks on, startling me. I've hurled my phone across the hall, so I fumble around the backup dancers to retrieve it as they get into a new formation. In unison, the women drop slowly into a deep squat. I'm dumbfounded by them and the way they move their bodies. Technically, I should be more at ease. I'm half Cuban and half Puerto Rican. Cuba Rican. Or Puerto Cuban, depending on who you ask. But I grew up on salsa and merengue. *This* is reggaeton.

Salsa and merengue have rules. There are basic steps you can repeat for the stretch of a song and you'd be fine. Reggaeton, on the other hand, is lawless. Anything goes with this kind of sexy dance music that combines rap with Caribbean rhythms, and it's *way* more sensual. There's a lot of touching of one's body, grinding, getting down low, rolling, bending, ass-shaking, and head-twirling. Reggaeton is salsa on ecstasy.

When I hear this kind of music, it has the opposite effect on me than what's intended. My body receives the signal, and somewhere deep inside there's a longing, but then I stiffen and take on a plank of wood quality. I don't even feel comfortable *standing* here. I suddenly wish I had a sexier stance.

I really didn't think this through. A few hours ago, I was desperate and about to lose my job.

"Dani, you may have already heard, but I wanted you to hear it from me." My boss, Maureen, VP of Marketing and Publicity at Ocean Records, had called me into her office.

"Don't you have a flight to catch, Mo?" I asked, wanting to avoid this conversation.

"I still have a few minutes." She tapped the slim leather watch on her wrist without looking at it. "Grab a seat."

I had heard the rumor all day. We had been bought out by some huge conglomerate, and in the merger, there would be downsizing. Here we were, end of day on a Friday, and I'm pretty sure I read somewhere most layoffs happen on a Friday. It seems unnecessarily cruel to ruin a person's weekend like that. Mondays would be *way* better. Being sent home on a Monday would almost be a good thing, if you didn't like your job. But I happen to love mine.

The aspect of the record label business I'm assigned to is all about looking forward. There are lots of calendars to manage. Production. Marketing. Launch. Awards. Each phase of the process, neatly divided into tabs on an Excel document.

"We've acquired a label out of Puerto Rico." Maureen's voice ended high-pitched with excitement. Late sixties, Mo wears a chic bob of thick ginger hair that's always perfectly smoothed down behind her ears. "We're expanding into reggaeton."

I sat up in my seat, confused. So far, the rumor was way off.

"Unfortunately, that may come with some cutbacks here. But any expertise would be invaluable. Do you follow the reggaeton scene?" My stomach tightened.

So the rumor was at least partly true. There *would* be layoffs. I quickly read into what Maureen was saying. If I could attach myself to this new genre, my position as marketing coordinator was secure.

Maureen isn't just my boss; she's always been my guardian angel. She mentored me all through my college internship and, when it ended, created an entry-level position just to keep me on. I've learned so much from her in the past seven years. I admire her ability to connect with artists. She always has lunch with them when they're in town and gets invited to their weddings.

Mo is in complete control and born for this job. She *and* her office always smell like an expensive candle, and her skin is flawless and matte. I've never seen her break a sweat. If she has any personal problems at all, they're tucked neatly away somewhere in expensive canvas boxes.

As far as I could tell, Maureen's one and only fault is always assuming that just because my parents are from the Caribbean, I have extensive knowledge and passion for all music ever to emerge south of Texas.

"Oh my God, yeah," I blurted out. "I'm very familiar with reggaeton. Been following it for a long time."

"Coming out of Puerto Rico?" She raised one of her eyebrows.

"Well, yes. Of course." The look of relief in her eyes made me feel instantly guilty. "Where else would it be coming from? Am I right?" I was a devious snowball plummeting down a mountain. In my defense, I thought I'd have time to research. As music genres go, reggaeton hasn't been around all that long. I could be an expert by Monday.

"But do you like it?" This time her face was more serious.

My cheeks froze in a half smile, hiding the preparation of another lie. *The only time I listen to reggaeton is when it's forced upon me. Like my little sister, Meri, playing it whenever I drive her anywhere. I could only define it in vague terms: Sort of like reggae, kind of like hip hop, always with the same incessant beat. The kind of music that makes you want to get an extra job so you can buy your sister a car.*

"Do I *like* reggaeton? No, I don't like reggaeton, I *love* it." I leaned back in my chair and exhaled. "Reggaeton is my life. I just can't get enough of it." *When Meri forces me to hear it, I zone out using different techniques.* "I know everything there is to know about it." *Humming other songs is effective. "The Hills Are Alive" works well.* "I love how each song is so different and you can really hear the nuances, you know, the, uh . . . the sounds." *Last summer Meri and I drove to the Keys, and after three hours, I could feel my brain slowly turning to mush.* "But my favorite thing is, um, how this new wave of reggaeton artists are always pushing the limits of the genre, you know?" *Because the same must be true for every artist in every genre, right?*

Mo's face lit up. "That is great to hear. Who's your favorite up-and-comer?"

"My favorite? Oh wow. My favorite up-and-coming reggaeton artist . . ." I spoke slowly to gain some time and scanned the wall behind her. There was the picture of her with one of The Rolling Stones members and another one with Yo-Yo Ma. "There are so many . . ." I said pensively and looked out the window. "It almost feels wrong to pick just one. Like choosing a favorite child, you know?"

I tried to keep it together, but it felt hopeless. I was sinking into the plush chair. I tried to think up an elegant way to excuse myself and thank her for her mentorship all these years, but I couldn't look her in the eyes. I stared off at the view of the green tops of banyan trees outside her window, and the delicate wisp of a single cloud on the bright blue sky...when a name popped out of my subconscious.

"El Rico." At that answer, Maureen's smile became almost too big for her small face.

"What a coincidence!"

"Yeah?"

"Well, this is just amazing. Isn't his voice magical?"

"Magical. That's exactly how I would describe it."

"I knew this would be the right fit for you." The lines around Mo's eyes spread out like sunshine. "You'll get a chance to step into a leadership role. It'll be a small team, so it's not going to be easy. You'll have to wear a lot of hats."

"Are you kidding me? I love hats!" Mo smiled at this. I knew nothing about the label we had acquired, but the only thing that mattered was I had secured my job. I was taking charge and Mo's excitement was contagious. The room felt electric with possibilities.

I was so grateful my sister loved reggaeton. And thankful El Rico's name had somehow lodged itself in my brain. Like all reggaetoneros, he must always say his name in his songs. Just in case we forget who we're listening to.

This could mean better job security. Ocean had released successful albums in the world music scene, but hadn't had any major luck in a long time. A reggaeton artist could go mainstream. Sure, for every Bad Bunny and Daddy Yankee, there were plenty of flops. The genre didn't guarantee success. But if my sister had heard of this guy, he had more potential in the United States than the Bosnian ska band we had been promoting the last few months.

"Do you want to meet René?"

"Absolutely." *Who's that?* I wondered but I was on autopilot. I'd figure it all out later. I was about to thank Maureen for always believing in me, when she told me El Rico was making a guest appearance at a concert tonight and I should pop by for a quick introduction and to get a quote for the press release about his new album.

"What a coincidence that René 'El Rico' Rodriguez is your favorite, right?" She did her best attempt to roll her *R*'s, her compact frame shaking with excitement.

"Yes, absolutely." The skin on my face froze, like the runner-up of a beauty pageant pretending for the cameras that everything's fine. She offered to drive so I wouldn't have to deal with parking.

While I considered feigning a stomach flu, Maureen told me she trusted me. That she was relieved it was me representing the label. How great it was for him to meet someone who really knew him and cared about his music. Mo hadn't met René yet, but she'd had a few meetings with his manager.

"I hear he's not much of a talker. Let him know you're here to help every step of the way," Mo encouraged me as she pulled up backstage.

"Of course," I said, feeling dismal, and slowly opened the door to let myself out.

"He only just recently signed and is recording his first album in a few weeks. Let him know Ocean acquiring his label is a good thing. I don't want him to think we're out of touch," she added.

"Oh, no. We wouldn't want that."

Right then, his manager met me at the door, so I've had absolutely no time to learn a single thing about the guy.

There's a painful pulsing all along my forehead. I'd love to track down a cold towel, but at any moment the door will open and I'll need to step inside. *The one time I lie. The one time I don't stick to the rules.*

I wish I'd had time to request a cameraman, then James could be here with his supportive presence. As one of our regulars for press interviews or behind-the-scenes of music videos, he's reliable and tech savvy. He would have made me feel better and I probably could have used his cell phone. Somehow his budget cell plan always mysteriously secures a signal whenever mine won't.

I take a deep breath. If I could just formulate a few poignant questions, I'd feel more confident. One of the backup dancers flips onto her hands, creating a shaking halo of bootie for the dancer in front of her. The loud music ricochets off the bare walls and isn't letting me concentrate. The lyrics in the song are about wanting to undress all the girls "in el club," as well as all the girls "outside el club."

I can't think of a single question that isn't insulting. *What do you think about the blatant machismo often found in your genre? Are you all for it? How do you make the boring, repetitive beat found in every reggaeton song all your own? That's gotta be a challenge.*

I try to think back to when my sister introduced me to his music. The beats and the vocals sound faint and mumbly in my memory, like they're being played underwater.

Whenever we drive anywhere, Meri and I take turns playing music for each other. I bring in classic punk or new alternative artists from our label. While Meri's turns are almost always reggaeton.

I take a deep breath and decide I have no choice but to go with a less-is-more approach. Pop in, shake his hand, introduce myself, tell him how excited I am to get started and show the world what he's all about. All I need to do is get him to say something fun and interesting about his new album.

The song ends and the dancers finally disperse. Now the sounds of the packed arena stomping their feet and cheering echo down the hallway.

The door opens and René's manager steps out. "All right, we're good. You've got five minutes." I thank him and he waves goodbye, leaving me there.

Five minutes? Five minutes sounds like an eternity. Thirty seconds would be plenty.

I step inside the room and a security guard shuts the door behind me.

There's a large clothing rack near the door preventing me from seeing too much at first. Chill rap music is playing. A relaxing beat with soft Arabic flutes. The whole room seems warm and soothing, and completely the opposite of the cold hallway. I step slowly around the rack and take in the dressing room. Dark wood-paneled walls, well-worn golden velvet sofa, black floors. One wall is a large mirror with old-fashioned stage lights around it.

A makeup artist is sprinting about, a barely clad stylist is sifting through a box of clothes, and a girl in a large floppy hat is lounging on the couch watching me. She's the only one who seems to have noticed my arrival. I muster a half smile in her direction and then turn to face the mirror on the far side of the room. I feel instantly nauseous. My vision goes blurry in what I can only imagine is some sort of stress-induced blindness.

I'm in a house of mirrors.

There are three guys standing next to each other, dressed in the exact same monochromatic look. Thick, white turtleneck sweaters, white slacks, and white sneakers. The one on the right is looking in the mirror and getting his hair teased by a makeup artist, the one in the center is scrolling through his cell, while a stylist is helping the one on the left with the cuff of his pants.

My eyes dart from one to the other. One of these is the real René, but I have absolutely no idea which one.

Chapter 2

I'm with the label. I *should* be able to pick René out of a lineup. From the corner of my eye, I notice Floppy Hat Girl is watching me. Long legged and sprawled out on the velvet couch without a care in the world. Everyone else in the room is going about their business, letting me just stand here.

Seven years of being around musicians, a lot of whom were way more famous, and I've never felt like this before. Worried I'm going to throw up or hyperventilate.

I take a deep breath and focus on the René in the middle. He has a scruffy mustache attached to a thin, scruffy beard. I check the others for wigs or prosthetics, but all three guys seem to have similar bona fide facial hair. They're not identical triplets, though. One is slightly shorter, one's leaner, and the one in the middle has an amazing body and beautiful tan skin.

"This is awesome," says the one on the right. He has an accent I can't quite place, but it's definitely *not* Puerto Rican, so I quickly rule him out.

I check out the one in the middle. He catches me checking

out his reflection in the mirror and his dark, bedroom eyes perk up. A faint grin emerges on his lips. *He seems sweet.*

The one on the left steps away from the mirror, giving the stylist kneeling before him more room to work on his pants. His hand reaches out and pushes a strand of her hair away from her face. The move is slick and flirty. That's *gotta* be him.

I step forward and reach out my hand. "Hi René, I'm Dani from—" His chin tilts up, revealing a confused look on his face. "Ocean Records," I finish half-heartedly.

Floppy Hat laughs.

After a beat, I laugh nervously, too. "Oh, sorry, you got me. That's a great trick." I'm addressing the real René now. The one in the center, who's turned around and side-eyeing me. "I guess that'll be fun…to fool your fans." I'm moving my arms around more than I'd like.

"Are you?" He sounds suspicious.

"Fooled? Yes!"

"No, a fan."

My hands wave off the question. "Of course."

He grins doubtfully, walks over to the girl on the couch, and plops down beside her. Floppy Hat hands him a pair of dark sunglasses. "*¿Para esto me apuraron?*" he grumbles to her as he puts them on.

This is why they were rushing me?

I could pretend I didn't understand. That's what I *should* do. But I need to fix this. Plus, if I don't let him know I speak Spanish now, who knows what he'll say next? Besides, he doesn't have to be rude.

"Listen, I'm sorry," I say boldly. "I…forgot my glasses," I lie, defending myself. "I was in the hallway for so long and it was bright out there and so dark in here. My eyes were still adjusting."

René spreads his arms wide across the top of the couch, clearly annoyed.

He leans over and lifts a dripping golden bottle out of an ice bucket near the couch.

"Champagne?" He's offering but there's something curt in his tone. I can't believe how wrong I was about this guy. There's nothing sweet about him.

"No, thank you."

He dunks the bottle back in the bucket and it sloshes around in the melted ice for a moment before settling.

I collect myself. "So, are you—"

"So, are you . . ." he mimics, "nearsighted or far?"

At this, Floppy Hat sits up and squints her eyes at him.

"You know what, um, it's kind of actually more like *medium* sighted. I can read just fine. And far away is also pretty good. It's more like that, you know, five-to-seven-foot range that's a problem," I ramble, motioning at the distance between the mirror and me.

His eyes soften and his lips twitch as though fighting the urge to smile. At this, Floppy Hat folds a long leg over one of his. I could be wrong, but it feels like she's claiming her territory. René leans forward and gently taps her, making her lift her leg back up and away from his.

She adjusts her whole body, crosses her legs the other way, and snaps her head in the direction of the stylists and the extra Renés. "All right, guys," she yells, clapping a few times to get everyone's attention. "Can everybody wrap up? We need to get going."

Everyone shuffles out of the room, leaving me alone with René and his *girlfriend*? *Personal assistant?* Person who can throw her leg on him *and* order the team around.

"So, you must be excited to start working on your new album?" I say enthusiastically, trying to smooth things over. "Anything you can share about it for our press release?"

"You speak Spanish?" he asks, ignoring my questions.

"Yes. I'm half Cuban, half Puerto Rican." *And half hoping this gets me a few points.*

He raises his chin and drops his gaze to my blazer. "Half Puerto Rican," he repeats. "The good half." His voice has dropped to a sexier octave.

"Well, I don't know about tha—"

"I'm just kidding. You should loosen up."

My jaw tightens. I have an aversion to being told to "loosen up." I've heard it a lot. Like *a lot* a lot. Every single time I've tried to pick up a sport or a musical instrument. How can I "loosen up" my wrist *and* hit a ball at the same time? It doesn't make any sense. It's not like I haven't tried. The problem is, I don't know how loose is loose. I have two extreme settings: stiff or completely undone. Like when they shut off the inflatable tube guy at the car dealership. Neither of which can serve a tennis ball.

"Do you dream in Spanish?" His voice is low and casual. I don't know if it's the unexpected and *somewhat intimate* question or the way he's delivered it, but he's cut through all my wires and I'm suddenly calmer.

"That, um, actually, I think I might."

"Yeah?" His face brightens with interest.

"My college roommate told me I talked in my sleep in Spanish." He nods approvingly. "She went out and bought a Spanish dictionary because she wanted to make sure I wasn't saying anything about her."

René smiles wide. It's a sweet, friendly smile. The kind you'd never expect from someone this good looking.

"What about you?" I'm trying to play it cool, but it feels like someone's started a fire inside my blazer.

"That depends." He pulls his sunglasses down. "Will my answer be on the record?"

At this, Floppy Hat adjusts in her seat impatiently. She grabs loose strands of her sandy blonde hair and brings them out in front as though someone's about to take her picture. René is perfectly still but there's a lot of movement on her end of the couch. If I weren't busy trying to get a handle on my own situation, I'd feel bad about hers.

"I would hope so. I *do* need a quote for the press release. Do you ever get ideas for songs in your dreams?" I'm impressed with my determination to get the job done.

René pushes his sunglasses back in place and leans over to Floppy Hat. "Can I have my phone?"

At least I *hope* I'm getting the job done. And that I'm only just imagining the abrupt change in his demeanor. That just because he's scrolling through his phone doesn't mean he's gone back to ignoring me.

"You said you're a fan, right?" After a few quiet moments of scrolling, he stops and hovers a finger over his phone screen menacingly. "So, I'm wondering, are you a fan of my old songs or the new stuff?"

He taps the screen and a reggaeton song takes over the speakers. It's nothing I recognize. Just the same repetitive beats. "Yeah, mmmm." I pretend I'm tasting something delicious. Something I've had before and I'm so happy to be eating again. But I can't even tell which of the two men singing

is René, let alone where this particular song lies in his reper-
toire. The only thing I know is that I've begun to sweat. Like a
lot. "Amazing. I love . . . this era."

"How about this one?" A woman's voice comes on, then,
after a few stanzas, what I presume is René's. Of course, *his* cell
phone would get a signal down here.

Actually, I *have* heard this song before, but had no idea it
was his. I bob my head along to the beat, trying so hard to
remember the words. I'm actually moving my mouth, attempting to keep up with the lyrics.

René's barely moved a muscle. If we *were* having a moment
a few seconds ago, it dissipated the moment I brought up the
press release. His stupid, gorgeous face is actually enjoying
watching me squirm.

"What's the name of this song again?" René hollers over the
music.

My stomach flinches. This can't be happening. I can't believe
I'm being quizzed about René "El Rico" Rodriguez for the second time in one day. Please, music gods, don't let me lose my
job over a reggaeton song.

Someone knocks hard on the door, saving me.

A woman walks in holding a red leather jacket. René lowers
the volume and hands Floppy Hat the phone and his sunglasses.
He gets up and takes the turtleneck off, revealing a strong chest,
most of which is covered in tattoos. He also has a sleeve of ink
that travels up one arm and wraps around his neck.

He slips on the jacket without a shirt underneath and checks
himself out in the mirror. He's got this whole brooding bad boy
thing going. Will definitely help with sales, I think. And he has
nice lips. Some would even call them luscious. But his roller
coaster of a personality takes away from the overall appeal.

I glance around the room, pretending to be interested in the shade of the paint on the walls. When I look at him again, he's watching me. I do my best to maintain eye contact, while ignoring the warm churning happening in my stomach. Between the sweat and the heat, it's now officially a sauna inside my blazer.

Floppy Hat snaps a picture of him with her phone, then he steps away and poses for another. He clearly enjoys the fashion angle of the job *and* he's got swag. I'll give him that. He takes the cell and turns the camera toward her. She takes her hat off and extends her legs off the couch, striking a pose.

"How about recording the album at Ocean Records' studio in Miami?" I ask, trying to get a handle on things. "That will be nice. We're really close to the ocean."

"Nothing like the beaches back home," he says, handing the phone back.

"Believe me, I know," I say with intense passion, then tap my hand anxiously against my thigh because I've never been to Puerto Rico.

He takes the jacket off and hands it to the stylist. He stands there, hands on his hips, looking at me like he's actively trying to solve a puzzle. "What do you miss about our beaches back home?"

Maureen was wrong. She said he wasn't much of a talker, but he sure asks a lot of questions. And he's incredibly comfortable being shirtless in front of strangers.

I smile nervously. "Oh, you know..." His dark eyes get smaller and I feel he can see right through me. He knows I have absolutely no idea what I'm talking about. *Fried cod on Flamenco Beach.* The memory of the song my father used to sing all the time distracts me. I pause and decide I don't want to lie. Not about this. "Actually, I've never been," I say at last.

René eyes me silently for a moment, then steps away. He's helped into the turtleneck and takes a seat back on the couch.

I need to change the subject. *Keep calm and carry on.* I've always appreciated that expression. Well, that and any motto that implies forward movement. "So, can you share *anything* with your fans and any potential new fans about the album?" I'm desperate.

"Nothing at the moment."

"How about influences?" I spit out.

"Sure."

"Any you care to mention?"

He looks away, considering this, then looks back to me. "No."

Carry on. Even when there's a large boulder in your way. One that wants to be difficult on purpose.

"How about—"

"What do *you* think I should say? Since you know me *so well.*"

I fight the urge to shuffle in place. "Okay. I think it can be simple. You're clearly excited to get into the studio. You could mention what an amazing opportunity it is to work with Ocean." I'm making it up as I go. "How you're hoping our diverse, international roster will open doors to some unique collaborations," I suggest, remembering that the two songs he played had other vocalists in them.

René grunts. After a long pause, he shakes his head and exhales deeply. He seems upset. I don't understand what's happening. A dark cloud has floated in above him.

"We should get going," Floppy Hat says gently, trying to help.

I want to cheer him up too. Bring him out of whatever hole

he's crept into, but I have no idea what's upset him. "Listen, everyone at Ocean is amazing. You're in good hands, I promise." René doesn't budge. "The music always comes first. In fact, we're going to make an in-depth behind-the-scenes of your album." I remember Mo had mentioned this in the car. I turn on my best peppy professional sales pitch. "The goal is to really capture every step of the process." This was my idea at the last company off-site. We were brainstorming ways to support an album with more impact, and I suggested an intimate portrait. Being there when the ideas sparked, having original content for each release, not just the first single. I thought it would especially help fans connect with new artists. Get them invested and subversively bring the attention back to the music and away from the disconnected nature of social media and music videos. Looking at René now, especially his inability to answer a simple question, I could see why Maureen had suggested we do our first one with him.

René shakes his head slowly. "That's not happening."

"Really, it will be great." *Just keep on keeping on.* "It'll be fun. We want to make something beautiful. Something intimate."

René lifts his head toward Floppy Hat and they look at each other for a moment. They seem to be speaking telepathically.

"This way we can really tell your story, as an artist. As a *Puerto Rican* artist," I add, grasping.

"So"—he turns toward me—"you understand the importance of keeping things authentic."

"Yes. Absolutely. That's *exactly* what I'm saying."

"I'm so glad we're on the same page. And it is a great idea. A behind-the-scenes, something authentic and intimate in the only place that can really happen."

"Uh-huh. Yep." My steam is dwindling.

"So you agree. My album can't be made in Miami," he announces, eyes narrowing.

"Huh? I'm not, that's not up to me—"

There's a double knock on the door, and Ángel steps inside. "We have to go," he says, addressing the room.

Floppy Hat slips out of the room in a blur. René follows her, then stops by the door to look at me.

"Thanks," he says. There's a broad smile on his lips, but it's rude. It's a rude-ass smile. My whole body tenses, but I smile back as professionally as I can.

René's manager is watching me from the hallway, holding a thumb up. "How'd it go? Got everything you need?"

"Oh yeah. And then some." Feeling numb, I step outside and let the door slam shut behind me.

Chapter 3

"WHAT DECADE WOULD YOU SAY DESCRIBES YOUR MOOD?" I glance up from the computer.

My mother's face scrunches up and her body shifts from left to right. "My mood is my mood," she responds finally, tired out.

"The twenties?" I suggest. "Or maybe the sixties?" She shakes her head, disgusted with these options. Like those decades personally wronged her.

"Right, we'll come back to that one." I check that there aren't any pets beneath me and nudge the kitchen stool closer to the counter. I click on the arrow and the next question pops up on the screen. "Would you describe yourself as a sunrise or a sunset?" I'm filled with hope she'll get into this one.

"What does that have to do with the windows?"

"This helps them get a sense of your personality, so they can put that into the design," I explain.

"They should come meet me." It's Saturday morning and she isn't going anywhere but Mom's long black hair with its single patch of gray is freshly washed and blow-dried, and she's wearing her favorite lace choker. The thin black one that makes her look like a lounge club singer.

"They will. But we need to do this first. I'd say you're a sunrise."

Her shoulders rise and fall as if to say, "Tomato, tomahto."

Dejected, I click on "sunrise." I considered filling this out on my own, but I really wanted her to get excited about the project. *And less upset about me taking on another big expense for our house.*

Last year it was the roof that needed replacing. I only have three payments left on that. Now we need to replace all the old windows with new storm-impact-proof ones.

Our roof guy recommended it. He said hurricane-force winds can break through windows and lift the entire roof off a house. I've had nightmares about it ever since. In my dreams, our house gets picked up by a tornado and dropped haphazardly in dangerous places. I wake up and our small, Spanish-style house is hanging precariously off the edge of a cliff, or in the middle of a busy airport runway.

I'm afraid we're one hurricane season away from a "We're not in Kansas anymore" situation. Still, my stomach constricts at the thought of the cost. I tap my thumbs nervously on the counter to try to drum away the anxious thoughts racing through my mind. Like how I sent the deposit check to the design team exactly one week ago. Before I heard about the potential layoffs. And before my "El Rico" debacle last night.

He's completely knocked me off my game. What did he even mean about not wanting to make the album in Miami? I push the thought away and focus instead on my failure to get a single usable quote from him for the press release.

I should have stuck around for the performance, but I was

desperate to get out of there. Had I stayed, I could have scoped out his Miami fans and asked them a few questions. Hearing what they had to say about René recording his first album could have been interesting. More interesting than what he gave me anyway. Which was nothing.

"Okay, this section helps them assess your ideal color palette."

Mom grins and raises a single eyebrow. "I can do the curtains myself," she offers.

I know what she's trying to do. She's trying to save me money, but I want to skip all that and get to the part where she's excited to get something done right. What could be better than custom-made window treatments by the very people who are making the windows?

"Trust me, they're really good at curtains and blinds." *And tearing down walls.*

I haven't told her about the biggest part of the project yet. She's not happy about the windows or the curtains, so there's no telling how she'll react when she hears I'm having them replace the small window in the sunroom with a floor-to-ceiling, wall-to-wall glass panel. It will brighten up the entire house and let the outside in. She'll be able to enjoy her garden more. I'm sure she's going to love it. I just want to make the house safer *and* nicer.

"I have no doubt you can do the curtains, Mom. But they'll use an actual tape measure and not their arm," I tease.

She humphs. "Don't make fun. My arm is exactly one yard. *Almost* exactly."

I let out a sigh, grateful an almost tense moment is over. Working together on anything for the house is such a delicate balancing act. I know she needs me to help with big things like this, but then she gets upset when I want to do them properly. When I hire actual professionals and not her friends. Or when I have the audacity to pull the proper permits.

Mom refills my coffee, then using a spoon, smacks large ice cubes in the palm of her hand until they resemble the crushed ice she knows I like but our old fridge quit making a while ago. She pours them into the glass and I smile. I want so much to make her happy, but sometimes it feels like an impossible task. She has no idea the amount of vendor research I've done or the fact that I've personally spoken to past clients for references.

"Okay, just a few more," I say brightly, getting us back on track. "Where in your home do you first go to in the mornings?"

"The bathroom," she teases.

I can't help but laugh. "*After* the bathroom."

"To the sunroom, to feed Baby."

"What about when we don't have Baby?"

She purses her lips, not wanting to imagine a time when we won't have the injured duck she took in a month ago. In addition to our full-timers—three dogs and two cats—Mom takes in fosters all the time. We'll often have a litter of kittens in the tub so tiny, they don't know how to pee yet. She's up all night rubbing their bellies in a circular motion after they drink. And now we have a duck. I have many concerns about the duck. Wildlife violations and all that. But Mom was born in Cuba, and Cubans fix things. The crushing lack of resources forces you to be, well, resourceful. "Resolver" is Mom's favorite word. One must resolve things for oneself. You don't hire professionals, or buy tape measures, or call the city when a duck appears on your lawn with an injured leg. In her defense, the duck's limp *has* gotten better.

I'm losing her. Mom's light hazel eyes, almost green in the sunlight, are staring out the kitchen window. She doesn't seem to age, my mom. In the living room, there's a large black-and-white photograph I took of her for a college photography class. To me, she still looks exactly the same. In the picture, she's holding a small cactus in each hand near her boobs, with the widest, most mischievous smile. Dad loved that picture, said I captured her essence.

"Do you like to entertain?" As soon as I've read it out loud, I try to read Mom's face. I wonder if she's gone where I have. To the memory of all the parties we used to have. To Dad and his band performing here near the kitchen. Moving the furniture in the living room against the walls and filling the house with salsa music. How he'd leave the band in the middle of a song to dance with her. Walking away from his shiny mustard-colored conga and abandoning his friends on the *guiro*, *maracas*, and the *clave* to fend for themselves.

I shove the memory away. *Keep your face to the sun. Take the money and run.* Just a little trick I do whenever I feel stuck or overwhelmed. I summon a catchphrase or a song lyric and move on with my life. Sometimes I make one up. Anything uplifting can become a mantra when you need it. *Get on the bus, Gus. Chug along, little Suzie. Buy some new pants, Dan.*

Some might call it avoidance and to those people I would say: *When you're going through hell, don't pitch a tent.* "Let's just get to the next one." I try to move things along. "Describe your idea of—" I stop myself. *Describe your idea of a perfect date.* There's no need to go there. Mom hasn't been on a date since Dad passed away six years ago. She rarely socializes at all.

Her mind seems to be fluttering around. I worry the

questionnaire may actually be depressing her. "You know what, let's just get to the best part." I click past a series of questions.

Who doesn't love before-and-afters? And there are some breathtaking ones on this site. I stop when I find what I'm looking for. A picture of a gloomy living room side by side with its transformation, a bright, gorgeous sun-drenched space. A small-windowed wall now has a floor-to-ceiling glass panel like the one we're getting. I turn the laptop around with flair.

"*Ay,*" she winces, waving a hand in the air.

"You don't even want to look at them?"

"It's too much money. We shouldn't do it."

"I got this. I've already signed the contract, I told you. And sent the deposit."

She looks me in the eye and gives me a weak smile. "Okay, okay."

I feel the familiar jab of disappointment.

This shouldn't be such a struggle. It's clearly what's best for the house. The place that's morphed, grown, or shrunk depending on our needs. Like when Dad passed away, I turned the garage into an in-law suite we could rent out for extra income.

I can't do anything about the decor, but I'm in charge of the finances and general upkeep.

Our house is pale pink, with a matching low perimeter wall that keeps the wild plants in. The yard is spotted with palms that are neglected yet somehow thriving. The grass grows in patches and there are pavers that don't lead anywhere. Inside, there's dark floral textured wallpaper, large comfortable couches, and a farmhouse dining table. The vibe is Copacabana meets Little House on the Prairie.

"They're so talented, you're going to love it. It's going to be okay, Mom."

I'll just have to wait for the right moment to tell her about the extent of the project. For now, just making sure she doesn't demand I cancel the entire thing is a win. Based on this bizarre questionnaire, I can see why she may not trust these people to pick out her curtain rods, let alone knock down a wall.

Chapter 4

I'M STARING AT A PICTURE OF RENÉ WITHOUT A SHIRT ON. *FOR strictly work reasons, of course.* He's humorless behind his dark shades, head tilted up. I drag the mouse, zooming in on one of his tattoos, and make a note. *Puerto Rican flag on heart.* I've spent the day on the couch with José José, our elderly dachshund, cuddled beside me while I crammed on all things El Rico.

The verdict? Attitude aside, he's extremely talented. *And in demand.* For over a decade, he's been writing songs for other artists, collaborating on major hits, and recording a *lot* of duets. As far as I can tell, he's been the secret ingredient to almost every successful reggaeton dance hit of the past few summers. All little tidbits of information I wish I knew yesterday.

Another major takeaway: He's as big a jerk in his songs as he is in real life. On almost every single track, René's the bad guy who threatens to steal your girlfriend, succeeds, then leaves her hanging.

Still, his voice is unlike anything I've ever heard. It's perfectly imperfect. Sure, he only pops on for about twenty seconds in a duet, but when he does, his unique voice cuts through and marks its territory in a song. I can't believe he's thirty-one, practically a spinster in recording artist years, and hasn't been signed until now. Maybe that's why he's wary of record labels.

He has a loyal fan base. There's an entire Reddit thread dedicated to discussing whether he and his personal assistant and stylist, Camila Gómez, aka Floppy Hat, are secretly a couple. He's also been linked to a few of the women he's collaborated with and a handful of models. René is extremely private. The spokesmodel for a brand of designer sunglasses, he never takes them off. His social media presence consists entirely of curated images of his sunglasses casually strewn about wherever he goes. Sunglasses in a recording studio. Sunglasses at a restaurant. Sunglasses on the edge of a hot tub.

I've dug up every "El Rico" interview to be found online. There are only a few from early on in his career. None of which were particularly helpful. He doesn't open up to *anyone*. Granted, most interviewers back then only wanted to hear about the more well-known artists he was collaborating with.

So I'm hoping his tattoos will help me learn something about him. Thankfully, there are innumerable shirtless photos of him online. I find a picture of him from behind and jot down more notes. *Research significance of large bird on his back. Is a phoenix a real bird?*

I'm feeling less confident than I would hope after this many hours of René research. My biggest concern is that he will demand to work with someone else. *Someone who knows what he looks like.* Then again, it's been over twenty-four hours. If he were really upset, my boss would have heard by now. I hold José José's sweet face in my hands. "Right?" He leans in, resting his head in my hands. "By the way, blink twice if the duck is pestering you."

"Mom, I need a *despojo*," my sister, Meri, announces as she flings her bedroom door open.

She's wearing a tight yellow tank dress and has crafted ornate twirly shapes on her eyelids with yellow liquid liner. She's standing, head tilted back melodramatically, waiting for a reaction.

"*¿Por qué?*" Mom calls out as she walks over.

"First, I can't get Juan out of my head, and now this test. None of it is going *inside* my head."

"Okay, let me see if we have eggs," Mom replies casually.

"You need a spiritual cleansing to help you memorize better?" I ask, not looking up from the computer.

"Pretty much, yeah." She doesn't sound like herself. Her voice has a gruff, tired quality. She drags her feet and plops down next to me on the couch. "So, how did it go? You have to give me a little more than 'It was fine,'" she begs, inspecting René's physique on my computer screen.

"It was okay." Thinking about last night makes me feel nauseous, but I can understand Meri's excitement. I've finally met someone at work she actually listens to, but I don't want to burst her bubble and break the news that René's a complete asshat. *Or admit that I didn't recognize him.*

"What did he say? What was he wearing?"

The memory of René standing in front of me without a shirt on begins to take form, so I shake it away. "Let's talk about your test." I close the computer, and Meri drops her head dramatically. "Are you sure you don't want me to hire the tutor? You know, instead of an egg."

Meri sits up. "No, it's fine," she says firmly.

"Seriously, the offer is still there." I know it's not the best time to suggest it, seeing as the window deposit will wipe out my bank account. Private tutors aren't cheap, but I found one that has great reviews for visual learners like Meri. It took her four years to get her AA, and for the past three years, she's worked as a sales rep for a well-known beauty brand while she's attempted to pass the nursing entrance exam.

Nursing wasn't what I expected for her. She spent most of her teen years watching or creating makeup tutorials on social media, but I'll admit I was relieved. Nursing is secure. Nurses make good money. Nurses make overtime. Double, if they're sent to a city where they're in high demand. Still, the college admits students only once a year for the fall. So for the past three years she's been stuck in a continuous loop. *Study for the test, take the test, fail the test, wait for the test.*

Mom hands Meri an egg and steps outside. "You want one?" Meri asks, waving the egg in the air.

"No, I'm good."

"*Are you?* Have you heard from him?" Meri sounds concerned.

"Who?"

"Your ex. You forgot about him already?"

"Oh, James," I say, relieved. "No, I haven't forgotten about him. We're fine."

"Do you miss him?" She's motionless in front of me, determined to get to the bottom of things.

"No."

"That's kind of sad."

"No, it isn't." It's been two months since we broke up, I want to add. But then I remember that Meri won't think that's much of a defense. James and I dated for a year and I wasn't especially sad when it first happened either.

I see it as a win that we've been able to slip right back into friendly colleague mode. Isn't that the best of all possible scenarios?

"I knew it. You didn't seem *perdidamente enamorada*." Mom purses her lips, contemplating. She's standing by the double doors that lead to the backyard, listening to every word.

"That's a good thing. I don't want to be 'lost in love.' That sounds awful. 'Lost' isn't a healthy relationship goal, Mom."

"He was too serious," she continues, disregarding what I've said.

"I liked that he was serious. *I'm* serious."

"That's true." She sounds disheartened, as though disappointed of the reminder.

As they step into the yard, I can't help but feel more left out than usual. They're so alike. Meri cooks like my mom, makes Cuban coffee like her. Try as I might, I've yet to achieve the damn *espumita*. They're both excellent dancers and will break into salsa at the slightest provocation. My sister could dance before she could walk. *Literally.* And anytime Meri's heartbroken, Mom is there, ready to jump into action. Wave an egg, read her tarot cards, or drop some seashells into a cup of water to help lure the guy back.

I know she's proud of my accomplishments. First in the family to get a degree, my job at the label, but I have this feeling nothing would make my mom happier than to find me sprawled out on my bed, in tears over a guy. Heartbreak, she understands. This cold, unfeeling daughter, she does not.

Before James, my previous relationship lasted three years, and that one also ended amicably and tearless. Who wants to be lost in love? No, thank you. I prefer to know *exactly* where I am at all times. Where does falling get you?

I watch through the window as Meri, under Mom's guidance,

slowly waves the egg around her head, and then her whole body. I hate that my sister is still hurting over her cheating ex.

Of all our differences, our taste in men is the most distinct. Meri always seems to fall for the wrong guys. The hot ones who talk a good game, then turn out to be untrustworthy liars. I prefer no promises to broken ones. I love a man who's rational and restrained. It's why I think Spock is the sexiest character on *Star Trek*.

Mom grabs the egg from Meri and takes over the cleansing. They look like the Witches of Eastwick out there, waving an egg around in the moonlight. There's a tugging in my chest. Meri's only five years younger, but when our dad died, I felt that gap widen. I could see in her eyes how afraid she was. She's strong-willed but extremely vulnerable at the same time, and I wanted so much to take the worry and heartache away. For Mom too. Even now if I could bubble-wrap them, I would. Put *them* in an egg carton.

Mom holds the door open for Meri, who walks through the house holding the egg out in front of her. "Now just throw it out into the street, into the intersection."

"I know," Meri says.

"Well, that's done." Mom sounds certain she's cured whatever was ailing my sister.

I wish I could believe that were true. Because at the moment, I'm picturing Meri walking down the street, throwing the egg out into the busy intersection, hitting a passing cop car, and getting arrested.

Chapter 5

I GET TO WORK FEELING LIKE I'VE DONE SOMETHING WRONG. Something *other* than lying to my boss about knowing who an artist is. René's words have haunted me all weekend. *My album can't be made in Miami.*

It doesn't help that Maureen has gone uncharacteristically silent. I managed to put something together for the press release and sent it to her last night, but I haven't heard back.

After some digging, I tracked down an online chat room of René enthusiasts. And it felt like a small miracle when I found a couple of fans who were at the concert Friday night. They were kind enough to meet me for a drink and give me a few comments for our press release about René's new album. To hear them talk, you'd think he was reggaeton's answer to Bob Dylan. *A poet. The voice of a generation.* Sure, if Bob were into girls who wear "*nothing but thongs to the club.*" A lyric from one of René's collaborations I have problems with. Mostly to do with logistics. How are these girls getting to the club? Are they riding in a taxi in their thongs? Are they sitting down at the club? Are they leaning against a wall in line for the bathroom? It's impractical and unhygienic.

René's fans were a little wary of the big record deal, but they said as long as he didn't sell out, they'd follow him anywhere.

I drop my things off at my desk and head toward the common area, past the bright Art Deco Miami furnishings, the photographs of artists and all the autographed memorabilia on the walls. Acoustic guitars, electric guitars, a surfboard.

Work has always been my safe place. For the past few years, my job has helped me feel balanced. It's been filled with long, predictable days of coordinating and planning. Sure, back when I was an intern, I dreamed of working on the creative side of marketing. I wanted to be the one who had the vision and who collaborated directly with the artists. Over time, I slipped into the parts of the job where I was most needed. Like helping bring *Maureen's* ideas to life, so *she* has time to work with the artists. It turns out, I am the queen of breaking down concepts and corralling them into calendars, tracking budgets and hiring designers. I feel needed *and* appreciated.

Not today. Today, I'm uneasy. I've finally been assigned an artist and it's *my* vision I'm supposed to be implementing, but I may lose my job before I ever get the chance.

I reach the common area with its high ceilings and modern, rectangular blocks along one wall that form stadium seating decorated with colorful cushions on every level. I take a seat in the center of the top row and look over in the direction of Maureen's office. I try to imagine a scenario where everything works out. There's always a chance that René didn't have his manager call to tell her what happened. You never know. Granted, best-case scenario, I'm still assigned to work on promoting

René's album. I wouldn't even know where to start. How do you promote an enigma? A cocky, obnoxious, difficult enigma.

If anyone can smooth things over, it's Mo. She's the artist whisperer. She manages to keep them happy while still having their respect. I've yet to see her lose her poise, no matter how outrageous a request.

We have a band that demands everything in their dressing room be blue. Blue rug, blue furniture, blue light bulbs in all the lamps. One legendary crooner's rider includes having someone vacuum their dressing room just before a show. Not because they're neat-freaks, but because it relaxes them to sit there and watch.

As the stadium seats fill in with executives and staff from every department, my cell phone pings. I pull it out of my blazer and click on the unread email from the window design firm. It's an automatic reply, letting me know they received our completed questionnaire. Too bad after today, I may not be able to afford them. I switch the phone to vibrate, set it down, and contemplate what it would be like to get fired after they've ripped our old windows out.

"Dani, pray for me." Alba, my most stylish coworker, takes a seat in front of me. She's wearing a dress with a cool sticker-like graphic of pizza slices all over it. "I'm interviewing 'Tokyo or Paris' after this."

I wince in commiseration. "Good luck with that." "Tokyo or Paris" is how we've been referring to one of our new artists. A young socialite-turned-singer who came across a tad snooty in her first round of media when she said, "I think I was at a nightclub in Paris when I first had the idea for this song. Or maybe it was Tokyo?"

"She was in a choir when she was little." I lean forward.

"I didn't know that."

"Yeah, that's how she started out. Have her talk about that and maybe sing one of her favorite songs from choir. That would help make her more approachable, and I think she'd enjoy it."

"I love it." She grabs my hands and shuts her eyes dramatically. "Thank you."

"You're welcome." I feel my body unwind itself, and I exhale for what feels like the first time in two days. Too bad Mo wasn't here for this exchange. Maureen's the one who makes the introductions at these functions. She's supposed to get things started, but she's nowhere in sight.

There's some confusion down in the front of the room. The heads of Sales and Legal seem to be in a heated debate, while our VP of Human Resources stands awkwardly a few feet away. My heart kicks into overdrive.

Mo must be somewhere putting out a fire. That's the only thing that would keep her away. What if *I'm* the fire? What if she's on the phone with Ángel right now? I don't know what else I would do. This is the only job I've ever had. If I'm forced to leave here without Mo's support or reference, where will I be?

"Sorry for the delay, folks." The head of Sales is now holding a microphone and addressing the crowd. "Thanks for coming, everyone. Unfortunately, Maureen isn't...available at the moment." He glances off in the direction of her office. "We want to welcome this young man from Mexico City. I've only just met him, but we're really excited to have you here, Fabian."

A lanky guy in his early twenties walks into the room holding an acoustic guitar. "Thank you for having me," he says, adjusting another microphone on a stand.

We have presentations like this all the time. It's a great perk getting paid to listen to live music, but I always feel bad for someone having to perform in an office on a Monday morning. The bright lighting and phones going off at reception can't possibly set much of a mood, but they do their best to try to win us over.

No matter how much work I have, I never miss one. Even if it means I'll have to stay late. For a new artist, having to sing your heart out on a Monday morning is bad, but doing it to a bunch of empty seats would be worse.

I love a performance day. The energy is so special. It reminds us that we are the keepers of something new. It's ours to support, promote, and help grow. We're a part of something being born. Sure, the artists are doing the cool part but our role is critical. We're basically the doctors who help get the baby out into the world. The forceps, if you will.

Fabian begins with a sweet pop song. It sounds more like he's talking than singing but I can see why we've signed him. He has a smooth, beautiful voice. Though the poor guy is standing still and looks visibly nervous.

Nearby, a phone begins to vibrate loudly against the wooden seats. I glance around, ready to judge the owner silently, when I realize it's my phone, which has fallen between the cushions. Maureen's name flashes on the screen.

The only thing more off-putting than Maureen's absence from this performance is Maureen calling me *during* the performance. Before I can answer, it stops ringing and I find she's also sent a text.

Come to The Dragon. ASAP

I rise to attention and then immediately hunch over in an attempt to make myself seem smaller. I head down the steps, ignoring the confused glares of the entire office. I make it to the front just as Fabian hits the chorus. I bob my head supportively to the beat, all while power-walking in front of him as nonchalantly as I can.

As I reach the hallway to The Dragon, my pace slows. Along the walls, there are framed platinum and gold records and an extra-long modern purple couch. All of our recording studios have been given powerful, albeit cheesy, names. There's also El Matador and Kilimanjaro. The wide door to The Dragon has a narrow glass window so I peek inside. Maureen's talking to someone just out of sight. These doors are professionally soundproofed, so I can't hear a thing. Her body language isn't reassuring. Arms crossed, shoulders slumped. Okay, I'm officially panicking.

I brace myself and open the door.

"There she is." The man's voice is dripping with feigned excitement. I turn to my left and find René leaning against the back wall of the studio. He steps out of the shadows and walks toward me.

It takes me a moment to react. The entire weekend, I stared at pictures of him hiding emotionless behind hats and sunglasses. At the arena, he wore dark sunglasses most of the time. Now, he's standing here and there's no wide-brimmed baseball hat pulled down over his eyes, no dark wraparound sunglasses covering half his face.

Looking at his bare face now, I'm somewhat taken aback. His dark eyes are so expressive, filled with bravado yet somehow vulnerable at the same time. And those lips—it's downright criminal and counterintuitive to every marketing bone in my body that he hides this face. He's wearing baggy gray pants and a tight iridescent shirt with the sleeves rolled up tight around the shoulders, showcasing his strong arms.

I lock eyes with Maureen and hers widen. I can't tell what

emotion she's transmitting. Exhaustion? Concern? Shock that I had the audacity to show up to work today?

She's like a gentle mom, but can be tough when necessary. If Maureen comes down on you, it's because you've messed things up royally. I've only seen her get upset twice. Once with a coworker who leaked confidential information to the press accidentally and another time with a particularly difficult record producer. Both times she kept her frame compact and never raised her voice. The only way you could tell she was angry was the vein bulging out of her forehead.

"Is it true?" Her tone is brusque but there are no signs of a vein on her forehead. Unsure which part of my disastrous meeting with René she's just heard about, I shrug slightly. "I'm just very confused." She sounds wounded.

"I was just explaining to Maureen," René chimes in, "how it all happened."

"Oh yeah?" I offer noncommittally.

"I was telling her how we just got to talking, about this and that. And how"—his dark eyes sparkle at me conspiratorially—"you know, you just knew me so well. Knew *my music* so well." I don't like his tone. It's dripping with sarcasm and performance. I can only hope Mo isn't picking up on any of it. "You just knew exactly what I needed. It was like you read my mind, right?" He pauses, waiting for me to agree.

Feeling like I have no other choice, I nod, though my neck no longer feels all that flexible.

"And fun. We had so much fun," he adds for Mo's benefit. She twitches nervously, trying to keep up. "Then"—he steps in closer, with a big announcer voice—"I told you how happy I was to have signed with a label who knew me so well, with a team so thoroughly up-to-date with me and my music. That's when I threw out the idea and you agreed with me. You said it was the only way." He blinks and looks right at me. "My album has to be recorded in Puerto Rico."

A nervous chuckle escapes me. I stand there dumbfounded for a moment. Suddenly, it all clicks. René hasn't told Maureen about any of my flubs, but he's clearly holding them over my head.

"So you can imagine my surprise," Maureen begins to rattle off, and when I pull my eyes away from René, I see it. It's happening. The vein on Mo's forehead is alive and pulsing. "Why would you even suggest that," she says between her teeth, "without consulting me?" I open my mouth, but she continues, "Knowing full well it's more...affordable to keep it here"—she gestures a hand around the large room—"where René's supposed to start recording in just a few weeks, in the state-of-the-art studio we own and therefore don't need to rent. Where we already employ a talented technical support team. Right here in Miami, where so many artists live and work and are readily accessible to collaborate with." I've never seen Mo have to work this hard to keep it together.

She's clearly distressed about having to talk about any of this in front of René. I notice, for the first time, the absence of Ángel. It's uncommon for an artist to stop by our office without at least one person from his team.

I glance at René, who's been watching me. He rubs his neck and tilts his head. His eyes are actually pleading with me to play along. He *really* wants this. And I want to keep my job, but I'm not sure how to do both.

"Yes," I respond, dragging the word. "Yes, I did because..." Each syllable fluctuates between high and low, and Mo, visibly baffled, hangs on each one, anxiously awaiting the end of my response. Looking past her, I take in the studio. It's massive and professional but also cold and lacking in personality. Enormous soundboard, a recording booth so big, I've seen it house an entire jazz band with their instruments.

"Because..." With an eye on Mo's forehead vein, I speak slowly. "I think it's the right thing for him. I mean, this will be his first solo album ever. He's finally putting himself out there. He has good reason to want to keep this on his turf," I reason, officially sounding like the newly minted El Rico expert I've become in the last forty-eight hours. "René's fans will follow him whether he makes the songs in his closet or here in our studio, but..." As the words sprinkle out of me, I realize I believe what I'm saying. I *do* know what he needs. "He *should* make this album in Puerto Rico. The proof is on his chest, in the tattoo he wears next to his heart." I toss in a little more info I picked up for good measure. "I'm sorry for not consulting with you; I got caught up in the moment and knew you'd want him to be comfortable and start things on the right foot. But of course, you have the final say."

The vein on Maureen's forehead hasn't retreated, but René's features have softened. He's clearly surprised I've rallied and defended his cause with such gusto. He's squinting at me, clearly happy, and I feel a buzz all through my body.

"But no press," René interjects, snapping me out of it. "Not until I'm done with the album. Remember?" He prods me, as though this is another thing we've discussed.

I've gone stiff again. The gall. I haven't even gotten Mo to agree and he's already piling on another request.

I shake my head no, but my mouth says, "Right, right. We *did* talk about that." I gather myself, refusing to be rattled. Mo watches us with curiosity. "And that's why I told you we'd be doing the in-depth 'behind-the-scenes' of the album." Take that, El Rico. Two can play at this game. He flat out said he wouldn't do this when I brought it up back at the arena. "It's perfect, actually. The behind-the-scenes will feed the press whatever it needs, so they'll leave you alone. You see," I focus on Mo, inspired, "René's main problem is, he's in a vulnerable place at the moment." René shifts uncomfortably, clearly wondering where I'm going with this. "He's been hiding behind his sunglasses and whoever he's collaborating with for too long and he needs to come out of his shell," I say, sure of myself.

"Fourteen collaborations in eight years." I shake my head, as though these are terrible stats. "Now, it's just going to be him. Of course we need to keep the press away. René needs all the help he can get, so he can branch out in new directions. Because let's face it, how many songs can one write about cheating, am I right?" I raise a shoulder at Maureen. "And you agreed"—I glare at René—"you said, 'I repeat myself a lot and I'm stuck in a rut.'"

He lets out a patch of air. "Stuck in a rut of hit songs," he replies as though correcting me. And holding himself back from a more biting response.

"Stuck nonetheless," I announce, pushing on. "No more doing what's become comfortable and second nature. You said you were done recycling the same old tired ideas and—"

"That's not what I—"

"Recycling, upcycling, I can't remember exactly. Something along those lines."

René's mouth puckers. He's cross but also clearly impressed he's got a worthy adversary. I match his pucker, and a zap of energy courses through me.

"Wow, well, that all does sound good." The vein has

vanished. "I hear you, Dani." Friendly, motherly Mo is back. "And I hear you, René. Just remember this all comes from your advance. The more you spend, the more pressure we put on your album. But if we can keep the budget under control, I can get the higher-ups on board about Puerto Rico."

René is visibly relieved. He pauses, taking both of Maureen's hands in his. "Thank you." He's soft-spoken and sincere. When his hands finally release hers, I'm wholeheartedly expecting them to head over in my direction. Instead, he uses them to slip on the pair of sunglasses that have been hanging from his shirt. "I should get going."

"Of course! We'll walk you out." Mo sounds more like herself.

We walk down the hall in silence, with Mo vigorously typing into her phone and the sounds of the performance still happening ahead of us in the common room. René has us stop at the end of the hall to watch while remaining just out of view.

Fabian is still standing in the same spot. This time, he's belting out a fast-paced dance song. It's extremely peppy. The kind of song you hear when the credits are rolling. When everything's been resolved. Up and down the bleachers, torsos sway to the music. René is moving to the beat, too. Not a care in the world.

Meanwhile, I feel tense and frustrated. I fight the desire to look at him. Where's the grateful nod in my direction? Any form of acknowledgment would be nice.

The crowd breaks into applause and René slips away from us. We follow after him, pressing our way slowly past the swarm of coworkers eager to get back to work, dispersing in every direction.

When we reach him, René is in the middle of complimenting

Fabian. "You sounded incredible, like you had a full band up there with you," he offers. Fabian is nodding vigorously, trying to take it all in while clearly being star-struck.

"This is good." Maureen leans over, flashing me her phone. "Ángel's assuring me he can keep the budget under control." I gaze at her and smile absently. "I'm glad you're running the creative on this one." She squeezes my hand. "You've clearly got a handle on it." My throat is a tightly knit pretzel. "Now that it's in Puerto Rico, I wouldn't have been able to do it anyway," she explains, eyes on her phone. "Things are crazy here, but I'll try to make it down there for a weekend."

My breath shallows as more of my new reality sinks in.

"When was the last time you went to Puerto Rico?"

"Oh"—my voice trembles slightly—"I've never been."

Mo tears away from her phone and smiles approvingly. "But he's refusing to do any press until the album's done"—she's switched into problem-solving mode—"so we have to cover every step of the process. You'll need to go deep, get meatier material, you know?"

"Sure, sure." I'm trying to remain calm, but inside, alarms are going off. I wasn't able to get the guy to answer a single question the other night. Most of the time, it felt like he was interrogating *me*. And just now, he didn't push back against us filming a behind-the-scenes, but I'm certain he would have if Maureen hadn't been there.

As she responds to a message, I watch René and Fabian posing for photographs. The look on the newbie's face is pure joy over having El Rico fawning over him so generously.

"Oh," Mo says, reading a new message that's popped up on her phone. "Sounds like they have an affordable solution already in mind."

"Yeah?"

"It's the previous home of some actor who had a recording studio built in, so we'd save on that. It's on a small island just off the coast from San Juan."

My body shivers, as though it's experienced a chill. "Oh, that's great." There are a few islands, I reason. *There's no way it's the same one.*

Chapter 6

WHEN I TOLD MERI I WAS GOING TO SPEND A MONTH IN Puerto Rico, she went through all the stages of grief in a matter of seconds. There was denial, anger, bargaining. "I don't believe it. You're lying. This isn't fair! I'm going to be saving people's lives and nothing like this will ever happen to me. Take me with you. I could be your stylist. I'll carry your suitcase."

I'm hopeful she's moved on to acceptance as she swings a straightening iron close to my ear.

"That's so much better, thank you." I admire the half of my head that's sleek and controlled.

Meri looks at her handiwork and smiles at my reflection in the mirror. When I attempt to do this myself, I end up with visibly jagged edges where I've held the iron for too long. I look like an anime character.

I admire her reflection lovingly in the mirror. Her dark brown hair falls over her shoulders, and a few lighter-colored strands frame her face. My little sister always looks so put-together. I don't know how she finds the time.

Just being with her calms me. Her room is the same size as

mine but feels cozier and more lived in. The furniture is larger and fills up the space, so it wraps you up with its four-poster framed bed and thick warm throws. Mine has more of an IKEA showroom vibe to it. In my defense, I've been planning to move out for years but keep pushing the date. Secretly, I'd hoped to be in my own place by my thirtieth birthday, but that's only six months away. At the rate I'm going, forty seems more feasible.

Meri divvies up a new patch of my hair to work with and eyes me suspiciously in the mirror. "So. Culebra Island, huh?"

"That's right." I do my best to seem unaffected.

"How are you feeling about it?"

"Great." She's got enough going on right now. The last thing I want to do is worry her. No need to tell her that for the last two weeks, I've simultaneously prepared for the trip and hoped a meteor would fall at just the right angle at the Miami International Airport, so there aren't any injuries but it's also impossible for anyone to get on a flight for a very long time.

Meri eyes me tentatively. "Really? So you're not feeling sad or any kind of way you want to talk about."

"Nope. I'm really happy about it. But it's not like we'll have much free time. We'll be in the studio every day."

She stops what she's doing and looks into my eyes, holding the straightening iron up in the air. "And James is your camera-man," she says, getting back to work on my hair. "Won't that be awkward?"

"Why? Everything's gone back to how it was before we dated."

Meri purses her lips like she doesn't believe me.

When Maureen explained we could afford only a one-person show, I immediately thought of James. He can run camera and sound, and he owns his equipment so we'd save money on rentals. I didn't even give it much thought. James was the logical choice. So what if we haven't had an actual conversation about anything other than work since we broke up two months ago?

"Seriously, I just want to make something beautiful," I tell Meri. "This was my idea, you know? To shoot an in-depth making of an album."

For the past few weeks, I've watched a lot of music documentaries and I've decided I want to make something original and inspired. No tired interviews of artists sitting by a soundboard or a wall of speakers, no boring shots of them recording in a booth that never feel spontaneous.

I want to capture the magic. Do I wish I were going to be doing it with another artist? *Yes.* But I'm not going to let that minor setback get in the way of doing a great job. "You can't get another first and ten without a couple of fumbles," I say more to myself than to Meri. She reaches over me to grab her phone off the dresser and taps away diligently, hiding the phone suspiciously away from me.

"What is that?" I try to get a glimpse of her phone.

"Nothing."

I try to snatch the phone from her, but she pulls it back.

"Here, I'll read it," she says and clears her throat. "'Meri, keep your eyes on the prize, not the bumps on the road,'" she declares in a monotone voice. "'Runners don't look back, because if they do, they'll lose the race, or fall, or both.'"

My mouth drops and then I start to laugh. I've sent my sister a ton of inspirational quotes, but I didn't know she'd been keeping a list.

"Is that supposed to be my voice?"

"'The future is a risk, but "no risk, no glory." And trust me, "glory" is always waiting just around the bend.' That one's weird, but I love it."

I can't help but smile, then moan. "Fine, I'll stop sending them."

"No, please. Never stop," she says.

When she finishes my hair, she combs through it with her fingers. "I can't believe it. You're going back to our roots." Meri sounds satisfied. "How did Dad's song go? He used to sing it all the time." She starts humming the tune and immediately I feel a familiar ache in my chest. I want to tell her to stop humming it. Instead, I stand and pretend to look for something in her closet.

It's complicated. I feel like someone's playing tug-of-war with my heart. There's the pull of finally getting to see the place our dad was from and loved so much. *Wrote a whole song about.* But then there's a yanking in the other direction, because I'm not sure I'm ready to see it without him. His biggest dream, other than hearing one of his songs play on the radio, was for us to go there together. But we were always too busy or too broke for a vacation.

"Do you want to borrow something?" Meri asks excitedly.

I check out the multitude of colors and patterns in her closet. "No thanks, I'm all packed." Whenever Meri finds me something while out thrifting that fits and I feel good in, she's noticeably bouncier and her eyes light up. She spins around the room, eyeing me from different angles, hoping I haven't changed my mind. It's the sweetest thing. You'd think she'd just cured me of some ailment. Though I do believe, for her, feeling your best does have healing powers.

"How are you so chill? You're about to spend a month with René. I wouldn't be able to sit still. I wouldn't be able to sleep."

I can understand what she means. At work, René's group-
ies have revealed themselves to me over the past few weeks.
The head of HR and even hard-core music buffs have come by
my desk to chat about him and what I know about the new
album.

"Why do you *actually* like him?" I sit back down on the bed,
facing Meri.

"What do you mean? He's a bonbon. A chocolatey sweet
bonbon."

"But you don't know anything about him. No one does."

"I know a few things," she says slyly, like she has a secret.
"Check it out." She digs her laptop out from under a stack of
textbooks on her nightstand, finds what she's looking for, and
turns the computer screen toward me. It's a picture of René kissing Natalia, two-time Latin Grammy–winning pop star from
Colombia. They collaborated on a duet two summers ago and
ended up dating for a while after that. It's a selfie, so one of them
must have been holding the phone while they were kissing.

"Where did you get this?" I ask. While I came across a few
paparazzi shots, I didn't find anything this intimate online.

"I'm just a really thorough fan," she announces
self-righteously. "Fine. This was on Natalia's social media. I'm
always on the lookout for pictures like this, and save a screen-
shot before they get deleted. Which happens every time celeb-
rities break up and start seeing someone else." She pulls up
another photo of Natalia and René getting ready for a night
out. "But I don't share them with anyone," she says, defending
herself.

"So you're a stalker who also respects their privacy?"

Meri doesn't hesitate. "Exactly. And if you want to send me
some more for my collection, that would be *so* appreciated." I

shake my head, so she continues, "You're going to have so much access, Dani. I've never asked you for anything like this before."

"Because that would be unprofessional." Inside, I feel something soften. Early on, just after we lost our dad, I felt Meri trying to keep up with me, and grow up ahead of her time. So, stalking aside, I kind of love when Meri does silly, immature things like this. Like when she asked for sparkly pink roller skates last Christmas.

Meri clicks on the next image. René and Natalia, embracing by a pool in their bathing suits. I read they were inseparable for a while, until he cheated on her. *Big surprise.* I linger on the image longer than I would like. He seems so happy.

I close the computer and a wave of exhaustion hits me. I shut my eyes and try not to think about the overwhelmingly difficult task ahead.

When I open them, Meri's bent over and looking through a stack of papers by her bed. After a moment, she sighs.

"What's going on?" I ask gently.

Her eyes tear up. "I bombed it. I failed the practice test."

"Oh no. I'm so sorry."

"It's just like I'm blocked or something. I don't know what to do."

"What about the tutor?"

She blinks and takes a deep breath. "It's so expensive."

I wrestle to get the words out. "No, it's not. Let's do it." The tutor I found boasted a high success rate of helping students pass the nursing entrance exam. Meri comes closer each year, but has never secured the minimum scores for acceptance. The next test is three months away and I can't, for the life of me, imagine how she will feel if she fails it again.

"Thank you. Maybe just for a month." Meri sighs.

"Whatever you need, seriously."

Using Meri's laptop, I enter my credit card information on the tutor's website, and it's a relief when it goes through. Instantly, I feel the purpose and satisfaction that come whenever I can help my family. Now I just have to keep it together the next four weeks. Make sure I'll still have a job when the bill comes in.

Chapter 7

THERE'S A YOUNG WOMAN WEARING A POOFY NEON PINK VEIL by the baggage carousel. She's blindfolded and her ears are covered with bulky purple headphones. And just to be sure nobody gets it wrong, she's also wearing a BRIDE TO BE sash across her chest.

Her friends hover around, taking turns holding her arm so she doesn't wander off or bump into anything. Once in a while, she sings along to what they've programmed to keep her from hearing any clues. When she does this, her friends chime in, too, and dance around. They're wearing matching T-shirts with a picture of a guy's face on it, presumably the groom.

I'm full-on staring. We all are. The captive audience waiting for our bags in San Juan.

One of the girls gawks at someone walking by. I follow her gaze and find James. Behind him, a late afternoon haze is coming through the airport windows.

"That would be my nightmare." I gesture in the direction of the girls as he approaches me with a luggage cart.

"Oh yeah?" He rests one foot on the cart and tucks a hand

into his pocket. James exudes the ruggedness and accountability of a guy in a J. Crew catalog.

"How come?"

"I don't see the logic in it. It's like, 'You're getting married, so let's celebrate by taking you somewhere you didn't choose.'"

"Fair enough." He nods once.

"What if I don't like where you've chosen? And how can I pack appropriately? What's even in her suitcase?"

"Maybe they packed it for her," he offers.

"That would be an even bigger nightmare."

He chuckles and I can't help but smile, relieved we're in a good place. Meri's wrong. It's a good thing neither of us was heartbroken. This is the best kind of relationship. The kind where, if it ends, you slip right back into being friends like nothing ever happened.

Now that I'm here with him, I try to think of something I *have* missed. I liked spending some weekends at his place in South Beach. But it's not like we ever actually went swimming because I felt the current at that part of the beach was too strong. Sex was a solid B+, but frankly, I don't miss that either.

A suitcase pushes through the rubbery black curtain, and my shoulders shudder. I tell myself it's just a healthy mix of nerves and excitement. Every step today has been a step closer to the island and there are only two steps left. Collect bags. Get on ferry.

Things will be fine with René. He owes me now, I reason. I helped him get the label to agree to recording his album in Puerto Rico. At the very least, we should be even.

James gets to work, grabbing heavy equipment cases and methodically organizing them onto the cart.

"That's a lot of baggage," I tease.

"I brought extra cameras and backup equipment. I figured there won't be much on the island."

"Good thinking." James always plans ahead. It's a relief to have someone I can trust on this job. Someone dependable and patient. James is also the best-dressed cameraman I've ever worked with. He has an impressive collection of smart, button-down dress shirts. You'd never know he was going to lug around heavy camera equipment all day.

I see my bag and let it keep going for a moment before I reach for it. Only one step left. The ferry.

"See you in"—I check my watch—"four hours."

"You got it. Be safe." He nods and heads off in the direction of his connecting flight, while I head for the exit.

I'd like to believe it's René's fault I'm not taking the quick island hopper flight to Culebra with James. But the truth is, I feel personally responsible that we're starting this album over budget.

So I'm determined to cut costs wherever I can. With only two flights going to the island a day, they were actually a bit pricey, so I opted for the ferry.

The cab takes over an hour to get to the dock just outside of the city. But even with traffic, I arrive with plenty of time to make the five o'clock ferry. My suitcase slips out of my hand with a thud and I drag it toward the dock. I swear my bag feels heavier than it did in Miami.

A mixture of tourists and locals are already standing on the narrow gangway waiting to board the small ferry parked at the dock. Families with children in strollers, older couples, a group of guys lugging fishing gear.

I take a seat near the ticket counter because I'm feeling a bit carsick. Then again, I *did* spend the entire ride responding to work emails and texting Meri to check in on things back home.

A couple of backpackers walk up to the counter and inquire about ferry tickets. *What kind of person just shows up to a ferry an hour outside of the city without a ticket? Without any assurance they'll be able to get on?* To my surprise, they secure tickets. Good for them, I can't help but think. Ah, to be young. Though, to be fair, they don't seem all that much younger than me.

At 4:30 p.m., the boarding announcement is made and I join the small flock. The sea is choppy, so the gangway and the boat rock back and forth. I should probably wait a few more minutes for the motion sickness from the cab ride to pass before acquiring a new one. I decide to check the vending machines I spotted near the ticket counter for crackers.

After a few splashes of cold water on my face and a can of ginger ale, I make my way back to the dock. My eyes scan the horizon. I can't believe that in about an hour, there will be no more steps. I'll be on my dad's island. Focusing on work is the only way I know to get through this. I walk onto the bridge but there's nothing at the end of it. The ferry is gone. I snap my head and find it, bobbing and dipping over the waves just past the next dock.

My watch says 4:41. Was that the 4:41 ferry? Or was that actually the 4:30 ferry and it was running late?

"Excuse me." The ticket window attendant is in the middle of building a tower of rental boogie boards. "Where's the five o'clock ferry?"

"That was it."

"But"—my breath catches—"it's not five o'clock." She looks at me like I've just said something unrelated. "Why would it leave early?"

The attendant finds someone to talk to and then comes back to me. "It was at capacity, ma'am. Everyone was on it."

It's not my first "ma'am," but they haven't stopped stinging. "But everyone *wasn't* on it. I wasn't on it."

The guy at the airport ticket counter is judging me harshly. His eyebrows shoot way up to the middle of his forehead when I tell him what I need. They remain there as he punches into the keyboard.

"For today?" He seems way too young to work here. *Definitely too young to be judging me.* "It's not recommended buying a ticket for the same day—"

"I completely agree, believe me"—I glance at his name badge—"Joaquin." I'm still catching my breath from sprinting through the airport, the mysteriously increasing weight of my suitcase threatening to yank my arm out of its socket. Having missed what turned out to be the last ferry of the day, I'm back at the airport.

"I was going to take the ferry but it was overbooked." I dig out my license and place it on the counter for him. "But then it took off early and—" I stop myself midsentence.

I might have a sixth sense. One that alerts me to any stuck-up, womanizing reggaetoneros in the area. Because I swear I'm able to sense René before I see him. Or maybe it's the way the group behind me went completely quiet, and I heard someone whisper, "That *is* him."

"*¿Hola? ¿Como estas?*" René walks up and cheerily greets the attendant at the next ticket counter. He drops his duffel bag on the floor and pulls out his wallet. I'm not sure if he's seen me.

Though I'm only about three feet away. "I just need to know where my gate is," he says, handing her his ID.

I want to say something nice and professional. Something that kicks us off on the right foot. But my brain feels like slush. The cab ride back to the airport left me with a fresh batch of nausea, and the race through the airport in search of this hard-to-find, small nondescript counter of hopper flights to the islands has left me spent.

"Daniela"—Joaquin picks up my license and then sets it back down—"I'm not seeing any seats on the last flight."

At this, René looks over at me. I can feel him standing there, watching me smugly.

"Can you please check again?" I do my absolute best not to sound like I'm exhausted or in trouble. René looks carelessly stylish as always. Large red sweatshirt, reflective mirrored shades, and a baseball hat.

"Let me check one more thing." I think my attendant has recognized René, and it's why he's typing even more vigorously.

René takes his ID back from his attendant with an appreciative smile. *"¿Hola. Como estas?"* He echoes what he just said moments ago. The woman's eyes narrow, confused.

"I'm so sorry." He brings a hand to his head. "It's just, I have this problem. It's actually my *main* problem. It appears I repeat myself. But you'd already know that if you'd heard my music."

My whole body tenses. This is *not* how I wanted to kick things off. I shut my eyes. I didn't expect René to forget everything I said, but I'd hoped that after Maureen approved his request to record the album in Puerto Rico, he'd agree that my ends justified the means. I'm about to try to acknowledge him and make light of the whole thing, when my attendant abruptly stops typing.

"Next available flight to Culebra isn't until tomorrow night."

"What?" I can't even attempt to hide the desperation in my voice. I can't miss René's first day in the studio. I wanted to get there tonight so I could get settled. Get a lay of the land. "What about flights to the other island? Can't I take a ferry from there?"

"Yes, maybe. Let me check."

"Just come on my flight," René gruffly blurts out, still looking at his attendant.

I turn toward him. "Oh, René! Hi." I loosen my shoulders and flash my best attempt at a carefree smile.

He turns to address me. "Ángel chartered a plane. There's plenty of room." His face is stern behind the mirrored shades, emoting nothing.

"That's okay. This is fine, thanks. We got it all sorted out." I cannot even fathom imposing or inconveniencing him like that.

"It's Gate 7B." René's attendant hands him a printout of his ticket.

"Thank you. Thank y—oh, see that. I almost repeated myself again." His tone is more agitated now. "But I held back, because I hate being stuck in a rut."

I scoff loudly. "You know what I hate?" I tell my attendant. "People who push their luck when someone's already going out of their way to help them. Like right now, as you are in the midst of trying to assist me, it would never even occur to me to add more and more requests or be purposefully difficult." I've snapped. How dare René be upset with me? It's just one too many things right now.

René lets out a laugh. I can't tell if it's a pissed-off laugh or if he actually finds what I've said amusing.

"Because that would be rude and greedy, wouldn't it?" My attendant stops typing and looks up at me curiously. "I'm sorry, don't mind me. Please don't stop looking." My voice is low and friendly.

René shakes his head and tosses his duffel bag over his shoulder. Is that all he's bringing for a month? A single, measly, seemingly weightless duffel? He's hovering, I think, begrudgingly waiting until my flight is resolved. There isn't anyone in line at his ticket counter, so his attendant is waiting too.

"There's one seat on the last flight to Vieques Island. There's a late ferry from there to Culebra you should be able to make."

"Oh, thank goodness. I'll take it." I exhale. "See," I snap at René. "I'm perfectly fine. You can go." I wave a hand at him for good measure.

"That will be one thousand two hundred and thirty-eight dollars."

My heart sinks deep down into my chest cavity. "Oh." Upon hearing me, René drops his bag. I can feel him watching me. I ignore him, and place my backpack on the counter, unzip it slowly, and dig for my credit card. What have I done? That's four times the cost of James's flight.

I hold the credit card in my hand and take a breath. Finally, I look up at René. One glance is all it takes. He's able to read my mind. Or possibly the desperation in my eyes.

He grabs my license off the counter and hands it to his attendant. "Can you please add *Daniela Maria* here to my flight's manifest?"

I'm hit with a wild combination of emotions. There's gratitude and intense relief I won't be accruing the enormous hit to our budget. Plus a dash of annoyance—and something else that I'd rather ignore.

René takes my hefty suitcase before I've had a chance to protest and we set off.

"Thank you." I turn to him as we wait in line at airport security. I brace myself for a snarky comment or for him to rub it in my face.

"No problem," he says simply, his face soft. I stare at him for a moment, unsure what to think.

As we walk past a kiosk selling handbags, René recognizes the attendant. I imagine from flying out of here so often. He gets close enough to tap the shoulder of the older woman behind the cash register. She turns just in time to see him, and waves eagerly at him. My heart warms for her. He's just made her day. Her month.

Then we make it through the airport, are driven by a van to the tarmac, and walk up the steps to the small private charter jet...in silence.

There are four large leather seats. I take one in the first row and René does the same, sitting across the small aisle from me.

The sound of the engine isn't encouraging. It's weak and tinny, like it doesn't actually have the strength to pick up this plane. But the nose tilts up and we're in the air instantly and my body loosens up a tad.

Below us, San Juan's Spanish fort cuts a jagged edge along the water. I can see waves crashing against the shore, and exactly where the water shifts and darkens to a deeper shade of blue. Islands covered in small green mountains come into view in the distance.

"There's the big island and then there's a hundred little ones. And Culebra is the most beautiful." I hear my father's voice. I see him hovering over a map on our kitchen table. I try to brush the memory away, but it resists and lingers a moment longer.

"Here there are turtles, here the ocean drops thousands of feet and there are whales." My father didn't just love Culebra. He loved the water and the little islands surrounding it.

I still can't believe I'm actually heading to the place I heard him obsess about my whole life. Of all of Puerto Rico's inhabited islands, Culebra is the rawest. The others are more popular with tourists and have more restaurants and hotels. Culebra is a lot of untouched beaches, sea turtle sanctuaries, and wild horses. Or so my father's song goes. *Horses living free, rolling in the sand.* A few hundred families have lived there for generations. Despite the limited resources, exposure to hurricanes, and the fact that kids have to be ferried to another island for grades 9 to 12.

René removes his sunglasses and pulls a pair of headphones out of his duffel bag.

I need to fix things. The only way I'm going to make it through a month on this island without my heart breaking from thinking about my father is by diving into work.

"Listen, um," I start, and he shifts his body toward me, a blank look on his face, "I just want to say, I'm sorry if I… offended you the other day."

He's eerily calm. His dark, bedroom eyes expressionless. "Which day?" He blinks. "The day you didn't know who I was and didn't know any of my music?" He taps his bottom lip for a few drawn-out seconds. "Or the day you finally bothered to do your homework and looked me up?"

"I, I don't—"

"Because"—he doesn't sound upset, just casually matter-of-fact—"both days were pretty offensive."

Air escapes my lungs. "I mean, you *were* being difficult." I match his calm, neutral tone.

"Because I spoke my mind and asked for what I needed?"

"Well, yes—"

"Listen, I can see why it's tricky." He glances down at my outfit. Black linen blazer, blank tank, jeans. "Everyone makes judgments." When his eyes find mine, my hands need something to do. I let them adjust the seat belt and tighten it around my waist.

"You see, that day at the arena," he continues with a smirk, "I played two songs for you, neither of which you knew." I want to correct him. Tell him I did recognize the second one. *Sort of.* "And guess what? Neither song was mine." My mouth drops open. Shit. He *did* trick me. "So you don't know me, fine. A tad worrisome, seeing as you work for my label, but fine. But not knowing the pioneers, the kings of reggaeton, songs that have been around since the early nineties. Now *that's* offensive. For someone who claims to love music, not to mention someone with a parent from the place where this music blew up." I flinch a little, unable to conceal the sting of his last sentence.

I swallow hard. What I *want* to do is ignore him. Or worse. I suck in my lower lip to hold back the curse words that are on the tip of my tongue. *Keep calm and plow on.* "When I first met you, I was just…nervous. This is my first solo assignment," I admit, because I need to fix this. "I *do* love music." I'm somehow keeping my cool but still on defense. "And not just as entertainment. In high school, I petitioned for a music appreciation class to prevent bullying." René shifts in his seat and I can tell I'm not the only one still seething. "I presented all this research about how people who like a variety of music tend to be more open-minded and conscientious."

"That makes sense." He's agreeing but still scowling.

"Right? They said they would implement it but they never did."

"That's too bad," he commiserates, though in a tone that's still sparring.

"I know." I inhale deeply. "I just want you to know that I don't *just* care about music, I care about people and how music changes their lives." *Though the jury's still out on songs about butts.* "So I'm going to work hard on this and on your entire campaign."

After a few moments, he nods slightly and slips his headphones on. I have to force myself to look away, though my heart is racing and I'm still breathing fast.

For the rest of the flight, René listens to music, his legs stretched out in front of him, and I self-soothe with my mantras. Anything to prevent myself from replaying everything he said to me.

The plane starts to descend quickly and my grip tightens around the armrest. Soon we're so close, I can see sailboats floating in the bay. I lean against the window, scanning the island for any semblance of a landing strip.

As though he's read my mind, René leans across the aisle. "Don't worry, it only looks like we're going to hit the mountain. The runway's just on the other side."

"Thanks." I'm wary but hopeful his attempt to comfort me is a good sign.

I let my head drop back into the seat. The sun is gone, but it's left streaks of pink behind the clouds. I exhale deeply and slip my hands in my blazer pockets. The feel of the cassette tape in my right hand makes my chest tighten. When I told my mom where René was recording the album, her first reaction was silence. Like she had gone somewhere for a moment. When she returned, she said, "The old house is gone, but you can go to the places in the song. He'd love that."

Today, before I left for the airport, she handed me the plastic audio cassette. The white label beige now. *Daniela*, in my dad's neat cursive.

I didn't have the heart to tell her I wasn't going to do any such thing. "I won't have time. I need to focus on work. Where would I even play this?"

"A lot of old cars have them. You could find one." She squeezed me close and kissed me warmly on the head. "You worry too much."

I wanted to point out that she worried too little and push the cassette back into her hands. Instead, I let it slip into my pocket. Better to be a delayed disappointment than an instant one.

Chapter 8

"I GOT THIS FOR YOU AND JAMES." ÁNGEL, RENÉ'S MANAGER, leads me to a bright red golf cart. "There are some taxis on the island, but it's not always easy to get one."

"That's very nice. Thank you! Has everyone arrived?" I can't help but watch René as he drives off in the yellow Mustang that was waiting for him in the parking lot of the small airport.

"A few folks got here last night. A group of them are out on the boat now. Everyone has agreed to being filmed. The producer and technicians."

"Oh, perfect."

The road is dark with only an occasional streetlight. The farther we get from the small airport, the more the island seems uninhabited. We hit a bump. Followed by another quick succession of bumps. Then we ride over a deeper hole and both of us bounce a few inches above our seats. I press down on my blazer pocket, holding the cassette in place through the fabric.

"How do you think René's feeling about the behind-the-scenes?" I ask, making conversation.

Ángel is quiet for a little too long. "He'll be fine. He's a professional," he adds, his whole energy filled with pride. From my research, I know he's part of René's tight circle of friends. He, René, and Camila all met at the visual arts college in San Juan. Thanks to René, he has a growing roster of clients.

Twenty minutes later, we pull off the road and are waved on by a guard standing near the fence. We park in an open field next to the yellow Mustang and two large SUVs. The instant the cart stops moving, we're blasted by sounds. Crickets, other chirping creatures, frogs, and a wind chime with deep tones. They all take turns, working together as though they were a band. *Chime, chirp, chirp, co-kee, chime, chirp, co-kee.*

Ángel leads me across the lot toward a dark patch of trees. "It's a really special place. I wish I was staying."

"Oh?" I don't hold back my disappointment. He's been my main contact the past few weeks as we've prepared for this. The way things are going, I could use his support.

"I'll be heading out tomorrow. But you're in good hands. Let me show you around and we'll get you some help for your bags."

He opens a small wrought iron fence. We make it to the top of a mound and golden lights come into view, illuminating a narrow wooden walkway that splits off in different directions. More warm light spills out from the handful of small cottages sprinkled on the next hill. Beyond the glow of the lights, we're surrounded by the darkness of lush vegetation.

The photos on the website were deceiving. The property is much smaller in person. Everything is more compact and closer together. Each cottage is a miniature beach house. Narrow rectangular structures with circular windows, each with their own tiny front porch. There are hammocks here and there and an outdoor seating area with wicker chairs in the shape of flowers. It's opulent but also quaint. Like a bougie fairy village in the middle of the forest.

"You and James get the second floor of that house." Ángel points to a cottage on the bottom of the hill. "We have a great cook from San Juan staying with us," he continues. "She'll be preparing all the meals. She's left dinner in your room. The kitchen is in the main house, and over there's the pool."

This was the former home of a well-known Mexican telenovela star. He used the separate cottages as guest houses and a gym. Now it's a boutique hotel typically used for yoga retreats. For the next month, the label has rented out the entire place for René to record his album.

Ángel points at one of the wooden paths. "That way's the beach and the dock. We're on a tip of the island so we're surrounded by the ocean on three sides. Wait till you see it in the morning." His enthusiasm is endearing. "There's a neat vintage bar on the second floor of the main house, and the studio's just over there," he says, pointing back toward the pool as we arrive at my cottage.

"What time will we get started tomorrow?" I feel nerves kicking in.

"I'm not sure. But René's personal assistant will put a schedule under everyone's door at night."

"Oh, okay." I force a smile, sad to see him go.

I say goodbye to Ángel, and climb up the narrow steps. There are two doors down the hall from one another. The one at the far end has its key dangling from the knob, so I head toward it.

The room has unpretentious retreat vibes. There's an antique wardrobe and a bed with a wooden spindle headboard covered with mosquito netting. Over a small table and chairs is a dark painting of Mona Lisa with an eye patch. Thick wooden beams run along the ceiling, which is decorated in thatch that comes down the corners of the room and all the way to the floor.

The room is also stuffy. It takes me a moment to figure out how to open the large circular window opposite the bed. Pushing it away does the trick. I slide the glass door open, too, and the sound of waves crashing immediately fills the room along with a warm, gusty breeze.

The balcony is inviting. There's a plush lounger with a wicker base and a collection of different-size cactuses in colorful pots. I look outside to the ocean and the empty boat dock at the end of the slim, meandering deck.

I snap a few pictures of the room to share with Meri later, push aside the mosquito netting, and sit on the edge of the bed.

A strong breeze lifts the curtain, and the scent of the ocean flows through the windows. *Tomorrow is a new day. Buck it up, Buttercup.* I want to feel more confident about the weeks ahead. I've written up pages of interview questions to hit René with at different stages of the recording process.

I know I can help René if I can just get him to open up. *We'll also need to work on making him seem less cocky and obnoxious. But baby steps.*

I unzip my suitcase with intention. This is me officially getting down to business. I blink and hold up a pair of white denim shorts, perplexed. There must have been some mix-up at the baggage claim. I don't recognize any of these clothes. But beneath a few more items that aren't mine, I find my black linen blazer. *Meri.* She must have slipped these in my suitcase. I'm relieved to find she hasn't taken out any of the things I packed. She's simply added a bunch more. More *color*. A lime green wraparound dress, bright pink silk camisole, a red strapless top I've seen Meri wear that is, in essence, a glorified bandanna, and a yellow lace lingerie set with the tags still on.

We're the same size, but my sister and I have such opposing styles, we never borrow each other's clothes.

I snap a picture of the open suitcase and text it to her. **How dare you make my bag this much heavier. I hope you're happy. I could be in jail right now for lying to airport security when they asked if I packed the bag myself!**

In truth, I feel loved. She's always trying to help however she can. Though I feel neither one of us has packed properly for this place. Everything here is so close together. It hadn't occurred to me that I could walk to the kitchen for a glass of water and run into René. I wish I'd packed something to wear around at night. There has to be a happy medium between pajamas and a blazer.

I take the quickest shower of my life, thanks to the small, shiny brown frog perched on the shampoo bottle. I text Meri a photo of said frog and get into bed, tucking the netting around me in tightly.

Tomorrow, we'll hit the ground running. In bed, the clear plan I had for tomorrow crystallizes into something better. We'll capture René getting settled, meeting his musicians and technical crew. We'll be there to film the exciting first moments. All I have to do is not let him press my buttons. *And pretend I'm on another island.*

I text James that I'm crashing early and make a plan to meet in the morning to go over the schedule. At some point tonight, Camila will slide it under our doors. She's probably out on the boat and will get to it later. I imagine it will be fairly simple. A basic itinerary with studio hours, breaks, and mealtimes. Feeling exhausted from a lack of sleep over the past few weeks leading up to this, I set my alarm for 7:00 a.m., a reasonable hour. Musicians are never up too early.

Chapter 9

I WAKE UP TO A LIZARD STARING DOWN AT ME FROM THE other side of the netting. But not just *any* lizard.

One that's bulked up and muscular. A bodybuilder with humanlike shoulders. I slide out of the bed, trying not to disturb it, and glance at the bottom of the front door. My heart sinks. *No schedule.*

I tell myself it's nothing personal. Camila's just terrible at her job. Or maybe she ran out of printer ink. Doesn't matter, I tell myself as I get dressed. I don't need a schedule. I'm just going to go down there and get to work. I'm running on optimistic adrenaline. Brought on mostly by Meri's texts early this morning.

FROGS?

You're seriously sending me photos of frogs when you could be sending pics of René?

Unbelievable.

Also, I'm 10 minutes early to tutoring! Thanks again!!

The thought that my notoriously late sister is so eager to get the help she needs makes me feel lighter. And knowing I'm the reason it's all happening, well, that just adds an extra bounce to my step. *This* is why I'm here. For her and Mom and our soon-to-be watertight house.

I check my reflection in the mirror and take a deep breath. I'm feeling pretty good in my navy twill blazer, white tee, and ripped-up yet still professional-looking jeans. I feel first-day-of-school jitters bubbling through me.

Nothing can stop me. I'm going to make the best behind-the-scenes of the making of an album of all time. It's going to be creative and insider-ee.

All I need are two basic elements:

1. Intimate interviews. This is where the artist shares their innermost thoughts and feelings, how things are going and where the ideas are coming from.

2. All-access, behind-the-scenes footage of the creative process. This is the good stuff. Nice, close-up shots of the artist, pencil in hand maniacally writing lyrics, stepping inside the recording booth for the first time, addressing the camera directly, letting the viewer inside their world. As if to say, I'm *happy* you're here. I *want* you here. Here as I brush my teeth or go for a swim to let off some steam. Imagine if we'd had a behind-the-scenes of Michelangelo as he took a break from carving *David*? Having a slice of pizza as he stared at the slab of marble, contemplating

where to hit it next. Looking at the camera and saying, "This is taking a lot longer than I expected."

I make for the door, but a glimpse at the view outside my balcony stops me in my tracks.

There are clusters of palm trees on the beach, bent over and reaching for the sea. To my left and right are the other cozy cottages surrounded by more palms and fruit trees.

It's a ridiculously picturesque view. Off on the horizon, there are small white crests of waves. Nothing seems to be moving, like in a postcard. And surprisingly, there's zero humidity. Only a soft, warm breeze. Suddenly, it's all too intense, and I have to pull the curtains shut.

The door to James's room is open. I find him sitting on the floor, under a table. He's in the process of organizing a mass of cables into neat piles.

"Hey, there you are." He's in a great mood. He stands, his cheeks flushed from work. "Here, I brought you a coffee." He hands me a bright yellow mug off the bedside table. "Cream, no sugar."

"Thanks!" I take a sip. It's almost room temperature, but it's delicious. James has clearly been up for a while. I can tell he's moved around the furniture in his room to make space for a fold-up table with his laptop. The equipment cases are sitting on his bed, and lights are organized by size against a wall.

His room has very different décor. Mine has 1800s antiques with modern art; James's is funkier. It's like the 1970s idea of the future. *The Jetsons* with lots of pink.

"Hey, nice lava lamp."

"Right?"

He gets back to work, lifting a large case and dropping it

onto his bed with a thud. Inside, there are three cameras, each one tucked safely inside foam dividers. The one on the right catches my eye.

"I have that," I say without thinking.

"Really?" He looks perplexed. "I didn't know that."

"You know I used to take pictures." Whenever James came over to our place, he'd admire the few prints I've let Mom display on the living room walls. The photograph of her holding the cactus. Ten-year-old Meri in a bright red diner booth, biting into a slice of lemon. A self-portrait I took in front of a large mirror, where the camera obscures half my face.

"I didn't think you still had it."

"I do. Mine's a much older version than yours." No need to disclose that my father and I bought it at a pawn shop. "I should probably sell it."

"I could buy it from you. Do you have any lenses?"

I feel a prick in my chest at the thought of letting it go. "Yeah."

"Nice," he says, his back to me as he plugs a power strip of charging camera batteries into the wall.

"Can we get going soon? I'd like to get down there right away."

"Sure, sure. Right behind you." He snaps a case shut and heaves it onto the bed.

We step into the hallway and make our way down the stairs. "I'm anxious to see the studio."

We're outside, stepping onto the wooden path, when it dawns on me that James hasn't brought a camera or any equipment with him. "I guess you'll come back for the gear once you've scouted the studio? So you can set up?"

I hear him come to a stop. "Oh, we're all done."

I turn around and see he's standing a little taller. "What do you mean?"

"Here, I can show you." Motioning back in the direction of the stairs.

"Where? In your room?" My stomach lurches. Something doesn't feel right.

He pauses, a bit taken aback by my questions. "Yeah, on my laptop. I can show you where we were allowed to put the small cameras."

Allowed?

I climb back up the stairs as quickly as I can.

James opens his laptop, and one by one, four small black-and-white squares appear on the screen. Each a fuzzy view from a different angle of the recording studio. The cameras are placed high up on the walls. I see two guys walking around, neither of which is René. As they cross the room, they pop in and out of the different boxes on the screen.

"What is this? Why are the cameras set up like that?"

"That's where René's assistant said we were allowed to put the cameras." He clears away a few things on the table. "I ran the cable through the window so we could sit up here. She didn't want us in the hallway."

I let out a puff of air and stare at the screens. This is not what I had in mind. I need to be *inside* the studio. I want something intimate. I want to capture the first creative moments that kick off the album. This isn't up close and personal. This is convenience store security footage.

When I reach the recording studio door, I take a deep breath.

I push the door in slowly. Inside, there's a technician beneath the soundboard and another guy up on a ladder, with a nail gun adding soundproofing to the ceiling.

My eyes dart around the room, at the tiny cameras up near the ceiling. No wonder the images are so terrible. It's so dark in here. There are moody, neon lights set up under the tables, making the room look more like a night club. I feel so let down by James. Why didn't he push back, or come find me?

I step back outside and practically collide with Camila.

"I thought you were all set up?" She steps around me and pulls the studio door shut.

"Oh, good morning." I gather myself. "Yeah, it appears so but—"

"And René won't do any interviews," she interrupts me. "Just so you know. He really wants to focus on the album. We'll worry about all that later." She doesn't sound rude. Just matter-of-fact bomb dropping. "If you really need them, we can always try when the album's done," she offers. She's actually attempting to be gracious, though she still comes across less than hospitable. I think it's something to do with her eyebrows. They're more angular than curved.

She's wearing a flowy long-sleeve crop top that ties in a bow beneath her bra and a long skirt with an extended slip. Her style is chic yet messy bohemian. Her long, wavy hair is tangled in places, and she's perspiring ever so slightly.

Thoughts are sliding around in my brain, but no sentences are taking shape. What I *want* to say is that an interview conducted later will be too far removed. I want to know how René's feeling *right now*. This morning.

Camila sways from side to side, eager to walk away, so I hone my negotiating skills. I gather myself and extend a hand. "I'm Dani, by the way. We haven't met properly."

"Right. Camila." She gives my hand a faint squeeze.

"Listen, I know you have no reason to trust me." I pause to

redirect. No need to focus on the past. "But I really want to make something beautiful here. I have big plans. We just have to be allowed in there with our actual cameras so we can film how it's going *and* interview him. Here. Regularly."

"There's nothing I can do. Not today. Let's talk tomorrow." Her tone says this discussion is over.

Stunned, I walk back to James's room and take the seat he's placed next to his so we can watch the movement on the monitors. It's like we're on a stakeout, only much worse. We're powerless detectives. If anything happens, we won't be able to do a damn thing about it.

Chapter 10

WE CAN'T EVEN HEAR WHAT'S HAPPENING. THE MICROPHONES on the cameras James set up around the room aren't the best quality. Plus, they're so far away from everyone, I don't know if we're listening to the beginnings of a bass line or the hum of an air conditioner.

I consider calling Ángel or Maureen, but even if they *did* manage to convince René to let us in, it wouldn't be the ideal situation. It would be better if René *wanted* us to be there. Camila did say, "Not today," and that really could mean "tomorrow." So I decide to hold off before calling for help. Still, there must be something we can do in the meantime.

"I can't sit here all day," I tell James, collecting my things. "Grab your gear."

Together, we scope out the common rooms and find a lounge near the pool. I keep an eye out for Camila, while James drags the comfy, seventies-style couch into the center of the room, shuts the curtains, and lights up the space for interviews.

New plan. I'm going to wait outside the bathroom across from the studio. Eventually, someone will need to use the toilet or have a snack, and when they do, I'm going to ask them to pop into the lounge and give us a few minutes for a quick interview. As long as we avoid René and the studio, we're not doing anything wrong *is what I keep telling myself.*

Three hours later, we've recorded our first interview. Sure, it was only with one of the studio technicians but anyone involved on the album is fair game. You never know who could have something interesting to say or shed some light on how things are going. *Any* light would be great. Maybe coming at it from different angles will help us weave together the tapestry that is René and his first solo album.

Unfortunately, Gustavo, a middle-aged man with a full beard and long hair that feathers back, only just met René this morning. Though he *did* work a festival last year where he performed. So while I still don't know anything about the album or how René's feeling today, we do know the following:

The exact kind of microphone René prefers onstage (Sennheiser SKM 2000)

Gustavo is big fan of the NY Yankees

Energy waning, I head out again and casually lean against a column near the studio. From where I'm standing, there's a clear view of the yard straight through the common area. Everywhere there are walls missing, completely letting the outside in.

Outside, a woman nimbly climbs a ladder leaning against a tree. With a few twists, a plump papaya snaps free and she drops it down to an older woman waiting below. I go back to pretending to be reading something on my phone, in case Camila or René pops out of the studio.

A few minutes later, someone appears at the end of the hall and I snap to attention. I recognize him immediately from the platinum-dyed hair. He's wearing black sweats and red leather high-top sneakers. *Santiago.* The relatively unknown producer René has chosen to work with.

He's had some success with local artists, but this is the first time he's worked on an entire album. He walks briskly toward me and I can't help but feel a rush of optimism. If we can interview Santiago, the day will not be a total loss. In reggaeton, the producer is an integral part of the music. When they're not reworking existing music, they're composing original beats. Plus, Santiago and René are also friends. He'll *know* things.

He walks into the kitchen, so I gather myself and walk toward the counter.

Keep on trucking. And put everyone in the truck with me.

"Hey, Santiago." He stares at me, unblinking. "I'm Dani. I'm with the label."

"Oh yeah, nice to meet you." He shuts the fridge, walks over, and gives me a kiss on the cheek.

"I'd love to interview you for the behind-the-scenes, if you have a few minutes."

"Sure, now's good." There's an easy enthusiasm in his voice.

As I guide him to our interview room, I feel like I can breathe again.

"Have you been to Culebra before?" he asks as James sets him up with a microphone.

"No, this is my first time." I try to sound bubbly and push down the lump forming in my throat.

"What?" He's genuinely surprised. "We'll have to show you around. We're going on a hike tomorrow morning. You should come." Santiago has a refreshingly down-to-earth and open demeanor. He's also a little flirtatious.

"That sounds amazing, I'd love that." This could be a great opportunity for us to bond. If by "we," he means René will be coming, that's even better. I can convince him to grant us access to the studio and let us stay in there for the next four weeks.

"Okay, we're rolling," James announces.

"So, Santiago, how's the first day going?"

"Good. We're just getting started. René has a lot of ideas and I'm showing him a few things I've been working on, you know."

"How's he feeling? Is he happy?"

Santiago considers this and shifts around in his seat. "This is a dream come true for René. A famous actor used to live here and made the recording studio, which we've obviously updated a bit, but René was telling me he used to ride his bike by here when he was a kid and look inside the windows."

"That's sweet," I respond, moved. "I thought he grew up south of San Juan?"

"He did, but he spent a lot of summers here."

"Oh, I didn't know that." There's so little René has shared about his personal life, it's nice to finally get some intel. I jot down a note to ask René about his summers on the island. It would be a great story to include in the making of the album.

"Yeah, he was always writing songs. Mostly rap when he was just starting out. But he was teased about it a lot at school. Even by his cousins." Santiago shakes his head. "He'd spend the summers out here with his grandparents. Get away from it all, you know. He'd come to this house hoping to see the owner in here making music, but I guess the guy was never home."

Poor kid. My feelings about René aside, it's awful hearing he was treated this way when he was just trying to do his thing. I'm relieved he wasn't dissuaded. *You showed them.*

"How do you think he's feeling about recording his first solo album? After a career of guest appearances," I add in my best professional interviewer voice.

"I don't know." He seems genuinely stumped by the question. "I think he's been happy. He's thrived. Reggaeton is layered, you know. You bring this, I'll add that. It's all about community. To be honest with you, I think he's liked that it hasn't just been about him. But you know what"—he sounds as though he's just figuring something out—"ever since we started talking about this project, and today, in there"—Santiago points in the direction of the studio, his eyes narrowing—"I can see this fire inside. René's always been fearless but I think he's ready to see how far he can push things."

Santiago leans farther back into the couch. "In fact, he had a plan, but he wants to throw it all out. Now that he's here, he wants to experiment."

"Really?"

"Yeah, I know he wants to have some piano, some guitar. Not a lot of artists use real instruments in reggaeton. You can get away without them, but René can play both so well. He wants to do something different."

While it's great to learn so much about René, it's unsettling there isn't an actual plan for the album.

"It's going to be huge," Santiago continues, excited. I get the sense he's noticed the look on my face and is trying to reassure me. "You know"—his tone shifts to something more somber—"René is loyal. I'll never stop thanking him for bringing me on. But I think it's because we're both from here, had similar upbringings, same exposure to music. We grew up with the same music playing in our houses." He chuckles and then pauses. "Still, I know what he's gone through to get here. He could have worked with anyone. Someone who could, like, guarantee him some hits."

I'm taken aback at his openness. "Are you scared of letting him down?"

He shakes his head. "He knows what I can do," he says, scratching his chin. "When someone believes in you like that... I don't know, it sets you free." He pauses, then smiles. "You know what I mean?"

I smile back, feeling the lump in my throat return. I know *exactly* what he means.

Life. It's all just a matter of perspective, isn't it? Whether something is good or bad depends on how you look at it. Or what you might have had for dinner.

Take right now, for example.

The sun is setting, my first on the island, since it was already dark when I got in last night, my jeans are rolled up, toes in the warm sand, and I couldn't possibly feel less relaxed. The beach on this side of the property is a long, narrow strip of pure white sand, with water so crystal clear, I can see a school of fish swimming near the shore. It's all a little *too* perfect. I came out here needing some air, but it just isn't working. There just isn't enough air.

An hour ago, James and I were in the dining room of the main house. We each had a beer and he was being kind, congratulating me for pivoting to make the most of the day. And he's right. The interview with Santiago was a step in the right direction.

And I'm going on this hike tomorrow. If René comes too, I can find a moment to talk to him. Explain my vision for the project. Then again, there's always a chance Camila will come and not be too happy to see me. I could be making things worse, but I have to try.

Then the dinner buffet was set out, along with its mouthwatering aromas. I stared at the three perfect scoops on my plate and my breath slowed. Red beans, yellow rice, and mashed green plantains drenched in garlic and olive oil.

Last night we had pasta. Today we had omelets for breakfast, and burgers for lunch. This was our first authentic Puerto Rican meal.

The plantain mash was an explosion of flavor that melted in my mouth. Since my dad died, my mom laid to rest his cuisine too. Anything that reminded her of him was too painful. Our kitchen went back to being strictly Cuban, and Cubans do different things to their plantains. The flavors were so unbelievably delicious and familiar, they brought back a memory just as intense. It took shape before I had a chance to push it away.

Dad and I doing karaoke of his favorite La India song. Well, not so much karaoke, just us singing along to the song as it played on our TV in the living room. The Puerto Rican goddess's powerful voice booming behind us.

We knew the words by heart about a woman whose man had just been stolen. The lyrics were kind of funny for a father and daughter to belt out so animatedly. Along the lines of: *You can have him! He's all yours! Don't call me when he does the same to you!*

Afterward, when we sat back at the dinner table, hoarse and spent from our performance, he said, "We should perform that on your wedding day. We'd take the house down." Then, he quickly followed it with, *"Eso si te quieres casar."* Letting me off the hook, in case marriage wasn't for me.

The memory was so clear. *And painful.* It made me feel restless and slightly claustrophobic. Never mind that we were in a part of the house where all the walls were folded away like accordions.

Now I'm outside, but it's not much better. It's just all so absurdly spectacular. Deep blue sky, clouds dressed in pink. My throat feels dry. I don't have time for this. It's going to take all of me to get this job done. I need to be on my game. I can't go falling apart every time they serve mashed plantains and beans. I can almost hear my dad clarifying, *"Habichuelas."*

My breathing shallows and I leave the beach. Climbing the stairs two at a time, I focus on my feet and take deep breaths. The winding wooden-decked path guides me to the right, where it circles around the wide trunk of an enormous tree.

There's an overlook, and beyond the deck, it's a hilly slope down to another sliver of beach. There isn't a banister by the edge, so I stick near the tree.

When I finally look up, I realize I've found an even more beautiful view. There's an island directly ahead, covered in green mountains. It looks like it might be close enough to swim to. The sun is setting behind it, making the water shimmer. It's so overwhelmingly beautiful, my eyes instantly water.

"Are you fucking kidding me?" I blurt out, throwing my hands up.

A figure peers out from around the tree, making me jump.

I gasp and immediately start wiping the tears off my cheek.

"I'm sorry." Sitting on the deck, legs dangling over the ledge, is René. Except he looks so *very* different. Though the only change I can gather after a quick scan is that he's wearing reading glasses. "*¿Estas bien?*" he asks.

"Yeah, I'm fine." I step out from around the tree.

"Do you need to be alone? I can go."

"Oh, no. You're good." I notice he's been scribbling into a notebook. "I wasn't *crying* crying." I feel the need to clarify. Though there may be a ton of real tears waiting in line, that is *not* what just happened. I was just moved to tears by the natural beauty.

His eyes wander down to my bare feet, and a glint of curiosity washes across his face. I glance down, relieved I had a pedicure before I left, but then I find what his eyes must be lingering on. *Toe rings!* I'm wearing toe rings. Meri and I got matching ones on a whim at a little shop in Midtown a few months ago and I haven't taken them off since. They're dainty, whimsical silver things on my second and third toes. I wiggle them around self-consciously.

"You don't have to be embarrassed about crying, not with me."

"Really, I'm not crying." The shock of running into him is slowly wearing off. "I'm just"—I motion to the sunset—"I'm just overwhelmed."

I haven't seen him since the flight yesterday and I have no idea where we stand. Having been locked out of the studio today, I'd say we weren't in a good place. But at the moment he seems unguarded. *Maybe it's just the reading glasses.* He's like a more down-to-earth version of himself. Apart from the glasses, he's in a silky, striped fifties-style shirt and swim shorts.

I wipe away the last of the tears from my face. "Hasn't that ever happened to you? Been moved to tears by something unexplainable?" He shakes his head. "It's happened to me a few times. With music," I add. "The first time I heard Radiohead's 'Creep.' He hit that high note and it was like"—I bring my hand over my heart and squeeze my eyes shut as though in pain—"it hurt. It felt like the truth slicing through me. I think it's because there's no BS in something that clear, in that perfect pitch."

"Radiohead, huh?" He sounds betrayed. I can't tell if it's because my music tastes are so far away from reggaeton or because he's jealous that Thom Yorke's had this effect on me.

"Yeah." I smile, relieved that my breath has steadied. "This is the first time it happened with a place."

"You said it's happened a few times with music. What other artist has it happened with?" I pick up a hint of betrayal still there, and I feel warm all over. Mostly because you gotta love a man who listens.

"Okay." I exhale. "But don't laugh."

His eyes widen with intrigue. "Okay."

"It wasn't a band or anything. It was"—I pause—"*The Lion King.*"

René laughs. An endearing broken cackle. "Sorry, sorry."

"It was the Broadway musical," I defend. "It came to Miami, and I took my little sister, and right when it starts, you know, it's that beautiful chant that starts with one high note, and well, I wasn't expecting it. Has that really never happened to you?"

"No, but now I wish it would." He's so sincere. With just a few short words, he's managed to make me feel special for having these experiences. "But I can see how it would happen. This place has an energy, I always feel so grounded here. No matter what situation I'm coming from, it pulls me in. You can't fight it."

"Yeah, you can't fight it," I repeat, except I say it like this is a bad thing.

His brow furrows, trying to understand.

"Well, I'll leave you to it." I gesture to his notebook.

"I heard you interviewed Santi."

I freeze, feeling caught. My brain immediately floods with the fear that he's going to make us delete the one good thing we captured today.

"Sit." He taps the spot on the ledge next to him.

I have to chuckle at the way he's said it, as if it were a command. "Is that an order?" I glance hesitatingly at the ledge. "Do people always do what you say?"

"Yeah, pretty much," he quips, making me stand even more rigidly in place. "I'm just kidding. Dani, would you like to sit down? You're making my neck hurt."

I exhale and take a seat closer to him, but still a safe distance from the ledge.

"So"—a tinge of concern on his face—"what did Santi have to say about me?"

"He said you spent a lot of time here growing up." René nods slowly then looks off at the sunset. "How did you two meet?"

"At a party." He pauses. "He's good friends with my ex."

The ex you seemed so happy with and then cheated on?

"And how did you meet Camila?"

"At a party, back in college. There was a telescope in that house and we spent the whole night outside looking at the stars."

"So many parties. I guess away from the cameras, you're secretly an extrovert," I tease.

"Yeah, I'm an extrovert all right. I single out a person at a party, take them outside, and spend the rest of the night really getting to know them one on one."

I'm so wrong, my face flushes. "Sorry."

"It's okay."

"Santiago also shared a few things"—I try to shimmy the conversation back to work—"about you being teased as a child."

"Bullied, more like. Probably why Ángel and Camila are closer than most of my family. They loved me when I was still figuring my shit out," he says with a smile. It's a big playful grin but it's also vulnerable, and I can't help imagining what it would be like to be on that short list. "It's hard to trust people in this industry. The business side of it, reporters," he adds, eyeing me. I nod as though I understand fully. As though I'm not on *that* list.

"What about your family?" he asks. "One of your parents is from Puerto Rico, right? Which one?"

My breath skips. "My dad." I don't bother correcting his tense. I look at the sunset I've been avoiding this whole time. The sun has slipped farther away, and the color of the water is now a golden rose that sparkles like glitter.

"Which part of Puerto Rico is he from?"

"Here, actually."

"Really? Culebra?"

"Mm-hm." My throat feels dry again. I've got to switch topics. Fast. "Listen, today was"—I weigh my words—"a good start, but I'd like to cover the process more...thoroughly. An interview would be great." I power on, though René has pulled his cell out and is scrolling through a slew of messages. "We just need access. Right now, for example, you're here writing lyrics, I guess? We need shots of that."

He tucks his phone back and takes his glasses off. Sensitive, contemplative Rico evaporates before my eyes. "You can talk all that through with Camila."

"Right, um." I try to mask my disappointment. "But I think if I could just tell you about some of the ideas—"

"Actually, I need to get going." He pushes back from the ledge.

"Oh, okay."

"I hadn't realized how late it was." With that, he stands and walks away. "Talk to Camila," he calls out behind him. He may as well have said, "Have your people talk to my people." The phrase lands without even a smidge of commitment.

Chapter 11

"ARE YOU SERIOUSLY WEARING A BLAZER IN PUERTO RICO?"
Meri's face gets bigger on my cell.

"Not all day. I took it off at lunch."

"Oh, you took it off at lunch, thank goodness for that," she
says mockingly.

The light catches her face, and her eyes look puffy.

"Have you been crying?" My voice is tense with concern.

Things rarely get her down. It's really impressive. She's who
you'd want by your side if you get bad news from the doctor.
She'd squeeze your shoulders and say, "We're going to beat
this," so unflinchingly, you'd believe her.

"No."

"Are you sure everything is okay?"

Meri lets out a moan and rolls onto her side. "Not really."
My stomach drops. "I cannot believe how expensive the tutor
is." She sounds miserable.

"Oh, don't worry about that."

"I can find someone else. I'll ask around at school."

"I've already paid for the sessions. It's okay, I promise."

"Well," Meri says, dejected, "the first tutoring session was awful. *I* was awful."

Now I'm the one moaning. "I'm sorry. I'm sure it will work out. You're just figuring out her teaching methods. Give it a moment."

"I was just hoping this time would be different. At the end of the session I totally expected her to say, 'I'm so sorry but I can't help you.'"

I don't know what to say. I still can't believe she's taking the test again. I don't know why she's putting herself through this. She's got it in her head she needs to get an actual BSN instead of an RN degree, but she never scores high enough.

She's so bright. There's just something about this test. It's become a monster she can't beat. In the meantime, she's done nothing with her associate's degree. And the pressure to pass this test only grows.

"I just...what if you spend all this money, and I still don't pass?"

"You don't need to worry about that."

Meri laughs weakly.

"Just stick with it. It will get better."

"Okay." She seems somewhat convinced, even if I'm not. I was only trying to help by hiring the best tutor I could find. Someone my parents would never have been able to afford. But now I feel I've added more pressure on her.

"But I had volunteering tonight and that went great." Her face brightens. "There were a few new moms and two of the counselors from the program. They were so freaking sweet."

"Oh, good. I'm glad." Meri's been volunteering at a women's shelter for a few years. She created this entire program where she gets the beauty company she works for to donate makeup for the shelter. She says it's not about what other people see. It's about helping people feel their best, so they can go out and conquer the world.

"Marisol wanted a new look for job interviews. She's the one with the genius toddler who already knows how to ride a bike."

"Oh yeah?"

"And, Dani, she cried when she looked in the mirror. And I had only done one eye." Meri's face has lit up.

"That's amazing." I pump a fist in the air. It's always surprising to hear about my little sister's interactions with people in the world. She was so shy as a teen, she couldn't even order for herself. "Tell her I want the tacos," she'd whisper in my ear as the waitress hovered next to us. "She'll have the tacos," I'd repeat casually.

"And you got this, okay," I add. "Give the tutor another chance. If it doesn't go well, we'll get someone else."

Meri opens and closes her eyes in agreement.

"Onward and..." I can't think of how to finish the thought, which makes Meri laugh. "Don't put it in reverse."

"You are out of control. How'd it go today?"

"I don't want to talk about it."

"That bad?"

I nod silently.

"You'll figure it out."

"How's Mom?" I ask, needing to change the subject.

Meri goes silent.

"Is *she* doing okay? I texted her a few times today, but she hasn't responded. Can you put her on?"

"Um"—Meri hesitates for a moment—"I think she went to bed already."

"All right." I try to hide my concern.

"Listen." Her tone makes my neck muscles tighten. "She found out about the plan for the big window when they were here today taking the measurements."

"No," I moan. "I completely forgot to tell her."

"It's okay. We talked when I got home. She's fine now."

A deep, exhausted sigh escapes me. "I should get going."

"Wait. You know what I think?"

"What?"

"Dani, you should be focusing on yourself. Doing your thing." She sits up and props the phone down on something. "Stop checking on us. We'll be fine."

Stop worrying about them? Why does that sound so unreasonable? "I'm not worried about you guys."

Meri eyes me suspiciously. "Cut the cord," she says coldly. "To us, the house. You know what you need?" she practically shouts, as though having a eureka moment.

"Please don't say empow—"

"Empowerment selfies."

Whenever she's feeling down, this is what Meri does. She takes sexy selfies she doesn't send to anyone. Empowerment selfies are my sister's coping mechanism. Nothing brings her more confidence and vitality than a photo shoot of sexy selfies.

"No, thanks. Some other time I'll try it, I swear."

"You always say that, and you don't. Trust me. Take a sexy picture of yourself in bed right now. You look good. I like your hair like that."

"You like my hair poofy like this?" I've been trying to preserve the smooth, straight look Meri gave me before I left, but it's been no match for a day and a half of being this close to the sea in a room without AC.

"It's not poofy, it looks fantastic." I flash her a half smile, so she continues. "It will help, I promise. You should be kicking ass like you normally do. Just try it; it'll make you feel powerful."

I promise her I will, and when we hang up, I let myself fall back onto the bed. I guess it's worth a try. I *do* feel powerless at the moment. Over literally everything.

This island. Work. My debt. Meri's test. Mom ignoring my calls because she found out about the windows. How lately, anytime I try to help, it backfires on me.

I grab the phone and turn on the camera function. I snap a bunch of photos of myself, turning my face to the left and right, puckering my lips. Looking dreamily off in the distance.

I click through the pictures, ready to receive my confidence boost. And instead, I snort. I look like a forlorn bank teller.

I sit up and slip off the blazer. I'm about to take more photos when I glance over at the balcony. The light from above kisses the potted plants and the wicker lounger, but there's nothing except an empty void behind them. The dark sky makes the entire balcony look like it's floating in space.

A pop of yellow would look so cool among all the brown. Without giving it another thought, I take off my shirt and jeans and dig out the lace lingerie that Meri snuck into my suitcase.

I check myself out in the mirror. The lace top makes me look bustier than I am, and the matching bottoms are a sexy French cut I would never have bought for myself. And Meri's right about the hair. It *does* look good.

Setting up the cell phone takes longer than I expect. But I'm already feeling better.

I prop the phone up on a chair near the bed and reach the lounger, but the camera's flash goes off when I'm on my knees and facing in the wrong direction.

I check out the image, and unattractive angle of buttocks aside, it's really cool. The balcony is framed perfectly by the curtains, but I wish I had better resolution on the phone. For the first time in a long while, I wish I had my old camera.

Ready to try again, I hit the timer, make it to the lounger, and lie on my side. I direct myself as I wait for the photo to go off. *Be wistful, like you're on a magic carpet ride.*

I throw one arm up over my head haphazardly, so it settles on the floor. I shut my eyes and tip my head back. I remain still waiting for the timer to go off. Nothing happens. I open one eye and then shut it. After another long while, I consider getting up to check the phone, but I'm convinced the flash will go off as soon as I move.

"Are you okay?" The deep voice is coming from somewhere above me.

I'm frozen for a split second as my brain tries to convince itself they could be talking to someone else. Then my legs coil into the air and I jump inside the room.

"Sorry, I didn't mean to scare you." There's a cheekiness in his tone. "Just wanted to make sure you weren't dead."

My heart bangs on the walls of my chest. I'm not having a heart attack, but I wouldn't rule it out yet. I wrap the curtain around me like a towel and peer out.

René "El Rico" Rodriguez is standing on the roof of the cottage next to mine. I thought there was nothing but a roof there, but now that it's lit up, I can see it's a rooftop garden. René's leaning against the railing looking down onto my balcony. He's wearing a long white robe and the wind is moving it around, exposing his bare chest and black shorts. He looks like a very unprofessional Jedi master.

"Hey, fine. I'm fine," I do my best attempt at a wave while

still holding the curtain around me, and I retreat back into the room. Mortified, I shut my eyes and stand against the wall.

"Let me know if you need help coming up with a caption," he yells out.

"Excuse me?"

"For your selfie. If you need help with the text, just let me know. You know, for whoever it is you're going to send that to."

A nervous laugh escapes me. "A selfie? I thought you said you were worried I was dead."

There's a pause. "I was. I thought you were taking the selfie and *then* died. Or you fainted or something."

I scoff. "That's not what I was doing."

"Don't let me stop you. I can go inside."

"You don't have to do that," I say assertively.

"There's nothing wrong with it. Nothing to be ashamed of."

I feel heat flushing my cheeks. I open my mouth to defend myself, but I'm too embarrassed to say what I was *really* up to. Besides, he doesn't need to know I'm an amateur photographer. *Or I used to be.*

The camera flash finally goes off, startling me. It lights up the balcony outside. I'm sure I hear him laugh as I dive for the phone, clutch it into my chest, and stand quietly against the wall again, unable to move.

"Still okay?" he says after a moment.

I can't believe he's still talking to me. "Yes."

I lose my grip on the curtain and let out a yelp. I place a hand over my mouth, hoping he hasn't heard me.

"You sure you're okay in there?"

"Yes. I'm fine. Of course I'm fine," I blurt out defensively. I can't help it. I'm so wound up and in shock.

There's silence. I actually think I may have scared him off.

"You don't sound fine."

My face goes hot. "Well, I am. I'm..." I almost say *fine* again. I'm breathing too fast to think. "Great. Really, thank you."

"Just so you know"—his voice is slightly less obnoxious—"it was too dark for me to really see anything."

"Okay. Um...I appreciate you clarifying that."

"Do you believe me?"

"Should I?"

Silence. "I'm pretty trustworthy," he says finally.

"*Pretty?* As in not entirely?"

"No, as in 'I'm pretty *and* I'm trustworthy.'" He laughs at his own joke as I roll my eyes and smile.

There's a pause again. I'm standing against the wall looking into my room, but I can still see him there, in my mind's eye, standing on the roof with his tan chest and white robe.

"Well, have a nice night," I yell out, and rest my head back against the wall.

"You too," he says after a beat. A few moments later, I hear the clang of a metal door.

Chapter 12

As I step outside, I see Camila in the front passenger seat of the black SUV. There's someone else rummaging in the trunk.

I tug at my denim shorts as I walk across the parking lot, wishing I'd gotten more sleep. I woke up in the middle of the night and the world was eerily quiet. Every cricket and frog seemed to be asleep. Even the waves were still. For a moment, I forgot where I was. A few hours later, the bugs were wide awake and buzzing. And so was my brain, busily reliving my balcony fiasco with René.

This morning is my chance to turn things around. This hike is my opportunity to bond with him and get on everyone's good side. Anything is more productive than watching security footage of René all day.

"*Buenos días*." Santiago steps out from behind the vehicle.

"*Buenos días*. Can I help with anything?"

"No thanks, we're ready," he says, shutting the trunk.

"Hi," I say to Camila as I get in the back seat. She turns ever so slightly, gives me a weak smile, and goes back to some sort of craft project on her lap.

"Ready?" Santiago turns on the car, and we pull onto the street. I was fully expecting René and possibly more of the crew to join us. With just the three of us, it feels an awful lot like I'm intruding.

We drive along the narrow roads for about thirty minutes, windows down, listening to a selection of low-key music. Santiago's playlist is a broad mix of reggae, a cappella hip hop, and mellow flamenco. Most with salaciously sensual lyrics.

The entire time, Camila either grooves to the music or hunches over a large Chanel handbag. She's sewing neon-colored thread along the seams at random, making a few of the squares pop and customizing her bag in the process.

"That looks really cool," I say, tapping her shoulder. I admire her valor at defacing what looks like an original and then making it better.

"Thanks," she says, lifting the bag to inspect her progress.

"I love it." I lean back into the seat, feeling more self-assured. Let the bonding commence.

Maybe it's a good thing René isn't here. I can focus on making some headway with Camila. And even try, as Meri suggested, to disconnect from the issues back home for a few hours.

We stop at a fruit stand on the side of the road and Santiago hops out to get us some fresh mango juice. Camila's absorbed in her sewing, so I take the opportunity to catch up on work emails.

There's one from a coworker asking me for a copy of a recent press release. Maureen is copied, so I draft a response so cheery and upbeat, anyone who reads it will think I'm doing fantastic and everything is perfectly fine.

Absolutely!! Here it is! Don't hesitate to ask for anything else!!

"A bowl of fresh-cut mango," Santiago says as he gets back in the car and hands us our juices, "would be part of my last meal." He pronounces it "man-go," the way my dad did. My chest drops and my breathing slows.

To focus on work, I reread the email I've just sent. Crap. *Too exclamation points.* I sound like I've downed a crate of energy drinks.

"Mine too," Camila says after a long sip. "Though I'm not sure it goes so well with the *rest* of my last meal. Mussels in Dijon and white wine, warm French bread to dunk into it, and a side of fried artichokes." Santiago moans supportively and I smile at the thought, feeling grateful that she's sharing. "René's last meal," she continues, "is *mofongo* and his mom's *fricasé de pollo.*"

"Oh yeah," Santiago says in agreement. "What's yours, Dani?"

"I don't know, I never thought about it. Would definitely include some Cuban bread slathered in butter and then dipped into coffee."

"Nice!" Santiago says, and even Camila nods approvingly.

We pass an overlook with views of a deep blue lagoon surrounded by mountains. I think back to the meal I had last night and wonder if there's a limit to how many courses you're allowed for your last meal.

The road climbs up a hill and then winds down again, and we turn into a small parking lot. We park near the start of the trail, and even from the car, I can see it gets steep right away.

"The hike's a little challenging, but it's worth it," Camila says as Santiago shuts the car off, his eyes watching me through the rearview mirror.

"Oh, okay. I'm excited," I say, masking my concern.

I didn't pack for adventurous trails. I mainly stuck to items that coordinated with my blazers. So, while Santiago and Camila are both looking fashionable and rugged, I look like I just crawled out of bed. Santiago's wearing a bright blue shimmery windbreaker over a bare chest, swim trunks covered in a floral print, and black hiking boots. Camila's in a low-cut, golden one-piece swimsuit, flowy violet shorts, and a pair of dark brown hiking boots. Meanwhile, I'm in a washed-out brown T-shirt I use to sleep in, the white denim shorts Meri packed for me, and my teal running sneakers.

A few steps into the trail, we're enveloped by the forest. It feels a few degrees cooler, and everywhere you look, there are different shades of green. Towering trees covered in dark green moss and then wrapped in light green vines.

Santiago leads the way, and I walk behind Camila, trying to avoid the thicker sections of mud on the path. Camila seems preoccupied. From time to time, she pulls her phone out of her back pocket, checks for something, and then puts it away.

"Ah." I've stepped into a deep patch of mud.

Camila turns around. "Try to keep to the sides."

"Yeah, good idea, thanks." I yank my leg and pull up a bare foot. The mud has kept my sneaker. And the sneaker has kept my sock. I drop my head back and let out a deep sigh. I bend over, balancing on one foot, and pluck the shoe free. "So how did both of you guys meet René?" I ask. I already know the answers, but I just want to make conversation.

"We met at college. René was studying music, I was in the fashion program." Camila hops between two stones, avoiding a muddy patch. "And he met Santi through a mutual friend last year."

"Well, that was lucky."

"Oh, there was no luck involved. It was totally planned. I get full credit for bringing them together." She pulls her phone out again, checks it, and puts it back. "No signal out here."

I groan a little to let her know I commiserate. "So how did it go yesterday in the studio?"

"It was good." The concise response sounds slightly irritated.

"And what's on the agenda for today, when we get back?"

She pulls her phone out of her pocket again as she walks. "I guess we'll know when René gets back to me."

It starts to rain, but most of it gets absorbed by the treetops before reaching us. We walk for a while, enveloped by its hollow tapping on the leaves.

A half hour later, Camila and I are standing alone in front of an enormous waterfall. Santiago has snuck off to pee in the woods. I'm in awe of this waterfall. It's more of a *waterwall* because it clings to the surface of a massive dark stone wall. It's a beautiful, clear-moving curtain, and it's so tall, the thunderous sound of the water continuously falling is hypnotic.

Did my father know about this place? I wonder if he ever came here? I look around and feel my chest tighten.

"René and I came here a few years ago." Camila pulls me out of my thoughts. "It feels like a long time ago." She sounds melancholic and it makes me speculate if they do, in fact, have a romantic history they've kept private.

"That makes sense. A lot's happened since then," I offer, taking a stab at comforting her.

She blinks in agreement, then steps around a tree to get closer to the river. There's a giant, translucent leaf near her face, and once again, I wish I brought my camera.

"Do you mind if I take your picture?" I ask her.

"Not at all!"

I pull out my cell and position myself so I can capture the silhouette of her face through the leaf. The lighting is perfect, her gold bikini shimmers, and everything is filtered by a canopy of trees. I feel as excited as I did last night on the balcony, exploring the best angles and playing around with the composition.

Camila loves the photos. And so do I. Her petite profile through the leaf looks like an olde-time fairy portrait.

"That's beautiful. Send them all to me!" It's clear I've chosen the right way to Camila's heart. "Whenever we have a signal," she adds with a sigh.

Santiago returns and we continue with the hike until we reach a fork in the road. The route to the left is overgrown bushes and an unruly climb, while the one on the right has steps made of logs carved into the dirt to help hikers.

"It's this way." Camila points to the trail on the left. "You're going to love this."

My interest piqued, I push on until we reach a clearing. Ahead of us is a large sloping rock surrounded by lush trees with a waterfall in the center that feeds a small clear blue pool.

"This waterslide is so much fun," Santiago says.

I check out the waterfall again and frown. Sure, the face of the rock *does* sort of have a natural curve to it, but I wouldn't call it a waterslide.

I stop at the foot of an enormous tree and take a seat on top of one of its aboveground roots. "I didn't bring a swimsuit." *I wish I had.* We've been walking for a while and my skin is sticky with sweat and rain. The idea of a cool, refreshing swim sounds amazing.

"Just swim in that," she says, waving at my outfit. "We've got towels in the car."

I stare at the waterfall. It's pretty grand. *And steep.* Still, I feel I should do it. This place is so ridiculously special. The late morning sun is a welcoming spotlight on the waterfall and the pool. It's, like, who would come all the way out here and *not* do this? I imagine us all after the plunge, bonding in the pool.

Santiago and Camila start climbing the face of the rock, their bodies bent over, using their hands to keep them steady. I take a deep breath and start to follow them, my mud-encrusted shoes struggling to get a grip on the slippery rock.

We reach the top and I peer over the sliding path, trying to map out how our bodies would handle all the rocky twists. We're about thirty feet above the ground. The fact that this is at the end of an unofficial trail has me questioning whether it's safe.

Camila takes off her shoes and then slips off her shorts. "You just do it like this." She sits down on the top of the waterfall, folds her arms over her chest, and scooches herself off the edge, gliding down the natural curves of the rock and into the pool below. The way I imagine an oyster looks slipping around our intestines.

"You want me to go first?" Santi can tell I'm nervous. He takes off his windbreaker and shoes.

"Come on! The water feels amazing," Camila calls up to us.

Santiago doesn't give it another thought. He sits, crosses his arms in front of him, and sets off. It's like he's made of rubber. He glides gently down and over the bumps, twisting along the turns, and splashes into the pool.

Alone on the top of the rock, I feel my heartbeat pick up. The bumpy, rocky path the water has carved over centuries into the stone doesn't get any smoother the longer I stare. Maybe if there were some sort of protection to go between me and these rocks? Like a sled, or a boogie board. We're just so far from a doctor.

"Just go for it," Camila yells. "You'll be fine!"

I wave and sit down, smiling.

I scooch an inch forward and then another, cool water splashing hard against my back and rushing down all around me. Camila and Santiago have swum farther away but they're still egging me on.

Fortune favors the bold. Even the nutty ones, I hope.

I try again but then stop mid-scooch. The feel of cool stone and water pulsing beneath me sparks a memory. I can hear my father singing the song he wrote for me. The song he'd sing at parties and sometimes like a lullaby to put us to sleep.

> *feel the heartbeat of a hidden waterfall*
> *give up fear for flying*

There's a verse about this place in the song. He *was* here.

In a bit of a haze, I scooch again and I'm off. My whole body tenses up like it's physically trying to stop the memory, while also stopping my body from plummeting down the steep incline of this non-waterslide. I'm supposed to slither down smoothly, but instead I stiffen and take each corner like I'm in a pinball machine.

I scream as I hit the water. My knee throbs and my lower back is on fire. The force of the fall from such a height pushes me deep down below the surface.

When I resurface, and I'm done coughing, I assure Camila and Santiago I'm okay. Convinced it's safe to leave me alone, they swim to shore and slide down the rock wall a few more times. The water is cool and refreshing and slowly numbs the sting on my knee.

I dunk my head beneath the water, then look up. I'm quickly

stilled by the contrast of the brisk water from the neck down and the hot sun on my face. Thick vines connect the trees that tower around the lagoon, and bright red wildflowers freckle the green on the ground. I feel completely enveloped, as though inside a tropical snow globe.

Chapter 13

"René's taking a break from the studio today," camila tells Santiago, relaying a message she's listening to on her cell as we drive back to the house.

A break? A break from *what*? How can you need a break when you're just getting started? Maybe he wants to hole up in his room to work on new lyrics? Especially if he's really thrown away what he came here with.

"He wants you to call him, Santi." Camila sounds pissy.

Whatever René's up to today, I'm no closer to getting access to filming it. Any points I may have won on the hike to the waterfall, I lost on the way back. I had to limp slowly the whole way to the car, which gave the mosquitos more time to bite us. And they seemed especially drawn to Camila.

My leg is stretched out on the back seat. I adjust my knee ever so slightly and check out the missing layer of flesh on the side. I'm fine. Just a little shaken up. The first aid kit Santiago found in the car had an antibacterial spray. This was sprayed generously on my knee, my left elbow, and on the rug-burn-looking rash along my spine. My body feels bruised, sticky, and dry. When we pull up to the house, Santiago hands me the antiseptic spray. "Here, you should probably reapply."

"Thanks."

We say our goodbyes and I limp away feeling spent. Instead of heading for the cottage, I step off the decked path and decide to meander around the compound. The grounds are mostly manicured but there are areas that haven't been touched. In those spots, the fruit trees grow haphazardly. There's plantain, papaya, and mango. Man-*go*. I wobble aimlessly past an over-grown garden.

Pretty soon, I can't go any farther. I turn around and everywhere around me is too prickly to pass. I have no idea how I got in here. I'm about twenty feet into these bushes. I take a step toward the right and something sharp grazes my scraped knee, making me wince. I've been fighting back tears since I crawled out of the lagoon, and they're threatening to come out.

My phone buzzes with a call, and I answer it even when I see it's from Maureen. Anything is better than dealing with these emotions.

"Maureen, hi." I try to sound like I have everything under control and not like I'm in the middle of a prickly bush field I'm going to need to be airlifted out of.

"Hi, Dani, how's it going?" she asks sweetly but getting right to the point.

"Well." I pat a fresh layer of warm sweat on my forehead. "I'm just getting back from spending some quality time with René's producer and assistant."

"That's great. And how's René?" I can tell she's smiling. "Have you been able to get him to open up yet?"

"You know, he *has* opened up...in some ways." I picture

René on his rooftop last night, his undone robe flapping in the wind.

Maureen lets out a sigh of relief through the phone. "That's good news. Tell me about the interview."

"The interview?" My throat gets all itchy. "We did interview some of his team, but not René just yet. I'm...focusing on, building trust first, you know."

"That's probably the best approach," she responds approvingly. "You know what, Dani, I have to say, I'm relieved you're there. You share the same culture, you're so familiar with his music."

Her words couldn't feel further from the truth. Especially not after the hike. Logically, I know I don't have to slide down a secret waterfall without getting hurt in order to belong here, but that's how I feel. Like I've failed a test.

"Send over what you've taped so far," Mo says, wrapping up the call. "I'm excited to see!"

"Absolutely, we can do that. We'll send you something right away. And...we'll get an interview with René soon. Thanks for believing in me, Mo." My voice almost cracks toward the end. We hang up and my arm dangles heavily by my side.

There's a loud splash behind me and reggae music kicks on from the direction of the pool. *Great.* If René isn't going to make music today, I hate that we're also missing capturing him as he unwinds.

To rub salt into my own wounds, everything rises to the surface. How upset Mom is with me and how stressed out Meri sounded because of the tutor I hired for her. I fight back tears and try to move, but the prickly plants poke my leg dangerously close to my injured knee and I let out a moan of frustration. Everything hurts. My knee throbs, and my back feels itchy and tender. The feeling of being stuck is overwhelming. I don't know what to do. A few tears escape and travel down my cheeks.

I can't hold them back anymore.

I have the strangest feeling I'm being watched. I hear a crunching sound behind me, so I turn around and my heart climbs up near my throat. René is in the clearing, walking away from me. I have no idea if he's witnessed my teary moment or heard me on the phone with Maureen. So I just stand still, choosing to remain stuck for a moment.

Chapter 14

I haven't convinced myself to try moving again when I hear someone calling my name. "Dani!" James is jogging toward me. "René's giving us an interview," he explains when he's close enough. "He suggested we do it in your room and I told him that'd be fine. I hope that's okay."

I register this, then dart out of the weeds, my hand framed over my knee for protection. Did René hear me talking to Maureen? Maybe he heard what happened to me on the waterslide and he feels sorry for me? Whatever the reason, I don't care. This is it, we're in. I could send Maureen a snippet of this interview right way and it'll be like the past day and a half never happened.

"I need to jump in the shower," I blurt out as James carries camera gear into my room.

"Sure, just let me know where you want to put him." He surveys the room.

"What about over there?" I point to the far corner, near my bed, where the thatched ceiling comes down to the floor.

"That works."

"Great." I leave him to it, and study the contents of my closet. As much as I'd like to wear jeans, my knee will need something softer. Reluctantly, I pull out the lime green wraparound dress Meri packed for me.

I take the quickest shower of my life, skipping the hair since I won't have time to blow-dry it. Meri's dress fits like it was made for me. It hangs just above the knee and is made of a soft, sweater-like fabric that wraps around my body.

I let the bun down and it falls into big, pretty waves. I adjust a few loose strands, and they're surprisingly compliant. Who knew sweat, lagoon water, and rain that's been through sticky trees would make the perfect hair product?

I step out of the bathroom as James is finishing up. He places the camera on the tripod and snaps the viewfinder out for me. He's lit the warm thatched texture in the background with an amber light, and framed the shot in a way so the white curtains from the sliding glass door are on the right, flowing with the breeze. It's the perfect tropical vibe for the making of this album. *And also resembles a photo shoot for a light beachy beer.*

René must have known this room would be ideal for the interview. He could have toured all the rooms when they first arrived, or maybe the thatched walls and ceiling can be seen from below. As long as him wanting to come in my room has nothing to do with catching me taking pictures of myself in my underwear last night.

I find the questions I prepared back home for our first interview and tuck them into my clipboard. A wave of nervous energy courses through me as I review them and scribble down new questions at the bottom of the page. Avoiding a few that pop into my head. *Did he really not see me? If he did, was he disappointed I wasn't wearing a G-string?*

René could arrive at any moment.

The problem is, I'm starving.

Someone brought in a tray of sandwiches while I was in the shower. James ate his, but I'm eyeing mine with distrust. I can't imagine it will be easy to eat. It's enormous, for one thing. Slices of juicy meat, lettuce, and tomatoes encased in two large pieces of fried plantains instead of bread. How can I eat this gracefully, without it falling apart in my hands? Maybe if I ditch the plantains and just have the rest with a fork and knife. Then again, it seems a travesty not to have it the way the chef intended. Wrapped in plantains crisped to perfection with all those crumbly salt flakes on top.

I'm standing by the door, sandwiched stuffed into my mouth, when René walks in with Camila.

"*Hola.*" He breezes in and introduces himself to James first, then turns around and straightens up at the sight of me.

I throw a finger in the air asking for a second while I break down the sandwich I practically had to dislocate my jaw to get my mouth around. I don't regret it, it's so good. But this is going to take a moment.

René takes a look around the room and our interview setup. "*No, no. Aquí no,*" he says, determined, and steps out onto the balcony. "I meant *outside*. It's so much better out here for photography"—he eyes me knowingly.

I start coughing uncontrollably. When I recover, I follow him outside.

René sets his things on the floor, leans against the railing, and poses. He's wearing a light pink terry cloth shirt and matching shorts with the designer's logo sewn down the edges. The outfit, the dark sunglasses, the puckered lips. He couldn't be flashier if he tried. And yet... the sun is low in the sky, bathing him in a warm glow, and the guy looks amazing.

"Sure, this is good." I'm trying to keep up and seem flexible, but inside we would have had been able to control the lighting. Now, we're in a time crunch with these dark clouds gathering and the setting sun.

James gives me a supportive thumbs-up, steps outside, and expertly slips a microphone inside René's shirt. Camila squeezes out onto the balcony too, holding a shiny black display case lined with velvet and overflowing with colorful lacquered sunglasses. René tries out a few options for her.

"I like these." Camila pulls out enormous red ones.

He checks out his reflection in the sliding glass door. He doesn't seem sold, but he leaves them on.

"What do you think?" James has sprung into action and set up the camera beside me on the cramped balcony.

When I look through the viewfinder, René shifts his pose for me. Chin up, face tilted, hands in his pockets. It's a great shot. His shirt is completely unbuttoned so the eye is drawn to his chest tattoos, and then his stepping-stone abs, which lead to the tight skin around his belly button. Then, I notice his rooftop garden directly behind him in the shot and instantly feel heat in my cheeks.

"Looks good, thanks."

"Great, I'll hit record and watch the monitor from inside, so you can stay out here."

"I don't know anyone that's ever hurt themselves on those slides." René pulls his glasses off to inspect the wound on my knee.

"Well, now you do."

"What were you saying up there? I heard"—he motions to Camila inside—"you were talking to yourself before you went down."

"I wasn't talking to myself." *Was I?* "Oh . . . I was just trying to remember the lyrics of a song."

"Strange time to remember a song." René's eyes narrow with interest. "Which one?"

I let out a short exhale. "You wouldn't know it."

"Try me."

"No, you *couldn't* know it. It was a song my father wrote."

"He's a musician?" René using the present tense again is a jab to the throat.

I stare at him for a moment, unsure how to respond and whether now's the time to clarify. "Yes." I hear my voice drop.

"*Qué padre*," he responds, impressed. I concentrate on how fitting the expression is. It means, "*That's cool*," but also technically, "*What a dad!*" "What's the song about?"

I feel slightly disoriented. "I think we should get started before we lose the sun." I check his image through the view-finder one more time.

"Do you want me to look at the camera or you?" René slips his glasses back on.

"Me, please." He tilts his head obediently. "And do you want to take your sunglasses off?" I press boldly. I don't know why, but I get the impression he doesn't *actually* want to wear them. "It's easier for people to connect with you if they can look you in the eyes."

René seems surprised; his eyebrows are peaking over his sunglasses.

"How about these?" Camila's back, brandishing a pair of aviators clear enough to see through.

He drops his head, pulls his glasses down slowly with both hands, and passes them over to Camila. He slips on the new pair and looks right at me.

"Much better. Trust me." And they really are better. His dark, bedroom eyes are also vulnerable. And somehow, knowing you can see them, has changed his demeanor. It's as though a weight has been lifted. He's still a Casanova reggaetonero, but now, he also seems gentler. And *way* less arrogant.

I can't help but savor the victory. *I'm here, I'm doing this.* I take a deep breath to steady myself. "Let's dive right into the album. How do you start such an undertaking? Lyrics or the music?"

He takes a beat, and adjusts himself on the railing. "It depends. Sometimes we have a beat we want to start with, sometimes I have a chorus we build on. It doesn't matter where we start, though." He shifts again.

Happy enough with his response, I glance back at my clipboard. I have pages of questions and I'd like to get in as many as I can.

"Why *El Rico*? I know it's common in reggaeton, but why have a nickname at all?"

He looks at me, his face stiff. "Why Dani, and not Daniela?"

I'm worried I may have struck a nerve. I don't see why. He's never explained where the name comes from before, but now should be different. He's stepping out on his own; he should be able to explain something so fundamental.

A sigh escapes me. "I asked first, but okay"—I loosen my grip on the clipboard, and give in to his question—"it just never sounded right to me."

"Why not?"

"Daniela's too...something I'm not. Feminine or, I don't know, effervescent."

He cracks a smile. "*Okay*. So, it's along the same lines for me."

"Well, that's not an answer I can use," I jab, trying to keep things light. Light yet professional. Exactly the type of creative marketing director I want to be known for being.

"El Rico does whatever he wants and says things René can't," he adds begrudgingly. "And just to clarify, it's an alter ego, not a nickname."

"So it's El Rico who wants all the ladies to drop their panties on the dance floor? Not René?" I spit out, quoting lyrics from his songs.

His jaw shifts and he takes his hands from the railing and slips them into his pockets. I thought it was a clever follow-up, but he's scowling. He seems uncomfortable, and possibly hurt. Okay, so maybe there *was* a hint of mockery in my voice, but I can't help it if they really are ridiculous lyrics.

"Let's just move on." I glance at the list. "Any worries as you begin the recording process?"

"Of course." He's cold as ice. "But I try not to think about that. I get to make music with my friends for people to dance to. What on earth could be wrong with that?" It's as though he's defending himself.

I nod and glance back at the questions, feeling warm all over. I skip over the next two instinctively. *Why do you think you've finally gotten your own record deal? Why haven't you addressed what happened between you and Natalia?* Both seem too hard-hitting for the moment. Even if the last one would significantly help his image.

"Do you think my music is shallow?"

I tense and look up to see René rub his hand against his buzz-cut hair.

"What? No." I lower the clipboard.

I try to read his thoughts and they're not good. *So you didn't know me, or my music, and now you don't respect it.* I scoff to myself, brushing off the list of offenses. I focus on the clipboard I'm squeezing with both hands. "Let's talk about—" I'm about to ask him to share the story about coming by this house when he was little, when it starts to rain.

We both seem to have the exact same reaction. Stunned by the initial downpour and then amazed by the steady, warm shower. Our view is even more beautiful now that it's draped by water falling through the late afternoon sun. We're above the trees so we can see the rain moving in sheets over the ocean.

The overhang above the balcony covers us completely, so there's no need to worry about the equipment getting wet. The rain loosens up the dynamic between us a bit. The earthy smell of cool rain on hot grass neutralizes things.

"René," Camila calls out sternly from the bed. "Talk about the old track you want to remix."

"We're not doing that anymore," René responds, looking off at the rain.

I catch a hint of offense in the way Camila is combing her fingers through her hair. Like heaven forbid he change his mind about something and not tell her.

Suddenly, René rises excitedly. I follow his gaze to a nearby branch. He takes his sunglasses off, picks up a small electronic device from the floor where he set his things down, and without any explanation, lifts both of his legs over the railing.

Chapter 15

René leans away from the balcony, one hand on the railing and the other holding what appears to be a high-tech wireless microphone.

"Come on," he calls out, "cover it with that." He eyes my clipboard, I assume because his fancy microphone isn't waterproof.

Camila and James are standing by the sliding door and I'm waiting for someone to say something. It's only the second floor, but with his whole body leaning out like that, it's still dangerous. What is he even aiming his recorder at?

I look back at René, and his eyes are on me. He's got this big, ecstatic smile on his face, encouraging me. Wondering why in the world I'm not out there yet.

I convince myself I can override the part of my brain that worries, and I thrust the clipboard at James. I lift a leg over the railing, and I'm over on the other side. Once I've got a grip on the railing, I take the clipboard back and lean out to join René.

I squeeze my eyes shut to avoid looking down, and stretch out my arm, covering his microphone with my clipboard.

When I open my eyes, I'm more aware of our proximity. René's face is only a few inches away.

Co-kee, co-kee. There's a tiny coquí frog on a leaf, his whole body smaller than a quarter. This is what René's aiming his microphone at. He puffs up each time he makes a sound.

I look down. "If the railing gives," I warn, "we'll be impaled by that spiky palm tree down—"

René shushes me, just as the rain picks up. I turn my face one way and then another, hoping to find a way to get less wet. I love the rain when I'm nice and dry *inside*. I've never really seen the romance in purposefully stepping outside to dance in the rain.

I squeeze my shoulders in, crunch up my nose, and narrow my eyes as though it's possible to create less surface area to get rain on. I'm frozen in this frowny defensive face, like someone's about to slap me.

René watches me, holding in a laugh. Imagining what I must look like makes me want to laugh too.

Other coquis are heard not too far away at different intervals but the one we're recording is quiet for a moment.

Over my shoulder, I see James on the balcony holding the camera now, recording us. I'm so close to René, I'll be in the shot, but at least we're getting *something* interesting. That is, if René's recording this sound for the album. I hope I'm not risking my life for René's random animal sound collection.

Co-kee, co-kee. Our tiny frog perks up again, his chin and belly taking turns inflating. René eyes me excitedly. I can't help but feel excited too. And watch the rain drip down the bridge of his nose, and over his full lips.

René's eyes dart down at my legs. I can feel my skirt is stuck somewhere high up on my thigh. At least the water isn't stinging my knee the way it did in the shower. Probably due to the adrenaline of dangling from a balcony. I notice that the waves on the beach have gone quiet and I decide to embrace the feeling of defying death while being completely drenched.

"That's good," René says suddenly, pulling himself toward the railing. Camila's waiting with a towel for him, but he turns and reaches for me instead.

With his help, I get back over the railing. Our eyes lock and I feel a warmness in my stomach. Then he winces, grabbing at his collar.

"Oh man, I'm sorry. Forgot about this." He hands James the now-soaking microphone that was attached to his shirt.

A few minutes later, we're both towel-dried and René settles against the railing again. It's raining more gently now and he's bathed in the warm last few minutes of light. I'm relieved he's agreed to continue with the interview, since we really haven't gotten much. He's taken off his wet shirt, but I don't think anyone will complain about a shirtless interview, and James has set up a new microphone over his head.

"You don't want to change?" René asks. "I can wait."

"I'm good," I lie. Meri's sweater-like dress feels like I'm wrapped in a drenched beach towel but we're almost out of light and I don't want to slow things down.

I take my spot by the camera James has set back up again for the interview and grab my clipboard. The pages are soaked and stuck together. I try to lift the top sheet and it peels right off, making René laugh.

"So, where were we? Oh, right," he says, "you were telling me everything you love about reggaeton."

"No, please," I say without any edge in my voice. I push a strand of wet hair off my face. Surprisingly, I feel more relaxed than I'd expect after dangling from a balcony in the pouring rain. Like I've had a couple sips of a strong cocktail. "What was that all for?" I ask, motioning to the frog.

"For the album," he admits. "I want to capture Puerto Rico. My culture." His face brightens and something softens inside me. "I'm so incredibly lucky." He takes in the view. "We used to come here all the time when I was a kid and camp on the beach. I just want to share it."

Now that he's loosened up, it's the perfect time to ask the kinds of questions that make the most sense for press. "This album could catapult things for you." I'm happily in a groove. "After all the duets, are you finally ready to be the leading man?"

He shakes his head disapprovingly. He grabs his cell, and after some quick typing, he looks back up at me and flashes a fake smile.

"How'd they turn out, by the way?" René asks provocatively. "The photos," he adds, motioning to the chaise on the balcony next to us.

The blood slips away from my face, making me feel instantly pale.

"Oh, that. Ha." I feign a nonchalant laugh. "Good." I glance over at James and Camila, who are sitting on my bed, listening to every word.

"Just curious." He's flirting with me. *Or pretending to.* He leans back, rests his hands on the railing, and strikes a new pose.

I can't help but size him up. I think everything he's doing is some sort of tactic to disarm me. Moving the interview out here, bringing up last night. He did this in the few interviews I watched too. He'd be all sly and flirty so they wouldn't even notice he wasn't actually answering the questions.

I glance at James inside and wonder if he thinks René is flirting with me. He seems fine. I try to imagine how I'd feel if he were the one getting hit on and decide I'd feel fine too. I can hear Meri's disapproving voice in my head. She'd say it's too soon for either of us to feel that way. But I disagree. We *should* want our exes to move on and be happy. *Shouldn't we?*

"You could have found a nice low-to-the-ground frog to record. Were you just avoiding my questions?"

He chuckles. "Why not? You're avoiding mine."

"What do you mean?"

"The waterfall," he reminds me. "Your father's song. I asked you what it was about."

"Oh, that," I respond, and René nods, satisfied. "Okay, fine. My father's song...yeah. It's about all of his favorite places here. And the waterfall we went to today was in it." René leans forward. "I realized it when I was up there."

It dawns on me, if I want him to open up, I may have to do it first. I'll just do that thing where I pretend I'm talking about someone else, and not my dad. "He actually passed away six years ago."

René's leans back. "I thought...I'm sorry."

"It's okay."

"What are the other places?"

"I don't remember. I haven't heard the song in a long time."

"I'd love to hear it."

"I actually have a recording of it." I look off and notice the light has changed dramatically. I lose myself for a moment in the beautiful sight of the sun retreating and what it's done to the sky and the ocean. "But it's recorded on one of those old audio cassettes," I say absently.

From the corner of my eye, I sense movement inside the

room. "We need to get going; we have the call to discuss the photo shoot," Camila barks.

"Sorry." He stands, dodging the boom microphone set up just above him.

"Sure, okay." I try to sound cool and like I'm not the least bit disappointed I opened up about all that for nothing. "Actually," I shout after him, "we'd really like to get in the studio with James and a proper camera. If that's okay." I can feel Camila's eyes on me. "I know you don't want to be disturbed, but we'll be discreet. You won't even know we're there."

"Yeah, okay," René says, "for a little bit." He turns to go, then stops at the door. "Have that cassette shipped. There's some old machines in the studio; there might be a cassette player."

"I have it with me." As soon as I say the words, there's a pinch in my stomach.

He tilts his head back in relief. "Bring it tomorrow."

"Okay, cool," I say even though it's not cool. It's not anywhere near the vicinity of cool.

Chapter 16

It's come down to the blazer. I'm torn between the light blue tapered and the beige double-breasted. The beige is comfy, unthreatening. It's ready for work but could also easily be grabbing a matcha latte on a Sunday afternoon. The tapered is all business. A mix of rayon and spandex so it gives without yielding its form.

Today's the first day we're allowed in the studio as a proper behind-the-scenes crew, so I want to make the right impression. I want to blend in, but also be taken seriously. Most importantly, I want everyone to feel they can trust me.

Yesterday's interview wasn't groundbreaking, but at least I had something to send to Maureen. James helped me prepare a clip of René describing how he wants to share his culture in this album, along with a few moments of him hanging off the balcony recording the frog sounds.

I slip the tapered blazer on and pull my hair into a tight ballerina bun.

My cell buzzes and I'm surprised to see who's calling.

"Hey, Mom, how's it going?"

"Here, fine. Did you see my email?" She sounds unsettled.

"No, let me check." Mom prefers sending emails to texts. Her main form of communication is an email. Even if she often sends a text to let you know she's sent an email.

I find her email and gasp. She's sent a photo of the wall where the large window is supposed to go, except it looks like it's been attacked by an ax. Three large sections of sheet rock have been cut out, exposing the insides of the walls.

"Did you see?" Her tone is accusatory. I wish I'd been there to help with all the things she must have had to deal with. Clearing the room for the workers, wrangling the dogs, who must have barked the entire time.

"Yeah, it's—"

"They made such a mess. All for nothing." As she speaks, she riles herself up.

"What do you mean?"

"They need to get an engineer because they couldn't find the structural load." The last two words sound studied. "They said it will take another week, but I don't believe them. Who knows when this is going to be fixed?"

"I'll call them."

"Meri's doing that."

"She's got enough on her plate, Mom."

"When you get home, this mess will probably still be here." She sounds frustrated.

"I'm sure it will all be done by then." I try to comfort her. "But I'm sorry about the mess, and the delays."

"I just wanted you to know so you're not surprised when you get the bill for the engineer. *Setecientos cincuenta pesos.*" She has switched to Spanish for the price because "seven hundred and fifty dollars" in English would seem fair. Whereas "*Setecientos cincuenta pesos*" said loudly and with more inflection sounds like a colossal rip-off. And it's worked. I feel the sting of the additional cost to the already costly windows *that* much more.

"How'd you sleep?" I find James at the small mosaic bistro table near the pool and set my breakfast tray down. "Good," he says, though he sounds otherwise. "Do you want to sit inside?" James inspects my outfit.

"No, no. I'm fine." I tug at the mock turtleneck beneath my blazer. "This is sleeveless."

"Okay." I pick up a hint of irritation in his voice.

I notice he's wearing the white linen button-down shirt I gave him for his birthday last year. We've yet to receive a schedule from Camila, so we agreed to meet for breakfast at 8:00 a.m. and set up in the studio before anyone arrives.

I turn my focus to breakfast. *Café con leche* and a bowl of *farina*. The burst of warm buttery sweet cinnamon has time-traveling powers. How long has it been since I've had *farina*? I move the spoon around the bowl, lost in the memory. Dad used to make it for us on the weekends, when he had the time.

James stirs his coffee loudly. Something is definitely on his mind.

"Everything okay?" I ask.

He pulls his lips in and takes a breath. "Yesterday was irresponsible," he says at last. "He shouldn't have pressured you to step over the balcony like that. You could have been hurt."

"I didn't feel pressured," I respond, somewhat defensive. "It was fine, I felt safe."

He nods, but I'm not sure he's satisfied with my response. "How's your injury?" he asks with the seriousness of a cop and points to the wrong leg.

"It's better, thanks. Just a little swollen today."

Being out in the rain with René feels like a distant dream. The waterfall, Dad's song. I purposefully left the audio cassette back in my room, hoping René will forget all about it. Now there's the busted-up wall, Mom's frustration, and the additional cost of an engineer.

We head to the studio in silence and I try not to think about how badly I need to keep my job. I just have to keep squashing the bad thoughts away and try to focus on the task at hand. *Is it me, or is James dragging his feet?* There are so many concerns to squash, with new ones creeping up by the second. My brain's playing one drawn-out round of whack-a-mole.

Inside the studio, Santiago is on his laptop and there's an engineer inside the recording booth moving equipment around. Santiago presses the button on the intercom connecting him to the booth. "René's getting his guitar, so we'll need that microphone." The engineer gives him a thumbs-up through the glass.

I exchange looks with James, and he heads across the room to prep his camera.

"Oh, check it out," Santiago calls out to me and points to something a few feet away from his console. I peek behind the long desk. Beneath the wide audio mixer is a stack of bulky equipment encased in stainless steel. Santiago leans over, presses a button, and a tape cassette deck glides out smoothly, like a mouth opening wide. "Did you need one of these?"

Chapter 17

WHEN RENÉ WALKS IN AND SEES ME NEAR THE CASSETTE DECK, his face lights up like a kid who's discovered a new toy. "You're going to play the song?"

There's a brief moment of doubt. How bad could it be to hear my father's voice for the first time in six years? What are the chances I'll burst into tears?

"Let me hear the song," René demands in a low, playful voice that catches me off guard.

I gather myself. "I forgot it in my room." I let my chest drop, feigning disappointment. "I'll bring it another time."

Even through the dark sunglasses, I can tell René narrows his eyes at me for a second, like he's trying to figure me out.

He sets his guitar down and turns his attention to Santiago. "You ready?"

"Yeah, this is what I was telling you about for the baseline." Santiago turns up the volume and a deep drumbeat comes on that ticks and tocks like a piano's metronome.

"It's laid back, I like it," René says, strumming his guitar.

James begins filming and I tiptoe past them to the far corner of the room. I squat amid the film gear and pick up the wireless monitor so I can watch James's shots.

With a few adjustments, Santiago has turned the groovy solitary drum into more drums that come in at different beats. He then uses the keyboard to create the beginnings of a melody. They jam for a little while and I find myself captivated watching the entire process along in the monitor. My heart perks up. *This* is what the making of the album should look like.

"Let's muffle it up," René says.

Santiago taps a few things out on his computer and plays it all back, including a new electronic steel drum. He programs a low snare to come in every once in a while, and both he and René get visibly hyped. Doesn't seem like much to get so excited about but I'm relieved we're finally recording something. Who knows, maybe this intermittent drum will be a very recognizable part of René "El Rico" Rodriguez's first single as a solo artist?

"Evasive, right?" Santiago makes adjustments and the sound of the beat changes slightly. There's an old-time record static noise added and the beats get deeper.

With a sense of urgency, René steps inside the vocal booth, his guitar in tow. I stand slowly and tilt my head a few times at James to nudge him into the booth with René. He opens the recording booth's door and steps inside. On my monitor, the camera tilts from a close-up of René's hands skillfully playing the guitar, up to his face as he starts to hum.

"How's that?" René asks Santiago through the booth's microphone and speaker system.

Santiago nods approvingly and drags things around on the large computer screen. So far, this is nothing like the studio sessions I've been to. For one, other than René's guitar, the music is being generated entirely with a computer.

Santiago taps the space bar, sits back, and hits play. They've created a new version of reggaeton's distinctive pattern: *boom chicki boom chic, boom chicki boom chic.* More sounds join in as the song intensifies, like a party hyping up.

I look at the time and scribble away in my notepad to keep track of what we're capturing.

11:07 am
Santiago gets up and waves his arms around
René stands, and moves his body slowly to the beat

11:12 am
Camila arrives and starts to dance
Camila steps into the booth
Camila and René dance together

I peel my eyes from the monitor to watch the real thing through the glass door of the recording booth. Camila twirls her hips, lips pouting. She turns around and backs up against René, thrusting her butt to the rhythm.

She's wearing a cropped tank top and tight jeans that hang low on her waist. She rolls her body to the sensual, steady beat and René follows along. They're so in sync, it seems rehearsed. As though it's a song they've danced to before, and not one René and Santiago just made up.

I wonder if there *is* something other than friendship going on between them. René notices me watching them, and feeling caught, I return to taking notes.

11:15 am
René tells Santiago to stop the track

Camila steps out of booth, sits on couch

I write quickly, then look at the monitor with curiosity.

"Play it again." René's tone is curt. Santiago does as he's told, and the music fills the room again. "When you hear this rhythm, what does it make you want to do?" He's looking straight at the camera lens. I lean into the monitor, trying to figure out what he's up to. He grins, sits back on the tall stool, and folds his arms, as though waiting for a response.

11:16 am
René interacts with the camera as though talking to
     future viewers of this behind-the-scenes

"Dani." René's voice resonates through the speaker system. My eyes widen. "What does this music make you want to do?" he asks, still looking at the camera.

I creep up until I'm standing. James holds the shot on René, and simultaneously looks over his shoulder in my direction. Now that I'm in plain view, René fixes his gaze on me. The beats play on and everyone in the room is watching for my response.

I flip through potential responses he could be digging for. *Smile. Buy the album. Share it with a friend.* "Dance?"

"I would hope so."

And *I* hope he hasn't noticed the flicker of irritation on my face. Relieved I've answered correctly, I slink back down into the seat.

"So, why aren't you dancing?" René asks, causing a thick, defensive knot to form in my stomach.

"I'm...I'm working." I manage to mask my exasperation.

"But you see"—René leans his head against the glass, pretending to be exhausted—"that's the thing. If the song doesn't make you move, then I'm not doing *my* job."

There's an unmistakable flash of annoyance on my face. I do not appreciate being put on the spot like this, but I don't want to say the wrong thing and get us kicked out of the studio.

"No *perreo* for you?" he presses.

"God, no," I utter without thinking.

René unfolds his arms and tucks his hands into his pockets. His shoulders slump, as he gets more comfortable in his stance. "Why not?"

"Uh, well." I measure my words. "I haven't quite mastered my *perreo* just yet."

"Really? That's concerning," he says, somewhat seductively. "What part of the dance do you need help with?"

The beat drags on. "Oh, you know." It's a struggle to keep my face from revealing my irritation. How could he already know where my buttons are? "I guess, mainly, the um, doggy-style part of it," I manage with a smile.

"And why is that?" His lips pucker.

"I, you know, the backing up on your dance partner. It doesn't look quite right when I do it."

"Maybe you're trying too hard." He flashes a mischievous smile.

"Maybe it's not for everyone," I snap, my face stiff. I'm trying so hard to remain calm, but I feel I'm speeding on an oily street and could skid out of control at any moment.

"I know what your problem is."

"Do you?" I say through gritted teeth.

"You need to let go. Loosen up." He shakes his shoulders around to show me.

What is it you're supposed to do, turn into a skid? Against it? Just let go of the steering wheel? I open my mouth to respond but I'm saved by a burly guy bringing in a tray of frothy espressos in see-through glasses. He sets the tray down on the coffee table and starts stomping his legs to the music, head bobbing along without a care in the world.

Chapter 18

IT ISN'T STALKING WHEN KEEPING TABS ON SOMEONE IS PART of your job. Just a part of the gig. Besides, I'm only peeking anytime I walk past my balcony. What? I'm supposed to *never* look outside? It's not my fault I have a clear unobstructed view of René, Santiago, and Camila as they have dinner on the long wooden table on his deck and later when they lounge for a while with their drinks on the comfy hanging chairs and the plush hammock suspended between two palms.

René has had most dinners out there with his friends while James and I have joined the technicians at the small tables in the dining room. While we're all living in the same compound, when it comes to meals, there's this unspoken upstairs-downstairs situation. Or people who *really* know him versus people who don't.

When Santiago and Camila have gone to bed, René settles on the outdoor couch with his notebook. My dad used to say the world can be divided into people who are content nibbling and those who want to swallow the world whole. *Comerse el mundo.*

René is definitely the latter. He's intensely alive no matter what he's doing or who he's with.

Earlier, when he was surrounded by his close friends, he was up and telling stories with fervor. When they spoke, he laughed, gasped, and even listened actively. Now he's alone, and every move is somehow artful. He crosses his legs, rubs his temple, and scribbles into a notebook. He's intense when he's still too.

I wish he'd let us film these intimate writing sessions and some of these meals. *And not just because I'd love to hear what he has to say when he actually opens up.* Seeing him unwind with his friends would be great for the behind-the-scenes of the album.

This morning I'm convinced things will improve. Different birds' songs overlap, and in the distance, a rooster crows. It doesn't hurt that I'm in one of my favorite outfits: tight black jeans, extra-long black blazer over a white button-down, with a thin black ribbon tied into a neat bow around the collar. René will *not* be getting to me today.

"I need to go check on some equipment I ordered," James says, stacking his dirty dishes methodically.

"Don't rush. I don't think René will be up anytime soon."

He finishes his coffee and stands. "What makes you say that?"

Because I was spying on him as he wrote late into the night. "Wild guess."

An hour later, when the studio door opens and René walks in, my heartbeat speeds up. He's wearing an unbuttoned Hawaiian shirt, orange shorts, and thick, white-framed sunglasses that wrap entirely around his head. He greets James and me with a "*buenos días*" that somehow sounds naughty.

After two hours, the back-and-forth improvisation between Santiago and René feels like unfulfilled foreplay. They start a track, creating loose guitar melodies and interesting snared-out beats, but after a certain point, they abandon it and move on to something else.

They seem to be having fun. Things get brainstormed, built up, talked about, grooved to, but then scrapped or put aside for another day.

I can make the footage we've captured work if René tells us about the lack of progress and how he's feeling about it. We only have access for another few minutes, so when Santiago steps outside, I take my chance. "Come on." I tap James on the shoulder and walk over to the booth. Gently, I push the door open and René lifts his head. "Can we ask you a few questions?" I lay on a super-sweet tone that I hope conveys, "I come in peace."

"Sure." Today he's wearing amber-tinted sunglasses and I wonder if he'll take them off the moment James and I leave the studio.

I take a seat on a speaker so I can be at René's eye level for the interview. It's a small room, so we're only a few feet apart. "How do you feel things are going today?"

"You look hot," he says, ignoring my question.

Is he seriously hitting on me? I scoff, adjusting myself and nearly fall off the speaker.

"Aren't you hot in all that?" he asks, gesturing at my outfit.

"Oh, no," I shriek, relieved, and then repeat in a regular voice, "No, I'm fine." I try but I'm unable to suppress a smile. Amused to have thought he was complimenting me. *Keep on keeping on.* "A lot of Latinx artists are crossing over these days. Is that something you think about?"

"Such a funny phrase. Sounds like you're dying. Like, you're *crossing over* to the next life or something."

"Doesn't that excite you?"

"I'm not going to cross over."

"Why not? Wouldn't it be a good thing?" I ask confidently, crossing my legs. I feel soothed by this quiet, muffled room. The puffy cushions on the walls zero out the sound completely. I feel like we could curse at each other in here and the room would swallow the words up as soon as they were spoken.

"I'm staying right here. All those people *over there* can come *over here* if they want to hear my music."

I nod, impressed. "Well, your *real* fans would follow you anywhere." I twirl the ribbon around my collar and glance at the composition notebook on the table. "Is that where you work on your lyrics?"

"Yeah, or on my phone," he says casually, extending his legs long out in front of him so his shoes are touching mine.

"When will we get to hear some?"

"Soon. I was up late working on something new, actually."

"Oh, were you?" I pretend I'm not fully aware what he was up to last night. "What's it about?"

He looks away, then back at me. It's quick, but I catch a flicker of something in his eyes. *Is he hiding something?* "It's . . . a work in progress." He looks away, I presume checking the studio for Santiago's return.

"I just want us to have a conversation." I need to keep things moving. "I know you don't like to give interviews, but let's just, you know, like, flow. I'll say something, you say—"

"When was the last time you flowed?" he asks, interrupting me.

I'm too shocked to speak. He leans forward slightly, waiting for my response.

"I don't know, like, what do you mean? I flow."

René scoffs. "When? When was a time you flowed?" The words come out of lazy, barely moving lips.

The first example that comes to mind is actually the other night, when I was taking my portrait on the balcony. The ideas were flowing as I adjusted the lighting and the composition. But there's no way in hell I'm bringing *that* up. I cough as though I've swallowed some unseen dust in the air. "Well, I've had so many great, *flowing* conversations with artists."

"How do you know?"

"Sorry?" I ask, needing clarification.

"How do you know they were flowing conversations?"

I stare at him, willing the sweat I sense forming to stay inside my skin at least until I'm out of this booth. "I could tell. I could *feel* it was flowing."

"Like with who?"

I huff, then swallow hard. "Stills Towers, the jazz pianist," I say at last. "We had an amazing conversation about improvisation and *that* really flowed." I sit taller, enjoying my mini mic drop moment.

"That sounds cool. I'd love to see that." René moves his lips over to one side, as though curious.

"I can get you a copy," I say cheerily. "The collabs you've participated in have been hugely successful." I tug at the ribbon around my collar again, and the bow comes undone. René's eyes drop to my now exposed collarbone as I tie it back up. "You're finally getting the chance to make your own music, to be the only voice for the length of a song. Do you worry it won't have the same kind of commercial success when it's just you? Is that why you're struggling today?"

René pulls his legs back toward him. "What do you mean?"

"Oh. It just seems like you've been blocked in here today."

"I'm not blocked." He sounds offended. *Have we not been in the same room for the past two hours?*

I nod and look down at the monitor on my lap, checking James's shot as I think of how to fix this. The close-up of René is gorgeous. His skin is splashed with the blues and yellows of the neon lights that wrap around the walls and door of the recording booth.

"A song is like magic. It just happens. Something channels through you and you're just a vessel. You feel these magnets pull you, and you go wherever they take you. You can't fight them."

Well, maybe you could fight them just a little.

"Do you know what reggaeton is?" He sounds unsettled.

"Yes," I say assuredly.

He grins and I feel the room get toastier. "What is it?"

This can't be happening. I literally can't handle another charged-up quizzing session. He waves a hand, motioning for me to respond. I gather myself, sit up taller, and try to look as comfortable as I can on this speaker. "It's...a style of music. A fusion of Latin and hip hop."

He shrugs dismissively as soon as I'm done. It was clearly not the answer he was looking for.

"Reggaeton is improvisation. It's whatever you want it to be. It's a blending of worlds and ideas. It can go wherever the hell it wants to go. It's a completely free genre."

"Lucky genre," I spit out, without thinking.

The slightest of frowns appears on his face. "What do you mean?"

James clears his throat and I use the distraction to check his shot in the monitor. "I don't know why I just said that." I return my gaze to René. "It's just, you know, something people say."

He scratches his scruffy beard, and the look in his eyes changes from raging rivers to something more swimmable.

As James and I walk back to our cottage, I pull off my blazer sullenly. We got some footage of the creative process and even some decent responses from René to go along with it, but at what cost? I feel like I'm going to pass out from the exertion.

"He's so difficult. And shut down. Why couldn't I have gotten Bad Bunny? He's super open in his interviews."

James nods patiently, then walks ahead of me, up the flight of stairs to our cottage.

"It's like he's getting to know me better than I'm, than *we're*," I correct myself, "than we're getting to know him."

Chapter 19

THE THREE DOTS ON MY CELL ARE DISQUIETING. THIS IS GOING to be one monster of a text when Meri's done writing it. While the dots have been rotating, I've brushed my teeth, crawled into bed, and tucked the mosquito netting as best I could into the mattress. The dots suddenly disappear and after a moment start up again. Something's wrong. Why would it possibly take Meri this long to respond to a simple "How was your day?" text?

Maybe Meri's done something she's afraid to tell me about. Something that's bad for her, like getting back with her ex. I pick up the phone to call her when it double-pings with two texts.

It was okay

just waiting for you to break the rules and send me a photo of René

There's no way this is what she's been typing all this time. She must have composed a text and then decided against it. I need to find out what she's holding back, but I want to tread lightly.

Me: I'm waiting too. For René to inspire my photographic skillz.

Meri: Your skillz? Ha! There's no inspiration needed when there are no wrong angles.

I picture René in the recording booth, and the way he looks in close-ups on my monitor. His shoulders, his strong jaw, and those full lips. She's right about the angles.

Me: When's the next tutoring session?

Meri: Tomorrow but

Again with the three dots. I brace myself for what she'll write next.

Meri: I'm going to wear my new tortoiseshell reading glasses. They make me feel smarter AND bring out the green in my eyes.

Me: Excellent plan.

We say good night and I lie in bed rereading the conversation for a clue as to what's really going on. She seems fine, I guess. But before I fall asleep, I find an accredited online program that helps RNs become RSNs. It would take longer and add a whole extra step, but the end result would be the same. I drift to sleep, comforted by the knowledge that if she does fail the test again, I can help her get what she wants without it. I can fix it.

It's enormous. The bright green iguana that's half on the balcony, half *inside* my room. I noticed it just as I was dialing into the weekly meeting with my boss.

"There isn't much in what you sent, but I know they're just getting started." Maureen sounds restrained.

"Yeah, that's right." It was hard to string together something worthwhile from the past few days. "The frog footage is really fun." I slowly push the sliding glass door, hoping the iguana will get the point, but the creature doesn't budge. It looks around the room like it's considering moving in. "I was think-ing that could be a big theme for us. James and I could go out and capture more of the beautiful nature." I hold the phone away, and hiss at the lizard.

"Sure." Mo doesn't sound convinced. "But Dani?"

"Yes?" The iguana backs up some, so I hold the phone between my shoulder and my ear and place both hands on the door, ready to slam it the second the lizard is clear.

"How are things going with you and René?"

"Um, great." I push the door until it's an inch away from the iguana's body. Nothing.

"Remember, it's all about mutual respect."

The creature scurries up the doorframe, but it's too big to get a grip. It slides down a few inches, then scrambles back up, its claws scratching at the metal trim. "Oh my god!" I step back. "Yes, I mean. Oh my god, yes. I agree."

"I'll be there this weekend for the showcase concert so we can catch up in person." I hadn't forgotten about the concert the label's hosting to introduce some of the new artists on our slate, but I can't believe it's only three days away. "So, what's on the agenda for today?" Mo asks.

There is no agenda. None that I've seen anyway. I can't tell her James and I just get to the studio early each morning and loiter around until Camila lets us in. "You know, just a regular day."

A lawn mower kicks on outside, and the iguana slips all the way down and ends up outside, so I slam the glass door shut.

"While I'm there, we can screen some footage together. Can't wait to see what you have by then."

"Mm-hmm." *Me too.*

Chapter 20

As the sun sets, the sky shifts through vibrant shades of sorbets. Dark grape, raspberry wisps, and then a deep orange. We still haven't been allowed in the studio all day.

James and I have been banished to wait in the common room. At least it's a beautiful space. An open-air room with a half-moon-shaped counter and barstools. There's a large comfy couch along one wall with tons of throw pillows. A steady breeze drifts through the room, and bachata music spills out of the kitchen partially visible behind the bar.

I've had *way* too much time to think.

About, for example, *other* marketing ideas I wish I'd pitched instead of the one that's landed me here. Anything would be better than promising an in-depth behind-the-scenes of an artist this difficult. *I mean private.*

My favorite idea was having *other* musicians who've worked with René come to his aid and help us promote him and his first album with their intimate stories. We could have called the campaign "Friend of a Friend," and leaned into René's mysteriousness. More importantly, I could be spending this month interviewing professionals. People who are accommodating and don't answer questions with a question.

Instead, I'm here pacing this room, never venturing too far and holding my pee longer than I probably should.

I've also had too much time to worry about Meri. And how I can't shake this feeling that she's keeping something from me. I hate to think she's going through something and doesn't feel comfortable sharing it with me.

Sure, I'm keeping a few things from *her* at the moment. I haven't told her about finding the waterfall in Dad's song. Or about René possibly seeing me on the balcony in my under-wear. I just don't want her to get the wrong idea. Or make a fuss when I'm trying to forget it ever happened.

I glance at James, sitting across from me, ready to spring into action. A door opens and I straighten up. The chef walks in from the kitchen, her short hair in tiny pigtails. She smiles wide at James.

Earlier today, when she was setting up the lunch buffet, I took it upon myself to clear out some dirty bowls on the counter left over from breakfast. I was frustrated from having to wait around to get in the studio, and just needed to feel helpful.

A few minutes later, there was yelling in the kitchen over the missing *raspita*. It wasn't my fault. I know the burned rice from the bottom of the pot is delicious, but I'd never seen it scraped out and served in its own bowl like that, like it was another side dish.

I check my work email again, but I'm all caught up. I can't imagine what Maureen will do when she gets here and sees how little access we have to the studio.

Today has to be different. I need more time with René. I need him to trust me. I slip my hand in my right blazer pocket and feel my dad's cassette tape. If I want René to give us more access, I'm going to have to go first. And this is as open as I can go.

He's asked about the tape a few times. I imagine it must be a musician thing, always up for hearing something new. Especially, for René, from a fellow Puerto Rican. Or maybe because René loves this island, and he knows that's what the song is about.

I hear the swoosh of the studio door gliding along the tile floor, and my pulse picks up.

"Now is a good time." Camila has stepped out of the studio. She runs her hand through her hair, combing it with her fingers.

There's incense burning, but otherwise the studio feels cold and dark.

René's in the recording booth. He's wearing a baby blue hoodie with white jeans, and at some point in the last twenty-four hours, he's had a fresh buzz cut. It's irritating how nice he looks.

"Is it true," Camila asks as I make my way to our corner of the room, "did you throw away the *raspita*?"

I force a laugh. "Yeah, sorry about that. Just trying to be helpful."

"*No ayudes tanto*," Camila says as she leaves the room. *Don't be so helpful.* She's only teasing, but her words hurt. I feel out of the loop as it is. Like when they use slang I've never heard before. *Bregando, pichear, pavera, puñeta.* I love hearing my father's accent, but it's been frustrating to speak the same language, and still not be able to keep up at times.

I tap the cassette in my pocket and try to regain my composure. René and Santiago seem to be on a break, so I pull the tape out and wave it in the air at René like I've got the winning lotto ticket.

He pulls his sunglasses off as he steps out of the booth and, without saying a word, takes the tape gingerly from my hand and bows his head.

As he hands the tape to Santiago, I remember the first time my dad played this cassette for me in his work van. He was dropping me off at school. "Look, my song is on the radio!" he joked. He was in such a good mood afterward, and I remember how happy I was all day because of it.

Santiago pops the tape into the player, and it occurs to me that it may not even work. There's a chance it's warped due to time, humidity, or heat.

"I'll be right back, if that's okay." James appears beside me.

"Sure." I watch him head out and feel slightly relieved. I guess because the fewer people around for this, the better.

Santiago hits rewind and the tape whizzes noisily. It stops abruptly and my shoulders rattle. René leans against the console and I drop slowly down onto the leather couch.

Santiago hits play. At first, there's only the low hiss of the tape. I'm hoping it works. And that I don't burst hysterically into tears. I'm squeezing myself in so tight, I might look constipated. When I can't hold my breath any longer, my father's voice comes through the speakers.

The song has a slow start, like someone winding up a clock. Then it releases, and both Santiago and René move to the beat of my father's conga.

I can picture his hand hitting the side of the conga from time to time. His ring tap, tap, tapping on the wood.

All the other islands are jealous
No one can blame them

My father had a deep, folksy voice. Gravelly and warm. As soon as René and Santiago hear it, I can tell they're impressed. The song is his love letter to this island. It's familiar and foreign at the same time. A shapeless memory. The longer it plays, the more it fills in, becoming thick and sweet with my father's energy. He sings about his favorite beaches, foods, and hearing live, traditional music under the stars.

Santiago taps his thighs to the music, and René shuts his eyes, savoring each lyric. Hearing it through these high-end speakers, I think my dad sounds pretty good. The recording isn't professional, but he's singing and playing his heart out.

"I know where that is," René says over the music. "It's really close by."

The song is a sweet celebration, and when it's over, I feel like someone's thrown a soft blanket around my shoulders. I look up and René and Santiago are exchanging amazed expressions.

"*¡Qué linda!*" Santiago applauds.

René stands. "It's beautiful."

My heart is pounding. I feel so grateful to them for listening and overwhelmingly happy for my dad. Proud *for* him. He would get a kick out of the way these professional musicians, artists I know he would have admired, feel about his song.

The next morning, I'm up early and doing something I shouldn't. Updating our department calendar. I was supposed to relinquish this task to Susana, the other marketing coordinator, while I'm gone, but there are so many events missing on this thing, I can't help myself. What's the point of having a calendar if it's not up-to-date? And don't even get me started on her disregard for uniformity. What kind of person abbreviates "music festival" in one place as "music fest" and then "music fstvl" in another?

I woke up feeling wound tight and tense, but as I sit at the small wooden table in my room and organize the calendar, my shoulders loosen. I don't want to give up the opportunity I've been given. Stepping up and leading the creative direction of a campaign has always been my dream, but at the moment, I miss these parts of my old job. So easy and predictable.

A gentle, double rap at the door startles me. My first thought is Susana's come to tell me to stop touching her calendar.

As I get up and cross the room, my spirits lift. It's way too early for James; there's at least another two hours before the breakfast buffet is set out. So it has to be Camila delivering the day's schedule. *Finally!* I open the door with abandon.

René is standing barefoot in the hallway. He's wearing a green camouflage tank top and hot pink swim trunks that reveal the full extent of his strong quads.

"*Buenos días.*" His essence is extremely vibrant for 6:00 a.m.

I'm wearing nothing but a long Blondie T-shirt, so I tuck myself behind the door. "Morning. Is everything okay?"

"Yes, sorry, I saw your light was on."

"Oh," I say quietly and nod.

"I want to show you something." He grins, one side of his lips rising higher than the other. It's a sweet, good-natured smile. *And so out of character, it throws a cog in my system.*

"Okay," I blurt out with an excitement that surprises me.

"Great"—his smile widens—"I'll meet you downstairs."

Chapter 21

RENÉ'S OUTSIDE MY COTTAGE, SITTING AT THE BOTTOM OF THE stairs. He hears the squeak I make stepping onto the wood and turns around.

"I should have told you where we're going." He stands and runs a hand across his buzz-cut hair. "It's outdoors." He's frowning.

I pause mid-step for a beat and then continue descending. "That's okay, I'm fine." I actually gave this some thought and put on a pretty versatile outfit.

He watches me incredulously but doesn't budge from the bottom step. "Are you *sure* you want to wear all that?"

I stand tall a few steps above him, starting to get irked. "Yes."

"Okay." He scoops up a tiny duffel bag he's left on the step and slips the band through his wrist. He starts to move then stops again. "Not even the blazer?" he cracks, teasing me now.

"No, I'm great." I whip up a smile. "And technically, *this* is a bolero."

"Well"—he fights back a smile—"in *that* case, we're ready

to go." He gestures at my large backpack, offering to carry it for me.

"I'm good." I transfer the hefty bag over to my other shoulder.

He leads the way on the narrow deck path and turns in the direction of the beach. I glance down at my outfit. Mid-sleeve black bolero, formfitting tank, above-the-knee skirt, and booties. This is actually my most laid-back work look, but no one said anything about the beach.

As we walk, my initial excitement wanes as the nerves over the unknown kick in. I take a deep breath. "So...how far away is it?"

"Not too far. Just a few beaches over."

A rooster crows in the distance. It's officially the hottest morning since I've been here. I'm already feeling toasty under these layers of fabric, but there's no way I'm turning around. And it isn't just because I don't want to admit that I was wrong. I really don't want to make him wait again while I change.

I stop when we reach the sand, then I bend down and pull off my boots and socks, a layer of perspiration already on my face and neck. I'm about to toss them in my already heavy bag when René stops me.

"Here." He jogs them over to a table near the back entrance of the property and carefully tucks them under one of the chairs to keep them out of the sun.

When our beach thins out, he holds the gate open for me and we come across another beach with a U-shaped dock filled with small sailboats.

We reach a taller gate. "I don't think we're supposed to go this way."

"It's fine," he says nonchalantly.

"Is it?" I point out the "Private Property" sign.

"What do you think's going to happen?" He opens the gate calmly. "It's quicker this way. It'll be fine. We'll walk fast."

I oblige reluctantly, and walk through. "Perfect." I shake my head. "When they stop us, we'll just say, 'Sorry, Officer, we thought this property was only private for people who walked slowly. Not us quick walkers.'"

René chuckles and then seems to get lost in his thoughts for a while as we walk along the pebbly shore. Every once in a while, he picks up a stone and makes it skip across the waves.

The private beach ends and we have to climb along a path of small boulders, balancing ourselves on one large rock at a time.

"Here we are, Flamenco Beach," René announces proudly as we turn a corner. "It's the last lyric in your dad's song."

I guessed this could have something to do with my dad's song, but I'm still visibly stunned. *And unprepared for this gesture.* The practically deserted beach is framed by a crystal-clear sea to the left, tall wind-breaking grass along the right, and a green mountain at the far end that jets out into the water. There's a wide stretch of powdery white sand that curves up and down like waves on the shore.

"It's beautiful," I say at last, still in a bit of a daze.

René opens the small bag dangling from his wrist and pulls out what appears to be a handkerchief but, with a flick, expands into a large towel. He drops down on one side, leaving room for me to sit on the other.

"Impressive."

"And it's quick-dry technology."

"You should be their spokesperson."

"They can't afford me." He smiles lazily.

I take a deep breath and let the warm air fill my lungs. René's scent slips in, too, so I get salty air with alluring undertones of musky, sweet cologne.

"Thank you for bringing me here."

"My pleasure." He eyes me curiously.

I feel like he may be expecting a bigger reaction from me, but I'm still in a bit of a shock.

As I look around, I can feel myself not letting it in fully. All my father ever did was miss this place. The food. The long drives on his only day off, so we could visit his friend's horses. His music.

It's been so romanticized, I'm almost surprised to discover it's a real place.

René stretches his legs out, leans back on his elbows, and tilts his head up to let the sun kiss his face. I watch him, his skin glistening, his sculpted body at ease. Even in hot pink swim trunks and expensive shades, he still looks like he belongs here. Like he's a natural fixture of this beach.

I, on the other hand, am sweating. Probably from the exertion of the long walk or the stress of breaking the law. It's incredibly nice of him to bring me here but I don't know quite what to make of it.

I take a few pictures of the beach, then set my phone down on the towel between us.

"Cute." René points to the image saved on my locked screen.

It's been my wallpaper forever. A picture of Meri and me. We're cracking up as we pose in a cardigan we're sharing, each of us wearing one arm. It's hard to imagine it was taken only a few months after our dad passed away. As an escape, we spent that Christmas with our aunt in the Keys. It was uncharacteristically cold, and we'd gone for a walk to check out the Christmas lights on the houseboats. Meri forgot a sweater, so I shared mine and we had the best time as we stretched out my cardigan and tried to walk around like that. It had felt so good to be silly. To make her laugh again.

"That's my little sister, Meri." René picks up the phone for a closer inspection. "She's not that little. We're only five years apart," I add in case he's wondering why we're practically the same height in the photo. "She's a big fan of yours, actually."

He nods appreciatively. "Is that you?" He sounds alarmed.

"Yes." Insulted, I try to take the phone from him.

"Sorry, it's just...you look different." He holds the phone next to my face. "You look older there than you do now."

He isn't wrong. My hair is flat and tucked behind my ears, dark circles under my eyes.

I focus on Meri's wide toothy smile. "She was the only kid in the world excited to get braces." I can feel René's gaze on me. "She wanted to grow up so she could be a woman so badly."

"I bet you were like that too. Wearing little blazers."

"No, actually"—I yank the phone from his grip—"I wasn't."

"So, why do you think your father included this place in the song?" He takes his sunglasses off; his dark brown eyes seem to be smiling. "What did he like about this beach?"

"Oh..." I look around, tiptoeing past the discomfort in my chest. "I don't know." Not too far off, two large seagulls glide effortlessly over the water, and then expertly dive in and out of it.

"Actually"—he reaches for his bag and pulls out a folded-up piece of paper—"I wrote out the lyrics."

"Really?"

"Yeah, last night," he responds matter-of-factly. "The digital transfer is still in Santiago's computer from when we emailed it to you."

"Oh, right." After we listened to the song, René had Santiago use the recording studio to transfer the old recording into a more reliable digital file for me.

"Okay." René reviews the list, getting down to business. "The waterfall you already went to." He glances at my knee. The skin is pink now and less swollen. "Resaca Beach," he continues, "is on the other side of the island. That one's a little harder to get to. I'll find out where we can hear some bomba music. And you've had *alcapurrias* before?"

"No, I don't think so."

"Really? They're so good." He studies the last line of the song. "The dock beneath the sea." He frowns. "I don't know what that is, but I'll ask around. I can help you do it all while you're here."

"No, no, that's okay. You're too busy to—"

"I want to." He hands me the lyrics.

"Thanks, I appreciate it." I slide my feet off the towel and onto the sand. Knowing I may actually experience what my dad most wanted for me is like setting something heavy down I didn't know I was carrying. And I feel some of my guard drop along with it.

I glance at the lyrics, my eyes lingering over the last line.

Last night I saw Flamenco Beach in my dreams

The memory rushes back vividly. My dad and his band performing the song at Christmas. Probably one of our last. The scent of a pig roast and the heat of family and friends crowded into the living room. He began improvising and adjusting the lyrics. *Last night, I saw Meri in my dreams. Last night, Dani was in my dreams.* We cheered as each person was included and waved their arms around, dancing.

"I used to think it was a happy song." I watch the waves, feeling René's eyes on me. "But it's really kind of sad, isn't it?" I let out a deflated half laugh. "Nothing but broken dreams and longing for a time and a place you can never truly return to."

René's quiet for a moment. "I can assure you as a fellow singer-songwriter, he *did* return." He gestures at the lyrics. "Every time he sang that song."

The thought is so refreshing, my eyes instantly water. "Thanks," I say, meaning it, and glance down at my feet.

"How did he die? If you don't mind me—"

"No, it's okay." I switch on the cool, distant approach I've perfected when I talk about my father. As though he were someone else. "He had a heart attack while he was at work." I tighten my ponytail with both hands. "One day he just didn't come home."

"That's . . . I'm so sorry." René's words are soft and deeply felt, and instantly push me closer toward the hole in my chest. "I never met my father," he says. "He split before I was born."

"Oh, I didn't know that. I'm sorry."

"It's okay. My mom's a badass." He half smiles, half smirks.

"That's good. Mine is too. And a little unpredictable."

"Nice," he responds like it's a good thing.

I have this strong urge to correct him. I try to focus on the seagulls. "Not really," I blurt out, unable to hold back. "For years, the month of the anniversary of my father's death she'd shut down. Barely come out of her room. Which sucked because he passed away in September, so the first year it coincided with Meri starting a new school." The words are flying out of me. "So I had to drive her myself and convince her that Mom was just tired. So no, it wasn't *nice*."

"I see." I kick myself for unloading all of that.

"Sorry. I don't usually talk about all that."

"No, it's okay." He gives me a warm, commiserating smile and I feel my whole body relax a couple of notches. "Sounds like they were lucky to have you."

"Yeah, I guess. I was lucky too, though. It was good...to have someone else to focus on, I think."

"You really don't talk about all this?"

"Actually, I never have," I admit more honestly.

His eyes shoot up. "Good. This is good." René puts a hand over his heart. "You have to get that stuff out."

"Do I? I've always found that *not* to be the case." Though I'll admit sharing how hard it was at first does make me appreciate how much better Mom is doing now.

"I grew up with my mom blasting classic Puerto Rican ballads." René extends his legs long out in front of him. "I thought everyone's kitchen had a radio that only played that kind of music. I'd come home from school and we'd dance together. If sad and sappy music wasn't playing loudly in our kitchen, something was wrong. We owed money or something." René pauses, seeming weighed down by what he's about to say. "I loved coming home and hearing sad music playing."

"I know what you mean. My mom loves those songs too. As long as the dejected lovers are looking at the same moon, everything's fine." I pretend to swoon.

"Well, obviously. Intense romantic melancholy equals happiness." I can't help but smile. "That's all I ever wanted." He looks into my eyes. "To make music that melts away your troubles. Makes you lose your inhibitions."

It's the most René's ever opened up about his childhood. I wish there was a camera here. Then again, he's probably being this candid *because* there isn't a camera around.

"Be honest—is this why you haven't wanted the cameras around? Because you're not making a reggaeton album at all, are you? You're making a sappy, romantic one and you don't want us there for it."

"I wish. Those songs are the best. Maybe one day I'll be dejected enough to write a ballad your mom would approve of."

I smile and shake my head, thinking about my mom. "She'd love it if *I* were dejected."

"What do you mean?"

"I broke up with someone not too long ago and didn't react the way she expected. But it's, like, what kind of mother wants her child to cry over a broken heart?"

"The kind that wants them to feel something. I'm going to have to side with your mom on this."

My mouth drops open, pretending to be shocked, while a little voice inside my head creeps in. *That's because you're the one who leaves them crying.*

"So what, you were happy it was over? What was wrong with this ex?" His bold demeanor seems somewhat weakened.

I glance back in the direction we came. "Nothing," I defend. "There's was nothing wrong with him. And I wasn't happy it was over. I just wasn't...affected. That sounds bad, doesn't it?"

"It's not good." He shakes his head good-naturedly. "All right, now *you* be honest"—his bedroom eyes switch on—"why are you always so stiff?" The smile on his face is mischievous.

"I'm not stiff." I force my jaw to unclench.

"Seriously. It's like you're not comfortable in your skin. Which I don't get, because you have really nice skin," he adds casually.

My cheeks fire up and the beach feels warmer. "Thanks. For

that *partial* compliment." He waves it off, his eyes still on me. "Why did you bring me here?" I ask, suddenly feeling bold.

He considers this. "You've never been before, so you needed to come," he says plainly. As though this were enough of a reason. "But I could tell you were hesitant."

I break into a half smile. "Am I that easy to read?"

"Maybe. Or maybe I can just tell when someone needs to do something they don't want to do. Like me when I have to do press," he adds more playfully.

A nervous chuckle escapes me. "It's true, though." I fiddle with his sunglasses on the towel. "It's hard to be here without him." Instinctively, I pick up his glasses and put them on. They feel nice. *And expensive.*

"Let me see."

I turn to him and pose.

"Ave Maria, que jevota." He blends the words together easily, barely annunciating. *Hail Mary, what a babe.*

My pulse quickens and everything suddenly feels hotter. As though steam were rising from the sand. He's poured water on hot coals.

I want to say something, but he's thrown me completely off course. My brain's been flooded with whatever it is deer get in their heads at the sight of headlights.

I take off the glasses and set them back down.

He fans his shirt. "How about a swim?"

"I can't. I'm not wearing a bathing suit."

"So?" He's baffled by my response. "Swim in that." He points to the tank top I'm wearing beneath my bolero.

"It's okay. I'm not too hot." I feel a bead of sweat slide down my temple.

He squints, fighting back a smile, then turns to his bag. He removes the small audio recorder he used on my balcony and heads to the water.

I watch him as I dig through my backpack for one of the protein bars I brought from home. I special-ordered them for Meri because they're packed with nutrients. As I peel it open, I'm actually taken aback by its girth. It's a brick of coconut, pecans, and sesame seeds.

A seagull shoots out of the water right in front of me, a fish shaking in its mouth. It's impressive but also off-putting because I hadn't even seen it go into the water. *How long can a bird hold its breath?*

Bringing the bar to my mouth, I watch as René aims his recorder at the waves collapsing on the shore. I'm about to take a bite when a seagull flies just above my head.

Before I've had a chance to react, another one swoops across the beach and snatches the entire protein bar out of my hand.

I sit there completely shocked for a moment, then start to laugh, in spite of myself. René's missed the whole thing. Which should be a relief, except I can't wait to tell him all about it.

Chapter 22

When I get back from the beach, the schedule has been slipped under my door. Coincidence? Maybe. But I've never been happier to see a sheet of paper.

4 pm
Piano delivery

5 pm
Piano tuned

6 pm
Interview

7–8 pm
Meal break

8 pm
Piano—new song

8:30 pm
Vocals—new song

Thanks to the schedule, James was able to get plenty of shots of an old Steinway upright piano being delivered. I may have gone a little overboard. I had him capture the moment from every possible angle, even lying on the ground as it rolled by him down the hall. I wanted to capture the instrument's elegance and build suspense. A reggaetonero having a piano brought into the studio is like Eminem requesting a harp. *Well, not quite. But pretty darn close.*

Knowledge may, in fact, be power because it's such a relief to finally know what's going on. To be on the inside. According to the schedule, René is recording a new song. One we have full access to. We've already got shots of the unique-to-reggaeton instrument getting delivered, and now James and I are on our way to interview René *before* he starts recording. We're finally going to film the *entire* process of a song. Catch the flubs, the last-minute changes, the moments of inspiration. All just in time before Maureen arrives.

As we exit our cottage and hop onto the wooden path that leads to the main house, James is trailing behind.

"Sorry, I'll meet you there." He looks a little pale.

"Are you all right?"

He nods, waves a shaky hand in the air, and walks briskly back down the path to our cottage. I hope he isn't getting sick. Thankfully, we're all set up for the interview in the studio. I could even start without him if I need to.

Inside the long hall that leads to the studio, my heartbeat accelerates. After we spent the morning together, I'm not really sure what to expect from René. He was so *nice*. On the way back, I cracked him up by reenacting a play-by-play of the bird's raptor-like attack on the beach. I laughed harder than I have in a really long time.

When we reached the house, he grabbed my boots off the bench and handed them to me, bowing his head as though he were my royal attendant. I yanked them from him, pretending to be annoyed. The whole interaction felt... well, flirtatious.

When I reach the studio door, I remind myself that this is a guy who flirts for a living.

Still, in seven years at the label, I've never spent time with an artist outside of work like that before. As I pull the studio door open, I can't deny I'm excited to see him again.

My eyes dart around the room. The studio is filled with people, but René isn't one of them. René's manager, Ángel, is back. He's near the recording booth, talking to Camila, and Santiago is standing by the console, talking to someone new. From where I'm standing, all I can see are her big, beachy blond curls.

"Hey, Ángel!" My voice comes out hoarse. "I didn't know you were coming in today."

"Hey, Dani." He walks up to me. "We just flew in." He motions to the woman talking with Santiago. I lean over, and when I see her, I know why he's omitted her name. No introduction is necessary.

"Hi!" I approach her for a handshake. "It's so nice to meet you."

A genuine, youthful smile appears on the woman's face. "*Hola, mucho gusto.*" Her voice is smooth and slippery. Natalia. The Colombian pop star René recorded a duet with last summer. And then dated for a while afterward. The one I read dumped him when he cheated on her.

She's wearing the brightest red lipstick, a black strapless dress, and at least a dozen thick gold chains. "Dani, René won't have time today," Ángel says, "but you *can* interview Natalia."

"Great." *And why would I do that?* The question is on the

tip of my tongue, but I don't want to reveal just how out of the loop I am.

"Also, I'll be around in case you need anything." Ángel opens the studio door. "I'm here until after the showcase."

"Amazing." *Though not as amazing as the lack of detail in Camila's schedule.* It didn't mention Natalia or why she's here. Or even Ángel's arrival. Though the fact that he's here today may explain why Camila sent out a schedule in the first place.

"Have fun," Ángel tells Natalia, who blows him a kiss in response.

Santiago and Camila also leave, and I'm left alone with Natalia.

It's disappointing getting knocked back down to "person who isn't privy to any relevant information," but I know enough about her to interview her on the fly. Even if I don't know why we're interviewing her. Her music is mostly pop with splashes of electronica, and her duet with René was her first reggaeton dance track.

"Natalia, let me have you sit in this chair."

She obliges, walking over. Her nickname, *Tranquila* Mankiller, suits her perfectly. Relaxed and sensuous, her whole body seems to run on smoother gears.

I switch on each light James has set up for the interview, careful to tiptoe around them so I don't knock anything out of place. *Keep your eye on the prize. Roll with the incessant punches.*

The studio door opens, and James walks in, his hair dripping wet. "Sorry I'm late." He seems tired.

"It's fine. You sure you're okay?"

"Yeah. I'm good."

"Natalia, you can just look directly at me. Let's start by sharing with us," *and with me,* "what brings you to Puerto Rico."

"Well"—she grins as though she has the juiciest gossip—"a

little birdie called me a few nights ago, and said René had a song for me." She juts her chin out seductively. "And when El Rico calls, you come."

"Sure, of course."

"I heard he had written a song that would be great as a duet and that I'd be perfect for it."

"That's... excellent." A duet with Natalia is practically a guaranteed hit for René's album. It's a solid choice to build on the buzz of their last collaboration.

"So, I moved things around, but I only have today. We're going to have to work really hard," she says, equal parts sweet *and* erotic.

"That's great." I suddenly feel agitated.

René's inability to open up even just a little about his album is upsetting. He shared so much this morning about his private life, but failed to mention that his ex, the Mankiller herself, would be gracing us today. Or that he was ready to record a new song.

Natalia takes a sip of her bottled water through a straw and crosses her legs. Her skin is flawless. Her long legs look like they've been airbrushed. There isn't a single blemish or scar. Has she really *never* cut her legs shaving? Been bitten by a mosquito? Scraped the side of her knee on a natural waterslide?

I try to pull myself together.

"What can you tell us about the song?"

"Nothing. They haven't shared the lyrics with me."

"Really?" It comes out a bit blunt. "Do you normally agree to be a part of a song you don't know anything about?"

"No. Never. I guess René wanted to keep it a secret, but I don't see why." She flashes a coy smile. "He knows he can trust me."

She's so sweet and adoring, you'd think he never cheated and they never had a tabloid-worthy breakup. "Are you excited to perform together again?"

"Of course. We always have such a great time together."

I've seen their live performances. René wrote the duet they recorded together, "*Cama en Llamas*" ("Bed on Fire"), and there was actual fire on the stage for it. The two were obviously still dating at the time, because there were very real flames between them as well.

"Why do you think René wanted you for this mystery song?"

"I don't know, I guess"—she thinks about this, shaking her shoulders friskily—"because he loves our voices together. And he sang on my album and now he wants me to repay the favor." *Why does everything this woman says sound like it's innuendo?*

"Why did *you* say yes to working together again?" As in, why are you here after René cheated on you?

"That"—she glances at the door—"is a good question. I absolutely love him. No matter what's happened, I think he's brilliant and I'll always jump at the chance to work together again." Her eyes radiate with affection.

Natalia reapplies a fresh coat of gloss to her lips, and my mind drifts back to the beach this morning. I can't believe I thought we were bonding and that he didn't tell me about any of this.

Natalia glances at me, ready for another question. The only one on the tip of my tongue, she can't answer. *Do you think I'm an idiot for believing René was actually flirting with me?*

Chapter 23

DRIVING A GOLF CART AT FULL SPEED ON A DARK ISLAND ROAD is strangely liberating. The warm breeze and steady clatter of the little engine are soothing, and each bump on the pavement sends me flying a few inches above the seat.

After the interview with Natalia, I helped James break down the lights because he still wasn't feeling well. I suggested he get some rest before we have to be back in the studio. But I needed some air. *And a little perspective.* Natalia and René recording a duet together again is huge. Who cares how I found out. We finally have access to something significant. Something I can actually show Maureen this weekend.

After about twenty minutes, I find the small dock right where it's supposed to be, with the open-air restaurant the chef said we should try.

The Rusty Anchor's style is loud and vibrant. Multicolored vinyl tablecloths, giant cardboard cutouts of beer ads against the walls, and pelicans everywhere. Porcelain pelican figurines, wooden pelican sculptures, pelican paintings. Maybe the owner said they liked pelicans once, and since then, it's all anyone's ever gotten them for Christmas.

There are a few couples waiting outside for a table, so I head straight to an open spot at the bar. I'm only a few feet away when I see Camila is seated next to the empty stool.

"Busted," she sings. Her intense vanilla-scented perfume now has a strong bouquet of rum. She smells like a boozy birthday cake. "Busted," she repeats once I'm seated. As though *she's* the one who just arrived and *I'm* the one who's been drinking. There's an avocado stuffed with crabmeat on her plate that's barely been touched.

She reaches over and gently taps the bartender's hand. "*Dame otro palo.*" Then, she whips her head to me. "'*Un palo*' is a drink." Her eyelids drag way down to where they're almost shut.

The bartender refills her glass with dark rum, then waves the bottle at me.

"No, thanks. I'll have a *palo* of sparkling water. And one of those, please." I point to Camila's dish. "And can you bring me the check, please? I'm in a hurry."

The bartender finds this amusing. I gather most visitors don't come to this island just to be in a rush.

Behind us, a dinghy pulls up on the dock and an older couple steps off it and right into the restaurant. A few feet away, a group of enormous dark blue fish are clustered by a table nearest the edge of the dock, where a child is tossing bread in the water.

A classic love song comes on over the restaurant's speakers, and Camila's head moves to the beat. The song is a well-known Spanish ballad and she's trying to sing along, but in her drunken slowness, she can't keep up with the lyrics. She repeats only a word or two a few seconds too late. *How come. Without you. Impossible.*

"So, how are you doing?" I ask as carefully as I can.

"Good. I'm good." She picks up her fork and pushes the crab meat around. "No, I'm *great*."

She's definitely *not* great. When my food arrives, an unsteady Camila bumps into me, knocking the crab off my fork. *Does this have something to do with Natalia's arrival? Is Camila jealous?*

I'm about to ask her what she thinks of the duet, when two teenage girls walk up to us and ask her for a photograph. They circle around her and take a bunch of selfies. As the girls walk away ecstatic and reviewing their photos, one of them shyly returns and tells Camila to send René a kiss. Camila promises she will, and I'm impressed. Ever an ambassador for René. Even inebriated, she's done a decent job.

"Is it hard sometimes, you know, working for René?" If Natalia's the reason Camila's drinking like this, maybe she wants to talk about it.

She watches me for a moment through the slim panel of eyelid that's still open. "It's not hard. All of this, it's not hard." She motions to the condiments on the bar.

I try to get her to have some water and food, but she only nibbles on a small scoop of crabmeat. I devour my meal and pay for the bill. "Do you need a ride back? How did you get here?" I need to run, but I can't leave her like this.

"She's gone too far," Camila grunts, ignoring my questions. "It's not right. You should have seen her with him." She brings her hands to her heart, eyelids hanging even lower. It's official—her eyelids are the drunkest part about her.

"Do you mean Natalia? Listen, I've got to get—"

"It's like she's forgotten what *really* happened. She's going to hear from me." She sounds definitive. "Don't get it twisted," she mumbles angrily to herself.

She attempts to unlock her phone but doesn't get the code right.

"She better be on her best behavior." She tries the code again and manages to get it right.

A sense of alarm washes over me. "Uh, I'm not sure about—"

Camila slaps her chest with her hand. "I'm the reason you're even here. Me!" She shouts this last word so loudly, our bartender looks up from the bar.

"Um, okay." I check the time on my phone. At this rate, I'm going to be a few minutes late. I ring James to let him know, but the call goes straight to voicemail. A jolt of panic shoots through me. He was going to take a power nap. I'm supposed to be his wake-up call. I try again and it does the same thing. I think he's shut the phone off.

"She's *not* getting away with this." Camila's voice quivers.

I lean my body over the bar and get our bartender to bring me Camila's check. "You can tell me all about it on the ride back."

She places a hand on my arm and squeezes hard. "Don't you think she's out of control?"

"Uh, nope. I don't think so. Not at all." My hands are shaking as I try to pull the credit card out of my wallet.

Then Camila slumps to the ground in one go, as though her knees have given out.

"Are you okay?" I find her folded up with her back against the bar, sitting on the footrest. "It's time to go, don't you think?" I squat and maneuver around until I'm sitting on the footrest next to her.

Camila's holding her phone out in front of her and I can

see that she's dialing Natalia. And that, for some reason, this is going to be a video call.

"If she doesn't like it, that's *her* problem!" Camila screams loudly into the phone, though it's still only ringing.

Everything in my body is telling me I can't let her make this call. Natalia getting yelled at by a wasted Camila is the last thing she *or René* need right now.

All I can see is the calendar. He only has a month to record this album, and almost a week has gone by with nothing but disconnected snippets to show for it. For the first time, he's going to make actual progress. Anything Camila has to say should wait. At least until she's sober. *And less angry.*

"Here, let me help you." I take the phone away from her and hang up the call. Camila lets out a shriek. Before I can say anything else, her hands are on my face.

"Hey, hey, come on."

"Give me that!" Camila howls, pulling down at my ears. The pain is surprisingly intense. I've got only one hand to protect myself, because the other's one keeping the phone away. There isn't any room for us to get away from each other. We're crammed between barstools and the bar, with people sitting on either side of us, and a family dining at the table a foot away.

Camila reaches my fingers and tries to peel them away from the phone.

"I'll give it back when we get home," I try to reason. Just then, her phone starts to ring. Natalia's full name appears on the screen. When Camila sees this, she squirms like a snake trapped in a small space.

Squabbling at such close proximity is painful. With all the pulling and pushing, everything hurts. My ears from being yanked on, my arm from holding the phone up high to keep it from Camila, and even my butt from the lip of this footrest.

But I need to resolve this below the bar. If I stand, photos of us could end up online.

"Camila, listen to me. There's clearly something important you want to say, and you have every right to do that." It's a struggle to get the words out without losing my grip on her phone. My face is strained, shoulders are hunched. I bring the phone near my chest, arm tucked in like a football player running the ball. "But believe me, whatever it is, it would be better in person."

Camila rages and digs her hands into my chest.

"Your little fingers are…so…strong." I free my hand from her grip, snapping my arm away from her too abruptly, and the phone flies out of my hand, sails across the few feet of dock, and plops into the water.

"I'm so sorry. Shit. I'm sorry."

Camila doesn't move or say a word.

"I'm sure you have everything backed up. The cloud still—"

Camila pushes the stool away loudly, and rises.

"I'll order you a new phone," I promise, struggling to get up. A man sitting near us at the bar watches us curiously, but otherwise I think our skirmish has gone unnoticed.

Camila walks slowly through the crowded restaurant, and I follow a few steps behind, feeling awful. We step outside and I try calling James, but it goes straight to voicemail again.

I reach the golf cart, but Camila is still shuffling slowly across the parking lot, dragging a large cardboard beer poster she's taken from the restaurant.

I feel trapped. This can't be happening. I need to get back to the studio. *What if James is still asleep?* I turn the golf cart on and pull up next to Camila, who abandoned the cardboard beer poster a few feet away and has stopped moving.

"Come on," I urge gently. "We're on the other side of the island. If you don't want to ride with me, let me get you a cab."

Camila shakes her head ever so slightly and sits down, right on the pavement. A passing car lights up her face. She looks drunker out here than she did at the bar. And like she's about to be sick. I park the cart back where it was, and help her move to the nearest curb.

Three excruciating hours later, I was able to get Camila to move again.

We didn't make it very far before I had to turn the golf cart around. Even at a low speed, the ride was too bumpy for her to handle.

So now we're back in the parking lot, sitting on the same curb again, waiting for her to feel better so we can try again. She's slumped forward, elbows on her knees, head resting in her hands. I'm sitting next to her and she squeezes my hand whenever she gets a wave of nausea, as though it were a contraction.

Using restaurant napkins, I've applied cold compresses to the back of her neck, and managed to get her to drink some water. My phone died over an hour ago, so I can only hope James made it to the studio.

Camila's definitely better. She's regained control of her eyelids, for one. I think it helps she's thrown up. I was so relieved for her when it happened. I sounded like the proud parent of a spelling bee champ. "Look at that. That's a big one! Great job!"

"I thought I was better." Camila's voice is hoarse.

"You *do* look better," I offer supportively.

"About *her*," she clarifies, slightly annoyed I can't read her mind.

"Everything okay?" asks a woman in a bright yellow dress walking behind us on the sidewalk.

"Yes, all good. Thank you. We just need to sit here for a minute."

"We slept together." Camila's hands are slightly covering her mouth, but I hear her just fine. And I'm pretty sure so did the woman, who looks back one more time, somewhat concerned.

"You and Natalia?"

She gives me a look that's more pity than annoyance. "René and I."

I feel an unsettling prick in my heart. "Really?"

"A long time ago." She stares at the pavement. "After being friends for a few years. And when I woke up, he was gone. No note. I didn't hear from him. He disappeared on me." She speaks slowly, without moving her head. As though she's wearing an invisible neck brace. "The next day he just came by, apologized for ignoring my texts, and told me our friendship was too important. I thought I'd be fine. *Eventually.* But you know when I knew that I wasn't?"

"When you tried to pull my ears off under the bar?"

A weak laugh escapes her. "No. Well, yeah, that too." She lifts her face. "Sorry."

"It's okay."

Camila squeezes my hand and I brace myself for her to be sick again, but whatever she was feeling passes. "Last year, when he and Natalia broke up." She lifts her head and locks her tired eyes on something across the street. "He and I were visiting some friends in Ponce and I saw this little dog. It was tied to a street post. Poor thing didn't look good, it was so hot.

"We got her some water and sat there with her for a while waiting for her owner to come. Built a little fort around us with an umbrella we had in the car." She cracks a smile. "She'd climb onto my legs, and then on his and..." She trails off, shaking her head ever so slightly. "I had this hope. The whole time, I kept wanting him to say it. *Let's adopt this puppy together. Let's be together. Let's be this little family forever. It wasn't Natalia. It was you all along.*" She whimpers.

I sit up taller, surprised she's sharing this with me. I squeeze her hand to show my support. I've seen this kind of heartache so many times. From my sister, who seems to be an expert at falling for the worst guys. And even from Mom, who for a long time acted as though she'd been betrayed by Dad for dying.

"If you felt that way, why did you stick around? Why put yourself through that?"

Camila stiffens.

"I thought about quitting, but their song was blowing up and he was getting all this bad press about the breakup. So I tried to convince myself it wasn't anything. Tried to think about the many years of friendship. He needed me." She shrugs her shoulders. "In a way, that made me feel better."

"Until tonight?"

"Yeah." She exhales loudly, then shakes her head resolutely.

"What did you do? About the pup."

"I took her home," she snaps defensively. "We left a note but no one called." Her eyes light up. "Chuchi's the best. If I had my phone, I'd show you a picture."

I chuckle and convince her to drink more water.

"The worst part is, I've been seeing someone. But I don't

think I've given him a real chance." She sounds disappointed in herself. "Maybe there's something there?"

"You never know. You deserve to be happy. Everyone does." It's what I've told Meri so many times. "Maybe it's time to stop carrying a torch and shine that light on yourself."

She squeezes my hand and draws a deep breath. "I think I can move on now."

Chapter 24

After I've tucked Camila in, I wash my hands in her bathroom. I look like we rolled back from the restaurant instead of walked. It turned out Camila was still not up for the golf cart, so we left it at the dock. Thanks to her short, mummy-like steps, it took forever to get back to the house.

I'm heading to my cottage when I hear voices coming from the fire pit at the edge of the compound.

"Hey! Where were you guys?" Santiago calls out as I approach. "You missed one hell of a session." I scan the faces around the fire. Two equipment techs, our chef, and René's manager, Ángel, are drinking beers.

"The song is so good," announces our chef.

There's a song?

"Everything was flowing. Natalia and René were on fire," Santiago says. "It's, like, basically done. There are a couple of things René wants to do with it, but it's all there." I slump onto a bench. "We couldn't stop listening to it. We called everyone in." Santiago's words hammer down on me.

"It's excellent," confirms the technician with the long hair.

"I think it could be the first single," Santiago adds.

"Where were you? Is everything okay?" Ángel asks. I can't imagine what it must look like, me waltzing in here at this time of night.

"I was taking care of Camila in town. She wasn't feeling well."

"Oh no, you should have called me." Ángel's voice is heavy with disappointment.

"You're right. I wish I had, but my phone had died when I thought of it. And Camila…didn't have hers." While it's all true, they sound like pathetic excuses. I feel like that one kid whose dog *actually* ate their homework.

"What about James? Where was he?" Santiago chimes in innocently.

"Asleep." I feel a tightening around my throat. "He wasn't feeling well either."

The group goes quiet, and after a moment, I excuse myself and walk away. There's a ringing in my ears, and all other sounds get muted.

René recorded an entire song. With his megastar ex-flame no less. While I was stuck on the other side of the island, living a nightmare called *Rehydrating Camila*. And the first reviews are in. It's a big hit, maybe even the first single. Apparently the process was spontaneous and inspired, and we didn't capture any of it.

I rest my head on the window as the cab drives past another beach. It's busier on this side of the island. Campers have set up tents on the sand, and small boats drift near the coast. The car pauses at a stop sign, and I watch a family make their way to the water under the harsh, early afternoon sun. They seem blissfully sluggish and relaxed. Which is completely at odds with how I'm feeling. I can't stop thinking about last night. Maureen will be here tomorrow, and I have nothing for her. Nothing of any substance anyway.

The cab drives past a strip of small, casual restaurants and drops me off in front of a modern concrete structure unlike anything else I've seen on the island. I'm meeting James here for lunch since René doesn't want to start until four today. I know this because I heard it from Santiago at breakfast, not because Camila was up early handing out studio schedules. After how sick she was last night, I don't think anyone will be seeing so much as a Post-it from her.

James headed out early to explore this side of the island, so we're meeting at the restaurant. I had a work meeting to attend about the concert tomorrow, where we're showcasing three new artists on our label. It sounds much bigger than originally planned. Hundreds of fans, influencers, and journalists are being ferried to the island from San Juan, and René will be performing as well.

When they asked me for an update, I did *not* mention the duet with Natalia. But I'm sure Maureen will hear about it tomorrow. Ángel will probably tell her about it when he sees her and I'll be forced to come clean.

I walk inside the hotel, and the soothing scent of a spa hits me. Planks of matte gray wood cover the walls, so the space feels relaxing yet sleek. The restaurant is straight ahead with views of the ocean behind it. A nice lunch with James is exactly what I need.

I need to forget about work for a few hours. *Forget about last night.* How we failed to capture something as big as El Rico reuniting with his ex for a new duet. Natalia left early this morning, so if there's been a reconciliation, we missed that too. The only thing I *did* get last night was a reminder of who René really is. No matter how different he seemed on the beach. Just look at Camila and Natalia, and all the other women who might be caught in his web.

I catch my reflection in a large mirror, and do a double take. I'm wearing the hot pink camisole Meri stuffed into my suitcase, with its plunging neckline and spaghetti straps, and my high-waisted black jeans. *I should wear more pink.* I tuck into a bussing station, take a decent empowerment selfie with a tall shelf of plates and fresh glasses behind me, and send it to Meri. I find James seated at a table in the center of the restaurant studying the menu. I feel instantly more relaxed. Being around James is like slipping into a broken-in pair of pajamas. Always there, always dependable. Well, except for last night.

He'd taken something for an upset stomach, and it made him feel groggy so he slept through the alarm. His apology this morning was sincere but quick. He's not the type of person who lingers on a problem. While I would normally appreciate this approach, I wasn't ready to move on. I wanted to sulk. I wanted to complain. And it stung a little that he didn't give me the chance.

"You look nice."

"Thanks. So do you." He's wearing the white linen button-down he knows I like.

He gives me a quick, easy smile before turning back to his menu. I go with the ravioli and a Puerto Rican cocktail made with rum and anise because it sounds nice and strong. James orders the pork chop and a Moscow Mule.

I study him as he calmly handles the waiter's questions regarding appetizers, salads, and what kind of water we'd like.

He sits tall and unwavering. A gale could blow through here and he'd probably still be sitting like that. He's always sturdy and reliable.

"I think you'd like this." He holds out his drink for me to try, and I take it.

"That *is* good."

"Have as much as you want." He always said the same thing when we were dating, and the drink would become *our* drink.

I try to imagine what it would be like if we *were* together. It would be so easy to slip back into this. Do I *want* to slip back into this? I decide to sit still for a moment and wait for my body to send a response.

An hour later, the message is clear. *No.* Though I haven't quite put my finger on why.

"How are things at home?" he asks.

"Good, the new windows are going in as we speak."

"Wow, that's great news. Did you go with the sliders? Or the awnings?"

"Sliders."

"Nice."

I give him an appreciative nod and look down at my plate. There's only one ravioli left.

I'd forgotten what a slow eater James is. I've had my half of the meatball appetizer and most of my ravioli and he's still working on his salad. His untouched pork chop is just sitting there looking drier by the second.

Not wanting to finish my meal before he's started on his, I set my fork down.

"There's something I've been meaning to ask," James says, his tone now serious. "Your father was from here?"

"Um, yeah." I'm rattled by the question, so I take a long sip of water.

"So...how do you feel about being here?" He's trying to be careful but there's no use. I no longer feel the breeze, only the heat rising from my core. "We don't have to talk about it if you don't want to."

"Thanks." I'm grateful he's trying to help, but I'm still trying to process how I feel about being here. Maybe René is right and I *should* let it all out.

"Check it out." To change the subject, James pulls his phone from his back pocket. "I worked on this commercial last week." It's a picture of an elaborate setup of multiple cameras on tracks around a shiny new luxury car in a bright white studio.

"That looks cool."

"I thought about buying those cameras, but that setup is pricey. I made a budget and I'd barely break even in three years, and that's if I got regular rentals."

I try to fight off a yawn but fail. "Sorry, you know I love budget talk, but I'm tired. Last night was...rough."

"You did the best you could. What more can you do?"

James is an incredibly hard worker, but he once told me his favorite part of his career was always being able to remain detached. *Light it. Film it. Go home.* But it's not like that for me. I love my job. I *want* to get the best out of René. I need to get him to open up on camera the way he did on the beach. And I need him to write and record another new hit song. Preferably by the weekend.

James finally moves on to his pork chop, so I scoop up a forkful of ravioli and pretend to love the feel of room temp ricotta in my mouth. When we were dating, I had the timing of our meals all figured out. I got into the habit of ordering foods that required assembly. Fajitas. Lettuce wraps.

James takes a small sip of his drink. "Here, have the rest." He sets the drink down in front of me. He's barely had any of it.

It occurs to me James may have ordered this drink because, when we were browsing through the menu, I said I wanted to try one. I also happen to know he ordered the appetizer because I love meatballs. It was always like this with him. Everything was frictionless and simple. I was never pushed or had to think. And I never had any idea what James really wanted.

I realize this is why, the whole time we've been apart, I've missed some things about our relationship, but I haven't missed *him*.

When we get back to the house, and pass through the ornate double wooden doors, we're immediately embraced by nature. There's a steady, cool breeze in the house. The glass panels have all been slid into the walls, so the place is opened up.

Music is coming from outside, so I take a peek at the pool. Santiago is out there, swimming with a couple of guys I've never seen before. We pass the kitchen and my phone buzzes in my hand with a call from Meri.

"I should take this." I stop walking.

"Okay, sure," James says brightly. "See you at four in the studio?"

I nod quickly and take the call. "Hey!" Meri appears on the screen, sitting in her car holding what appears to be an extra-large smoothie.

"Okay, that top is officially yours." There's a little tiredness in her voice. "Where were you? And more importantly, who were you with?"

I open my mouth to respond but the sound of flip-flops approaching make me panic. I step backward up the stairs that lead to the second floor of the main cottage. "Hold on," I whisper as Camila walks by wearing a crochet knit bikini.

I ordered her a new phone but it was too expensive to have it rushed same day to the island. I don't want to tell her it won't be here until tomorrow. Though I'm relieved to see her up and about. *Silver lining, Camila's alive.*

"Sorry, that was Camila." I reach the top step, find an open room, and shut the door. "It's a long story, but I don't want her to see me."

"Who are we avoiding, Daniela?" René's deep and sexy voice is behind me.

Chapter 25

Without letting go of the doorknob, I glance over my shoulder. The room is softly lit and cozy. There's rattan furniture and a vintage-looking bar along one wall. René is standing behind it, holding a cocktail shaker in the air.

"What's up? Who's that?" Meri sounds thrilled, as though she may already know the answer.

"Sorry, I'll just—" I say to René and pull the door open.

"*Hola*," he calls out, speaking to whoever's on my video call.

"*Hola, René*," Meri says softly and slightly creepily. I aim the phone so they can see each other.

"Ah, it's the sweater thief."

There's a pause on the line. "What?"

"He saw my screensaver," I explain.

"Oh, but did you tell him that was your idea? That was her idea." She's going a mile a minute, and I can feel her nerves through the line.

René gazes at me. "Take a seat."

"Yes, Dani, take a seat," Meri echoes.

I let go of the door and sit on the rattan barstool closest to it.

René motions for me to hand him the phone, so I hold it over the bar. His fingers overlap a few of mine as he takes it, causing a ripple of heat up my arm.

I look away and focus on the gorgeous room. There are a couple of golden sconces on the walls in the shape of suns on either side of the bar, and the lush wallpaper is covered in palm trees. I notice there are three glasses filled with drinks on a tray. The window is open, letting in the music playing out by the pool.

"So, can you tell me why your sister has a problem with Mother Nature?"

Meri giggles nervously. "What do you mean?"

"Since she's been here, she's wiped out on a waterfall, gotten stuck in a thorny weed patch, and been attacked by seagulls. Is this a new issue or has she been like this her whole life?" He sets the phone down on the bar and leans over, giving Meri his full attention.

"Really?" Meri sounds concerned. "A waterfall?" She flounders for a moment, surprised she hasn't heard about any of this. "No, not at all," she finally replies. "She used to climb trees all the time. She was really good, actually."

"Is that right?" He narrows his eyes and takes a step back to look at me. Like he's trying to locate the tree climber inside.

"Our mom would get so upset and Dani would tell her she didn't have to worry because she was 'one of the trees.'"

"No, I said I was 'one *with* the trees.'"

René's dark eyes look up at me and I'm suddenly aware of what I'm wearing. The pink slip top. The lack of a bra. As though reading my mind, his eyes run down my neck and onto my bare shoulders.

"So, it's just Puerto Rico she has a problem with?" he asks, eyes back on mine.

"I guess," Meri says, cracking up.

"And is the blazer situation a medical condition?"

My mouth drops, and a laugh escapes. He's wearing his reading glasses so he's back to being a more down-to-earth version of himself. Without the dark sunglasses, he's lost El Rico's brash bravado and now he's just Clark Kent. Or just René.

"Don't get me started, but yes, we're pretty sure it is." Meri's having such a great time. It's nice to hear the bubbliness in her voice.

"She's something else, your sister." He shifts to a more serious tone. "On the outside she's tough, and stubborn," he jabs good-naturedly, "and she tries to slink into the background, but the truth is she's excited and curious about everything." He looks at me and I feel my pulse pick up. "She's an observer. Maybe that's why she loves photography?"

Meri goes uncharacteristically quiet. "Yeah, I think you're right," she replies at last, her curiosity piqued.

"Okay, okay." My face feels flushed. It's strange to hear René theorizing about me. Or to know he's been thinking about me at all. *Curious and excited?* These are not words I'd use to describe myself. *More like shut off the world and plowing forward.* Then again, deep down, "curious and excited" sounds like the me I was before. Does he *actually* see her? Are there remnants of her still around?

I lean over the bar and pick up the phone. "Say goodbye to René, Meri. He has to get to the studio soon."

"No, wait. Why? I'm sure he has more questions. It sounds like he has a lot of concerns I can help with."

"Nope, he's all out of concerns. Aren't you?" I ask, playing along.

"Nice to meet you, Meri."

"You too! So nice! Wait, one last question. Please!"

Without hesitating, René reaches for the phone, his eyes conveying he's happy to comply. "Shoot," he tells Meri.

"*¿Que paso con Natalia?*"

My stomach drops to the floor. Only Meri would ask a question René has refused to answer every time it's been posed by journalists. Including some pretty well-known ones.

"You guys were so beautiful together," she adds, so innocently. As though she were talking to an old friend. I have no idea what René's thinking, I can't dare to look at him. I'm too busy staring at the back of the phone. Willing it to evaporate.

"Well, Meri. I'll tell you." He sounds somber but unruffled, so I look at him again. "She meant everything to me. One day we were talking about marriage, then she was off on her tour for three months, and when she got back, she ended things."

"What? Why?" Meri squeals, and my back goes rigid.

He taps the bar softly with his thumb. "Let's just say, if you're not tough enough in this industry, people can get in your head sometimes. Convince you"—he measures his words—"they know what's best for you."

My eyes widen. I can't believe he's opening up like this. I quickly fill in the blanks. Someone close to Natalia convinced her René wasn't right for her. *The label? Her family?*

"How horrible." Meri sounds as though she's on the verge of tears.

"Yeah, it was a really hard time. But we're in a good place now."

"I knew it, I just knew it. I knew you wouldn't cheat. I never doubted you."

"Thanks. I'm lucky to have a fan like you." He glances at me but I have trouble maintaining eye contact, seeing as I *always* doubted him.

"All right, Meri. I think we've taken enough of René's time." I reach for the phone and he waves goodbye to Meri before handing it back to me. "I'll call you later, okay?" I tell her.

"Okay, bye. Call me back. Have a great rest of your day," she rattles off quickly, trying to soak up every last moment of being on the line with René.

I hang up and slip the phone into my bag. "She's a really big fan. Thanks for that."

"Yeah, I remember you said that on the beach." He digs behind the bar for something.

"Why haven't you ever—" I try to bring up what he's just revealed about Natalia, but he speaks at the same time.

"What can I make for you?" He picks up a lime from a fruit basket.

A popular bachata song comes on the speakers outside, sending its relaxing vacation vibes into the bar. René's here offering me a drink and I can tell he's enjoying playing the part of bartender in this beautiful room. I scan the row of alcohol on the shelf behind him. There are old bottles with handwritten labels and brands of rum I've never heard of.

"I had rum at lunch so I should probably stick to the same. To be safe."

"You went with James?"

I keep my gaze aimed at the bottles on the wall. "Yeah." I try not to read too much into his question.

"He's your ex, isn't he? The one you were indifferent about?"

My mouth drops with a scoff. I nod feebly, wishing I hadn't told him about that.

"I figured. I was getting a vibe." He cuts the lime, squeezes a slice into one of the glasses, and stirs the drink vigorously with a long metal spoon.

"He's a good guy." I feel the need to defend him. "But we're just friends now," I say lightly, wanting to be done with the topic. "What are *you* having?" It slips out somewhat coyly.

"Here, you can try it." He places a napkin down in front of me with a flourish and then places his drink on it.

I smile and take a sip. "That's"—my face cinches up—"tart."

"You don't like passion fruit?"

"No, no, I do. I just wasn't expecting something sour."

"You want something sweet instead? I can make anything." He stretches his arms over his head and folds his hands behind his neck all cocky.

I scan my memory for a complicated cocktail. As he waits for my order, he places his hands on the bar and leans over, closer to me. His scent is warm and musky, like spicy wood.

"Damn, you're really concentrating. Don't hurt yourself."

I can't help but smile. "Shh, I'm trying to think of something really difficult." My voice has gone hushed, I don't know what's come over me, but that was *also* flirtatious. Something in his eyes tells me he's noticed. And in his body, too. Like every part of him has blinked in surprise. "Maybe something with egg yolk and bourbon." I tap a finger on my lips. "Or one of those drinks that requires a burned twig of rosemary."

"Burned twig—" he starts to repeat, then interrupts himself. "You have a nice smile," he says, impressed. "It's like...a square."

"A square?" I scoff. "How is that nice?"

"It's just the shape your mouth makes when you smile."

"No, it doesn't. That's anatomically impossible."

"It's nice. It's different. Different is good, Dani."

I try, but can't stop smiling, so I cover my mouth. "Oh, congratulations." I rest my elbows on the bar. "I heard about the new song." I may have messed up royally by missing it, but I *am* genuinely happy for him.

"Thank you. *Está buenísma*," he gushes, rubbing his face.

The disappointment over last night's fiasco feels raw again. I had the chance to film the creation of his new song and I missed it.

"That's awesome. I'm sorry we missed it." I can't believe he's gotten a song down that he's happy with. "And not just for work purposes," I add, meaning it. "I can't wait to hear it."

"Thanks. I wasn't planning any collaborations on this album. But"—he moves some of the glassware around on the bar—"it worked out." Something seems off about him all of a sudden.

"What's this new song about?"

"You know, it's a...it's a party track." Now *he's* the one unable to maintain eye contact.

Of course he doesn't want to share any details with me. He knows I'm not a fan of reggaeton. Or of *him*. I feel guilty all of a sudden. For believing the worst when it came to his breakup with Natalia *and* for not respecting the guy's music. Especially when my feelings have changed. I'm not ready to run out and buy every reggaeton album, but I do admire René's talents and how hard he works on his music.

"I'm really happy for you," I respond. "So, what's on the docket today? Do you plan to work on it some more? It would be great to get something on camera." It feels a little strange and uncomfortable asking him directly, but I'm desperate.

"Not really, sorry. I want to move on today." He turns and pulls a pear-shaped bottle from the top shelf. "I think you'd like this." He pours me a shot.

"Thanks." I bring the glass to my lips, and I'm hit with the strong scent of rum. I take a careful sip, but the warm liquid goes down smooth. "That is *really* good."

He puckers his lips proudly, and gets back to squeezing lime into each of the drinks on the tray.

"So, Natalia"—I gather the courage to press him—"why didn't you set the record straight? Why let people believe you cheated?"

"Why?" he repeats. "Same reason I don't do interviews. They take one look at me and make their judgments, and in the end it doesn't matter what I say. Do you really think they'd believe me?"

He has a point. "Okay, but why not have Natalia deny those allegations for you?"

"That's...a longer story." His eyes dart around the room and land on the window. "Speaking of coming clean, sorry if I blew your cover. I assumed your sister knew you got hurt on the waterfall."

"It's okay. No, I hadn't told her."

He takes a long sip of his drink. "Why not?"

I let out a deep breath. "I didn't want her or my mom to worry. I don't normally do that kind of stuff."

"And why is that?" I glance at the pretty drinks he's prepared, all ready to go on the tray. While René leans comfortably over the bar, with no intention of delivering them anytime soon.

"I guess I always try to be a good role model and wouldn't want Meri to take risks like that. I don't know"—a new realization sinking in—"probably also because *I* can't afford to take risks like that." Admitting this makes the bar feel stuffier. There isn't any room in my life for injuries. Or much of anything other than work. "I guess I had a lot of responsibilities when our dad died. I imagine it's like when you have kids. New parents are probably less likely to go parachuting," I declare, as though this were a well-known statistic.

I can't remember the last time I had more than one drink or stayed out too late. At first, I felt I didn't have a choice. Mom was a wreck. If I didn't go straight home after work, who would be there for Meri if she needed help with her homework? Or get her to school on time in the morning? Now, it's habit, I guess. Making sure I'm there to help everyone's week run smoothly.

"I see." He puckers his lips slightly and flashes me a disappointed look. As though he were just about to offer we go sky-diving. "I think you're too tough on yourself. Your sister seems all grown up now."

The muscles in my back loosen. I open my mouth to say something just as his phone pings with a text.

"Actually, Daniela," he starts casually as he responds to the text.

"Dani," I correct dryly.

"Dani," he repeats with a grin, and slips his phone into his pocket, "I need to go home soon. Why don't you guys come? If you think it'd be good for the making-of."

"Home, home?"

"Yeah," he says with a chuckle.

"Yes, that would be incredible." Capturing footage of René going back to his hometown almost makes up for the missed recording last night. Between the rum and this invitation, I feel my first sense of relief in days. "Yes. Please, and thank you," I list off.

"Well, you checked it all off there." René puts his hands on his hips.

"I'm anything if not thorough."

He raises an eyebrow and smiles warmly. He leans over the bar, pressing more of his weight on the counter. I seem fine, but I can feel sweat forming on the palms of my hands.

"On the way back, we can hit one of the lyrics in your dad's song."

"Oh, no, don't worry about that. I'll do it on my own time. I don't want to waste yours."

"It's not a problem." The bedroom eyes have woken up behind his glasses.

"Great, thanks." I feel winded and like I'm struggling to keep up.

His phone pings again with a text and he sighs. "I'll see you in the studio." He picks up the tray of drinks and heads out.

"Yeah, see you," I respond, a little delayed. And then I just sit there after he's gone, trying to catch my breath.

Chapter 26

Maybe going for a run at noon wasn't the best idea. There are tall trees and impenetrable wild brush on either side of this narrow street, and the sun is scorching the island and reflecting up from the asphalt. It feels like I'm trapped in a bubble of humid heat. My cell is tucked into my running shorts and I'm listening to Meri on headphones, so even my ears feel hot.

"You never have to get me another birthday present. You're good for life." Meri already expressed her gratitude on the phone last night. And in a biblically long text she sent this morning.

"That's a substantial amount of savings," I respond, catching my breath. "Of time *and* money. Thanks."

"I mean it. That was so cool," Meri squeals. "And that was sweet, him asking all those questions about you. You guys must be getting close working together, huh?"

"I wouldn't say that. I mean he's..." I pause because I don't know what to say. I've replayed our conversation at the bar so many times, but my feelings about it are jumbled.

He made me feel he wanted to stay and keep talking. Was he

flirting with me? *I know I was.* He was so sweet and open with Meri. Then again, that could have had nothing to do with me. That's just who he is, a charmer. René being René.

"He can be nice sometimes."

"Really? Tell me everything." She doesn't wait for me to answer. "Oh man, you have to admit he's even sexier in person."

"Yeah, he's okay." A couple of cars zoom by, so I veer onto the narrow path on the side of the road. "I just don't trust him, his whole act." I'm trying to jog quicker but I'm mostly hopping, jumping, and sidestepping to avoid the tree roots jutting out of the dirt. "And we're stuck here, and everything revolves around him and he's so"—I almost trip over a rock—"closed off."

I see the beach through the tangle of trees and stop jogging. "First he's all cool like he doesn't have a care in the world, then he makes you feel like he's actually listening and remembers things you say." *And offers to take you to the places in your father's song.* But what about Camila? Does he have any idea how she's felt about him all this time? "If this is how he treats women, no wonder they stick around."

"He didn't cheat on Natalia," Meri declares proudly, a point in his favor.

"And what's *that* all about?" Gruffly, I push aside branches as I make my way toward the beach. "Why let people believe you cheated on someone you loved? Doesn't make any sense. I think he's hiding something."

Meri moans in disagreement. "Though I did read he may have a secret tattoo"—she pauses for dramatic effect—"inside his lower lip."

My brain gets distracted by the thought.

"But what was he talking about?" Meri sounds worried. "What happened to you at a waterfall? And with birds?"

"Oh, nothing. A seagull took my food on the beach. It was funny," I say to calm her, and I hold back telling her about the waterfall. My knee is pretty much healed now anyway.

"Give me a second," Meri says. I hear someone approach her with a question about makeup brushes. Meri knows exactly what they need and why. It's a sweet opportunity to hear my little sister at work, being knowledgeable and helpful. She also sounds good. Maybe whatever was upsetting her has been resolved? It's amazing the effect Meri's happiness has on me. It boils down to this: if she's okay, I'm okay.

We say goodbye just as I find shade beneath a tree filled with dusty rose-colored mangos. I breathe in the warm breeze and take in the calls of unusually loud birds and the not-so-distant sounds of waves crashing. I contemplate the possibility of going for a swim in shorts and a sports bra.

At least I'm not in the studio waiting around like an idiot. Thankfully, Ángel has taken over the schedule. René isn't going to the studio until after lunch and then he'll perform at the showcase. He also plans to return to the studio, so we'll be working late into the night.

Who knows if we'll capture an actual song being recorded, but at least I'm finally feeling hopeful. Maureen arrived early this morning but went directly to the beach where the concert is taking place.

I have a new idea I want to pitch to her. The making of the album could center around in-depth footage of René opening the doors to his private life back home, and not so much in the studio. We could focus on how those aspects of his life influence his work, without actually seeing much of the work. *This is me, keeping calm and carrying on. Making lemonade.*

Out of the corner of my eye, a horse appears. It's not a baby but also not a full-grown adult. Golden auburn with a blond mane and tail, and a narrow patch of white on its nose. It's poking around a patch of dry grass near the beach. An ache forms deep in my chest.

"When I take you to Culebra, you'll see the wild horses on the beach." My father's voice echoes in a memory when I was little.

"Really? Why are they on the beach?" I asked.

"I don't know, nobody owns them. They're just free to run around. You see them everywhere."

"I want to go."

"We'll go."

Standing on tippy-toes, I reach a mango on one of the lower branches and approach the horse until I'm only a few feet away. Unsure if it's safe to have a wild horse eat right out of my hand, I toss the mango at him. As soon as it drops its head to grab it, I have a sinking feeling in my stomach. *What if horses can't eat mangos? What if it chokes on the large seed?* So I kick the mango. The thing flies off toward the beach, reaches a slope, and starts to roll quickly down a hill.

The horse trots in that direction, so I run after it. The slope is steeper than I thought, and my knees buckle beneath me. I drop down on the sand and the horse reaches the mango. It scoops it up, chews and chews, and then hacks a few times before spitting out the pit and ambling away.

Stepping out of the SUV, I see Ángel and Maureen standing on the stage that was built overnight for the showcase. Mo is a bold pop of color in a long, purple dress. It's late afternoon and the beach is buzzing with stagehands and tech crew making last-minute adjustments. In less than an hour, three ferries filled with fans, influencers, DJs, journalists, and promoters will arrive from San Juan at Culebra's ferry terminal, where busses are waiting to bring them to the beach.

While James unloads the camera equipment, I look off in a trance at the beach. Playa Tamarindo is one of the largest beaches on the island so there's plenty of room for the stage we've built. It's a simple structure framed by large speakers, and strategically placed in front of a row of tall palms. It's hard to imagine the stage isn't always there, ready for the next concert on the beach. Soon, three new artists will be performing, and René will join one of them for a song.

I step onto the sand, excited for the event. James and I will be covering the performances and interviewing the new artists. Artists who won't push back.

You know in the movies, where the sensible girl gets a sexy makeover? Well, that's not what's happened here. *This is more of an internal makeover.* I feel lighter and optimistic. Well, that and there's no blazer. I'm wearing a formfitting coral vest with matching slacks that cinch up around the ankles. My hair is half up, half down, and I've put on my largest gold hoop earrings.

"Hi!" I call out with confidence as I climb up the steps onto the stage.

I may not have much resembling footage of an artist recording actual songs, but René has given us access to his home life and I know that's going to impress Mo. I know from the chat rooms, his fans are begging to learn more about where he grew up.

Santiago appears on the other side of the stage to start the sound check, and Ángel turns to greet him.

"Hey, Dani. Puerto Rico suits you," Mo says after she gives me a big hug.

"Thanks. It's good to see you."

"I heard about the new song with Natalia." There's a trace of confusion in her voice. Probably wondering why I haven't told her all about it. "Ángel's brought me up-to-date. How did that go?"

My face goes rigid. The image of Camila pulling my ears under the bar flashes before my eyes. I don't know what to say. It doesn't sound like she knows we weren't there. "René is so happy with it," I say, deflecting. "It's a really great track. Everyone thinks it could be the first single."

"Excellent! I can't wait to hear it."

Me too. I smile wide and try to loosen my back muscles. It occurs to me that letting Camila call Natalia could have actually *helped* René. Maybe he's one of those artists who writes best when he's upset. I may have deprived the world of the best rage anthem ever written.

"But even better than that, René's invited us to his hometown. We're going to get a tour, meet his family." Maureen's eyes light up.

"Really? How'd you manage that?"

"Oh, you know. I learned from the best," I respond, tossing her a friendly compliment. She squeezes my arm sweetly and smiles.

By the time the fans have filled the beach, I know Maureen

is happy. She's watched as I've done poignant and fun interviews with the new artists who are performing tonight, interviewed a few fans, and even had James set up a camera on the stage so we could get a neat time lapse of the audience filling in.

James is the only one allowed to record the concert. Everyone in the audience has had to drop their cell phones into individual pouches, which will remain locked until the concert is over.

The late afternoon sun is still blazing, but the crowd is unbothered. They're swaying around happily to music pumping through the speakers. There's a sense of joy and privilege to be at the exclusive event. While there's buzz for the new artists who will be performing, everyone I spoke to is here to see René.

The music shuts off and the audience cheers wildly as Santiago walks onto the stage to where his DJ stand is set up.

"*Hola, hola, hola.*" Santiago speaks into his microphone with a big smile. "I don't think you're ready," he teases, making the crowd scream even louder. "You have no idea what you're about to experience." The crowd quiets down to listen. "I'm so excited for you but also a little jealous that you get to hear these artists for the first time."

I'm standing with James on a small riser in front of the stage. We have a great shot of Santiago and can easily turn and get shots of fans' reactions. Maureen is babysitting some of the VIPs near the soundboard behind the crowd.

Santiago introduces Lazaro Amparo, a young Puerto Rican rapper wearing a baseball hat on backward, who jogs energetically onto the stage. Right away, he kicks into a fast-paced rap song. After he's sung a few phrases a cappella, Santiago starts an updated version of a classic salsa track and then adds a live piano riff on his keyboard. It's a great party starter and the audience loves it.

The next artist, Tempo, is a more classic reggaetonero with a unique high-pitched voice that doesn't quite match his rugged, bad boy look. His performance is more energetic. He gets up close to the crowd, singing and dancing right in their faces with his low-hanging pants.

I keep an eye on the monitor, but once in a while I scan the crowd to make sure there isn't anything James should be aiming his camera at instead.

From where I'm standing, I can see the action happening just offstage in the wings. I tap James's shoulder and point it out to him. He complies and zooms into it, so I follow the action on my monitor. Backstage, René and Camila are dancing together. *Somewhat provocatively.* It's a great visual to have. René and Camila enjoying the new music. But I also can't help scrutinizing their moves. They're so comfortable around each other. He holds her close at times as they dance.

When James returns to covering Tempo's performance, I don't take my eyes off René. He's wearing white-framed sunglasses, and a white short-sleeve shirt with dressy white pants. He could be heading out to play a round of golf, except that none of the shirt buttons are buttoned up. His stomach and chest muscles are peeking through, his tattoos adding color to the overall look.

"How's everybody feeling?" Santiago calls out to the crowd. They yell back in unintelligible excitement. "Can you handle one more?"

"*Sí!*" the crowd shouts back in almost perfect unison.

The lights dim over the stage and Santiago kicks off a beat.

After a few moments, René's voice is heard. There's an effect on his vocals, but the audience goes wild with excitement.

René's still offstage and I watch him holding the microphone close to his lips, head tilted down. It occurs to me, I haven't heard René sing in person. Not actual words anyway. So far in the studio, we've only been around as he's played the guitar or hummed a few bars.

René steps onto the stage and the crowd whoops and cheers. The sound effect on his microphone goes away and his real voice kicks in. René's deep and raspy voice is mesmerizing.

"Everyone, meet Juan," René says, welcoming the young rapper who was waiting for his cue.

"This is the first single off my new album. It's dropping next week and you're hearing it here first," Juan says, addressing the crowd, and then to René, "Thank you, man. For making this possible." A faster drum layer kicks in, Juan raps his solo, and I watch the audience sway with the slow, melodic rhythms and his smooth vocals.

He raps about his first love and how he compares every woman he meets to her. When he's done, René steps forward to sing the chorus. His rap is more like a conversation letting woman after woman down. He dances as he sings, every move requiring zero effort.

It's not you, it's not me, you're just not her.

René connects to the audience so easily. When a girl yells something from the crowd, he waves and flashes her the sweetest grin. Even in sunglasses, he's completely real and it's the sexiest thing I've ever seen. I let go of the monitor so it hangs freely on its strap around my neck. When performing live, René "El Rico" Rodriguez sounds just like he looks. Slick, breathy, and smooth. Easy, yet certain.

He steps aside when Juan comes in for the bridge. I watch René and find that I'm practically holding my breath. My stomach is cinched tight, anxious to hear his voice again.

Chapter 27

A GIRL NEAR THE FRONT OF THE STAGE THROWS A STUFFED bear at René. In one fluid move, he catches, kisses, and tosses it right back to her. Is this what she wanted? To get the gift back having touched his lips, or was she hoping for René to take it home and cherish it forever?

Up on the DJ platform, Santiago is also a big part of the show. When neither Juan nor René is singing, he'll moan into the mic to hype the crowd with a "*¿Dónde está mi gente?*" or a "*¡Vamos Puerto Rico!*" Even a simple wave of his hand in the air gets cheers from the audience.

From time to time, René looks over in our direction and I wonder if he's noticed me on this platform. We're about three feet above the ground, so I guess it's possible.

Beads of sweat are forming along my cleavage. I can't tell if it's the actual temperature that's rising, or if it's the heat permeating off this crowd as they push their way closer to the stage and around our riser. Or maybe it's because of René's steady gaze in my direction.

And then, for the entirety of a chorus, he smiles at me. An easy, flirty, "I want you" kind of smile.

When he turns away, I reason with myself. There's no way that just happened. Did it? Was it all in my head? Is there more to René wanting to help me find my father's places? Why is he taking us to his hometown? I imagine him giving us a tour of his childhood bedroom. This quickly leads to a visual of René and me in the tight closet where he recorded his first songs. What I'm doing in the closet, I have no idea. If anything, it would be James in there with the camera.

I feel the weight of a small hand on my shoulder and flinch. I turn and find Camila on the riser next to me. "Hey, I need to talk to you." She leans in close. Somehow, I can hear her clearly despite our proximity to the large tower of speakers.

She's glowing and her boho chic style is more elevated today. She's sporting a short, flesh-toned dress made solely out of netting with just enough fabric to cover key areas. Her new cell is dangling at the end of an edgy cross-body strap made of tiny, interconnected locks.

"I wanted to thank you," she says in my ear. It's like she's developed a skill for throwing her voice deep into an ear canal, without resorting to yelling.

I lean in and try to send my voice the way she does. "I'm sorry about your phone. I shouldn't have gotten involved."

"No, I'm glad you did," she says firmly. "You were right. It wasn't the right time." She eyes the stage, somewhat menacingly, and rubs the gold charm on her necklace between her fingers. When she drops her hand, I see it's the same lion pendant René's worn a few times. "Is everything okay?" she asks.

"Yes!" I respond excitedly. "I was just admiring your cell phone case." It isn't technically a lie. The interlocking locks *are* really cool.

"Oh, thanks." She beams. "I made it."

She's so talented. If she ever wanted to quit being the world's worst assistant, she could make a killing with her bespoke designs.

The song ends and the crowd bursts into applause. René takes Juan's hand, and lifts it up to the sky. I turn to Camila. "Well, that was a success."

"Oh, they're not done," Camila announces, sure of herself, and walks off the platform.

Santiago kicks off another song and the reggaeton dance beat with a vintage feel gets everyone moving immediately. René seems surprised by this, and jogs over to the DJ platform, as Juan walks off the stage.

James sets the camera on a tripod. The concert is technically over, but there's clearly something brewing.

"I guess let's wait and see what's happening." I check the soundboard for Maureen, but she isn't there.

When I turn back to the stage, René is approaching Ángel in the wings. I try my best to read their body language. René doesn't seem happy. Ángel is clearly trying to placate him. With the song continuing to play for the crowd, René throws his arms up.

"All right, all right," René says into his microphone, walking back on the stage. "So here's the deal. I wasn't planning on sharing this one yet. But..." René pauses and looks over at James's camera. *Or was it directly at me?* "This one's for you"—he looks back at the audience—"before anyone else hears it. This is the first song we've recorded for my new album. I hope you love it as much as I do." The audience breaks into loud applause, whistling and whooping.

Maureen has appeared next to Ángel in the wings, and I can tell she's just as confused as I am. And probably running through all the same thoughts. No one in the crowd has their cell, so there will be plenty of buzz and press, without leaking the unreleased track.

James steadies the camera back on his shoulder as the crowd quiets down and pushes in tighter around us on the riser. Everyone's been waiting for this. René "El Rico" Rodriguez making his own music, not just appearing as a blip in someone else's song. The truth is, I'm excited to hear it too. I feel fortunate to be here, to be among the few who get to experience it before anyone else.

The song has a great beat. Unmistakably fun and light. James is holding steady on a wide shot so I tap him on the shoulder and point behind us, so he can capture a shot of the fans dancing.

René holds the microphone close to his lips and I feel something akin to protective. I hope everyone loves it. Obviously, he must feel ready to share it. Then again, he didn't seem to know he'd be performing it so I'm nervous for him.

He starts and it's slow and easy. Like he's just talking and I'm hanging on every word. James's camera has a long lens so now, in the monitor, I'm looking at a close-up of René's face. He holds the mic to his mouth again and I can't take my eyes away from his lips so close to the mesh.

He turns in our direction. His deep, raspy voice is captivating and I don't want to admit it, but I feel like he's serenading me. It's ridiculous and exactly how every girl here must be feeling, but I can't help it.

The song switches to a more fast-paced beat and the audience cheers René on encouragingly.

> *never met a Latina I didn't like*
> *until now*
> *but if you take off the blazer*

My body stiffens. Did he say *blazer*? Blood begins to pump loudly in my temples, as more phrases set off alarms. *Stressed. Repressed. No one wants your sexy selfie. When you hear this, you won't dance.*

At some point, I think the lyrics turn sensual, but I can't tell for sure. I'm stunned. Like a fish zapped by a moray eel, I'm floating away, eyes and mouth wide open. He *is* serenading me, except it's a diss song. He's *diss-enading* me.

Natalia's voice comes in when he calls out in Spanish.

> *Where are my Latinas?*
> *Right here, here, here, sí.*
> *Right here, here, here, baby.*

The chorus is a set of instructions. In essence: Take off your blazer, get up and dance, get off your high horse, ride me instead.

I'm gripping the monitor so hard, but I force my eyes to roam the stage because I can no longer stand to look at René's face. I find Camila near Maureen and Ángel in the wings. They're nodding their heads, pleased. It must be obvious to them. They must know. *James must know.*

This song is about me. I know because it's taking an

impossible amount of effort to stand here and not cry. To
pretend I don't feel humiliated. The chorus comes on again
and I physically shudder, because this time, the crowd is singing along. Of course they are. The stupid song is catchy as
hell.

Chapter 28

I FOUND THE CALENDAR IN A FANCY STATIONERY STORE IN Coral Gables. It was meant to be a gift for Meri, who was starting her senior year a month after our dad died. The high-quality daily calendar had thick paper with gilded edges, and at the top of each page there was an inspirational quote.

> Sorrow prepares you for joy.
>
> —Rumi

> You may encounter many defeats,
> but you must not be defeated.
>
> —Maya Angelou

> Things'll go your way, if you hold
> on for one more day.
>
> —Wilson Phillips

It was a time where I searched for Band-Aids everywhere. Anything that could help her. I bought two calendars, one for her and one for me to follow along and bring up in conversation. I guess I thought I could expand on the quotes, do some research to give her more context. It would be like a read-along.

I couldn't have known it would be exactly what I needed. The reminder that people around the world, from the beginning of time, it seemed, needed inspiring too. It helped me feel less alone.

Eventually I know Meri stopped using the calendar, because at some point she didn't know what I was talking about. But those steady, daily doses of wisdom got me through that year.

Now, if only it could help me get through the next hour. I feel completely exposed. *And* pissed. My blood is in a roiling boil. The audience is being corralled back onto the ferries, and we've set up a spot to conduct interviews on the beach behind the stage. Mo suggested we keep them brief, so we've already interviewed the first two singers and are now waiting to talk to René and Juan at the same time.

Maureen approaches James and me as she wraps up a call. "The only question is, do we want a collab as the first single? I'm inclined to say yes in this case," she rattles off excitedly into the phone. "Dani's here and covered all of it for the making-of." She winks in my direction and the knot around my throat tightens.

I don't know how to tell her we weren't there. If we had been, I wonder if I'd feel any better about the lyrics. If Mo knows the song is about me, she hasn't let on, and neither has James. The blazer lyrics would be the only tip-off, as the rest of the references are all moments that have happened since I've been here.

Still, it feels as though everyone on this beach knows René was singing about me.

I glance hesitantly over my shoulder to keep an eye on René. Ángel is guiding him as he makes his way through photographs with a handful of VIPs who were allowed backstage after the event. He hasn't changed his wardrobe, but I notice he's switched to neon green sunglasses that make him look extra smug as he poses. I snap my head back quickly toward the beach, take a deep breath, and review the questions I'd prepared before the concert.

I hear Ángel's voice approaching behind me and my heart climbs up my throat. Mo wraps up her call, greets René and Juan, and walks them over to the interview spot.

> Life is 10% what happens to you
> and 90% how you react to it.
> —Charles something or other

It doesn't help. It feels like nothing will. Not unless it's specifically suited for this exact situation. So I come up with one on my own.

> It only hurts if you care what he thinks.

Something shifts and I do feel better. I *don't* care what he thinks. *I don't.* I take another deep breath and address René with the grace of a professional who wasn't just publicly humiliated. "Do you mind taking your sunglasses off?"

He contemplates this for a second. "Sure," he concedes, takes a few steps forward, and hands them to me. I take them from him, without breaking eye contact, and let them slip into my vest pocket.

"So, René, why did you come here today? Why stop working on your much-anticipated first album, and make the time to come out here to support Juan?" I'm impressed with myself. There wasn't even a hint of sharpness in my voice. Though my heart is pounding in my chest.

"Well," he begins, his eyes locked on mine. "It's simple. This guy's amazing and he's my Puerto Rican brother. We have to be there for each other."

"Juan, what do you think about that? How does it feel to have René on your side?" *Instead of, you know, backstabbing you.*

"It means the world. He's someone I've always admired, so this is a dream come true. I've hit him up a couple of times the past couple of years and he's always been there to answer my questions and give me advice." I'm about to step in, but he continues. "For a moment there, I was having a hard time with a really difficult personal situation," Juan adds, turning to René, "and he helped me. René's a lifesaver." René puts an arm around him and squeezes. Juan reaches over and gives him a hug, his eyes watering. It's possibly the sweetest moment of male friendship ever captured on camera. Of mutual respect and gratitude. And it's so ridiculously at odds with how I feel about René, I don't know what to do with myself.

As they turn back toward me, I continue with the interview. "René, when it comes to mentors—"

"What did *you* think of my new song?" René asks, interrupting me.

I look around. "Are you asking me?"

"Yeah."

I remain still. *Is he serious?* What did *I* think? Is he trying to rile me up? "It's terrific," I manage with a grin. If there was someone I could personally thank for the word "terrific," I would. It's short and sweet and has the power to be ironic without anyone noticing.

René's eyes shrink and he looks a little wounded. *The gall.*

I glance at my notes but I'm unable to move on. My frustration is bubbling. I know I should stick to the script, but I can't help myself. "But…it's not always like that, is it?" There's a heavy pause. René eyes me, trying to read the testier tone in my voice. "Sometimes you hear a song for the first time, and you hate it. Am I right? It's only after a couple of listens that you see its potential. You know?" I have a headache. Probably brought on by forcing myself to pretend I'm not furious or hurt. "But that first time it's a gross, messy little thing. Like watching a baby giraffe trying to walk for the first time. You can't help but think, 'You're a mess, little giraffe. You should sit down for a bit.'"

Someone coughs and I'm suddenly aware of the presence of a small crowd behind me. I turn to find Ángel, Mo, Santiago, and Camila have all witnessed my rant.

"I *do* know what you mean," René says.

"You do?" I ask hesitantly.

"It's called the exposure effect. Sometimes you develop a fondness for something only after repeated exposure," he explains. He's picked up on my frustration and come to my rescue, I feel.

For the rest of the interview, I stick to the prepared questions. Though every time certain lyrics from René's song creep up, I think I'm going to be sick.

Five hours later, I'm in bed and tucked inside the netting. Outside, the waves are raging in surround sound. To the left and right there's the pounding of water on water. Stumbling, pushing, crashing over each other, like they're desperate to be first. The island seems as upset as I am.

I want to cry, but the tears are stuck inside. If I could get them out, I'd feel better. I'm sure it's like indigestion. I don't care what René thinks, I just need to get these tears out.

Part of it is the shock of it all. The extreme pendulum swing from thinking René could actually be interested in me, to... well, whatever it is someone feels when they write a humiliating song about you. Hate? Disgust? That you're a clown?

After the concert, I rode back to the airport with Mo so we could catch up before her flight. I knew I had to tell her, so I just got it over with. "We didn't get any footage of that song," I said abruptly, my heart racing. "René and Natalia's duet," I added for clarification.

She peered back at me from the front passenger seat. "None at all?" Even at night, in the darkness of a cab, I could see the vein on her forehead bulging. "You didn't get any of it?"

"No," I said. "But it's not—"

"Why not?" she interrupted. She wasn't just upset, she was disappointed, which made me feel worse. I could hear what it would sound like if I told her the truth. Camila's drunkenness and James's stomach bug. I knew Mo, and the vein that was now full-on bulging, preferred it when you just owned up to your mistakes. "I messed up. But I'll fix it. I promise."

Chapter 29

"HOW DO YOU KNOW IT'S ABOUT YOU?" MERI SOUNDS SKEPTI-cal. I have the phone on speaker on the pillow as I lie spiritless beside it. A strong, early morning breeze lifts the curtains and threatens to untuck the mosquito netting.

"It's obvious," I say dryly.

She's quiet for a moment. "And what do you mean 'it's a hate song'? Why would he do that?"

"I have no idea. All I know is I started packing last night." I feel a little embarrassed admitting this. I don't know if I actually meant to go through with it, but the act of opening my suitcase and throwing in a few things made me feel better.

Not only have I let Maureen down when my job is already on the line, but René ridiculed me in a song that will probably be a huge hit. Heck, my future generations will probably be ridiculed by it too. As I consider the scope, it only gets bigger. I wish I could sink into this bed and come out on the other side of the planet. Then I remember that reggaeton is pretty big in Japan.

"Do you think there's a chance you're overreacting?" Meri asks gently.

"It's about a girl who wears blazers," I say, interrupting.

"Oh, well, then it must be you," she teases me.

"*And* doesn't dance," I add to the list.

"A lot of people don't dance."

"And other stuff," I murmur, because I don't want to tell her René saw me taking selfies in my underwear. "I just know, Meri, believe me."

"Okay. If it *is* about you, which I'm not saying it is, this is a great opportunity for you to turn it around. See the positive in it. You made such an impact on the guy that he was inspired to write a song."

This is Meri's approach to life. She doesn't spiral. If a thought doesn't suit her, she doesn't let it in for too long. It's why she's been avoiding answering my texts about her upcoming exam or how it's going with the tutor. She only welcomes the positive. I, on the other hand, let all the bad thoughts in. I clear out my closet for them, offer them dinner and my side of the bed. I'm very comfortable focusing on the potential negatives. Bad things happen all the time. It's best to be prepared for them.

I turn to my side and away from the phone. I want to believe Meri's right. For a moment, I let in a kernel of doubt. Maybe the song *isn't* about me. Maybe only *certain things* are, and the rest he made up. The way a movie can be inspired by true events. There's the possibility the song was only *inspired* by true events.

No one wants your selfie. It's like a hot poker to the chest. There's no way the song isn't about me. But there's still a chance I can do a good job. I hear our dogs barking in the distance and smile. I'll be back there soon enough and everything will go back to normal. Better! We'll have new double-pane windows to keep us safe.

I shut my eyes and focus on the sounds of home. There's more barking as Meri feeds them. I hear Meri's slippers on the tile floor walking to her favorite spot on the couch in the Florida room. I can imagine Mom heading outside to feed the birds and the duck. Just then, I hear the squeak of the door that leads to the backyard and the sound of someone singing.

"Who's there?"

"That's Mom." I can tell that Meri is smiling.

"Our mother is singing?" I'm flabbergasted.

"Yeah, hold on," Meri cautions as she shuts the back door. "She's seeing someone," she whispers into the phone. "He's really nice. He came over last night and made the best Cuban fried rice I've ever had."

I spring up and grab hold of the phone, rubbing the sleep from my eyes with my free hand. "What now? What did you say?"

"Um...yeah. I don't know why she hasn't told you." Meri's quiet for a moment. "I mean, they just met and—" She stops herself and I hear another slam of the screen door and Mom's singing. I can't remember the last time she walked around the house singing. She sounds so carefree, so happy.

"Hold on," Meri whispers, waiting for Mom to leave the room. "I guess she was at lunch with a friend from her old job, oh, and she actually drove there, and *she* asked him out."

I'm dumbfounded. Mom went out? Mom *drove*?

"I'm sure she'll tell you soon. So, act surprised."

"Oh, that's not going to be a problem." My brain is slogging through what feels like mountains of information. Mom. A man. Fried rice.

We hang up and I stare blankly at the wall. *Focus on the positives.* Mom's met someone. She's actually put herself out there. But the negatives push down the door. Mom hasn't dated. She's barely left the house. She's barely left *her room!* She needs to slow down. What if she gets hurt? I mean, who even is this guy?

I drag myself to the table and turn on my laptop. I need to dive into work. I decide to hammer out a new marketing strategy to send to Mo. I review my notes on the footage we have so far and write out what I hope we'll have by the end of the month.

A calmer breeze slips through the room. I can do this. Pumped on nerves and adrenaline, I type out a new plan detailing how we can use the material. When it's done, I attach it to an email and contemplate a strong subject heading: NEW MARKETING STRATEGY. Eh, I don't like the reminder that there was an Old Marketing Strategy that hasn't worked out. REVISED CREATIVE FOR RENÉ "EL RICO" RODRIGUEZ. I quickly backspace to delete his name. Seeing it on the screen physically hurts. I take a deep breath and hit send.

I slip on the pair of black jeans that were lying near the top of the suitcase, put on my Fleetwood Mac tee, the one with Stevie Nicks on it and the lyric *Back to the gypsy that I was,* but then come to a halt in front of the small wardrobe. Three blazers are grouped together on the rack staring back at me. I scan the room. At the blazer on a hook by the door, at the bolero draped carefully over the chair by the window.

As I roll up my sleeves, I'm fully aware of the message *not* wearing a blazer today will send to René. He'll think, *I did it. I got to her.* But it's not like I want to stop wearing blazers indefinitely; I'm just not feeling one today. *This has nothing to do with him.*

As I corral my hair into a ponytail, there's a knock on the door. I'm expecting James, ready to head down to breakfast, so I'm completely taken aback to find Camila, and a loud "Oh" slips out of my mouth.

"Good morning," she says, letting herself in. She walks right up to my bed and rests a knee on the mattress.

"Morning."

"I just want to go through your morning in Salinas." Camila's all business, in a way I've yet to experience. "The car will pick you up in an hour." She lets out a deep sigh. As though communicating this has required a lot of effort. "Don't assume everyone and everything is okay to film, in terms of, like, family and friends. So just be respectful and ask René first."

"Sure, of course." I'm beyond surprised René's making good on his promise to take us to his hometown. But mostly relieved we can implement the new plan, the *revised* plan that I've just promised Maureen.

"You're not coming?" I ask, suddenly aware I'm going to have to go on pretending he's done nothing wrong.

"No, there isn't enough room."

I want to ask what she means by that, but she's distracted by something on the other side of the bed. I follow her gaze and find my half-packed suitcase. "I guess I should probably unpack at some point, huh?"

Camila raises her knee off the mattress and combs her fingers through her hair. "Well, text me if anything comes up." She stops by the door because something else has her attention. The blazer hanging on the hook. I watch as she looks around the room and finds the one on the chair. Her face scrunches, a detective scouring the room for clues. Her gaze lands on the closet I've left wide open, and the blazers hanging in there evenly spaced and facing in the same direction. I know there are only three of them, but seen through her eyes, I feel it may as well be the sales rack at Brooks Brothers.

Chapter 30

I wouldn't call it a helicopter. It's more of a large toy. One that's lightweight enough to be effortlessly wheeled around by our retired Navy pilot and a woman in four-inch heels.

I assumed we'd be taking a plane to René's hometown, but our driver passed the airport and pulled off the road into this open field near the beach.

I peer back at James unloading the gear. "Can you ask if we can attach our small cameras to the outside? The views will be nice." My voice is a little shaky.

"Yeah, sure." James seems unfazed by the helicopter, though he said it will be his first time on one too. My eyes wander past him to the road. The truth is, I'm more anxious about spending time with René then I am about the mini chopper.

He's meeting us here, and I'm just going to pretend everything is fine when he arrives. I don't have a choice. Today could be the answer to all my problems.

My phone buzzes with a call, but when I see who it's from, I send it to voicemail. I know exactly what my mom's going to say, and it's more than I can handle right now. How can I be expected to respond anyway? *Congratulations on your secret life?*

I put the phone away just as the yellow Mustang pulls up alongside our van. René steps out wearing dark sunglasses, a cable-knit polo, and what appear to be dressy ski pants. It's a bizarre look, yet he's somehow pulling it off. While he greets our pilot, I hop out of the van and check on James near the helicopter.

"Good morning!" René sings as he strides over to James and me. "You guys ready?"

"Totally!" I quickly turn to James. "Why don't you mic him up while I figure out where I want him."

"Where *do* you want me?" René teases.

I tense up. I can't believe him. What I want to do is laugh maniacally and say something like, "Nowhere! I want you nowhere!" It would be *so* nice to retaliate. To demand some sort of an explanation or apology. *Or royalties.* But I have to focus on work.

The tiny pod-like interior of this scaled-down version of a helicopter has two narrow seats in the front and one small bench in the back. If I put James back there with René, he'd be too close for a good shot. If René rides in the front with the pilot, we'd mostly get the side of his face. There's only one answer. James *has* to sit in the front, and I have to sit with René in the back. But the bench is so small, there's no way we won't be touching.

A few minutes later, René and I aren't just close, we're *over-lapping*. I'm annoyed that our shoulders are pressed together and that his right hip is tucked behind mine. But even more so, that I'm worked up and my pulse is racing.

The blades start spinning and the pilot's voice comes in

crystal clear over our headsets. "It looks like rain." He turns toward us, flashing what I bet he thinks is a reassuring smile. "But it's fine, as long as there isn't any lightning."

As though sensing my nerves, René gently taps his knee against mine a few times. I hate to admit it, but this small, friendly gesture actually helps. It also has the effect of a shot of caffeine and my whole body feels more awake.

We're off in a slight tilt that presses me harder against René. I try to pull myself away from him, but it's impossible to move. The seat belts have us pinned back against the bench.

We level off and rise as though we're inside a bubble floating over the ocean. James aims his camera at René as he looks out the window, and I feel myself breathe again.

"So, where are you taking us today?" I'm relieved I sound calmer than I feel over the headsets.

René runs a hand over his buzzed head and keeps it there for a moment. His face is so close, I'm forced to look at his dumb lips and that stupid, sexy scruff of a beard. "Couple of places. We'll go to my house and a few other spots. I want to get back to the studio, so we don't have too much time, but we'll make the most of it."

"When was the last time you were home?"

"Too long. I've been really busy." He seems genuinely bummed.

Soon, we're floating above the big island and following a river with lush green hills on either side. For a while, we follow a large road and then float over a bridge. The late morning light, still not quite above us, sends long shadows over the mountains.

About an hour later, the helicopter swings along a beach, turns inland, and starts to descend over an old racetrack. The no-frills track is on a narrow strip of land with the beach on one side and farms on the other. It's a long runway with tight hairpin turns on either end.

René leans over me slightly and looks out my window for a better view. Now, the only thing I can see is the back of his neck. "I worked there for a year after high school. Nothing better than having a racetrack in your backyard." His scent is overwhelming, and I can't help following the tattoo that climbs up the back of his ear. "I wanted to be a race car driver." René sits back against the bench.

"So, this was your first dream?" I ask, though it's more of a statement.

"Uh, no." He pretends to be insulted. "Music was my first dream. It's always been music ever since I was really little. But there was a while where I actually considered that."

"Because it offered better job security?" I ask playfully.

René fights back a grin. "Exactly. And just an overall safer work environment." His eyes linger on mine. While I've become more comfortable with the helicopter, something in his gaze makes me uneasy. Then I have a flash of him onstage mocking me in that song, and my chest aches.

I pull away and look out my window as we hover over the parking lot and land.

James steps off the helicopter first and I'm about to pull myself out when René bumps me gently with his shoulder.

"Hey," he says near my ear in a hurried tone, so I turn toward him. "How are you?"

"Wow, that is *not* what I thought you were going to say."

"What did you think I was going to say?"

"Get out of the way. Move," I list off. "Hurry up, I want to get out of my helicopter." René grins and then his smile is replaced with a curious look, like he's studying me. "I'm fine, thanks."

"Good." He sits back into the bench. "For a second there, I thought you were mad at me."

I exhale abruptly because it really is shocking. Is he kidding me? Does he think I don't know that song is about me?

I smile, doing everything in my power to avoid looking him in the eye, then I turn toward the door.

If I can get through today, I know I can get through the next few weeks. Today will be the toughest. It's up close and personal. The rest of the time we'll be back in the studio with other people around to buffer me from him. With every day that goes by, the sting of that song will get better. *I'm sure of it.*

James films René as he walks through a large garage, slips between two cars parked closely together and onto the track. He stops to admire a red Mustang with a large black stripe across the center. The place is empty other than a few personnel working on two identical white cars under a tent.

"Do you think they'd let you drive one?" I say, taking charge, my eyes glued to the small video monitor hanging around my neck. *This will be easier.* All I have to do is avoid eye contact.

René loves the idea and, after chatting with the mechanics, gets us access to any car on the lot. The sun blazes down on us and on this open track, but it feels good. It's a relief to be here, actually getting access to René's past. I love that it's colorful and sexy and certainly fits his "El Rico" persona.

I stick near James to avoid any unnecessary proximity to René.

"Do you think we should place the small cameras on the dashboard? Or on the windows?"

"Whatever you want. I don't have a preference." James sighs, setting equipment down near the car.

"Oh, okay." I peek inside the car. "Let's go with the dashboard." James seems testy. He barely reacted when I told him about the plan I pitched to Maureen. His response was something along the lines of, "Just tell me where to point the camera."

I turn and René is in front of me, nudging his audio recorder into my hand. "Can you aim it low to the ground when I drive by?" I'm struck by how tender his tone is.

"Um, sure."

I feel James watching us before putting his face behind the viewfinder again.

Holding on to the recorder, I tilt the video monitor toward me with the other hand and watch René settle into the car. He's promised the crew he won't be going fast enough to require the leather gear and full-face helmet.

I watch the dashboard camera on my monitor as René heads down the first straight. His wide, open-mouthed smile gets even bigger when he takes the first turn.

I squat, preparing for his next turn, and aim René's recorder through the fence that separates us. I make triple sure I've hit record and hold it steady. I feel betrayed by my body. I want to be unaffected by René, but I feel like a stupid teenager who's excited her crush has just trusted her to hold his backpack.

On the next corner, he veers off the pavement for a moment and skids on the gravel. At this, René lets out a shriek of joy as though it was more fun to mess up than to stay on the road in control of the car.

Afterward, while René poses for photos with the racetrack personnel in front of a souped-up white Mercedes, I consider my next move. Although this was visually impactful, the new idea I pitched to Maureen requires more. We need to capture intimate footage of René at home and with his family.

We'd start off with René showing us around his hometown, and then we'd see him in the studio working on a song. Each song could start with René sharing a different aspect of his story back home. It would be like flashbacks of his life. And then cut to the studio as he works on a different song. By the end of the album, we'd have a behind-the-scenes of the making of an album and a clear, well-rounded picture of the real René "El Rico" Rodriguez.

"It's just a ten-minute walk to our next stop," he says as he approaches us.

"Are you okay with that?" I ask James because he'll have to carry the camera gear.

"Sure."

"Oh yeah, I can take one of those," René offers at the same time.

"I'm good." He sounds fine, but I see irritation in his eyes.

Outside the racetrack, we walk through the small beachside town, past brightly colored homes on large plots of land. René takes his sunglasses off and tucks them into a pocket in his baggy pants. "This is Salinas." He speaks to the camera unprompted like a host on a travel show. "Welcome to my hometown. I spent my summers in Culebra with my grandparents, but this is where I'm from. We have the best food, the best beaches."

"Why not record the album here?" I ask.

"Too many distractions," he responds politely, turning back so he can look me in the eye. Is it me, or is he being extremely easygoing? I didn't even have to beg him to take his sunglasses off or narrate what was happening. Is it guilt? Does he feel bad for writing that song? Is that why we're here? I wish I could come up with a way to mention it. My anger would subside if he would just admit the song is about me.

René notices something at the end of the block and quickens his pace. "This sucks," he groans, walking up to a store that has gone out of business. He turns the knob and the door creaks open, so we follow him inside.

"This used to be a movie theater, Lalo's." René tilts his head as though remembering something. "I knew the owner passed away, but I assumed his kids would keep it going."

I look around, confused. Nothing about this place resembles a movie theater. They could have sold jewelry in here. There's a long row of display cases in the center of the room, empty shelves cover the walls from floor to ceiling, and there are more shelves across the large window that faces the street.

"On every one of those were his collectibles. Lalo collected everything. Superheroes, little toys, all the cars you can imagine, toy airplanes, and tin lunch boxes. I loved being in here, waiting in line for the movie. You always had something to look at. I don't think I saw everything there was to see. Once when I was, like, seventeen, I discovered a little troll collection down there." He points to the bottom shelf nearest us. "I was, like, how is this possible? I've been coming here since I was born. How have I not seen these scary-ass creepy trolls?"

I fight back a smile. René pushes in the double doors and leads us to a small theater. There are about twenty seats and a projection screen.

"The floor was always sticky. Always. I'm shocked it's not sticky right now. But the projection was fine, and he actually had a great sound system. I fell in love with movie scores here."

"I love them too." It slips out, swept up with his nostalgia. "Maybe you'll score one yourself someday."

"You never know." René ponders this as we step back outside.

"I didn't know you liked scores," James says to me as he stops to replace the camera battery. "That's cool. Any favorites?"

"Well, obviously anything from Hans Zimmer or John Williams."

"Danny Elfman?" René prods, turning around.

"Of course," I say with a smile.

René smiles back, then looks down at the ground. "*Planet of the Apes.*"

"Yes, and you know what else is great? Don't laugh. *Twilight.*"

René laughs. "Sorry." He forces himself to settle. "I haven't actually heard it, so I'll hold off on mocking it till then."

He's being nice but his words cause a little sting in my chest. They remind me he was fine mocking me onstage. Didn't hold back on that.

We turn down a street with a small grocery store and a few other businesses, and René stops from time to time to record different sounds. A dog barking behind a gate, chickens cackling, a truck announcing the sale of plastic chairs stacked high on its flatbed, and lots and lots of birds.

"Idalia's Taberna." René reads a sign just up ahead. "That's my mom's place."

While James films René being flanked by family and friends, I walk over to the bar, lean against the counter covered in shiny, ocean blue tiles, and take it all in. Some folks are having lunch at the small tables, while others are playing the video casino games that line the back wall. From the looks of the sleepy streets on the way over here, most of the town may, in fact, be here.

"This is my mom, Idalia." René has walked over with his arm around a woman a few feet shorter than him. "Mom, this is Dani, from the label." I can't help but take note that he hasn't introduced me as Daniela.

"¡*Bienvenida!*" René's mom has the same dark, almond-shaped eyes as René's.

"What can I get you guys?" René has stepped behind the bar.

"Beer, please," says James.

"Okay, sure. A beer sounds good, thanks." I watch as René grabs a cold mug out of a fridge and expertly slaps down the beer tap on the bar.

"So, the truth comes out," I announce.

René glances up at me for an instant and then returns to the beer quickly filling up. "Whatever could you mean?" he asks with a flirty grin.

"Oh, I don't know, the other day you acted like you'd never stepped foot behind a bar."

"No, I didn't." He picks up a coaster and twirls it across the counter and it lands directly in front of James, who's still film-ing René. Then he takes another one and flips it like a coin toss and it lands in front of me. "That was just you doubting my expertise." He pushes back the tap's handle and sets the beer on the bar for James. It's the perfect beer pour. Foam bubbling over the top without overflowing.

My mouth drops open. "That is *not* how I remember it," I tease. I shouldn't be so friendly. I should keep things profes-sional. I've been trying to maintain a safe distance from him all day, but now I can't help it. I can't miss the chance to tease him, to make him laugh.

"To be fair"—René turns toward me while pouring another beer—"I *was* a little lost that day. I mean, look around. You're not going to find a single burned rosemary twig."

"I think that's a good thing."

He nods and looks at me as he pours a third beer for himself.

"There's live music here on the weekends." René walks over to his mom, who's sitting at a high-top table near the bar. He waves for James and me to join them, so we collect our beers and walk over. I take the seat farthest from René. "I started singing here when I was three. Before she owned it." He nods affectionately toward his mom. "But she'd stand behind me, holding me on a barstool the whole time, because she was afraid I'd fall."

"I had to! He would hold the microphone with both hands and get so excited, he'd shake around too much." She doesn't take her eyes off him.

"She ruined my whole vibe holding me like that."

I'm grinning uncontrollably at their sweet interaction. "Do you have any pictures or video of that?" I ask, then look to René. "If it's okay with you."

"Sure."

"I think I have one or two pictures." She taps her hand on his forearm approvingly, then rests it there. I feel guilt bubble up for not taking Mom's call earlier. Of course I want her to be happy. I just wasn't ready to hear the excitement in her voice. I was afraid to hear her say the words and make it all official. And that no matter what I said, she'd hear the concern in my voice.

"Be right back." René stands and starts to head toward the table of older gentlemen in the corner of the room.

"Can James go?" I call out, determined to film anything he'll let us before our luck runs out.

"Yes, of course," he assures me, as though it's not even remotely a problem. Like I'm weird for even asking and he hasn't been a completely different *and difficult* person up until now.

"He seems happy." Rene's mom watches him as he walks away. "More himself," she adds. "The album must be going well."

"Um, I guess it's going okay."

"Ah no? Maybe it's something else?" She eyes me with curiosity. "I'd offer you lunch, but René told me he's taking you to a place your father loved. He was from Puerto Rico?"

"Ah, yes, he was," I respond, surprised to hear about René's plan.

"*¿De dónde?*"

"Culebra."

"*Ah, mira.* What a miracle." She leans back to get a good look at me. "Excuse me." She picks up a drink order at the bar and delivers it to a young couple seated at a table outside, then chats with them for a moment.

As I look around, my gaze drifts to a church across the street. It has a beautiful cupola covered in colorful stained glass. I love it here, I realize. This powerful feeling of belonging washes over me. One that I welcome happily. I find René and think, he shouldn't belong here either, but he does. The tattoos, the way he dresses. And yet he's so unapologetically himself, he belongs without trying.

"Renécito was baptized in that church." Idalia returns and

takes the seat closest to me. "He was over there boarding up all that glass to protect it from the last hurricane."

"Really?" I don't mean to, but I sound more shocked than impressed.

"Yes," she says defensively.

I feel bad, but that hurricane was just last summer. After René's big hit with Natalia. So I guess I imagined him... well, anywhere else in the world.

"That... sounds just like him!" I burst out. "Sorry about before. I was just having a hard time seeing him up there being... handy," I improvise, trying to make amends. "Not the philanthropic part; that's not the part that's hard to believe at all."

"He's does a lot," she continues, her tone softening. "He donates instruments to the schools in Salinas and scholarships. Always anonymously," she adds, still somewhat offended I've pegged her son all wrong. "He doesn't like attention."

An hour later, I'm standing inside René's childhood bedroom.

"The acoustics in this closet are incredible." René talks to the camera, the way he has all morning. Narrating, sharing stories about growing up here, and introducing us to old family friends and neighbors. "I recorded so many songs in here."

The walls in his room are painted light green and there's a small wooden bookshelf to the right lined with books. Above the twin-size bed is a window with dozens of glass strips like the one we're currently replacing in our kitchen back home. The smoky glass filters the light so there's a warm spotlight coming into the room. It reaches me where I'm standing, so I shut the French door to his bedroom to let the light shine through it.

The door is like a scrapbook. Neatly framed inside each glass panel is a different image. For someone who hasn't revealed much about themselves, René's bedroom door is a treasure trove of information. A carefully hand-drawn Pokémon, magazine cutouts of bands like Daft Punk, Eurythmics, and the Red Hot Chili Peppers logo. Sprinkled throughout are photos of him with friends or his mom. I focus on a picture of a young René standing on the hood of a car, holding a baseball bat. He's pretending to be tough, but not quite pulling it off. He looks the same, just shrunken down, without any muscles or tattoos. It's a really endearing photograph.

I hear a knock and find René pressing his nose against one of the glass panels. And I get an idea.

"What if we take your picture here by the door and post it across your social media?" I brace myself for René's reaction. "We could write something cryptic about the new album and how you'll be letting people in for the first time. Something about how revealing it is." *About me, but that's a problem for another time.*

René scans the door, then looks back to me. I know what I'm asking for. This would obliterate the cryptic social media tactic of the past few years; images of his sunglasses thrown ever so casually on tables and car dashboards.

"I don't know. I like to maintain some mystery."

"What if I said you don't come across as mysterious? More like stuck up and unapproachable." He raises an eyebrow but doesn't respond. "This is good. This is better," I explain, pressing my hand against the door. "If you're afraid it will make you weak to show some vulnerability, you're wrong. It's the opposite."

"Let's do it," he says softly.

I feel a fire light up inside me. The excitement of getting something right. Using my cell, I snap away, inspired. It's effortless, really. René looks so ridiculously sexy posing there. The door glowing behind him. His brown eyes sparkle with the warm light coming in through the window. He adjusts his stance so we can see more of the images on the door, and his cockiness takes on a different appearance. It's pride, a healthy one. Proud of himself, proud of his culture and where he comes from.

We've been together all morning and I've been expecting him to push back, tell us a room is off limits, or there's something he doesn't want to share. All day, I've been waiting for the other shoe to drop, but it never does.

Chapter 31

THE WORDS FLOW SO EASILY, YOU'D NEVER KNOW I WAS DRAFT-ing a text to Mom letting her know how totally cool I am that she's met someone. It doesn't even occur to me to mention I'm concerned about how quickly she's moving with him. Instead, I tap away, letting her know how deserving of happiness she is and how incredibly proud I am she's put herself out there. I throw in a bunch of Mom's favorite emoji, flamenco lady. They float there at the end of the text, dancing their little hearts out, adding just the kind of levity and joy I want to transmit.

I'm hoping this carefree hopefulness will last, but I think I'm just riding on a rush of endorphins brought on by how well it went this morning. It's gone even better than I'd hoped. Like, "I think I just saved my job" better.

"Has Maureen responded?" René asks, twisting around the front seat of the helicopter so he can see me sitting behind the pilot. We've agreed we're done filming for the day, so James is next to me, holding the camera on his lap. I can't help compar-ing how different it was to sit next to René. Right now, I don't feel any tingles of electricity. Only a large camera battery poking into my waist.

"No, not yet. We don't have a signal up here."

"True." He turns back around and taps his hands excitedly on his thighs as though they were drums. I can't believe he's excited about the post. I can't believe he *agreed* to the post.

While we were still at his house, I emailed Mo the image and text for her to approve. We landed on, *Soon, I'll let you in...*, first in Spanish and then in English. I love the image René and I agreed on. He's looking right into the camera, a sweet half smile, eyes literally sparkling in the sunlight. Behind him, the revealing images on his door are partially in view along with a glimpse of his bedroom.

We reach the ocean, and the helicopter veers right to follow the coast. With San Juan behind us, we begin to float down over a parking lot near a long strip of food trucks. René turns around. "We're going to get a bite here before we head back."

As soon as we land, I turn airplane mode off on my phone and send the drafted text to Mom. I admire it proudly then scroll through the last few texts I've sent her, all way less fun in comparison. Not a single playful emoji in sight. I'm checking up on the window installation, her health, and whether the repaired sink disposal is functioning okay. And is she really sure, has she tested it with something like a lemon?

Next, I check my emails and find a response from Maureen. It's simple and to the point, but I can tell she's excited.

Brilliant! Go for it!

I tap René's shoulder and flash him the response. When it registers, he keeps a straight face but stretches his hand out for a high five. I comply, but not without a smirk.

"How much time have we got?" James asks brusquely as he unbuckles his seat belt.

René turns to speak, but I beat him to it. "What's up?"

"I'd like to take a taxi to San Juan for a few things I can't get on the island."

"Sure, whatever you need," says René. "We'll be here at least an hour."

"Great," James snaps loudly. "Thanks." What's up with *him*?

"Hey, are you okay?" I ask James, once René is outside.

"Yeah, I'm fine."

"Are you feeling sick again?"

"No. I'm okay. Just a little tired, I think. Seriously," he reassures me, "I'll be back soon." He sounds more like himself, so I choose to believe him.

Once James is gone, I find René outside and review the social media post one more time.

"Are you sure?" I ask him before posting.

He nods once, and when I'm done, I hand his phone back, feeling accomplished and relieved.

"This is a strange place for so many food trucks," I say as we approach the crosswalk. "There's nothing around here." Across the street is an oasis of food trucks facing the two-way road with a narrow strip of beach behind them. The smell of smoke from savory beef being grilled on open fire pits reminds me I've barely eaten today. We've arrived a little late for lunch, so there aren't many people in line and the picnic tables on the grass in front of the road are mostly empty.

"It's a busy road, so it's an easy pit stop as you're going into or out of San Juan."

Different songs blast from the trucks, so as we walk past one, the song changes. It's like switching the station on the radio with your steps. I catch my reflection in a food truck window. My hair is all tussled like it's on vacation, and there's more color on my face.

"Everything here is delicious." René has stopped in front of a truck with large pictures of their menu posted outside.

I check out the options. Every single item looks delicious, except for one oddball, poorly lit sandwich in the corner. Possibly a quick last-minute addition.

René pulls a face. "That one looks like he had a rough night."

"I think that might be its mug shot," I whisper.

He laughs and my eyes drift to his one crooked tooth. It's on the top right of his smile and it leans in a little. It's the sexiest little tooth.

I try to ignore the confusing cocktail of emotions. There's relief in the ease between us, but there's also distrust and apprehension over the hurtful song he wrote.

"I think I'll just go back for something from the first place," I say, trying to regain control of my head.

"You can't come here and go to just one place. You have to hit a few. Try different things. They each have their own specialty. Here." René leads us to the picnic tables. On each one, there are a variety of hot sauces and a whole, raw onion holding down a small stack of napkins. "I'll go first. Pick a few things, and then you can go."

I watch him walk away and I'm surprised no one recognizes him. I wonder how he'll feel if this album blows up. Will he be able to come to places like this without bodyguards?

For the first time, I consider the possibility of working with him again. We'll have to at some point, I'm sure. One day I'll cover the filming of one of his music videos or see him backstage at an awards show. *God, I hope this album wins awards but not for the song about me.*

That's it. I have to ask him about the song. Now, while we're alone. I can't keep pushing it down. I'll get an ulcer. Who knows, maybe he does have a good explanation.

There's a bounce in his step as he makes his way back carrying a small tray of food. "Okay, here's my selection." He places a glass of juice in front of me. "Homemade passion fruit juice and empanadas. These are spinach and these have beef." He points to a small plastic container. "Mayo-ketchup," he announces. Then he shakes another one with oily green liquid in it. "And cilantro mojo."

I grab a beef empanada and take a bite.

"No, wait! May I?" René asks, leaning across the table with the cilantro mojo in his hand. When I nod, he pours the oil into the opening I've bitten into it. It seeps inside, and the whole moment feels bizarrely intimate.

If someone were watching, they'd think we were a couple. I sit up taller and try to push the thought away. What I need to do is find the right moment to bring up the song he wrote. I tap my forehead and feel a layer of perspiration. René's skin is also gleaming. There's a warm, intermittent breeze coming from the ocean, but it's no match for the early afternoon sun, and heat rising from the open-air fire pits that surround us.

I take another bite and my eyes widen. It's the absolute perfect burst of zesty beef, lemony cilantro, and warm, flaky crust. I shut my eyes, savoring the flavors. When I open them, a trail of oil is oozing down my wrist, threatening to drop onto my pants, so I stop it with my mouth. With my lips still on the back of my wrist, I catch René watching me closely as he chews.

I flash him an awkward smile, take a napkin, and wipe the rest away.

"It's delicious," I say at last.

"Your turn."

I walk away feeling a little ridiculous and like I need to get a hold of myself. I decide when I get back, I'll just place the food down and say something like, "Hey, there's something I need to ask you." Or more to the point, "Hey, we need to talk about the song."

I find a bright yellow truck and peer into their glass case filled with different kinds of fritters. I find myself wanting to impress René with my choices. I want to pick a few things that are delicious and maybe balance each other out. I get the vendor to tell me what everything is and decide on what looks like an elephant ear but is in reality codfish batter. The thing is bigger than my face. To add some sweet to the savory, I also get some fried sweet cheese croquettes.

I wonder how he'll react when I confront him. Another thought pops up as I watch the vendor grab our items with a napkin. *This feels like a date. A really fun date.* I don't know if it's the heat getting to me but I'm in a happy trance walking through a wall of smoke from the fire pits.

"*Bacalaíto*," René announces with glee, "and *sorullitos*?"

I nod with an expectant smile and admire my selections.

"I love these." René grabs one of the croquettes, dunks it in mayo-ketchup sauce, and takes a bite, devouring half of it. He groans with delight. "Unexpected grouping with the codfish but I admire your"—he pauses to think about how he wants to finish his thought—"creativity."

I shake my head, pretending to be upset, and take a bite of *bacalaíto*. I take my time, letting it linger in my mouth before swallowing. They've magically turned fish into an airy, fried doughy snack. It's thin and perfectly crispy on the outside, soft and chewy on the inside.

"I've never had this before." I rip another piece off and dunk it in the cilantro oil.

"Really?" René's flummoxed.

"My dad never wanted to go out for Puerto Rican. He was never impressed and spent the entire time comparing everything to the food back here. My mom used to make a few basic dishes, but nothing like this."

René furrows his brow and opens his mouth to speak just as his phone rings on the table. Santiago's name pops up on the screen. "That's actually why I wanted to bring you here." He flips the phone around without answering it.

My stomach does a couple of somersaults at the sight of René not taking a call because he's with me. Being the focus of René's full attention is overwhelming. I feel drunk.

"My turn," he announces, pushing himself away from the table.

I wish I could know what he's thinking. Is *he* having as much fun? Now that he's gone, I re-center myself. I need to ask him about the song. I'm running out of time.

A few minutes later, René returns and places a basket on the table with extra swagger. "*This* is the real reason we're here." He looks accomplished, like he's won some game.

"A giant corn dog?" I tease him.

"This is so much better than a corn dog," he explains, his face lit up. "It was in the song."

I tense up. "What song?"

"Your father's song. The line about *alcapurrias*."

I blink a few times but can't speak.

"I'm sorry, we can get them back on the island too," René says, concerned. "These are the best *I've* ever had so I thought I'd bring you here. But maybe that was wrong? I can take you to get some on the island instead."

"No. It's not that. It's just..." *What I want to say is, why are you being so nice to me?* "I know you have work to do. You have so few days. I just want you to know, you don't have to do any of this." The words spill out of me quickly in an irritated ramble.

He shuffles in the seat. "I know."

I let out a deep exhale and pick up the *alcapurria*. I take a bite and it's an explosion of flavor. Sweet and spicy mash wrapped around tangy, savory meat. "It's the best thing we've had today," I admit somberly. "The least attractive, but still the tastiest."

"Right? The dough is made of plantains and yucca. And then deep fried, of course."

"Of course," I say, feeling my throat tickle. I refuse to get emotional over a fritter. It's just impossible not to think of my dad. Suddenly, I can see him here. Walking around with that bounce in his step. Always open to strike up a conversation or make new friends. He would have asked the couple next to us where they were from and suggested things they could do in the area. He would have ribbed the vendors. Coming up with just the right thing to make a perfect stranger laugh.

I feel his absence so much more intensely here. Probably because it's become impossible to fight back the memories. Still, it's nice to let them in. To fill the hole in my heart with a clearer picture of him. To remember his zest and the way he left everyone he met better off than they were before.

"Hey," I say and take a deep breath, "thanks again for today."

He nods, glancing up at me. "Now we just need a proper interview." René scrunches his nose at this, as though he's smelled something foul. "Seriously, we'll really need one at some point."

He sits back in his chair, studying me. "You really don't let up?"

"Does it upset you there's someone in the world who doesn't bow before El Rico?"

"No, not in this case."

The directness of his comment sends me floating. "Seriously, though, all the wonderful footage in the world will need to have actual sound bites for us to share with the press," I add.

He grabs a *sorullito* and points it at me. "You don't dance. I don't do interviews. We all have our things."

Bringing up my not dancing reminds me of the lyrics of his song, and it takes all of me not to reveal the disappointment on my face.

Chapter 32

I take inventory of which parts of my body *aren't* sweating. I'm down to my ears and the bottoms of my feet. To avoid the evening bugs, I've kept the sliding glass door closed tonight. The sheer mosquito netting tucked around the bed feels like Saran wrap preventing the little oxygen in the room from getting to me.

I can't stop thinking about René, which only makes the room feel hotter. *He's sexy, that's all. It's natural to be attracted to him. I'm not immune to his good looks. I have eyeballs. That's all it is. Purely physical attraction.*

I consider calling Meri. I want to talk to her about René, and how he's been taking me to see our dad's favorite places. But last I checked, it was after midnight. *It's probably for the best.* I don't want her jumping to conclusions about what it could mean. I'm doing that enough on my own.

At least things with Mom are a little better. I called her this afternoon to catch up. She sounded so happy, it was hard not to be swept up in her excitement. Even if I think a part of me will be weighed down with concern until I meet this guy.

"So, Meri told you?" she asked me right away.

"About the Cuban fried rice guy? Yeah, she told me," I teased, trying hard to be on the same page.

"*Ese mismo.* Lázaro," she corrected me. "He makes me laugh, he's very funny. Oh, and he wants to teach me to play chess. I thought you'd like that."

Why would I like that? Because you think that makes him sound smart? I think that also makes him sound like a serial killer.

"That's so cool, Mom. I can't wait to meet him."

"And how is it going? Are you okay?" She sounded worried. "You haven't told me anything."

"Yeah, I'm fine. Why?"

"I'll light a candle to San Judas," she offered.

"Why? I haven't lost anything. Isn't he the saint for that?"

"He also helps with work things."

"Save the candle, Mom. Everything's going great."

And it is. *So why can't I fall asleep?* I grab my phone from the nightstand and check on René's post again. It's been up for eight hours and already has almost a hundred thousand likes. I scroll through the comments, a lot of which I've already read, and find the thread I'm looking for. These are the comments I read just before bed and are probably the main reason the room feels so stuffy and I'm still awake.

> Those eyes! Thank you Lord, no sunglasses.

> Amen! He's so hot and filled with desire

> I wish I took that picture!

> Yeah, who is he looking at?

Wait, can you see the reflection in the glass?

Can someone zoom in?

It's a brunette, NOT a blond!

It's not Camila!

SOOO TRUE! I see her! Who is that?

I kick off the sheets, slip out of bed, and slide open the door. Immediately, a strong breeze enters the room. Like it's been waiting just outside.

I'm letting it cool off my skin when I hear Camila's voice coming from downstairs.

In front of René's cottage, there are two figures deep in conversation, lounging on the round outdoor sofa. I've stripped down to my tank top and underwear, so I wrap myself in the curtain and take a step out onto the balcony, poking my head out the rest of the way. It's René and Camila. She's on her side, her hair a loose, beautiful mess. His hands are resting behind his head and he's looking up at the sky.

I crawl back in bed, tucking in the netting as I go. I can hear them, but I can't make out what they're saying. It's just animated storytelling in friendly tones that sometimes turn into whispers that seem more intimate, then René will say something that makes Camila laugh.

Things weren't so peppy between them when we got back earlier today. René arrived first and Camila was arguing with him while James unloaded the truck. The disagreement was still going on when James and I walked into the main house.

"How could you do that? I would never have posted you in that outfit." She was screeching, she was so upset. "Why didn't you call me?" They were in the middle of the hallway, so we had to walk around them to get to our rooms. Camila bit her lip, resting her hand on her hips while we passed, and then went right back to arguing. We could hear her the entire walk up to our cottage.

"Cami, it's fine. You can barely see what I'm wearing." René tried to calm her, keeping his voice several octaves lower, clearly displeased by her yelling at him like that.

She was upset she hadn't gone with us, but the whole thing was mostly about the photo we had posted without her signing off on his wardrobe. Now, they're out there chatting it up as though nothing happened.

How can they have this much to talk about? They've known each other for years. They work together. They see each other every day. You'd think they'd be all caught up by now.

They've gone quiet outside. I hold my breath and perk up my ears. *Snap out of it, Dani. What are you even listening for? Footsteps? Kissing?* It would have to be sloppy and slurpy for me to hear it this far away. Waves crashing, leaves rustling with the wind, but nothing else.

I hear Camila speak again and the knot in my stomach loosens. This is ridiculous. I find my earbuds on the bedside table, and listen to an indie pop playlist until I fall asleep.

An hour later, they're still out there sharing. I've dozed off and the breeze in the room is gone. I listen to their voices, to the rhythm of their conversation, and feel an ache in my chest. I'll admit I'm jealous. Not of Camila, I don't think. But of their intimacy. I let myself sink deeper into the bed. I've never had that. My relationships have always played out on the surface. Even with my family. Intentionally, I realize. There are so many subjects, my father, for one, I avoid so no one gets sad or misses him. I want to stay up late into the night talking to someone like that. I want us each to have that much to say.

Chapter 33

IT'S DARK IN THE STUDIO. THE NEON LIGHTS ARE ON, BUT they're dimmed way down. It's not going to be enough light for James, who should be here any minute. I walk into the recording booth to ask René if it's okay to turn on a few more lights, and I catch my reflection in the glass door.

I actually like my hair like this, loose and air dried. I don't know why I bothered packing my straight iron. I haven't used it once since I've been here. What's the point? It's no competition for the weather. The studio is the only air-conditioned room, so we're outside practically all the time. Every day we inch closer to summer, it gets warmer and more humid.

I push in the door, but it's stuck on something. I put my shoulder into it, but it still doesn't budge. I think René's blocking the door with his foot just to mess with me.

"Let me in." I get close to the glass. "I need this." I push on the door with both hands. "Please."

The door finally gives, swinging in abruptly, and I'm sucked into the booth.

I've landed on René. His back is flat against the foam-padded wall and my face is in his neck. I feel the warmth of him instantly.

"Shit, sorry. You smell nice," I say, then wish I could take it back. I adjust myself to look at him, just as he's pressing his lips together, fighting back a smile. He moves in and it dawns on me. *We're about to kiss.* I close my eyes and tilt my head back. "What is that? Gardenias?" I ask, unable to keep my mouth shut. I open my eyes, but he doesn't respond. Of course he isn't responding. Why would he admit to that? "Did you change colognes? This is nice, but I prefer the other one you wear." What am I saying? Who cares what the man smells like? "I mean, not that it's up to me what cologne you wear. Not that you care what I prefer. Actually, *do* you care what I prefer?" My cheeks flush and my heart is pounding.

He pretends to ponder this, puckering his lips. I nudge at his arm playfully and he grabs hold of my hand. In a blink, I'm the one against the foam wall and his lips are on my neck.

He runs his hands up my back and combs them through my hair, while he pulls me closer to him. I let out a moan.

I wake up with a jolt. It's two in the morning and my room is completely still. The waves are coming in gently, and the strong scent of sweet gardenias fills my room. It's intense. There must be a giant shrub just outside my cottage. "Idiot."

I slip on jeans that were hanging on the standing mirror and can't help but smile at my reflection. My hair looks an awful lot like it did in the dream. I slip on flip-flops and walk out onto the balcony. No signs of Camila and René. They must have gone to bed at some point in the past two hours. The lights in his cottage are all off.

I head outside and walk along the pool, toward the open-air living room. A few lamps are on and there's a large, fresh bouquet of birds of paradise and palm leaves on the coffee table. I step behind the counter in the kitchen and open the fridge, searching for a cold bottle of water. I hear footsteps and freeze behind the open refrigerator door. Which is the world's worst disguise, I realize.

"I just want to get it down." René's deep voice makes my insides twitch.

"I'm here for all of it. Let's see where it takes you," Santiago says, sounding farther away, like they've made it past the kitchen. Then I hear the smooth glide of the studio door closing.

I shut the fridge and walk over to the studio. When I make it to the door, I stand there for a moment, hand on the handle, and assess what I must look like. Potential bed head, no makeup, a T-shirt so worn, it was demoted to a pajama months ago.

They're going to work on a song in the middle of the night, and something about what René has said makes me want to be there. I want to know all about the song that couldn't wait till morning. I could take notes and be fully prepared to interview him about it tomorrow.

I pull the door and step inside. Like in the dream I just had, the neon lights are dim. Then to my right, in the recording booth, two heads turn.

Santiago smiles and René glances in my direction, but otherwise they don't make a fuss, so I wave hello and let myself in. Santiago adjusts a microphone and steps out of the booth. René starts to play a sweet, slow melody on his guitar. He's in a black tank, the wolf tattoo on his shoulder aimed directly at me.

Suddenly I have an idea. I slip off my sandals and I walk to the far corner of the room, looking ahead for the camera cases. I find the one I'm looking for, undo the clasps, and lift the foam in the center. I pick up the digital camera, the same one I have back home. Expertly, I slide in the battery and turn it on, the weight of it familiar in my hands. I click through the functions on the dial. With muscle memory, I find the photography function and turn it on silent mode.

I hold the camera above me and take a picture of the entire room, including Santiago at the console and René in the booth. Feeling confident, I walk up to the booth and, through the glass door, take a picture of René playing the guitar. Then I take another one, racking the lens manually, so only the wolf tattoo is in focus. I check the last image on the LCD screen and flip through filters until I've made it black and white. I love this camera. It gives you the perfect balance of grain and texture. It's digital without being cold.

I remember taking pictures of Meri in our backyard. Capturing her midair on the trampoline, or as she ran through the sprinklers. I smile, realizing I may be part of the reason she loves to take selfies. Then René's voice pulls me back into the room.

> *If I knew it would be our last kiss*
> *I'd remember it better than this*
> *But I can still taste the first one*
> *All night, sunrise*

It's a beautiful song and there's so much raw emotion. He whistles for a moment. He's run out of words but keeps the melody going. He looks off, lost in his thoughts. I watch him curiously. He doesn't seem to be searching for the words, more like listening for them. Ready for some invisible force to whisper them into his ear.

>   *how do you go from all or nothing to nothing*
>   *and from nothing to something that means everything*

He reaches the chorus and belts it out, his voice hitting higher and higher notes. I had no idea he could sing like this.

>   *you're the breeze I'm counting on*
>   *to take me to the finish line*

The lyrics and his voice make the hair stand on my arms. As though in my dream, I reach for the door to the booth, but René beats me to it. He stretches his foot out, pushing it open. The door shuts behind me, and everything is magnified. I can hear the sound his lips make when they part and the breaths he takes before he sings again. His voice, the guitar, it all vibrates in the air and bounces off the padding on the walls. I can feel it on my skin.

My body sways with the music. The next time he sings the chorus, I snap continuously as I move, and slowly push him out of frame. I take pictures of the long muscle on his forearm, of his right hand stroking the strings, and of the other one sliding up and down the neck of the guitar.

He's watching me now, a big smile on his face as he sings. He's either happy with the song or happy with what I'm doing. *Maybe both.* Somewhere deep inside, I know there's a way we can use these pictures, but I'm not really thinking. I feel weightless like I'm flying. Letting my instinct guide me.

be the breeze I'm counting on
take me to the finish line

The lyrics are so deeply romantic. Noticeably lacking in cheating, thongs, or sex on car hoods. When the song ends, a different part of my brain snaps back on. I switch the camera's functions over to video and press record just in time to capture René as he steps outside to hug Santiago, who shouts something excitedly in Spanish about writing a song in one take. I remain in the small booth and continue to film their celebration. And breathe in the traces of musk and sandalwood René's left behind.

Chapter 34

"Daniela, why don't you go first." Our general manager, Jaqueline Mendes, is on my computer screen. "How's it going?" She's sitting in the main conference room, the wallpaper behind her covered in colorful geometric designs. Narrow face, shoulder-length hair that flips out like a half pipe. Seated next to her is Maureen, offering a supportive smile.

My adrenaline is pumping. Everything's fine, I tell myself. There's nothing to worry about. Still, in the seven years I've worked at Ocean, Jaqueline's spoken to me only once and that was to bark, "Is that your car?" as I walked by. I almost said the red Ferrari *was* mine, she was *that* intimidating.

Jaqueline's assistant requested the meeting an hour ago, labeling it a "catch up" on the invite, which would sound harmless enough if it weren't so unprecedented. I've put on a fresh coat of makeup and I'm wearing my black blazer with a CBGB T-shirt. A look I hope screams, "Record label powerhouse who discovers underground bands after work." Never mind that it's ninety degrees in my room. Or that the outfit doesn't quite go with the vista behind me—sun setting on a

Caribbean island. It looks like I've got one of those fake backgrounds on.

"Well, it's going great. As you know, René took us on a personal tour of his hometown."

Jaqueline nods approvingly. "Yes, Maureen told me."

I feel my shoulders untense. Maybe that's all this call's about. The head of the label's just taking time from her busy schedule to tell me to keep up the good work.

"And as I'm sure you've heard"—I smile and sit up taller—"the picture we posted of him by his childhood bedroom already has over a hundred thousand likes, and a lot of the artists he's collaborated with have reshared the post." I catch a glimpse of Maureen shutting her eyes and nodding in relief. I get it. I'm relieved too. After a disastrous start, I've managed to turn things around. "And my personal favorite"—I'm impressed by how off the cuff and together I sound—"is that someone's started an entire subreddit dedicated to the joy of finally getting to look into René's eyes." Maureen lets out a conspiratorial laugh. "And last night"—I shift to a weightier tone—"René improvised an entire song, all while playing the guitar. Santiago had to play it back for him just so he could remember the lyrics and continue working on the vocals." I sound a little *too* impressed, so I tone myself down. "The song is so different than what anyone expects from him."

"Well, I can't wait to see *that* footage," Jaqueline snaps, after giving Maureen a knowing look.

"Actually," I continue, feeling less sure of myself, "it was after hours, so the cameraman wasn't with me. But what I did was…" I stop here and try to flash Maureen a smile, because I haven't told her about this yet. "I took photographs." Jaqueline's chin juts out, intrigued.

Last night, as Santiago played back the song, René sat close to me on the couch, so I could show him the pictures. "We have to use them," he said, and the word "we" sent something warm through me. Not only did he love the photographs, but he was finally seeing the behind-the-scenes as a project that was "ours," not just something I was forcing on him.

Being there together in the middle of the night felt like we were in another world. One we had just created. With him admiring the photographs while his heavenly new song played, the studio was some sort of magical womb. One with a really nice, high-end speaker system.

"René loves them. I think we can come up with a cool way to use them. They captured the sensitive moment more...respectfully than video. I'm glad James was asleep," I burst out. For a moment, I think the connection has dropped and left me with a frozen image of Maureen and Jaqueline looking baffled.

"You took photographs? Like with your phone?" Jaqueline doesn't mask her disappointment.

"No, with a digital camera, and I think if I can get René to finally agree to a proper interview," I argue, sounding more defensive than I mean to, "they could be really powerful."

Maureen pulls her eyebrows down. "Send them over!" She sounds overly excited, like she's putting on a front for Jaqueline. "I'll check them out and we'll brainstorm some ideas."

"Is he pushing back about the interview?" Jaqueline's revved up. As though someone's parked in her spot again. "Do we need to step in?"

I scratch at my ear and tighten my ponytail. I can't find enough to do with my hands. The desire to defend René is so strong. What I *want* to say, the words that are on the tip of my tongue are, "René's been making music for over a decade and the songs he's collaborated on with huge artists are almost always the best songs on those albums. It's safe to say he's done proving himself!"

"He's in no position to be pushing back on anything we need. Has he seen the photograph?" Something about her tone makes my adrenaline start pumping.

"What photograph?"

"Here, I'll send it to you." Mo types into her phone.

A moment later, I'm looking at a partially obscured photograph of Natalia sitting in a restaurant booth, dissolved into tears.

"Oh yes, I saw this." Meri sent me the image just before this call. I felt badly for Natalia and whatever she's going through, but I don't see what this has to do with René. "So?"

"Did you read the comments?" Jaqueline doesn't wait for my response. "People blame René. He's been skewered, saying how he's left her a mess. Unable to maintain a relationship."

"What?"

Tabloids are picking it up," Jaqueline continues. "It's been a year and people are *still* blaming him. The timing couldn't be worse."

This is why they've called me.

"It's ridiculous. They're on excellent terms. And I know for a fact René did *not* cheat on her." I shake a finger in the air for punctuation. "They've just recorded a song together."

"About that. We don't have *any* footage of them together? Is that right?"

I hesitate for a beat. "No."

"Anything of them together, having a good time?" she expands, as though there's some perfect material I've forgotten about.

I shake my head. "We do have a brief interview with Natalia in the studio." I think back to her responses. She was so adoring and admitted she'd come even though René had shared nothing about the song. "Actually, I'm not sure that would help. She kind of came across like she's still hung up on him."

Jaqueline sighs loudly. "Well, we have to do something."

"I'll talk to him. I'm sure he'll agree he can't continue to ignore this."

After the call, I let my hair down and run my hands through it, setting it free from the ponytail shape it's still clinging to. I take off the blazer and put it away, then sit back down in front of my computer. I respond to dozens of emails from journalists requesting information and press materials about René. I let them know it will all be ready in a few weeks and then add their names and contact information to the master Excel document.

Then, I find the file where I've downloaded all the photographs I took last night and send Maureen a few of my favorites. I still feel these were the right approach, but I wish I hadn't rambled off about them on the call like that. *I'm glad James was asleep.* What the heck was that?

My guard was down, that's all. I just need to build it back up. Convince René that he needs to open up about the real reason behind that breakup. People should know, Natalia dumped him. Not the other way around.

Two more weeks. I need to keep a steady head on my shoulders. I'll focus on getting what we need. Like a robust interview that ties everything together.

I step outside for some fresh air and follow the path that leads to the beach. It's dark out now, but James and I need to be in the studio in an hour for another late-night session. Santiago has spent the day working on the new track, while René and Camila took the small boat out. There's nothing to worry about, I tell myself. Outside, the night air feels cool and the moon is gone tonight so the ocean is a large inky blanket.

On my left there's a frame of wooden screens I've never seen before. I make my way through them and reach a garden with two large sculptures sticking out of the sand. I sit on the steps that lead to the beach to admire them. They're two silhouettes of heads looking up at the sky. From where I'm sitting, dozens of stars are framed inside them.

I slouch back, kick off my boots and let my feet enjoy the cool sand. Out of the corner of my eye, I see something on the stairs. There's a pair of yellow high-top sneakers. On impulse, I lean across the step and pick one up. It's hand-painted with colorful graffiti. I turn them around and even the soles are painted, making them look more like an expensive work of art than a shoe.

I bring it up close to my face to try to make out what it says when René walks into the sculpture garden. *Shirtless.* His sculpted tan chest is dripping wet and he's wearing short swim trunks that sit low on his waist and cling to his skin. He looks like a merman whose under-the-sea shift just ended.

"Hi," I say, a couple of octaves too high.

He stops in his tracks, surprised to see me. "Hey." He rubs at his wet hair and stands there for a split second, then moves again.

I set the shoe down as he rinses the sand off his feet at a faucet on the end of the deck. When he's done, he approaches me, his tight trunks at my eye level, and I try to ignore the sizable bulge.

"May I?" he asks, pointing at his shoes.

"Of course." I slide as far over as I can on the narrow step.

He picks up one of his shoes and pulls out a pair of socks tucked inside. Lifting one knee up at a time, he pulls on both socks. He's so close, I can smell the saltwater on his skin as well as the musky sweet cologne he wears as an undertone. Just like he did with his socks, he slips on both sneakers.

"Interesting," I say.

"What?"

"Nothing. It's just you put on both socks and *then* both sneakers."

"Yeah, so? How do you do it?"

"Uh...sock, shoe, sock, shoe. As is common practice."

He scoffs. "Always?"

"Always," I respond firmly.

He shakes his head.

"No, hear me out. When you put one sock on at a time like that, you have to put your foot down on the ground. Now *that* sock is exposed to dirt and debris. Dirt that is going to be transported *into* your fancy shoe. It's just senseless."

He lets out a single laugh. "Dirt and debris," he repeats quietly, squinting his eyes as he looks at me. "I'll consider it."

His body adjusts like he's about to stand, but then stops himself. "What do you think about those?" He aims his chin toward the sculptures.

I take them in again, more discerningly this time. "I like them," I say decidedly.

"Me too. They seem happy, don't you think?"

"Yeah. Though that's probably because they don't have any brains."

He snorts and nods. "I think you might be right."

We sit in silence for a moment, and I feel a pulsing between us.

"So, when did you get into photography?"

"High school. But last night was the first time I've taken pictures in a long time." I trail off, my mind flooded with memories. "My dad used to drive me to this dark room class every Saturday, and then wait in the parking lot until the hour was done. He'd inspect all my prints and tease me about how similar they all were. '*Chica, yo no le veo la diferencia*,' he'd say, holding up two prints of the same image. One could be completely blown out and awful and he'd still say he couldn't tell the difference." René chuckles. "I'd like to pick it back up again, to be honest. Though...I thought that part of me was done growing or was stunted or something."

He scoffs. "My best friend when I was little got a Saint Bernard puppy for Christmas one year."

"Okay? Abrupt change in topic."

"Stay with me," he says, "and the dog grew all out of order. Tail, legs, and then his head." I raise an eyebrow, amused by the bizarre observation. "What I'm trying to say, in a way I hoped you'd find poetic *and* insightful, is it doesn't matter how we grow, or in what order. As long as you keep growing."

"Ah. I guess it *was* sort of poetic." I tuck a loose strand of hair behind my ear. "You know, these are exactly the kind of deep thoughts we want to capture in your main interview." He exhales loudly but doesn't respond. "Seriously, we'll have a lot to cover."

"We'll see." He surveys my face and I do my best to maintain eye contact, but it isn't easy.

He arches his eyebrows like he's got something to say. He opens his mouth, reconsiders it, and then chuckles to himself.

His knee is doing a little nervous bounce. Is René squirming? *Because of me?*

There's a strong hold on my chest. Any attempts to rebuild my guard are crumbling with this push and pull between us.

I need to secure this interview. "Have you seen the picture of Natalia from today?"

He scowls and bites down on his lower lip. "Yeah."

"It would help if you spoke up about what happened between you two. It makes you look culpable that you haven't."

He lets out a sort of grunt. "What, you don't trust me anymore?"

A single laugh escapes me. "Oh, I *never* trusted you." It slips out and I'm sure I meant for it to sound playful, but his face drops. He nods a few times, then looks away.

As the silence drags, a million thoughts flood my brain. He's upset. Why is *he* upset? He doesn't get to be mad at me. Why *should* I trust him?

"Can you really blame me?" I'm gentle but blunt. There's something in his eyes, a flicker of concern. This is the course of action I've decided on. The only way to fix this is to break it down. Crack it all open. Right here and now. "That song, the one you recorded with her. With Natalia. The one you performed on the beach. Is it about me?"

He puckers, considering this, then looks away. "I didn't want to perform it that day," he says matter-of-factly. "Then Santiago just started playing it." I'm numb. This response isn't good. He's not denying it. "I took *some* poetic license, but yes, it is about you." He leans back on his hands.

A high-pitched whimper escapes me. I quickly grab one of my shoes and try to slip it on. It's too tight. I have to unlace it first and I hate that even on this dimly lit boardwalk, it's clear my hands are shaking.

"You didn't like it?"

I scoff exaggeratedly. "Why would I like it? It's an insulting song."

He scrunches his face. "I don't think so."

"*No one wants your sexy selfie?*" I quote loudly.

"*Not if you're repressed when you undress,*" he raps, completing the lyric. As though it were some kind of defense.

"That doesn't make it any better."

"You said yourself you couldn't dance, right?" he argues as though reviewing a list. "And you *do* wear a lot of blazers."

I squeeze my lips tight. I can't believe this. How is he not apologizing? "Just because something is true, that doesn't..." I'm so upset, I can't think of the words. "It doesn't make it less insulting." I try again. "If you're making fun of someone."

"I wasn't making fun of you. You didn't really listen to the song." He sits back up, concerned. "*I want to make you move, and move you, the way you move me.*" He's delivered the line slowly, as though reciting a poem. Okay, I don't remember *that* part of the song, but I'm not about to admit it. Besides, one nice line does not negate the rest of it.

"Yeah, sure, but first I have to take off my blazer, get off my high horse, drop the attitude, and take care of a bunch of problems I didn't even know I had. Believe me, I heard it. I wish I could *unhear* it."

"You heard it," he repeats, his face rigid, "but you weren't really listening. You heard what you wanted to hear."

I can't accept he's still pushing back. "There's no mistaking, *I never met a Latina I didn't like, until now,*" I quote defensively, and in a way that also sounds like I'm mocking the song.

He's quiet for an unnerving amount of time. I look at him, my body steady. For the first time in my life, I fight the desire to fill up the silence or to come to someone's aid. I won't make this easier for him. When he finally looks at me again, there's a wounded look in his eyes.

"I wasn't making fun of you," he says earnestly. "I'm sorry you took it that way."

All I manage is a shaky nod. We need to work together. I should tell him it's fine. That it's fine, even if it isn't. But my throat is tight and dry, and I can't get any words out.

Chapter 35

I'm giving him space. For an entire day, I've skirted around René. Yesterday, I stuck to the corner of the studio or out in the hallway, where I could use the monitor to take notes and direct James through our wireless headphones system.

It was easy enough to stay out of René's way. He sticks to a routine lately, so I pretty much know where he's going to be. He works alone in the studio in the mornings, goes for a swim or a boat ride in the afternoons, and then works with Santiago in the studio late into the night.

Maureen loved the photographs I took, so I worked on a few ideas on how we can use them. I also scouted locations for René's main interview but have yet to find the right spot. The only place I haven't seen is his cottage.

I have a feeling his room might be the perfect backdrop for this behind-the-scenes. I'll find a way to slip that in when I finally face him today to schedule his main interview. My plan is to use some psychology instead of asking if he'll agree to do it. Like I used to do with Meri when she wouldn't eat her vegetables. *Do you want broccoli or carrots?* I'm just going to walk right up to René and ask if he wants to do the interview tomorrow or the day after.

I have to try. We have a little over a week left and I worry the closer we get to the finish line, the busier he'll be in the studio. So today, as soon as I see him, I'm going to walk right up to him and ask.

Which is probably why I'm escaping at the crack of dawn. I borrowed James's digital camera and called a cab, but now we're still in the parking lot because I can't decide where to go.

"You don't know? You're more lost than me! That's saying a lot." The driver eyes me through the rearview mirror, his thick gray hair sticking out from under a red Kangol cap. Everything about this man feels warm and familiar.

"What about Resaca Beach?" I ask hesitantly, remembering it's in my father's song.

"Resaca?" he shouts. "*¿Estás loca?* You want to ruin my suspension?" He's pretending to be upset, but his eyes are smiling. "You can't get there by car," he shrieks. My dad used to do this. Act like he was all riled up over the smallest thing. Remembering this particular bit of his personality makes my heart ache.

"Oh, I didn't know. What about a golf cart?" I wonder how much he'd charge me if I get out of his taxi before he's had a chance to take me anywhere.

He waves both hands in the air dramatically. "I don't recommend it. Not with all the rain we had last night. There's nothing but a long dirt road to get there." One of his hands keeps swinging to convey just how long it is.

The shiny red golf cart is parked a few feet away. It's pristine, literally sparkling under the early morning sun. I try to envision myself taking it off-roading. I fly around in that thing when I'm on a paved road. Best-case scenario, I'll get stuck in the mud. I've been able to keep a low profile since René and I spoke on the beach. I don't want to have to call for help because I'm stranded.

I feel a wave of intense disappointment. I've been afraid of seeing the places in my dad's song. Worried it would be too painful or make me miss him even more, I guess. But today I think they would actually help. I couldn't miss him any more than I do now, and if I'm going to be sad, I want to be sad in his favorite places. I hear the song so clearly in my mind.

> *bomba es el latido de mi corazón*
> *Playa Resaca, mi pulmón*
> *en el muelle bajo el mar*
> *encontré la fé y aprendí a amar*

—

> *Bomba is my heartbeat*
> *Resaca Beach, my lungs*
> *on the dock under the sea*
> *I found my faith and learned to love*

Maybe there's somewhere I can listen to bomba music on the island. Maybe at one of the hotels? But it isn't going to be anywhere at seven in the morning. René was going to ask around about the "dock under the sea," but I don't know if he's had any luck.

"You can take a boat to Resaca," offers my driver. He has my dad's accent too and it has a soothing effect on me. If he were the voice on one of those bedtime apps, I'd fall right to sleep.

"It's okay, I don't have access to a boat," I reply, and then I watch as his lips pucker toward the one docked just ahead of us on the property.

"Are you from Culebra?" I ask, leaning forward.

He nods vigorously. "A few generations back on my dad's side."

I smile, impressed. "Have you ever heard of a dock beneath the sea?"

"*Qué?* No!" he shouts again, pretending to be offended that I've stumped him. "What's that?"

"Nothing. It's just a place I heard about." I tap the camera on my lap. "You know what? Can you just take me to *any* dock? Well, not on this side. I've pretty much walked this entire part of the island. Can you take me to a dock on the north side?"

"Which one?" he barks.

"It doesn't matter. You pick," I respond brightly, egging him on.

The whole way, I have a good feeling. I've never been a gambler but having this man who reminds me of my dad choose makes me feel like we'll find it.

The road we're on ends, morphing into a wide cement dock that stretches into the water with large boats parked on either side. I pay him, say goodbye, and head slowly toward the water.

This is definitely *not* it. No one has ever written a song about this dock. Functional and plain, with a two-foot lip around the edge. It's so high above the water, the only way this dock would ever be "under the sea" is if it were struck with some treacherous storm surge. Not to mention that it looks relatively new, so it probably wasn't even around when my dad was here. I stare at it and let out a heavy sigh. To my left, there's a row of beachfront homes. On the right, the road leads to a public beach, so I set out in that direction.

At least I've embraced the dress code. It's muggy out but I'm comfortable in these denim shorts and the strapless top Meri packed for me.

There are only a few people on the beach, I imagine because it's early. This side of the island smells different. The air is salty *and* sweet. The waves are calmer, there are more seashells on the sand, and the neighboring islands are way closer to the shore.

I photograph a black-and-golden-haired mama chicken walking on the sand with her two babies. Then, I linger, up to my knees in the warm water, and observe a human family wading in a few feet away from me. They're fully clothed and carrying everything they've brought to the beach on their heads and shoulders. A large cooler, a small child, a boombox, and grocery bags. They walk determined, their course fixed on the closest island, about fifty yards away.

They graciously agree to let me photograph them, so I stake the beach out for the best vantage points. They remind me of a family of ducks all in a row. On a mission, determined to get where they're going so they can have a good time.

When they're far enough from the shore, I frame out the beach and the island, so they appear to be in the middle of the ocean, but with the water always just below their waists. When I head back to the beach, my wet denim shorts dragging, I feel the unfamiliar lightness of doing something just for fun.

"Hold on"—Meri switches our call to video—"check it out. Altogether, twenty-seven dollars." She aims her phone at her latest haul of vintage finds sprawled out on her bed. A dark green handbag, a white beret, and a pinstriped pencil skirt. "I mean, how perfect is this entire outfit? You have to try on the skirt when you get back." She aims the camera at herself. "I think it's going to look great on you."

"I love it all. Very impressive."

"Hey, Mom really loved the pictures you sent. She wants to frame the chickens on the beach. You should take a class again."

"I actually thought about that this morning when I was out there. It was so much fun."

"Do it!" Her eyes ignite with excitement.

"Maybe. I just need to see what's going to happen with my job first."

"And then what?" she snaps, surprising me. "When do you get to take a day off? Or a proper vacation? There was that photography workshop in Mexico you used to talk about."

A laugh escapes me, the idea is so preposterous. "That was a long time ago. Although we really should go on vacation. The three of us," I add, trying to keep things light. "Whenever I'm done paying for the windows."

"The *windows*?"

"Why are you yelling?"

"Because you're always moving the goal post. It's always, 'I'll move into my own place when the roof is done, I'll take a class after Mom's knee surgery, I'll take a vacation when the windows are paid for,'" she rattles off. "When are you going to do what *you* want?"

"Are you mad at me?"

"I'm frustrated," she clarifies, gathering steam. "I don't think you even see the goal anymore. Not one of your own."

"I just said, I want a vacation."

She gives me a look. "And what about René? Have you talked to him?"

"Since he admitted to writing an insulting song about me? No."

"Why not?" She's cooled off a bit.

Yesterday I told Meri about my talk with René, and she went on and on about how she was sure he had feelings for me. She said she knew it from the day he spoke to her at the bar and that the song actually proves it. "You need to talk to him."

"Meri, he's a grown man. If there was something he wanted to say to me, he would."

"Not if you're icing him out."

"I'm not icing him out." I shift uncomfortably. My back is starting to hurt from sitting on a stack of beach chairs. "We still have to work together, you know. I'm just trying to keep things civil." I fight back a groan.

"You're not avoiding him?"

"I'm not avoiding him," I confirm, just as the need to adjust myself or stand reaches a peak.

"Where are you?" she asks, her curiosity piqued. "Is that toilet paper behind you?"

"No, I don't—" I look behind me.

"Are you...hiding in a closet?"

"What? No this is, like, a little office I've been using."

Meri shakes her head. "Unbelievable."

So what if I'm in the storage closet? René and Santiago are busy working on a song they started yesterday. A party track with clever lyrics about a girl he's trying to forget. It's sexy and reminiscent of The Weeknd with a reggaeton twist.

It's just been easier to stay out of his way. I'm about to explain myself to Meri when my video monitor comes to life signaling that James has started to record again.

"I should get going," I say, watching the monitor. "I need to..." The camera zooms in for a close-up of René's face and I forget what I was about to say. The sight of his dark brown eyes and full lips in high definition on my lap creates a stir in my stomach.

"Wait," Meri says. "I need to tell you something."

She looks away, her eyebrows knitted tightly and my mind starts racing. Has she gone back to her cheating ex? Is Mom sick? "What's wrong?"

She's gone silent. Whatever it is, she's afraid to say it.

"What's happened? Did you dent my car?" I joke, hoping to make her smile and push my mind away from negative thoughts.

"I quit. Yesterday."

"Quit? Quit what?"

"Nursing school. I'm not applying anymore. I canceled the tutor."

I sit up quickly and the beach chairs wobble below me. "Really?"

She nods, her face pained. "I'm sorry to disappoint you, D." She's so upset, tears have started to flow. "I'll pay you back for the loans, and for the tutoring and everything. Someday." She's talking so fast, I can't get a word in. "Don't worry, I have a plan. I'm going to focus on the makeup work while I figure something out."

"You don't have to have a plan, Meri." Her eyes get bigger, anxious to hear what I'm going to say. "This is good."

Meri drops her mouth open. This is clearly not the reaction she was expecting. "Are you serious?"

"Of course."

"I thought you wanted me to be a nurse."

"Meri, you've been miserable for so long, why would I want that for you?"

A wave of relief smooths out her face. Of course, I'm a little concerned about what she'll do now. But she's been so hard on herself, forcing a test she found so painfully difficult over and over. Of course she's done the right thing. She should be in an environment she can shine and feel confident in.

"I just want you to be happy."

She smiles feebly. "What about you?"

"What about me?"

"Are *you* happy?" Meri sniffles.

"Well, now's not the best time to ask me that." On my monitor, René and Santiago are on the couch. I have the volume all the way down, so I have no idea what they're talking about.

"I know you need to go." She wipes at her tears.

"No, it's all right."

"Really. We can talk later."

"Okay."

As soon as she's gone, I'm flooded with a sense of relief. I can't imagine how free she must be feeling. There's a dopey smile on my face. *Finally, something's gone right.*

Someone knocks on the closet door and I lean too far back, causing the beach chairs to slip out from under me. It's a harsh, metal clanging spectacle and I end up spread out like a starfish over them.

Chapter 36

"Are you all right in there?" Thankfully, the voice belongs to James.

"Yeah." I'm trying my best not to move but an especially pointy part of a beach chair is digging into my shoulder blade. "I was just wrapping up a call." I watch for his shadow beneath the door to walk away, but it doesn't. "Everything okay?" I sound concerned, like *he's* the one being weird.

"Yeah, they're just going to take a break."

"Cool! I'll be right out."

A few minutes later, when I open the door, James isn't there. Across the hall, in the kitchen, I see the fridge door is open.

"So, how's it going in there today?" I ask all casually and like I wasn't just hiding out in the closet.

"Not too bad." The deep, raspy voice makes my lungs deflate. The fridge door shuts, and René is standing there holding a stick of butter. Behind him, the dinner buffet has been cleared and the kitchen smells like strong coffee.

I decide to just run with it, like this is exactly how I meant to approach him. "Well, that's good to hear."

He sets the butter down, empties still-hot coffee grounds into a bucket near the sink, and repacks the espresso machine. For what feels like an eternity, I stand there not knowing what to do. He's wearing worn-in jeans and a Bruce Lee T-shirt with black leather sandals. It's probably the sexiest I've seen him. Keep your head in the game. Get him to agree to the interview. Now. Just do it.

"*¿Cafecito?*" He raises an espresso cup in my direction.

"Sure, thanks." I drag one of the stools so it's directly across from him and take a seat at the counter.

"Sugar?"

"Yes, please."

"Butter?"

"Butter?" I repeat with a laugh.

"You don't like *café con mantequilla*?"

"No," I say with a snort. "Well, actually, I do love *dunking* buttered toast in my coffee and then drinking up all that buttery drizzled residue the toast leaves behind. So, I guess this would save a step."

René chuckles faintly. It's enough to make my whole body relax. "Exactly. I prefer to cut to the chase." Taking his time, he scoops up a spoonful of butter and dunks it in my coffee a few times, so it softens. "My hands are clean," he declares, then pushes the butter off the spoon with his finger until it slips into the coffee.

"I believe you," I say, all breathy.

He huffs at this, keeping his eyes down. And I don't know how to respond. So I focus instead as he does the same thing to his own coffee. The melted butter, the finger, the hot steam rising from the espresso.

I try my coffee, letting the creamy butter on top slip in with the first sip and then melt in my mouth. "Wow, I might never have toast again."

He fights back a grin. "Cuts out the middleman." He takes a slow sip, his eyes on mine.

He declines my offer to help and washes everything up meticulously. I discover then and there that it's possible to be turned on by watching a man wipe down a counter properly.

When he's done, he leans against the counter. "I was looking for you earlier."

"You were?" *That's odd, because I've definitely been around and not hiding in a closet.*

"I need your help with something. I have an idea for the album I think would be great for the behind-the-scenes."

"Really? You got it. What do you need from us?"

"No cameras. Just you."

I sigh dramatically. "How would that be good for the making-of?" I can feel things are better between us again.

"Take pictures," he declares, like it's the obvious solution.

"Fine." I scoff. "I guess I can do that."

"Great."

"So, what is it? What's the idea?"

"Ah, you're just going to have to trust me. Do you think you can do that?" He's trying to make light of what I said the other night, but I can't tell if he's really over it.

I want to tread lightly. I can't acknowledge our conversation from the other night. I don't want to talk about the song he wrote. What I need to do now is move past it. And get him to agree to the final interview once and for all so I can finish this job.

Two days later, I'm standing in the middle of the parking lot, on the only small island of dry gravel. The rest of the front lawn is soggy with mud after all the rain from the past few days.

The guard at the gate was under strict instructions and said I absolutely had to wait here. Whatever René has planned, it's a welcome distraction. I haven't been able to stop thinking about my conversation with Meri. How long has she been considering quitting her nursing school path? Why didn't she felt comfortable telling me sooner? And why hadn't Mom told me about the guy she'd met? I can't shake this feeling that my absence has freed them somehow. Like as soon as I'm gone, everybody does what they really want.

"Ready?" René calls out from the front steps, a broad grin on his face. The sight of him looking so cheery and excited to spend time together has a multitude of effects on me. It's like being shot with a soothing tranquilizer that somehow also elevates my heartbeat.

"I'm not sure," I yell back, curious as to what he's up to. He motions for me to follow him as he walks around the main building. I don't know why he doesn't want James to come. The last two days René's been nothing but accommodating. Not only did he let us properly capture the recording of a new song, but we filmed him making his buttered coffee, getting his hair freshly buzzed by a barber friend on his patio, and having dinner with Camila and Santiago.

As I turn the corner and onto a small field on this side of the property, my feet come to a halt. Two large ATVs are being unloaded off a flatbed truck by a woman in a black leather jacket and matching cap. René is next to the truck, talking to the main studio tech.

"What's all this?" I ask when I'm close enough.

"Cool, huh? We need these to get where we're going."

"Uh...yeah." I check out the ATVs. *They're very intimidating.* They have bright yellow wheels, and a see-through shell exposing their motors and technology like an exoskeleton. They are so souped up, they're like giant mechanical bees.

The truck makes a loud rattling sound and I jump. Thankfully, René's missed my reaction. He's busy looking through the contents of a large backpack the tech has just handed him.

The leather-clad woman hits a switch that raises the flatbed back up, now free of ATVs. This all seems a bit extreme. I have no idea where we're going. Plus, the sun is setting. Am I expected to drive that thing back here in the dark?

"Hey, do you want me to put that in the storage trunk?" René asks, motioning to James's camera hanging on my shoulder.

"I'm sorry but I would need, like, a two-hour lesson before I can take that thing on the road. Maybe three."

He smiles and my shoulders soften. "I think you just need to—"

"If you say, 'Let go,' I'm going to get really upset."

He opens his mouth to speak.

"Don't say it. If you really want me to get on that thing, you're going to need to say something else." Even with my nerves frayed, I can feel a charged flirty energy between us.

"Let."

"Don't say it."

"Go," he whispers.

I exhale loudly and roll my eyes.

"I'm sorry." He gives my arm a little squeeze. "And I'm just kidding. Actually, you're going to need to hold on tight."

He's wearing baggy shorts and a black shirt with the faintest of florals. Only the bottom button is buttoned, so my eyes wander down his chest. *The interview.* "I'll do it, if you promise to give us a proper interview."

"Right."

"We're running out of time, and I really want to do it while we're here, while it's all still fresh."

"Yeah, I get it," he says, and I feel my chest drop with relief. "Can it wait until the end?"

"That would be ideal, actually. I just wasn't sure if you'd be too busy. That way we can cover everything. One big interview," I say to summarize.

"Fine. Yeah, we'll get it done." It's as though he's just confirmed a dental appointment.

The leather-clad woman introduces herself as Vega and hands me a helmet. She walks me through the basics, spitting out words like "throttle," "clutch," and "kill switch." She tucks James's camera into the storage compartment, and then helps me mount the thing like a horse.

"Can you put this away too?" I pull off my white linen blazer and convince myself my black silk tank and dark jeans I'm wearing can handle a little mud. I feel René watching me as I take off my ponytail and slip on the helmet.

"I'll go ahead and turn the headlights on for you," Vega says. "And when you speed up, make sure you lean forward so you don't flip back."

I nod, my lips in a tight smile. With her not so reassuring final words in my ear, I let my whole body settle into the seat.

Chapter 37

I'M ONLY AFRAID FOR MY LIFE ONCE, ON A STEEP AND GRAVELLY hill where I never quite feel enough traction. I imagine my ATV flipping backward with me on it. And how I'd die looking like a giant dice rolling down a hill.

After about thirty minutes, René veers onto a dirt road ahead of me. I pull up next to him feeling more at ease maneuvering a large, dangerous piece of equipment than I ever thought possible.

The whole way here, René checked on me occasionally. I tried my best not to read anything into it. *He's just making sure the record label exec isn't dead.* But each time, I felt a warmth in my chest. It was a beautiful ride with the ocean almost always in view. I loved the straight roads, where we'd speed up to over fifty miles per hour.

Without removing his helmet, René flashes me a thumbs-up to gauge how I'm feeling. I give him a thumbs-up back, then move my hand around, mimicking a thumb on a roller coaster. His eyes crinkle in response, then he starts off down the narrow dirt road, splashing right away through a large ditch covered in mud.

I follow him slowly, driving around the ditch while also avoiding the boulders and trees on either side of us. Eventually the muddy water gets deep. At times it rises above the wheels, and I have to lift my legs to avoid getting my jeans soaked.

The carefree, childlike rush I feel sloshing down the long, muddy river of a road, weaving around large rocks only to dip into an unforeseen small hole, leaves me buzzing. When we reach the end, my cheeks hurt from smiling. *I only wish I'd worn a more supportive bra.*

René hands me a thermos of water and takes my helmet. He grabs our things out of the trunks and places the helmets inside.

"Resaca!" he announces, his arms raised high like a true showman. "From your dad's song."

I feel my cheeks flush. "This is Resaca?"

"Well, the beach is at the end of that path."

I unmount the bike and my legs are wobbly. "I don't know what to say." I'm beyond moved he's brought me here. "Thank you."

"You're welcome." He leans against his bike. "I also asked around about a 'dock beneath the sea,' but nobody's ever heard of it. Maybe it was more figurative and not a real place?"

"Poetic license?"

"Yeah. We do that sometimes." He's being smug, but in a way I find adorable.

"You've got a little mud." I tap the bridge of my nose to show him where.

He laughs because we're both covered in mud. "Thanks." He wipes off his nose with a knuckle. "After you." The trail to the beach is narrow, so he lets me go first. "I also tried to find a concert," he says as we walk, "for the part about listening to bomba music, but the only thing I found was an event coming up in San Juan in a couple of weeks."

"Oh, that's okay. I appreciate you checking, really."

"Yeah, so . . ." His voice trails off.

The path spills us out onto a clearing and my breath catches. The sun is setting on a literal paradise. A cove with a white sandy beach, palm trees and mangroves, crystal-clear water, all enclosed by small green mountains. In a movie, pirates would hide their treasure here.

"I called a couple of friends and told them we needed the bomba to come to us." He points out a group of camping tents and tarps down the beach.

It's all too much to take in. "You know them?"

"Not *all* of them."

"Are you kidding me? You shouldn't have gone through all this trouble."

After a few minutes of introductions, I'm still trying to wrangle my emotions. I'm ecstatic, overwhelmed, *and* emotional. There's a dancer, two singers, and three musicians who are in the midst of setting up their tall, barrel-shaped drums around a hefty bonfire.

In addition to the tents, there are lounge chairs, coolers, and a pop-up table set up with food. I think this group intends to stay a few days.

"Takes me back to when I used to perform at my friends' parties." René is nearby, unpacking the backpack he brought with him. "I used to have to set up the audio equipment and the speakers, as well as perform." He undoes the cables wrapped tightly around a small microphone.

Something clicks into place. *It's not just for me. This is for the album.* Getting down to business, I unpack James's camera and take some pictures of René setting up small microphones on stands near the drums. This *would* be incredible for the making-of. The large bonfire, the loud crashing of the waves, the drummers starting to warm up.

"Please let me get James over here. I can't enjoy this if we're not filming it. It may as well not be happening."

"Do you hear yourself?"

"I do," I admit after a beat.

"It's impossible anyway. He'd need an ATV and I had to have these ferried to the island."

I let the weight of what he's said hit me. "There must be another way."

"You saw what it took to get here. Nothing else could make it."

"How did *they* get here?" I gesture toward the musicians.

"Some were dropped off by boat, some walked." He motions his chin in the direction of the mountains. "Besides, we should start right away before the sun sets."

He's right. Even if James *could* find a way to get here, it would be too late. Plus, clouds are beginning to gather. If I want to capture any of it, we need to start now.

René puts his headphones on to monitor the recording and, with a nod, gives the musicians the go-ahead.

A sole drum kicks off the music. The dancer starts to move, lifting her skirt and twisting it around herself. Then the other drums, the maraca, and the singers join in.

René appears beside me. "You know, bomba is perfect for you," he whispers, removing his headphones. "You don't have to keep up with the music."

"Go on," I say, intrigued.

"The dancer sets the rhythm for the musicians. They follow *her* lead. She marks the beat, not the other way around."

"Hmm, I like that." I'm transfixed as the dancer moves her waist and feet quickly, and then, as one of the drums echoes her moves.

A thin, older man dressed entirely in white bellows out a phrase, and then the others repeat it. The drumming and chanting seep through me, loosening every muscle. The deep, repetitive beats vibrate in my heart, and my shoulders begin to stir.

"*¡Eso!* There you go," René eggs me on. I smile and, feeling the music, begin to tap my feet.

René sets his headphones down and offers me his hand. When I take it, he holds it tight and uses his free hand to pull the camera strap off my shoulder.

I don't know what it is exactly. The dancer's improvisation, the rhythm of the drums, the comfort of being here— experiencing music my father loved in a place he wanted me to see so badly. But I want to dance and I'm not afraid about keeping up. More than that. I feel like the only mistake would be to stop moving.

René lifts our hands above our heads as we move. His face is inches from mine. The glow of the bonfire kisses his full lips and strong neck, enhancing his features. "Thank you," he whispers near my ear as we dance.

A little voice creeps in. *René would dance with any label representative who was here. He'd put his hands on her waist like this. He'd pull her closer and look at her like th—*

The clouds burst, dropping an instantaneous downpour on the beach, and we scatter in different directions. René rushes to the aid of the musicians and carries the largest drum into a tent. I grab the camera and toss the microphones and recording equipment inside the backpack.

I end up drenched and alone under a tarp with a battery-operated lantern hanging from a tree. I sit there, squeezing my knees in, dazed by the incessant, shocking amount of rain. I start to pull off my soaked boots and socks when René appears holding two beers.

"Thanks."

"So, it was short-lived, but what did you think?"

"I loved it. So much."

I take a long sip of my beer and consider making a comment about the rain. How I've never seen so much fall all at once like this. As though upset with my intention, the wind picks up, causing the tarp above us to inflate for a moment before coming back down.

"My dad loved bomba. He'd play it in his truck." I watch the bonfire wrestle with the rain. "I don't remember it sounding like this, though."

"It's very different live." I nod in agreement. "So, you like bomba, but you don't like reggaeton. What else *do* you like?"

"I listen to everything."

"Except reggaeton."

"I never said I didn't like reggaeton. Not out loud, anyway," I mumble, making him laugh. "Honestly? It was probably the only thing I didn't *use to* listen to." I give him a look, letting him know he's the reason this has changed. "So *now*, I really do listen to everything."

"Everyone always says that."

"No, really," I insist. "I love the Ramones, Fleetwood Mac, Marvin Gaye," I list out, "folk, funk, jazz, literally everything. Radiohead, as you know. I even listen to Cowpunk."

He tilts his head doubtingly. "Cowpunk."

"It's a subgenre of punk combined with country music."

René shakes his head, unsure about what he's hearing. We finish our beers and watch the bonfire slowly succumb to the rain. When it finally does, we turn to each other, mouths agape, as though we've just seen something way more impressive. Like a shooting star. There are tiny drops of rain on his buzzed hair, and on his scruffy beard and mustache. Like morning dew on plants. *Except I've never wanted to lick the dew off plants.*

"Are you hungry?" René asks. "Dinner should be ready."

"Yes!" I say, a little too eager. "Are you?"

"You should know this about me. I'm *always* hungry."

You should know this about me. It's the kind of thing you tell someone on a date. The kind of thing you share because it could be a valuable tidbit in *our* future.

While he's gone, I give myself a sobering pep talk. We only have a few more days here. He's agreed to the interview. I'm golden. All I have to do is keep things professional between us. Keep my *thoughts* professional.

A few minutes later, he sprints back carrying a small plastic bag. Before unpacking it, he lifts it, so I can appreciate how drenched it is. "So, I got some news, but why don't we eat first."

"Okay." I stretch out the word playfully.

He carefully unpacks the contents of the bag and sets us up with a miniature picnic, complete with two more beers. Sitting across from each other, we share a large wooden bowl of fish that's more sashimi than ceviche, soaked in lemon and some unidentifiable but ridiculously delicious spicy powder.

"Listen." He sounds somber. "I won't use the song on the album if you don't want me to."

"The one about me?" I feel an itch on my ankle. Sand fleas? Or maybe no-see-ums? Because I don't see them, but I sure feel them.

"The one *loosely* based on you."

I take a long sip of beer, feeling my pulse kick. "It's a great song," I say at last. "It's good for both of us if you keep it on the album. We can just come to some sort of arrangement. You know, in case it does well. Like if it goes platinum, I get a new digital camera."

"I was thinking more like a new car."

"Oh, me too. I wasn't done. I get a digital camera *and* a new car."

He laughs heartily, and his whole body seems to relax. I have an image of how things could be after all of this. Of the song becoming a connection between us. Maybe it isn't so horrible after all.

"Deal." He scratches the back of his neck. "I *am* sorry if it hurt you." His hand falls heavy on his thigh.

"I appreciate that." Suddenly, I'm more comfortable with the rain hitting my back from time to time because the tarp isn't big enough to shield us completely. "Wait, so what was the news?"

"The road's flooded," he announces nonchalantly. "Two of the guys are going to double up, so we can have that one." He points behind me. Confused, I turn to see what he means. It's a tent. An almost cylindrical-looking, narrow, single-person tent. A "there's no way I'm sleeping with René in that tent" tent.

"How do you know the roads are flooded?" I ask, in denial.

"They just told me."

"When?"

"When I went to get the food."

"Are you sure? Should we go check?"

"We don't need to. These roads flood when it rains like this. And they were already soaked."

"We have big wheels. I think we could make it."

As though objecting to my protests, the rain pounds harder on the tarp.

René gives me a look. "We could get stuck."

"We *are* stuck!" I have to shout, the rain is so loud now.

René slaps his neck. "Are you getting bitten?"

"A little," I lie. The truth is the itchiness around my ankles has escalated into an intense burning sensation. I feel hot stings on my neck and up and down my arms. We're under attack by invisible bugs armed with miniature blowtorches.

"I can sleep here under this tarp." He taps the sand we're sitting on. "You take the tent." Despite my hesitation, I know the truth. There's no way he can sleep out here. We *both* need to get away from these bugs.

Chapter 38

SOMEONE HAS SPRUCED UP THE TENT FOR US. INSIDE, STACKED together in the middle, are a thin sleeping pad, two small pillows, a sheet, a blanket, a large bottle of water, a flashlight that doubles as a lantern, and two oranges. It's good we have things to do right away. We don't need to speak or think about what's happening. There's the unified task of getting the tent ready. Move the oranges. Spread out the sheet.

"Are you sure you're okay with this setup?"

"Yeah, totally." I almost add, "I trust you," but I'm glad I catch myself. I don't want to bring up that old wound right now. Besides, I do trust him. It's me I'm worried about. I don't know what my arms and legs will do while I sleep. What if he wakes up in the middle of the night and I'm holding him in a tight death grip?

I scooch over near one of the pillows, and he positions himself near the entrance, sitting back on his knees. He peels his shirt off and lays it over his backpack for drying. Even in the dim light of the lantern, I discover little things about him. *The whirl of a cowlick on the back of his head. He bites his lower lip when he's concentrating.*

"Are you okay with me taking these off?" His hands pat his wet shorts.

"Sure." I look away and pretend to inspect my corner of the tent. He shuts the light off and crawls toward me. It's dark but my eyes adjust quickly enough to see black, hip-hugging briefs.

"Do you want to take those off?" he asks, pointing at my jeans. I realize I'm lying on, and therefore dampening, our shared blanket, so I quickly tuck myself under it.

"No, I'm fine." *I'll just have wrinkled legs in the morning.*

We barely fit. We're both on our backs, side by side, and my right shoulder is pressed against the cool tent fabric.

"You're shivering." I shut my eyes, embarrassed he's noticed. "Your clothes are soaked. Just take them off." He sounds more like a concerned friend than a guy trying to get me naked.

Obviously, sleeping in my underwear is the sensible thing to do. My silk shirt and jeans are soaked and cold. They're also extremely uncomfortable, like heavy chain mail stuck to my skin.

"I've already seen you in your bra and underwear, remember?"

"Uh, no. You said it was too dark to see anything."

"Did I? That's right."

"I knew it. Admit it, you *could* see me from your rooftop."

"I'll answer that if you admit you had no idea who I was when you first met me."

My mouth makes an involuntary deflating noise. "I could just go up on your rooftop and find out for myself."

"I want to see you try." His voice drops to pillow talk levels and I feel a stretching and squeezing. Like someone's playing the accordion with my rib cage.

"Fine." I sit up. "Bet you've never had to ask a girl twice before," I tease, trying to cover up my nerves as I struggle getting the wet tank up over my head.

"I'm just going to ignore that." He steps in to help me pull my top over my arms. I get the jeans to my knees but he has to take over from there. He crawls to the end of the tent and peels them off. He tries to make the task strictly utilitarian, to keep his gaze on the jeans. I, however, am not able to take my eyes off him. And the way he takes his time stretching out my things at the foot of the tent to help them dry.

"Thanks. I'm glad that, in this household, you're responsible for clothes drying."

"That works for me. What's your chore going to be?"

"I'm one hell of an orange peeler. So, whenever you're ready for that, just let me know."

He fights back a grin and I watch the outline of his body crawling back toward me. I lie back feeling a million times better. We settle under our blanket again and something feels different. My body temperature is more comfortable, for one. But things are more comfortable between us as well. Probably because I've accepted this is happening. I'm going to sleep in a tent on the beach with René. In my underwear.

When the rain picks up, René gets out from under the blanket and grabs his audio recorder from his backpack. He gets back under the blanket and aims it at the roof of the tent. I support him with my silence.

"Cierra los ojos."

Damn it, his deep voice is always sexier in Spanish.

"Okay." I close my eyes and tuck a hand behind my head. Right away, the muffled sound of rain pelting the fabric heightens.

With my eyes still closed, he shares his collection of sounds. Some from our trip to his hometown. Busy streets and places he's traveled to. Many variations of waves, the coqui frog we risked our lives for.

"It's amazing how a sound can make you feel," René says. "They ground me. That's why it's so important for me to include them in the album. Just hearing them, you know you're in Puerto Rico."

"Yeah, that's all very nice," I tease. "Just promise me you'll repeat everything you just said in our final interview."

He means to elbow me, but we're so close together, he ends up pressing his forearm gently against my side. The feel of his warm skin on mine makes my insides stretch and squeeze again.

"This is a good one." He lies on his side to face me and holds the recorder close to my ear. "Can you guess what it is?"

I shut my eyes again, feeling an easy sort of bliss. The sizzling of food on a grill, music in the distance, people talking. A broad smile stretches across my face. "The food trucks."

"Correct."

"I'm surprised I can remember a lot of these." I turn my body to face him. It's dark, but I can make out all the details of his face. "They're like audible snapshots."

"I do this all the time," he explains. "I prefer recording sound to taking pictures. A few seconds of my family at home at Christmas is way better than a fake photo session by the tree."

"Yeah, but it's so much harder to frame."

He scrunches up his nose in pretend protest. "I know you like photography, but I think sound is more honest. Audio has no judgment. It just is. It's hard to see without judgment. Impossible to capture a photograph without altering the truth."

"That's probably *why* I love photography." I move an arm up near my chest, trying to get more comfortable. "You have the control. You can make someone *feel* what you want. Take the gaze, for example. Where a subject is looking changes everything. If they're looking directly at the camera, it's a demand." The look in his eyes seems to intensify. "Or when a photograph is out of focus," I continue, my heart beginning to race, "it creates a sense of confusion for the viewer. It's uncomfortable."

He narrows his eyes and puckers his lips. "So, why aren't you doing it full time? What do you need? A place to stay? Inspiration?" He spits out offers generously. "I know people who support the arts," he says with a wink.

"That's very kind, but I've actually never wanted to do it professionally. I love my job. Photography is something that lets me…I don't know, express myself. I just never do it anymore. It's been a long time." I fidget, then rub at the tarp beneath me, feeling a pebble near my butt.

"How come?"

"It's been a while since I've had any time for anything that wasn't…productive," I admit with a wince. "It's been nice to have the chance to incorporate it into the making of your album. But I'm also glad we're getting video."

"And why is that?"

He adjusts an arm under his face and leans over slightly as the rain gets louder. It feels so good to be here with him, looking into his eyes. So easy to be open. Outside, the sky is falling, but in here, things are clear and safe. Even if I can't stop looking at his lips.

"Well, because getting to see you make music is pretty amazing. And you do this thing where you laugh when you like the way something sounds and things are working. I wouldn't be able to capture *that* with a picture."

He smiles and then his eyes move around my face, searching for something. "So"—he clears his throat—"what have you
been doing with your time? What's been more productive than
making art and expressing yourself?"

"Work."

"That's it?"

"Pretty much."

"Would you say you're a workaholic, Dani?" he asks in his
best therapist impression.

"I *am* starting to think so. Sometimes when I see a 'Now
Hiring' sign at a coffee shop, I'll think, I could probably work
here on weekends. Or squeeze in a few hours before work. Get
up early. Maybe six a.m. to eight-thirty a.m. Help out with
their morning rush."

Even in the dark, I can see his eyebrows furrow. "Is it
because of money?" he asks, still in his therapist voice. "Or are
you afraid of free time?"

I huff. "Maybe both." His face shifts from compassion to
concern. "What about you? What's the end goal, René? World
domination? International stardom?"

He exhales loudly. "Honestly? I want to sell out a stadium.
Just me." His sincerity washes over me. "When I've performed
in one for the collabs I've done, the energy is…" He makes an
explosive sound. "You feel all this love. Like the whole damn
city has showed up for you."

The accordion in my chest stretches wider and then contracts
even tighter. "You'll get there with this album."

He puckers his lips considering this. *God, those lips.* "Some
people think I should play it safe, stick to collabs."

"Does that worry you?"

"A little bit. I worry I'll let people down. And it would

suck"—he chuckles—"to be one of those artists that was doing great and then fucked it up when they went in a different direction."

"Well, I think you have to keep trusting your instincts." He moves his hand and it lands so close to mine, I can almost feel it. "You won't disappoint anyone. There's so much certainty in this new music. So much strength. Even when you're being vulnerable. It's so *real*, René," I say, meaning every word. "So true to yourself and where you come from. What's not to love? Is what...people will say," I tack on. "When they hear it. And..." I draw in a breath because our hands have made contact. "I genuinely think the behind-the-scenes of the album will help you. You're changing before our eyes. Well"—I have to collect myself because my heart is racing—"not really changing, more like shedding. Real instruments, real conversations with your friends, and no sunglasses. You've let us in."

"You're in all right."

My breath gets caught somewhere deep in my chest. His hand presses into mine and I slip my fingers under his. He opens my palm and traces it with his fingertips, mesmerized. When he gets to my wrist, everything feels warmer. My free hand moves up his arm. His skin is soft, yet solid with muscle. He starts to lean over and my hand tugs at his shoulder, bringing him in faster.

The feel of his pillowy soft lips on mine pushes me over an edge I hadn't realized I was so close to. The kiss is slow and tender. And slightly smoky from the rain on our skin.

A burst of laughter from a nearby tent snaps me back to Earth. I pull away, my heart knocking against my chest, and I lean back until I feel the tent fabric behind me. He settles back too, the way he was a few moments ago.

I need a minute. I need to get a hold of myself. "Thank you, um, for bringing me here. Too much." I'm not making any sense. My brain hasn't fully powered back on. "I'm so grateful. I don't like surprises, but now, I think I may like them. You have single-handedly changed how I feel about surprises."

"Glad I made an impact."

I have to chuckle at how short his sentence is compared to what I'm feeling. Then, I think about going home in a few days and my chest aches.

"Dani..." he starts but stops short.

"Seriously, though, I loved it." My mind has spun off without me. "And the whole thing was so effortless. The musicians, the—"

"Now, I wouldn't say *that*." His voice is deep and warm. "I booked the four-wheelers, called half of San Juan to get the bomba together. It's actually the most planning I've ever done, thank you very much."

After a beat, I start to laugh and he joins in. "Of course. I'm sorry, I didn't mean—" Maybe it's the nerves but I laugh so hard, my stomach crunches. When I finally stop, we're closer together again, my hand on his chest. And he's looking at me. *Really* looking at me.

This time, it's me who leans in. We kiss harder and with more intention. His hand finds my waist, then moves up my bare back. My mind shuts off. The only thing I know is I want to live this. I want to be here fully. Be here *with* him.

I trace the tattoo around his neck with my lips, desperate to be closer to him. When he opens them, there's a pleading in his eyes. "What are you doing to me?"

"Whatever you want," says other Dani.

He comes alive.

I take mental photographs of everything. The way he looks at me when I reach back and undo my bra. His hands on my hips, fingers stretched out, grasping. His full lips on my stomach. Each kiss a warm bomb setting off ripples.

I know my bare back looks good in this light. Our weathered, narrow tent is a faded shade of red, so the early morning sun is coming in faded, too, casting a reddish pink haze on everything.

Am I actually trying to flex my back muscles? Yes. Yes I am. But I'm not sure if anything's happening. Other than I'm starting to strain my neck.

I'm not even sure René's awake. All I know is, I've woken up on my side, in a partial spoon with him, his thighs pressed against the back of mine. Last night, it was cool in the tent, but it's a warm sauna in here now. The heat weighs me down. Outside, the waves sound like low, rolling thunder as they pull away.

The idea that I can catch the sunrise gets me moving. I find my bra, throw on René's shirt, and step outside.

Two surfers have found the beach. They're sitting on their boards in the distance, patiently waiting for the sea to give them something. The sky is dark blue, except behind the mountain where the sun is rising. The rain has stopped, but there's a strong breeze rustling through the palm trees that sounds just like rain.

I shut my eyes, drunk from little sleep. For hours, René and I lay on our backs, arms and legs intertwined, and talked. About music, his mom, my sister. About the time he performed after having just sprained an ankle. And how I had felt strangely orphaned when I learned my dad had died. René said he thought it was because the parent who understood me the best was gone. This led to a lengthy conversation about the need to be understood.

I told him how, growing up, I never really felt American or Cuban or Puerto Rican enough.

He finally shared why he's rarely given interviews. How the first song he wrote for someone made him so much money, he was terrified he'd come across like an idiot or say the wrong thing and fuck everything up. He was too young and shy but then it all sort of stuck and grew from there. Mysterious El Rico, the sunglasses.

We talked about the best drummers in the world. How much he liked a particular freckle on my shoulder. I feel undone in the best possible way. I bring a finger to my lower lip and rub a sensitive spot. *There was some biting.*

I've never felt so in sync with someone. Or had so much fun. The sleeping pad rustled so loudly beneath us, it was a game trying to keep quiet. Shushing, laughing, moaning uncontrollably. *Not necessarily in that order.* Every kiss was a release that brought us closer. He wasn't even El Rico anymore. *Except for when he pulled out a strip of some luxury brand of condoms I'd never even heard of before.*

The ocean is inviting. The clear line separating the shallow beginnings from the deeper, darker water is far away. It seems ridiculous that I've yet to go for a swim the whole time I've been here. I hang René's shirt on the corner of our tent and head to the shore.

The water is so warm, it surprises me. When I'm about waist-deep, I float, spread out like a starfish. The way the mountains wrap around this beach makes me feel held, so I let myself drift. With my ears below the surface of the water, the only thing I hear is sand shifting. For the first time in my adult life, I'm not trying to fix anything. I know Meri and Mom don't want me to worry about them, so I let them go too.

Something taps my foot and I pull it away, splashing my arms in distress. After I've rubbed the salt out of my eyes, I see René in front of me. "I can't believe you just did that. I thought you were a shark."

"I'm sorry. I didn't mean to scare you." I can tell he regrets it, but he's also got a big smile on his face. "I thought you saw me coming. But I should have known better, you seemed so relaxed."

"I *was*."

He drops deeper into the water. "What can I do to get you back there? Do you want to be alone?"

"No," I respond without a beat, though I'm certain my mind is conflicted. Last night had felt safe. In the tent, each moment was special but also unreal. Now, in the raw morning light, the real René "El Rico" Rodriguez is before me and I'm unsure what last night may have meant to him. Come to think of it, he's got a whole song where he compares himself to a shark. "Do you think the roads are okay by now?"

He's about to respond when a wave comes out of nowhere and crashes into us. We end up close together, so I take a step back.

"Please don't."

He dips his head back beneath the water and comes out, face dripping.

"Don't what?" I think I know what he's saying, but I'm going to need him to spell it out.

"Don't pull away." He's just loud enough for me to hear.

Three short words, but they're raw and vulnerable. They shoot oxygen through my veins, and the need to reciprocate beats out any idea I could ever have of keeping things professional. I reach out and grab hold of his arm. It takes a millisecond for him to respond. He slides forward, bridging the space between us.

This kiss. This one is by far my favorite. It fills me up. My heart feels bigger, like it's taking up all of my chest. It's salty, of course, but also so damn sweet. Not in a bad-for-you, processed-sugary kind of way. It's thick, pure, top-notch honey. Delicious *and* nutritious.

"Were you able to sleep?" he asks when we come up for air.

"I think so. 'Rainy night on the beach' might be my new favorite bedtime soundscape."

René grins, an ease washing over him. "I'm just sorry the music had to end so soon last night."

"It's okay. It was incredible."

"I'm glad I was able to make it happen. Hey, I got you to all the places in your dad's song. Well, all but one," he says.

My hands wrap around his face and I kiss him. "Thank you." I rest my finger on his dimpled chin, visible through the scruffy beard.

"You're welcome." They were amazing back on land, but beneath the water, his hands feel like satin on my skin.

The waves have calmed around us, and so have I. Stilled in the certainty that there *is* something between us. I rest my head on his chest and find the surfers. Lying flat on their boards, paddling away around the mountain.

Chapter 39

"I THOUGHT YOU SAID YOU WERE GETTING US A HEALTHY snack?" James has found me in the kitchen, his camera idling on the edge of his shoulder. Behind him, the sun is almost gone, and there's a row of palm tree silhouettes.

Caught in the act, I try to smile sheepishly, but my mouth is too full. I've just taken a huge bite of an *alcapurria*, the rest of which I'm holding in my bare hand because I didn't bother to get a plate. Or a napkin. It's crispy and fresh and almost as good as the one I had with René at the food trucks. This one is filled with warm, spicy crab meat. "This is so good. You have to try one."

"On our first date," he says, his face stiff, "you told me fried foods were like dinosaurs. They became extinct, as far as you were concerned, when you discovered how quickly they clog your arteries."

"Wow, um, good memory. And, I mean, that's obviously still true. But everything in moderation, right? So, when in Rome!" All of this comes out a little too manic as I wave the fritter around. I can't help it. Since René and I got back this morning, I've been floating.

"I had gotten you a box of donuts from that place on Lincoln Road. The one that always sells out, so you have to get there early. You wouldn't even taste one," he says dryly.

I've taken another big bite so all I can do is nod for a moment. "I know, and I'm sorry. I was really strict about trans fats back then."

Under his watchful eye, I stuff the last of it in my mouth and try my best to hold back a reaction to the sweet and salty deliciousness. A few minutes ago, when I saw the platter of fresh *alcapurrias* cooling on the counter, my first thought was René must have told them. The chef hadn't made them since we've been here, and I think there's a real possibility these were a little gift for me.

James sets the camera next to me on the counter. "I'll be right back."

He's been quieter than usual today. Just as René and I turned our ATVs onto the dirt road that leads up to the house, James was jogging alongside it. I waved hello, but I couldn't tell if he waved back because we accidentally left him in a cloud of dust. I can't imagine what I must have looked like to him, driving up after a night away on a huge, splattered-with-mud, all-terrain vehicle.

René texted Camila last night so I knew James would have received the message about the roads. He'd know we were going to have to spend the night on the beach. But still, it must have been off-putting to see me pull up like that with René. My hair loose with salt-water-crusted curls, rolled-up jeans, and a crumpled-up tank top.

"Hey, what's up?" René said to James. Then he flashed me a sweet smile and walked inside the house.

"Are you okay?" James asked, eyes on René as he walked away.

"Yeah, I'm great. I just need to be hosed down."

Selfishly, all I could think about in the moment was that he had robbed me of a proper goodbye with René. Thankfully, there's a plan. One we'd made this morning, before we left the beach. We're going to meet at midnight by the statues. I pull my cell out to check the time and feel a fluttering in my stomach. It's 7:45 p.m.

James returns from the bathroom just as my phone buzzes with a text from Meri. I notice a bunch of missed calls from her I didn't see since my ringer's been off all day in the studio.

Daniela Maria, you CANNOT leave me a message like that and then not answer your phone.

After I had a very long shower, I tried to call Meri but it went straight to voicemail.

Meri, I was so wrong about René. You are not going to believe what happened last night. Call me back.

I thought I was being discreet, but Meri would be able to hear *exactly* what happened in my voice. I couldn't help it. I felt chemically altered and giddy. Most of all, I was so excited to share it with her. In the last twenty-four hours I'd finally cracked a code and figured out how *not* to feel like her parent anymore. I had my sister back, and our relationship could be fun and light again.

We need to get back to the studio, so I send her a quick text promising to call her as soon as I can, and put the phone away. "Ready to head back?" I ask James.

"Yep." He slings the camera back on his shoulder. "Though it looked like they were about to wrap things up."

I pull the studio door open with gusto, my entire body excited to be near René again. Right away, I register the song they're blasting inside. All day I've been floating high, but for the first time, I drop closer to the ground. My plane hits an air pocket. René's near the console, arms out in front, dancing to "Take It Off." The song about me and my blazers is playing so loudly, it's deafening. All for the maximum appreciation of his VIP guest.

Seated on the leather couch, moving to the music, is the person who's consumed René's attention all day. Carlos Miguel. Puerto Rico's prodigal son, actor, singer, and humanitarian. He was waiting for René when we arrived this morning.

Carlos Miguel started out on a TV show about a boy band. It was hugely successful, and when he outgrew that, he joined a real boy band, toured the world, won a Latin Grammy, and for the next ten years or so, had a succession of hits. I never met him before, but have heard good things. He gives off the air of a man who's lived through a lot and now likes to reside in the present moment. A simple man, who arrived in a compact yet spectacular yacht he parked on our dock. He was all tight leather pants and unbuttoned poofy shirts when he was younger, but at fifty-something, he dresses like a retired pro skateboarder. Brown curls, stretched-out paisley tee, long shorts, and white Pumas.

They've spent the day together in the studio, and all day, James and I have had front-row behind-the-scenes access. Carlos and René obviously knew each other, but I wouldn't say from their interactions they were close. Today's felt like one long man-date between two talented artists taking turns displaying their mutual respect while listening to René's new songs.

Though the morning started out with some confusion. Carlos was under the impression there was something for him to record for the album. René easily clarified the mistake, but it got awkward when Santiago pressed the issue and suggested track after track they could incorporate Carlos Miguel's vocals into. The subject was eventually dropped, and Carlos stuck around, only too happy to simply listen to the album.

He spent the afternoon on the couch, listening and giving his feedback from time to time. It's great to have footage of them hanging out. It's easy to see it's meant a lot to René to have Carlos here.

René and I haven't spoken since this morning. I caught him looking at me a few times and it felt special to have this secret between us. All day I've fanaticized about, oh, I don't know, pulling him into a closet for a super-speedy, albeit satisfying, make-out session.

Now, while James steps around the console for close-ups, I press my back against the cold glass of the recording booth. I haven't heard this song since René performed it at the showcase and it hurts when I hear some of the lyrics. *So much.* Worse than it did that day on the beach, for some reason. René glances briefly my way, so I widen my eyes and force my head to bob to the beat.

By the time the song ends, I'm solidly back on the ground. Carlos loves it. He agrees it absolutely *has* to be the first single. I wait for a sign from René. A smile or a wink. *Anything.* Something to let me know he no longer feels the way he did when he wrote that song. But I don't get one.

James and I walk down the hall and turn in the direction of the pool, just as Camila's coming in the opposite direction.

"They're out by the pool," she drones, forcing a faint smile in our general direction. She's flawless today. Her makeup

looks like it's been airbrushed on, and she's wearing a beautiful, flowy, peach dress. Yet, there's something off about her. All
day, I've picked up a strange vibe. Like she's secretly miserable.
Her eyes are puffy and her voice is hoarse, as though she's been
crying. It occurs to me that *everyone* seems off. Santiago hasn't
been himself today either. I wonder if the same thing is upsetting Camila, Santiago, *and* James.

The living room's removable wall is gone. The space opens
dramatically out to the pool and is lit solely by a lamp that curls
over the deep burgundy velvet couch.

Carlos is alone on the couch, cradling an acoustic guitar.

"I think it's called *Searching for Sixto*, something like that.
The documentary I was telling you about. You have to see it,"
Carlos says to James as we approach, then adds to me, "René
will be right back."

"I'll check it out, thanks," James replies.

"Thanks!" I echo. "Can I ask you a few questions while we
wait for René?"

"Absolutely."

"What do you think about the album?" I stuff my wireless
earphones back into my ear.

He waves a hand in the air, like the answer is obvious. "It's
incredible, it's..." He shakes his head, searching for the right
words. "It's going to blow everyone away. People think they
know El Rico, and that's the magic of this album. It's bigger
than anyone's preconceptions. I love it. I couldn't be prouder."

He's right, of course. It was impossible not to get swept up
in their shared excitement today as they listened to the album.
And as René made strides on incorporating the bomba music
from last night into one of the songs. It's one of my favorites
on the album, bringing the traditional, vivid feel of bomba to a

modern dance party track. So I get it, and I'm happy for René. The most important person who could show up at this juncture did. Of course he's been distracted. And of course he'd want him to hear *all* the songs.

We have a plan, I remind myself. In less than three hours we're going to see each other again. "Let's meet tonight at the mindless statues," René said just before we got back on our ATVs to leave the beach.

I felt weightless when we were together. But after hearing "Take It Off" again, gravity's pulling me down. And it feels *stronger* than before.

René reappears, flying over the steps waving a shiny, silver trumpet in his hand. He crosses the room with a bounce, and takes a seat on the couch next to Carlos.

"Where did you find that?" Carlos roars excitedly.

"It was a gift from Camila."

Carlos rests the guitar on his lap and leans forward with interest. "*¿Sabes tocarla?*"

"Not at all," René responds, making Carlos crack up. "What do you want to play?"

Carlos thinks for a moment and then begins to play the guitar. I recognize the tune, but then second-guess myself because there's no way Carlos Miguel is about to sing Carole King's "It's Too Late." He slows down the melody, and adds his sweet, overly emotional voice, making the song feel more hopeful. René lifts the trumpet to his lips and joins in. It's messy and slightly off key, but somehow it fits. Carlos smiles in agreement as he continues singing.

I tap James on the shoulder and signal for him to switch up the angle. We step out of the living room and get as close as we can to the pool. I check the new shot on the monitor. From here, the dimly lit living room resembles a stage. It's a really cool shot, but makes me feel so disconnected from René. Like I'm a satellite that's simply passing by on its orbit.

Neil Diamond's next. They never quite take any of it too seriously, but at the same time give all of themselves in every performance. They improvise for a while. Using an app on his phone, René creates a drum beat and makes it play on repeat. He then adds a bass guitar and a bell and somehow all that belongs too.

Between songs, they drink beers and Carlos shares some details of a tour he's been planning. When René talks about his upcoming tour, my breathing gets short and jagged as it all sinks in. Who René is and what he's about to become when this album is released. I truly don't know what I was thinking. How could I let myself fall for him like this? I touch my lower lip, searching for the sensitive spot, but it's all better.

Chapter 40

ON MY MONITOR IS A CLEAR, HIGH-QUALITY IMAGE OF A SUPER-
star struggling to maneuver his boat away from our narrow
dock. It takes him a few tries but eventually he gets it. René is
in the foreground of the shot, waving goodbye, and I'm standing beneath the pergola near the pool.

I check my cell. One hour and twenty minutes to midnight.

I turn the monitor off as René and James stroll back to the
house. When he reaches the lawn, René stops and looks off in
the direction of the cottages.

"Can we talk?" he says.

"Does it need to be right now?" I can't see Camila, but I can
hear her through René's microphone.

"Yes." He seems tense. "Let's go over here."

What could this be about? Does this have something to do
with her attitude all day? He guides her to the steps that lead
down to the beach as James reaches me.

"Do you want anything from the kitchen?" he asks, his
forehead damp from hauling the heavy camera around in the
muggy night air.

"No, I'm good." As I follow him inside, I pull one of my wireless earpieces out, but leave the other one in. I tell myself I'll take it out in a second. When I reach the kitchen. When I step onto this floor tile. Okay, the next tile. With René's breathing in my ear, I make it across the grand common room, and take a seat on the bench by the window. From here, I have an unobstructed view of René and Camila on the beach.

"Are you going to tell me what's going on?" René says at last. "*¿Qué te pasa?*"

"Hey." James takes a seat in front of me and sets the camera down. In my earpiece, I can hear the waves crash loudly on René's microphone. I peek at the camera on the table. Though it's no longer recording, it's still turned on, which explains why I can still hear him.

"Me? What's wrong with *you*?" Camila snaps defensively. "I cannot believe you denied Carlos a track."

"Did you tell him to come?"

"No. Santiago called him."

"Yeah, that's what he said, but going behind my back doesn't sound like Santiago. It sounds like you."

"No, you *did not* just say that to me!" Camila shrieks, making my eyes widen.

This is so wrong. I cannot listen to their conversation. I need to take the earpiece out, but my arms are too heavy to move.

"You know, can I just say," James starts, nudging in closer to me on the bench, "you are *not* yourself." Behind him, I see René and Camila on the beach. She's standing so close to him, no wonder her voice comes in so clearly through René's mic.

"What do you mean?" I refocus my gaze on James.

"I mean since we dated. You're a totally different person."

I sit up. "Is this about the fried foods?"

James sighs deeply but doesn't respond.

I don't think René's responded either.

"Do you even know why I ended things between us?" James tilts his head.

"I know you mean well, Cami. But you need to trust me."

"Trust you?" Camila's indignant. "How could I? I had to hear it from Santiago you were seriously thinking of killing Natalia's track."

"Uh, I think you said we were better off as friends." I pull more hair over my earphone.

"Yes, but do you know why?"

"No."

"So, why didn't you ask?" James sounds wounded.

"See? I knew it!" Camila shouts. "That's why I told Santiago to play it onstage for the press. So you'd have to keep it."

"What?" René's dumbfounded.

"Because..." I pause, trying to keep my head straight. "I assumed it was bad. Something bad to do with me," I elaborate quickly. "Besides, the past is in the past, it's all good. You know me, I prefer to look forward."

"I *thought* I knew you." James sounds pained. "And I disagree. Sometimes it's important to look back. Especially when it could help you now." He gestures toward the studio. I look off in that direction, pretending I have no idea what he could be referring to.

René huffs in my ear. I glance in his direction and see he's looking down at the ground.

"There *is* something I need to tell you," Camila says in a low voice.

James is talking to me so I try to tune her out, but I can't. And removing the earpiece isn't happening. My arms feel like lead. Is Camila finally going to tell René how she feels about him? Maybe she's been waiting until he was done with the album? Other than fine-tuning some of the songs, he's technically done.

"Did you hear me? I said I'm in love." Camila sounds like she's speaking through gritted teeth.

"No. No way," René barks dismissively. "You're kidding me, right?" He sounds distressed. I glance out the window past James.

"Why? What's the problem?" Camila shouts, making me lean away from the window.

"Believe me, I know what Santiago's like with women." René's got a hand on his head. "How long has this been going on?" he asks.

Camila says something under her breath that I can't make out.

The room is spinning and I don't want to hear any more. I need to pull the earpiece out, but James is looking right at me. René seems more upset about Camila seeing Santiago than he is about her meddling on his album. And he sounds worse than upset; he sounds *jealous*.

James's face comes back into focus. I know he's been talking for a while, but I've missed it all. And now he's just sitting there, waiting for me to respond.

"Could you, um, expand on that?" I ask, leaning in.

"Expand? On how you were when we were together?"

"A little bit, yeah."

"Well, how about robotic, distant, frigid."

"All right. That's enough. I got a clear picture now."

"I always felt like you were somewhere else. Like you were checked out." I tap the hair over the earpiece to make sure it's still covered. "I just kept thinking you'd eventually open up or let me in," James continues, "but you never did. I knew that you'd lost your dad, but anytime I asked you about it, you shut down. And then I turn around and"—he checks the kitchen to be sure we're still alone—"you're sharing stories about him with this guy. Playing him a song your Dad recorded. Dani, I didn't even know your father was a musician."

"I'm sorry." It stings to be reminded of this, even if it felt necessary for me at the time. "So why didn't you stay in the room when I played it?" I try to defend myself.

"Because I was hurt." He's aghast. "You weren't playing it for me. You were playing it for *him*." He rubs his forehead. "We dated for a year, Dani. And you open up to *this guy*?"

"You sound jealous."

"I am, but not because I want to get back together," he says, and waves a limp hand in my direction. "I'm just saying, it would have been nice to get this version of you. The trusting and open one."

His words are a kick in the gut. He's wrong, for one. I'm not feeling very open at the moment. And as far as trust goes, the earbud in my ear would say otherwise.

"I just want to say, keep it up." James presses a hand on mine. "I'm happy for you."

"I don't know what more you want from me! I've given you everything, René. Everything!" Camila's yelling now. Loud enough for James to hear. He turns to look behind him, so I yank out the earpiece.

Chapter 41

I took my time washing my face. Scrubbing in perfect circles, as though I were in a commercial for a sudsy facial wash. I opened all the windows and the sliding glass door, but didn't bother tucking in the mosquito netting. Now I'm lying here watching it hover above the bed like a tethered ghost.

Last time I checked, it was a quarter to midnight. I'm not going. There's absolutely no way. I need to prepare for the interview in a few days and focus on getting this job done. On *keeping* my job. I still have to cover Meri's tutoring bill, and the hefty final invoice for our new windows should be arriving any day now.

I can't let all these feelings get in the way. Everything I've promised Maureen is hanging on this interview. Every idea they've loved requires René really opening up.

This morning he had me floating and high on life. Now I'm still feeling high, but no longer in a good way. More like on a tightrope.

My head is a mess of thoughts. The way René reacted to finding out about Camila seeing Santiago didn't just sound like a concerned friend. There may be some feelings there he's never explored. Then again, I've only known him a few weeks and I've seen Santiago hit on me, our ayurvedic chef, and a mango fruit vendor. If he's been seeing Camila this whole time, there could be reason for concern.

I check my phone on the bedside table. It's 12:04 a.m. I rise in a state of panic. What if he's still there, waiting for me? I can't just *not* show up. I slip on sandals and take long, quiet strides down the hallway.

When I reach the arch that leads to the sculpture garden, I clock what I'm wearing. "Shit." I'll be *saying* I want to keep things professional, but my silk pajama shorts will be sending a different message.

Maybe he isn't even there. I try to force the idea, but the truth is, I'm basically sprinting because I know he is. This doesn't offer me any kind of relief. Instead, it feels as though someone's raised the tightrope, making it even farther to fall. He'll be there but this is El Rico we're talking about. There's no scenario where this doesn't end badly for me.

Possibly worse than it did for Camila. Like with her, he'd have this fling with me and then keep me around at the label, heartbroken but forced to flutter about working for him.

I turn the corner and find him sitting on the steps, facing the sculptures, his back to me.

Hearing my footsteps on the deck, he looks back. "I was beginning to think you were blowing me off." His smile makes me feel physically incapable of holding a conversation.

I try to smile, but my face is numb. I reach him, then stand for a moment debating what to do. Can't this be quick? Do I really have to sit down?

"You okay?" he asks, his head tilted up, watching me.

"Yeah, I just…" I take a seat next to him and trail off. The peace I feel just by being near him is completely at odds with the hostile thoughts squirming around my mind. It's warm out and the waves are muted tonight. They're coming in low and long, reaching up onto the shore, then retracting slowly back into the sea.

"How are you?" he asks patiently.

"I'm okay." I take in the empty, smiling heads of the sculptures and then turn toward him so we're facing each other. "Listen." I have to shove the word out.

René's head and chest draw back slightly. Just enough for me to notice. He knows what I'm about to say. Nothing good ever comes after "Listen." "Listen" is the beginning of an end, a preparation for a letdown. He's come here thinking there'd be more kissing. Possibly sex on this beach. None of which can begin with "Listen."

"I'm sorry if I was distant today," he interjects, "with Carlos here and—"

"Oh, I totally get it. And it's for the best. Not to worry, we're on the same page."

"I'm not sure we—"

"Well, we're *practically* on the same page. Same chapter!" I correct myself. "Anyway, what I want to say is, we need to…" I wish my voice wasn't so shaky. "Keep things professional. It's just better for work…and everything."

René snaps his gaze toward the beach and we sit in silence for a moment. "Do you regret what happened?" His earnest tone tugs my heart.

"No. I don't regret it." These words come easy.

"So why not see where it goes?"

See where it goes? Why would I stick around and let these

feelings grow, only to be let down and heartbroken at some later date? "I can't do that. Besides, it was just one night, right?" I feel my cheeks burn.

"Did I do something to upset you? I'm trying to understand what happened."

I have nothing to say. Nothing I *can* say anyway. I can't admit I was eavesdropping and heard Camila crying. I can't tell him I want to avoid ending up like her. Or that James saying I was more open, more myself with René has also somehow contributed to this shutdown.

"Tell me. Give me a chance to . . . I don't know, try to fix it." He lets out a nervous laugh.

I have to look away. I scan the darkness that is the horizon and rest my gaze on the lights of a large, barge-like boat in the distance. Of all the reasons pushing me to this, I decide to bring up the one I know I can defend.

"It's obvious, just like in the song." I brush off a few grains of sand sticking to my skin just below my ankle. "When you played it for Carlos, it was clear to me this was, we shouldn't . . ." I stumble. René's forehead has creased and it's making me lose my patience. I can almost hear his thoughts racing, still working it all out. What *isn't* he getting? I clear my throat. "When I heard that song today, I felt attacked all over again. And that's just not how I want to feel."

He exhales, exacerbated. "I can't believe you still haven't heard the song."

"What? Yes I have. Tonight may have only been the second time, but it's plenty."

He doesn't speak. His legs are crossed and stretched out in front of him, and one foot has begun tapping the other intermittently.

I let out a long sigh. *Keep your eye on the prize. One step in front of the other gets you…* How does that one end? *Gets you somewhere eventually.*

"René," I begin calmly, "this is exactly why we can't do this. We need to focus on next week."

"Next week?" he repeats, clueless.

"Well, it's your last week in the studio and"—I pause—"there's the interview."

This does it. His feet have stopped tapping. Bringing up the interview has ended it. I can see it in his eyes. I've switched on a harsh, cold white light and sucked the warmth out of the night air.

"Well, I'm just gonna," I mutter as I stand. "I'll see you tomorrow." I wait a beat for him to say something, a burning sensation spreading in my chest.

"Cool, yeah." René scratches his scruffy beard.

I walk away, fighting the urge to look back one more time. When I reach the arch, before I turn the corner, I give in.

He's sitting in the same position, facing the sculptures. Except this time, he seems farther away and impossibly still.

Chapter 42

A WEEK LATER, I CLIMB THE METAL SPIRAL STAIRCASE FEELING numb and wobbly. It was Camila's idea we use René's rooftop for the interview. There's a Zen-looking garden with oversize fanned palms, plush rattan furniture, and a clear view of Culebrita Island.

"What do you think?" James asks, stepping away from the camera.

We've set up the interview beneath a pergola wrapped in climbing plants.

"Yeah, Dani, how do I look?" Camila beams. James asked her to sit in the interview chair so he could adjust the lighting.

I take a seat and look at the monitor. It's absolutely perfect. Camila's glowing under the warm lights and series of sun reflectors James has set up, Culebrita Island framed on her right.

"Beautiful."

Camila's been so much happier this past week. Things between her and René seem to have smoothed over, though they haven't spent as much time together. She and Santiago are now open about their relationship. They spent their afternoons in the pool, while René and Ángel took the boat out. Ángel flew in a few days ago to help facilitate the checkout.

René and I have barely spoken. He's been busy fine-tuning all the songs and recording a new one I love. A genre-blending sexy jam that combines reggae with salsa.

"We're all set." James is in a better mood, too. He and I have slipped comfortably back to a good place and we've even gone jogging together a few mornings. It seems getting things off his chest helped. Everyone around me seems better off after unloading their feelings. But not me. Anything I've unpacked while I've been here feels stuffed back in again. I'm like one of those jack-in-the-box dolls. All wound up and ready to pop.

I grab the clipboard out of my bag and take a deep breath. René will be here any minute.

I need to be creative. I need to be persuasive. This interview needs to wrap everything we've filmed over the past month with a tidy bow. I know the label will see this as the ultimate test. For him *and* for me. If René can't give his own label a proper interview, how will he handle the endless rounds of press needed to promote the album in the coming year? And how can I keep my job if he won't open up after I've had a month to get him to warm up to me? What will that say about my ability to connect with artists?

I hear the clang of the metal steps. Ángel arrives and, after approving the interview look, joins Camila on a bench near the pergola. Does it concern me they're going to stay for the interview? A little. But having some familiar faces around for René can't hurt.

When I hear the next set of steps on the metal staircase, I find I'm all out of inspirational quotes. I know I can do this. Well, I *have* to do this.

René appears on the roof wearing head-to-toe white linen. He's had a fresh buzz cut and, as always, looks magazine-spread-ready.

"Hold on." He takes his sunglasses off, and Camila pops over to take them from him. I see the move as a personal favor and sink more comfortably into my chair.

"Well, first, thank you for doing this." I only mean to sound professional, but it comes out a bit frigid and it hurts treating him like this, like he's just another recording artist.

He uncrosses his legs, stretches the fabric out, then crosses them again. "It's what you need, isn't it?"

"Well, yes," I stammer. "It's what the project needs."

"Right." He forces a smile.

I smooth down the pages on my clipboard. "Okay, why don't you tell us how you felt when you first heard you were getting a record deal."

René looks at the camera and then looks away, as though collecting his thoughts.

"You know what?" I lift the clipboard in the air. "We don't need these." I open the bag hanging from my chair and tuck the questions away. "Just keep your eyes on me, and take me through the process of putting together your debut album. As though you were just telling me a story. If you miss anything, I'll ask you about it at the end."

"Sure, that's fine." Our eyes lock, and we both smile. His acquiescing, mine offering support.

"Two years ago, I took a meeting with a label," René begins. "Not Ocean," he clarifies. "The last thing I'm thinking is that it's for another duet. It can't be. Those usually don't require this kind of formal meeting. They had this huge food spread, and I was signing autographs and taking pictures. The president's daughter was a big fan and she was there with a group of her friends. When we finally got down to business, it turned out all they were offering me was the duet I did with Natalia. Of course I was honored, but it was hard to focus on that." He pauses. "I thought my life was about to change."

It's a relief this approach is working but I'm taken aback by just how well. He's being so *open*.

"Since I started out, I've been making other people more famous. And I..." René clears his throat. "I don't know when exactly, but that had stopped being enough." This isn't feeling like an interview. It's as though he's talking just to me and the camera isn't even there.

"When Ocean Records bought out the Puerto Rican label I had signed with, I had a hard time trusting them at first. I believed they didn't care about me or know anything about my music." He flashes me a grin and I feel my cheeks go hot. "But then they let me come here and do whatever I wanted. It's been a dream come true. I guess it's like with any relationship—things can't be one-sided. You have to trust people have your back and hope they know you'll have theirs, no matter what happens." He glances over at Camila and smiles warmly.

For the next two hours, René talks about each song on the album—his inspiration, the music, the desire to make something authentic and new. When he gets to the song about me, I realize I'm holding my breath.

"I meant for it to be a solo album, but there is one duet. The idea was kind of forced on me"—he shoots Camila a playful look—"but it ended up being an important piece of this album. Having Natalia participate on a track"—he pauses—"provided some closure I didn't know I needed."

He looks at me, his gaze softened. "I never cheated on her. You asked me"—he squeezes his eyes shut and corrects himself—"*people* have asked me why we didn't set the record straight. Well, I'll tell you." He leans in. "She wanted to defend me back then, but I asked her not to say anything. You see, being dumped simply because she didn't want to be with me or I wasn't famous enough didn't really work for the El Rico brand." His eyes have gone glossy.

"René, I don't—" Ángel tries to interrupt but René waves him off.

"It's fine, right? This is the kind of stuff you wanted, right?" There's hurt in his voice. "You see, early on, I created this seductive, arrogant persona. A weasel. He served me well, and I'll admit at times I lived up to it. But I've outgrown him and I've decided this album is going to be called simply *René*."

There's nervous laughter coming from Ángel and Camila, but I can't look away.

"Okay, well"—I let out a breath—"you've covered every—"

"Are you sure?" He sounds defeated. "There has to be something more. For example, I've never said where 'El Rico' comes from. They assume it's salacious, but 'Rico' was my nickname growing up. It may be hard to believe, but I wasn't much of a talker when I was a kid," he says dryly. "I loved my grandma's cooking. One day she was feeding me and 'rico' was my first word. How's that? You think you got enough?"

"Yes," I say firmly.

"Here's another one," he continues, ignoring me. "People are always curious about the hidden tattoo on the inside of my lip. It's not very El Rico either, but..." He lifts his hand to his mouth. "James, you're going to want to zoom in," René says, tugging at his lower lip.

"No," I say.

"It's fine." His hand tugs down at his lip.

"Seriously, stop!" I shout, rising from the chair.

I feel a range of conflicting emotions. Relief, because we got everything we needed from the interview. *And then some.* But there's also this sticky, uneasy feeling. *Why did he do that? Did René have to be so damned obliging?* And what could he possibly be thinking by dropping "El Rico"?

I wrap the cord around the video monitor and hand it to James, who immediately unwraps it. I try to break down one of the lights, then remember I don't know how.

"Are you sure you want to go back?" James sounds worried.

"Yeah, I need to get home. The earlier the better," I respond coolly.

"You don't want to enjoy another day here?" He reaches beneath a chair for a power strip. "The flight change was only a hundred bucks. We could go snorkeling."

"No, thanks." I take a seat, but then get back up. "But I'm glad you'll get to enjoy the island." James watches me carefully as he packs a light into its box.

I walk to the other side of the rooftop and find my cottage just across the garden. This is where René must have been standing the night he saw me in my underwear on the balcony. Instantly, I feel exhausted and my body aches. Like I'm coming down with something. *He was telling the truth.* The view of the lounger *is* partially blocked by the railing.

I find James sitting on the ground, taking a break.

I grab a bottle from the cooler and take a seat next to him.

"Cheers." He holds his water bottle in the air. "You did it."

"Yeah," I say half-heartedly. "It was touch-and-go there for a moment, huh?"

"Thanks for bringing me." He unrolls the sleeves of his shirt. "I hope I was able to get you what you wanted."

"Yes, you were great." I feel like we're no longer talking about work. "Thank *you*. For everything."

We sit there watching the sun set, feeling mutually spent. The two of us on this roof, unable to move, feels like we're wrapping up more than this project.

I rest my head back on the planter. "Um, so, when my dad passed." James turns to look at me, waiting for me to continue. "I found this home improvement catalog on his nightstand." I feel my eyes sting. "There were all these pages folded to items he must have wanted. A picnic table, outdoor lights, a screen to hide the trash cans. It took me two years, but I bought every single one of those things." The last of the sun dips behind a cloud. "I know this sounds strange, but I was glad to have something to focus on."

James leans over and hugs me. Gently at first, then tighter, and I let the air leave my body.

"Thanks for sharing that." He squeezes me tighter. "Best gift you've ever given me."

"Really? Better than the coffee bean cuff links?"

"The ones that looked like poop emojis?"

I nod.

"Yeah. Even better than those."

Chapter 43

I FEEL LIKE I'M ON A CONVEYOR BELT. MOVING ALONG, DOING what I need to do without putting up a fight. I find Ángel, Santiago, Camila, and René at the fire pit. I'm leaving early tomorrow morning, so I need to say goodbye and thank them for everything. What I *want* to do is slip away quietly into oblivion, but being social and polite is part of the job.

René's the closest, but I start with Camila. I get a perfectly cordial hug from her and a kiss on each cheek from Santiago. Ángel makes me promise to let him know if there's anything I need for the behind-the-scenes. When I get to René, he stands, hugs me briefly, and says something near my ear I don't quite register. *Suerte? Cuidate?* Good luck or take care.

"Thanks, you too. And hey, you can . . . let Ángel know if there's anything you don't want us to use from the interview." I hadn't planned to say this, but I want to give him the chance to change his mind. "What you said about Natalia, for example."

He looks into my eyes and takes a deep breath. "Do whatever you want with it."

I nod a couple of times and try to seem breezy as I walk away, the pebbled path crunching loudly beneath my feet.

After a long, much-needed embrace by the car at airport arrivals, Meri spits out a series of fun-loving updates, catching me up on the happenings at home. *Mom's a redhead again, don't ask why Benny Moré has a limp, oh, and the duck is gone.*

"What do you mean, 'the duck is gone'?" I throw my suitcase in the trunk of the car.

"Mom released him." Meri eyes me suspiciously as I take the passenger seat. "Is that my dress?"

"Yes. Why?"

She looks doubtful. Like she can't believe I'm wearing it. "Nothing, I love it on you." She grins affectionately.

"Where did she release him? Did she take him to the lake?"

Meri turns to me, probably to be sure I'm being serious.

"I think so. Why?"

"There are some gators in that lake. Do you know if it was in the morning or at night?"

"I don't know!"

I look out the window and try hard not to envision an alligator swallowing Baby whole the moment Mom turned around. He was in our care for two months. He probably forgot how to forage or behave around other ducks. What if they no longer want him around? I'm certain Baby will either be eaten by a gator, starve to death, or die of loneliness.

"So?" Meri glances at me. "What happened with René?" She seems to be holding in a scream of excitement.

"Nothing." I harden my face. "I mean, we had a really good

time, but nothing came of it, obviously. Which is totally fine by me. It was just a one-time thing."

Her face scrunches up, confused. "What happened?"

"Nothing. Just like I knew it would. It's all good. It's fine." I throw a hand in the air. "In fact, I think that's why I was so comfortable around him. *That's* why I had such a good time. Because I knew it was just an in-the-moment thing. It's fine."

"The more you say, 'It's fine,' the less I believe you."

I shrug. "Whatever. He agrees, we're on the same page."

Meri's eyes narrow. "Did he actually say that?"

"Not exactly. Not with those words."

"What words *did* he use?"

I exhale loudly. "I don't remember." I'm unable to mask the shift in my tone to something more irritated. "I'm sorry, I really don't want to talk about it right now."

I desperately want us to start being more honest with each other, but I physically can't say another word about René. I just want to get home and clean the grill or pull the weeds between the pavers. Thankfully, I have the weekend before I have to go back to work. Before I'm forced to relive it all by reviewing the footage from the past few weeks. For the next two days, I need everything to be as it was.

We pull into the driveway, and for an instant, what I need flies out the window. *Literally.* The new windows have completely altered the look of our home. I mean, they're sturdier-looking, for sure. But they're more modern than what was there before and the house has lost some of its quirky personality. It takes me a second to get used to them, and to recognize our home again, behind the blooming flamboyant tree in the front yard.

I drop the bags by the door and follow Meri to her room.

It's as though her closet and large dressers have spit up all at once. Tops, skirts, accessories, handbags, everything she owns is either on the bed or arranged into small piles on the floor.

"You're purging," I say excitedly, gently pushing a mound of colorful earrings out of the way so I can sit on the bed.

"Sort of. I want to move the furniture around and they're easier to move without anything in them. But look, that pile is for donation." She beams, knowing I'd be proud of her. I see where she's pointed and find the smallest pile of the bunch. I'm not sure I'd even call it a pile. It's a faded leather handbag with a purple bra on top.

"So, how are you feeling?" I ask carefully.

"I know what you're thinking," she says, standing in front of the tallest dresser, "but I'm not changing my mind about nursing."

She pulls a drawer out and dumps it all on the bed. Inside are all items that should not have been living side by side. A workout bra, thongs, belts, sunglasses, and a large bottle of hairspray.

"That's not what I'm thinking."

"I'm sorry." She glances at me, and the look in her eyes is so sincere, it makes me melt. "Believe me, I tried."

"I know you did. I just wish you hadn't forced it for so long if that's how you were feeling."

"It was, I don't know. You've always done so much for me, I just..." She trails off, unable to finish her thought.

"You thought you had to pay me back by studying something I'd approve of?"

"I know you never said that. It just felt that way."

As Meri disappears behind the bed to grab another drawer, I feel slightly defensive. Then again, all those times when I thought about telling her to quit and try something else, something always held me back. Nursing was safe and steady. I had convinced myself I was just being supportive, but deep down it was what *I* wanted for her.

The sound of Meri laughing brings me back to the present. She's holding a small eyeglass repair kit. "You know when you're looking for something, you never find it? Do you know how many of these I have now?" She tosses the kit on the donation pile, pushes a tall dresser over a few feet, and takes a few steps back to admire it. There's something different about her. She seems lighter, more enthusiastic. For one, she's genuinely enjoying making this mess. Perfectly content to sleep in it if she has to, until she figures out where she really wants things to go.

I head to the kitchen and stop to admire the large window in the dining room. There's a pup on his bed and a cat in her tree enjoying the warmth of it. I scan the house, not finding anything that needs doing. It's strange, Mom not being here. She'll be home later from an overnight trip to Palm Beach with her new boyfriend. I imagine this is what a parent must feel when their kid goes away to college. Missing them, while at the same time knowing it's what's best for them. And for you.

Standing in front of the kitchen sink, I'm transfixed on what must be Mom's latest floral creation on the windowsill. I pick it up in awe of her talents. It's a small cat made entirely out of daisies and other flowers sitting in a wicker basket. It has delicate snapdragons for whiskers, and she's added felt triangles for ears and small googly eyes on a sunflower. It's the most adorable thing I've ever seen.

I place it carefully back on the shelf and notice a few smudges on the new kitchen window. I grab the stepladder and the window cleaner from under the sink and get to work. I spritz generously, satisfied to have something to do. After I've wiped off the smudges, I put everything away and I'm almost out of the kitchen when I turn back to admire my handiwork.

What I expect to see is a sparkly, clear window. Instead, the only thing I notice is I've missed a pretty big smudge near the top. Probably because it's behind one of the three glass pendant lamps that hang over the sink. Back on the stepladder, I spray and wipe again, but the window cleaner doesn't get it out. It's less of a smudge and more like tape or glue residue or something. I find the retractable knife in the miscellaneous drawer, get back on the stepladder, and delicately scrape it all away. Feeling lighter, I step off the ladder, and the knife taps against one of the lamps as I pull away.

The glass pendant falls and shatters into pieces. I'm stunned. I mean I *barely* tapped it with the knife. That glass shade must have been hanging on for dear life to have fallen so easily. There's broken glass everywhere. In the sink, on the counter, on the floor. And Mom's floral cat has fallen headfirst into the sink and come completely undone.

I don't even know where to start. Everything is so much worse off. There are small shards of glass on so many surfaces. The naked bulb is hanging there next to two lamps, looking disorderly. I'll need to buy a whole new lamp. The floral cat. My chin starts to quiver and I burst into tears.

I wake up to a blurry redhead sitting next to me on the bed. Her hand is so impossibly soft on my forehead, I think I might still be sleeping. I try again with one eye closed and one open. "Mom?"

She comes into focus and the first thing I do is marvel at her hairdo. Expertly brushed over to one side in a low ponytail. Glamorous yet unwavering, like a contestant on *Dancing with the Stars*.

"I'm so sorry about the lamp. And the cat."

"Did you like it?"

"The floral cat? It was beautiful...before I decapitated it."

She chuckles and pushes a strand of hair away from my face. "Good, because that's my new business idea," she announces.

"Oh yeah?"

"I'm going to make arrangements in the shape of people's pets." She throws her head back, to punctuate the idea. "They send me a photo and I'll ship them a floral bouquet that looks like their cat or dog."

"That's...brilliant." I can't help but see all the potential problems. Has she considered what it would cost to ship fresh floral arrangements? The cost of packaging? What defining features of someone's beloved pet will she *really* be able to capture with carnations? But instead I say, "People love their pets and they're willing to do anything for them."

"That's what I was thinking." She squeezes my arm. "I could start in Miami, so I can deliver the arrangements myself, obviously. But it's still a big city, so we'll see."

She rests her hand on my forehead and I shut my eyes again. I feel simultaneously better and worse. I'm not sure I can cry again, without replenishing my fluids first. Earlier, I threw myself on the bed and cried so hard and for so long, I gave myself a headache.

Low, guttural howls came from somewhere deep inside. And

when they'd subside, I'd see René again. Standing by the fire pit when we said goodbye. And I'd get right back to the business of howling.

After a while, the pain loosened its grip and I started to laugh. Grateful to be feeling anything at all. I think I'd stopped believing I had the potential for this kind of pain in me. It would come and go in waves like: *Yeah! I'm alive. Oh, but it hurts so bad. Wow, I can feel things! But whoa, it's painful.* The lows were so painfully low, but during the breaths, when I came up for air, I felt almost euphoric. I may have also had a high fever.

"What time is it?" I ask Mom groggily. There aren't any lamps turned on in the room, but my door is open and light is spilling in from the hallway.

"It's almost midnight."

"And you're just getting home?" It's my lame attempt to sound like a worried parent.

Mom laughs. "Yes, and?" she asks, playing along.

"Nothing, I'm glad."

There's a knock on the door and Meri peeks in. "Hey." She comes in and sits on the foot of the bed. "Do you want something to eat?"

"No, thanks. I'm not hungry."

I sit up and catch a glimpse of myself in the mirror hanging behind the door. I wipe at the smudged makeup, rest against the headboard, and let out a deep sigh.

"What happened?" Mom asks delicately, and I feel Meri's hand give my leg a squeeze.

For the briefest of instances, I consider *not* telling them. *Push it all down and carry on.* The words come on like a song programmed to automatically play when your alarm goes off. But I can't push another single thing down.

"René," I start, and the tears come again. I wipe them with the back of my hand, already exhausted. "I think we really," I try again, but it hurts too much to say out loud in one go, "connected." I've never cried like this in front of them. *Ever.* "But I got out before I could get hurt." My skin seems to tighten, making me feel smaller. "But it hurts anyway." The tears come again, and Meri gives my leg a squeeze. "So that sucks. I was afraid of being heartbroken, but here I am"—I raise my arms and plop them back on the bed—"broken anyway." Out of the corner of my eye, I swear I see a grin on Mom's face. "Are you . . . smiling?"

"I'm sorry." Her eyes seem glossy too. "It's so good to see you like this."

"Suffering?"

"No," she says with a laugh. "Well, yes, in a way. I'm proud of you. This is a good sign." I give her a look like she's lost her marbles, and I cover my face with my hands. "I always thought you were embarrassed about loving like this. Maybe you thought it was weak or shameful. But it's brave."

All I can do is nod. I agree with my mother. I look to Meri for support, but she only nods too. We all finally agree on something.

"He made me," I begin, needing to say out loud what I've been too afraid to admit to myself, "want something for myself." Mom shoots Meri a look, like she's not quite following. "What I mean is, I never really cared if I had my own family or my own . . . anything. I was happy enough the way things were." The tears begin to flow again. "But he made me wish I had my own life, so I could share it with him." Mom pats my shoulder. "But how do you do this?" I blubber. "How can you ever trust someone with . . . all of that?"

"By trusting." I wait for more, but that's it. That's all she's got to say. I let myself cry. I feel Meri's hand on my foot and Mom holding my arm with both of her hands. It's like they're performing some sort of heartbreak exorcism. And I let them.

When I catch my breath again, I tell them all about hearing Dad's song and how René took me to almost all the places. I share the photos I took and Mom picks a few she'd like printed out and framed. The island feels far away. I can't believe I left this morning. I think about how there was one more place in the song we couldn't find, the dock beneath the sea and shrug at the futility. There will always be things I won't know about my dad. And I start to cry again.

Chapter 44

I FIND THE ONLY PRINT SHOP IN THE DESIGN DISTRICT THAT'S open on a Sunday. "Give me a second," says the twenty-something-year-old in a denim apron. His name tag says "Dash," but he takes his time, ambling down the hall and into a back room.

Yesterday, I slept in and then Meri dragged me to a dance class. It turned out to be, more specifically, a pole-dancing class. She had never tried it before either, but Meri wrapped her legs around the pole like a pro and got a lot of height. I mostly got friction burns. When the teacher told us to crawl on the floor, but "make it sexy," I looked like a soldier trying to save Private Ryan. *But baby steps, right?*

Overnight, there's been a monumental shift between us. I'm no longer the only person who gets to play caretaker. Meri's become my rock, and her solution in my time of need is to get me dancing.

Tomorrow, I'll go back to work. It won't be easy promoting René's album launch, to hear him sing in the footage, and rewatch his interview over and over so I can distribute the best sound bites to the press.

Dash returns and places an enormous paper bag flat out on the tall counter between us. I pull out the 32-by-23-inch color print and swell up with pride at the photograph of the family I took in Culebra, knee deep in crystal blue water, waddling like ducks in a row.

I went with a white frame, white matte border, and museum-ready, reflection-free glass.

"It's really nice." Dash leans over and rests his elbows on the counter. "Did you take it?"

"Yes, in Puerto Rico."

"Cool composition."

"Thanks."

In the image, I'm directly behind them, so it feels like the viewer is heading off to the island too. The little girl sitting on her dad's shoulders turns back toward the lens with a huge smile, happy we're coming along.

I'm proud of it. And actually happy to let Mom gush over something I've done and hang it on the wall.

I can't help but admire the details and quality of the print. The colors are more vivid than I remember. The family's excitement and anticipation for the day ahead leap off the paper. There's a sense of movement and clarity of purpose, and your eye travels along naturally to where they're headed. A stunning island covered in palm trees.

Now that it's this size, I can see the small, sandy beach they headed to, surrounded by a wall of palm trees tightly packed together. There are also a few other people on the island I hadn't noticed that day. I lean down, filled with curiosity about one particular figure. My mouth drops. There's a person standing just off the edge of the island, far from the shore. And seemingly walking on water.

Chapter 45

I PULL THE DOOR WITHOUT HESITATION AND WALK INSIDE THE gourmet food market across the street from work. I didn't tell Maureen why I wanted to meet, nor did she bother to ask. For the past six weeks, we've come here almost every day. We've had lunch, coffee, or late afternoon pastries at the café tucked inside this market as we finalized and then executed the marketing plan for René's album.

It was impossible to detach myself as I put together the behind-the-scenes pieces and sent them off to the press. Practically every single one of my coworkers came by to marvel at René's piano playing or gawk at him swimming in the pool, the bird tattoo on his back gliding beneath the surface of the water. It wasn't easy, but at least René's happy with everything we've done. *Or so we've heard from Ángel.*

Maureen is sitting at a corner table, wearing her chic red reading glasses and hyper-focused over a thick stack of documents. It's 11:00 a.m. and there's a waitress placing drinking glasses on the empty tables ahead of the lunch rush.

"Have you seen this one?" Mo asks, looking up from her reading as I sit down.

René's first single was released last night at midnight, so this morning, Mo's assistant distributed printouts of every single article, online post, and review.

"Which one?"

"*Billboard Global.*" Mo picks up the top page. "'If there were any doubts whether René Rodriguez was worthy of his close-up, they melt away before he gets to the chorus.'"

"I have," I say, wishing I could see René's face when he reads it.

The bomba song ended up being the first single. The traditional music blended with Santiago's reggaeton beats and René's vocals created a joyful dance track people are already calling the perfect summer hit. We made a phenomenal teaser for it that combines the photographs I took of René recording the drummers on the beach, with video of him adding vocals in the studio.

"I ordered us something sparkly," says Mo. "Hope that's okay."

"Sure, why not."

"There's a great piece in *Variety.*" She flips through the stack of printouts. "I just saw it."

"Is it the one that describes René using a bunch of hyphenated words back to back? 'Genre-bending, multi-instrumentalist, soon-to-be chart-topping, global-phenom'?"

"No, but that one's good too. And did you see the one in *Marketing Magazine* online?"

"Yeah, I did see that one, but please don't let that stop you from reading it out loud."

Mo smiles wide and holds up the document. "'Kudos goes to the marketing team at Ocean Records,'" Mo begins, "'for their unconventional campaign to promote René's much-anticipated first single as a solo artist. For twenty-four hours, fans could experience the song before anyone else by stepping inside private dance booths that popped up in select cities across the country. The queues were long, but listeners left happy, and with the ability to preorder the album at the booth, the buzz and sales generated have paid off.'"

The dance booths were my idea. I wanted people to experience the passionate rhythms without any distractions, the way I had on the beach. Besides, I knew it's what René wanted after all, to make people move. While it's nice to get a shout-out, it has a bittersweet sting.

Our waitress places two glasses filled with pink bubbly on the table.

"To you," Maureen toasts. "Congrats, Dani."

"To us," I amend and take a large gulp for some liquid courage. I know I have to shift the subject soon enough.

"'Whether it's with his heartfelt lyrics'"—Maureen has moved on to another article—"'or his pop-up dance booths, René Rodriguez is more *Rico* than ever.'" She flips through the papers.

"Actually, Mo, I need to talk to you." I haven't told anyone about my decision. Not because I'm afraid Mom and Meri will try to change my mind—I just want to make it official first.

"Is everything okay?"

"Yes," I say and decide to spit it out because Maureen's intense joy has switched to just plain intense. "Everything's fine. I just wanted to tell you why I asked to meet up." The lines around her eyes and forehead flatten out again. "I quit."

Maureen is stunned silent, still holding one of the documents out in front of her.

"I'm officially giving my notice, Mo," I continue, excitement spreading down my arms and making my hands shake. "I'll give you plenty of time. It doesn't have to be for a while, actually."

Mo sets the document down. With everything going on, I know I'm leaving things on a good note, but I still hate feeling like I'm letting her down.

"I just want you to know I've loved working together and appreciate every opportunity you've given me. But...I'm moving to Puerto Rico."

"Dani, I—"

"I'm sorry," I interrupt. I'm so nervous, I need to barrel through the speech I've prepared. "I just know from our calendars how far out you count on me, so I wanted to give us enough time to find my replacement. I won't leave you hanging, Mo. And if you hear of anything in the San Juan office or can put in a word at other labels there, that would be great. It doesn't have to be right away. Could be in six months, or maybe even a year. Whatever you need, Mo." It's a huge relief to get it all out, so I down the rest of my drink.

Maureen reaches across the table and gives my hands a squeeze. "How about next month?"

I cough as the bubbles come back up my throat.

"Your counterpart there just gave his notice a few days ago." Mo's eyes widen. "He wants to open his own yoga studio. The kind with a monthly membership," she adds as though this were an important detail.

"What?"

"You'd still report to me, but you'd basically be running your own show. We could pay for your move." The conversation has shifted and now it's Mo trying to convince me to leave. "And put you up for a month while you look for a place to live."

I'm speechless. The idea has been forming since I got back. I've been feeling this intense need to stretch out. It started as just wanting to go back for a visit. That grew into an idea for an extended stay. Then yesterday, at our weekly team meeting, I just *felt* it.

To commemorate the release of the first single, Mo played the final mix of the song for us in the conference room. The bomba music and the sounds of the beach that seeped into the song as René recorded it, they were all calling me back. The rhythm was telling me to move. Not just to get up and dance, but to *move* move.

Now, though I'm still sitting inside a café, nestled inside a fancy supermarket, I'm already there. It's all happening. Limbs are being stretched. I'm learning to make *alcapurrias*. I'm photographing Old San Juan on the weekends.

I told myself I would be practical. To save up money so I could venture out even without a job. But here's Maureen saying I can go right away, and with the safety of working for the same company, doing a job I love.

"Yes, of course. Let's do it," I say, all dopey-eyed and ecstatic that I get to be adventurous *and* practical.

I can see Mom's and Meri's faces when I tell them. They'll probably want to take the credit. Say it's all thanks to the magical egg cleansing I let them do for me when I got home, or the glass of water Mom put by the window with some seashells in it.

Mo jumps into an excited speech about all the new artists I'll be working with. "But"—she tilts her head down, bringing me back to the moment—"I'll need you to start right away, so you won't be able to finish up René's campaign. Will you be okay with that?"

I lean back in my seat and feel the tightness around my heart slacken for the first time since I've been back. There's a year of work ahead on René's first album, promoting the album's release in a few weeks, then the next two singles, the tour, the awards circuit. "Yes, I'm fine with that. The pieces are in a good place. I can hand it all off."

Maureen doesn't know what happened between René and me. How could she know this is exactly what I need? It's a miracle within a miracle. I can finally start to move on from René. And move on with my life.

Chapter 46

I'VE MADE A TERRIBLE MISTAKE. I'VE BEEN LIVING IN SAN JUAN for a week, and everywhere I go, I hear René's first single. The song is on heavy rotation. It blasts out of every other car that passes me as I walk to work. It plays inside grocery stores and restaurants. Two teenage girls passed me on the sidewalk yesterday singing it a cappella. *A cappella!*

And now, as I wake up, it's seeping in through the walls of my new apartment. I press the pillow around my head and cover my ears. The universe has a twisted sense of humor. Or maybe I shouldn't have moved to a place where everyone loves the guy I'm trying to get over. The label put me up in a hotel for a month, but I moved out of it yesterday after only a week. This was the first place I saw, and as soon as I had the key, I ordered a mattress. In the span of an afternoon, I had a new home.

The window in the kitchenette is my favorite feature. It has art deco vibes and lime green textured glass. I open it and René's song comes in louder. I shut my eyes and brace myself for the ending. The song winds down with sounds René recorded himself. I miss him so much, I feel seasick hearing the waves crash and the chorus of one particularly recognizable frog.

I can't let it get me down. It's my first morning in my own apartment. I have so much excited energy, I don't know what I want to do first. I consider walking the hour and a half to El Viejo San Juan, but I'm too hungry. And I don't have any food. Or plates. Or even a table and chairs.

My new neighbor Beatriz recommended a few shops for furniture thrifting. She's a sculptor and her boyfriend, Pablo, is a tattoo artist. They live below me and were the ones playing René's song just now. I met them last night and they've already invited me to a party they're having in a few weeks. They also said I was free to use their terrace whenever I want. Framed by walls of hanging plants, the terrace in front of their apartment has a barbecue, a large wooden picnic table, and two comfy outdoor bean bags.

So far, San Juan hasn't been the switch off of René I was hoping for. But there's plenty of newness and temporary diversions. As soon as I'm settled, Meri's coming for a visit. In the meantime, she's found a reggaeton dance class near work for me to try. The last month in Miami, we were inseparable. Mom too. The three of us made dinners and checked out Meri's favorite thrift stores. I also met and played chess with Mom's new boyfriend, who's actually very considerate and kind. He'll call her on the phone just to play her a song that's made him think of her, and I love that there's music in her life again.

Walking back from the grocery store, I see a familiar face just as I'm reaching my gate. Pale pink tube top. Hair and miniskirt looking a bit frayed at the edges. Camila.

"Dani? What are you doing here?" She glances suspiciously at my building.

"I just moved." I lift the enormous bags of groceries as proof.

"Wow, I hadn't heard. Congratulations."

"Thanks. Wait, do you live nearby?" I think we're both surprised by how excited I am at the possibility of having her as a neighbor. I can't help it—it's comforting to run into someone I know on my first day in my new home. Even if that someone is Camila.

"No, I'm meeting a friend for brunch over there." She points at a café down the street. "What made you move to San Juan?"

"I transferred, so I'm still working at the label." The heavy bags are starting to hurt my hands. "Do you want to come up?"

We take the flight of stairs up to my apartment, and the moment we step inside, she says she loves it. I glance around the room, feeling the same joy and excitement I experienced when I first saw it.

It's cozy and eclectic, with high ceilings, oversized windows, and a terra-cotta-tiled floor. There's a small, triangular balcony, and if you lean out far enough, you can see a sliver of the beach two blocks away. And it's also only a fifteen-minute walk to work.

"When I walked in here yesterday, they had all the windows open and the breeze was so strong." I drop the bags off in the kitchen and join her in the living room. "It reminded me of Culebra. So I took it, right on the spot. And how are *you*?"

"Great." She takes a few steps to the French doors that lead out to the balcony. "I'm strictly styling René now." My smile drops. "We got him a new assistant," she adds, turning around. "Probably for the best, huh?" She gives me a knowing look.

I want to nod or smile, but something's messing with my equilibrium. For the past five weeks, I've eased myself out of any direct work on René's album, but up until last week I was still copied on every email. Every single time I saw his name in the subject heading, it was like a thumbtack prick to the heart. Even though it was followed by words like REVISED BOOTH SKETCH or TOUR MERCH APPROVAL VERSION 2.

Since I moved here, I haven't been cc'd on any emails. Or invited to a single strategy meeting. It's what I needed. Hearing about René hurts too much. And those were just work updates. I hadn't thought of the danger of being around Camila. I'm not ready to hear about René from such a direct source.

"That's awesome. Congratulations," I manage, shuffling my weight. "We should hang out soon," I say, changing the subject. "Once I get some chairs."

"We should," she agrees with a smile. "I'll let you know when I get back from the tour. Have you seen all the looks I've picked out for René?"

"No," I admit, my voice deep. Before I can think up a reason to stop her, Camila's next to me and scrolling through hundreds of photos on her phone. René is everywhere. His hair and scruffy beard are more grown out. I feel like a punching bag receiving quick-hitting jabs.

She scrolls quickly, so I only get a vague sense of what he's wearing. Tank tops. Colorful pants. Shimmery shirts. Baggy jeans. He's posing for the camera, humoring Camila, enjoying the looks she's put together. But when she stops too long to show me a favorite outfit, it's a jab, punch, or uppercut.

"Gorgeous. I mean, *it's* gorgeous. The styling. You're so good at styling."

"This one I absolutely love." She pulls up a photo of René leaning on a car in a leather ensemble. In this one, he seems kind of down to me.

"How's he doing?" I blurt out nervously.

"Good. He and Santiago are in Mexico."

"Oh, right." I remember he was going to be doing press there.

"He's excited about the concert. It's two of his biggest dreams: selling out a stadium and launching a tour here."

"Mm-hmm, that's right." In two weeks, René will be performing here in San Juan the night before the album drops. I know it's his dream, but selfishly, I can't help wondering when it will stop hurting to hear about him.

"Hey." Camila takes a step away from me. "That day on the roof, during the interview, why did you stop René from showing his lip tattoo? That was so...weird."

"Oh, um, you know what, we didn't need it." Camila studies me as I stumble. "I just...I could tell it was important to him," I say in a more serious tone, dropping the act.

Camila's face doesn't budge, but one eyebrow curls ever so slightly. "Yeah, it is."

For two weeks, I've made every excuse *not* to visit Culebra. I mean, how could I *not* try all the restaurants in a two-block radius of my new apartment? And, like, have you really lived in a city before you've visited at least one of its museums? Plus, I needed chairs for the balcony, plants, a toilet plunger, door stops, and curtains.

I'm not out of excuses, but today I took the day off and hopped on the first ferry. René is performing tonight, and the stadium is in the dead center of San Juan. Close to my new office and close to home. *So Culebra it is.*

Tiny, shimmery fish jump in and out of the waves the boat is making, like dragonflies. From the landing, I take a cab to the neighborhood where I spent the morning taking photographs that day and retrace my steps. It's a weekday and still early in the morning, so the beach is empty, except for an older couple, who wave hello as I walk past them.

I strip down to a bathing suit and throw my beach cover-up and sneakers into my backpack. Ahead of me, the island seems farther away than I remember. I gather myself, hold my bag over my head, and start to wade in.

The water is at the height of summer warmth. Every once in a while, I look back to see how far I've come. When I'm about halfway, the older couple is sitting up on their loungers, watching me. I'm about waist deep, heading out to sea, holding a large backpack over my head. Even with their hats and sunglasses on, I can see the concern on their faces. I consider yelling out an explanation. Something, like, "Hey, don't worry! The water is shallow all the way to the island. I photographed a family doing this not too long ago." But I decide a little mystery never hurt anyone, and I keep on walking.

It's a struggle to get onto the beach. Like quicksand, my feet sink in with each step. I have to crawl to avoid toppling over. This is when I realize it isn't sand at all. Instead, each grain is actually a miniature stone or seashell sediment.

I make my way farther up the shore, where the ground is more walkable. I don't know if it was the quicksand or the heat, but I feel weak. As though I've already run a race. Wading waist deep in the ocean for a few minutes is more tiring than it looks. I pull out my water bottle as I walk along the deserted beach.

As I approach the end of the beach, I have mixed emotions. I think this may actually be the last place in my father's song. But I have a strange feeling I'm going to lose something else the moment I find it. If I'm right, I'll have nothing left to find.

No more of his wishes to fulfill. This, I realize, is why I've been avoiding coming here until now.

I see the spot I've been searching for. An area where the water comes right up to the trees. This is the place where I saw the figure in the photograph walking on water.

When I reach it, I brace myself and face the sea. My shoulders drop. It's a dock all right. Sunken a few inches below the shimmering, clear water and made of large planks of wood. It juts out about thirty feet in front of me before it disappears from view.

I hang my backpack on a branch and set up my camera, programming it to take a picture every ten seconds, and then I walk to the shore.

Unceremoniously, I step onto the dock. Out in front of me, the water glides off the surface like it's on ice. You'd think the thing would be covered in seaweed, but it isn't. Instead, the water has weathered the wood in other ways. It's swollen in parts, or rubbed soft like foam. Initially, I was afraid it'd be too slippery to walk on. But now that I'm standing on it, I'm more concerned it'll crack and I'll fall right through.

I take a deep breath and start to walk. I'm ankle deep in the crystal-clear water, and the wood is soft and gives a little with each step. About halfway, I stop. It's creepy walking this far out. Up ahead, I can't tell how deep the water is. Tall waves break near the end of the dock before they ripple gently onto the shore. If I get hurt, there isn't anyone around to hear me call for help. I've left my phone and the rest of my things on the shore, and I didn't even tell anyone where I was going. But I did manage to set a photo timer, so if someone recovers my camera, they may get to see the exact moment I fell through a crack.

I remember my dad's song and the lyrics about this place.

on the dock under the sea
I found my faith and learned to love

Suddenly, I'm ten again, up in a tree with him egging me on from below.

"I don't think I can go any further," I called out, pointing up to the next branch. "It's too far away from this one."

"Keep going. It only looks that way now."

I push on, my eyes watering. The farther I go, the higher the water rises over my calves. Overcome with emotions rushing up and through me, I reach the end. As the next big wave approaches, there's fear and excitement, like the panic that grips you on the roller coaster just before the drop.

I tighten my leg muscles to firm up my stance, and my toes grip the foamy wood. The next wave crashes and I let out a long, happy shriek until I've run out of air.

Remembering I set up the camera, I turn around for the ultimate empowerment selfie. I raise my hands in the air, brace myself for the next wave, and count to ten.

I turn back around to take in the view one last time and feel so at peace. Everything is a message from my dad. Everywhere I look, there's a reminder that he's here and that I belong. The birds, the fishermen on their small boat passing by. They wave at me and it's so sweet. If they only knew what their kind smiles mean to me right now. When they're close enough, I can hear the music they're listening to. Is that? No. *There's no way.*

Chapter 47

Never met a Latina I didn't like, until now
It's the blazer that's got to be off, not your rhythm
But if you play me your B-side, I'll want you beside me, baby

"This is for a Ricky Martin concert." The security guard inspects the backstage badge I'm still wearing around my neck. "From last year," he adds, turning it over.

"Really?" My heart is beating at a disturbing pace, but my face is perfectly still. Call it instinct, but I feel the less overacting I do in this situation, the better.

"In Orlando." He pulls the badge *and my neck* closer.

"I must have grabbed the wrong one." My tone is so nonchalant, it's bordering on boredom. I happen to be using the lanyard as a bookmark, so it was the only one from my extensive collection I had on me.

I dig through my bag. Not too desperate or too hurried. With my performance, I hope I'm conveying: *I absolutely have the correct pass somewhere in here. I'm so certain, I'm not even stressed.*

The frustrating thing is, I was granted access a few weeks ago. Gabriel, the coordinator who took over my position, included me on the list. I know he's here and could easily get me inside, but I may have been a little *intense* when I stormed over to his cubicle demanding to be taken off the list. In my defense, I'd already asked him to stop copying me on every single email about René. So when I saw the access badge email, I snapped.

"It was just as a courtesy since you're going to be living in Puerto Rico by then. In case you wanted to stop by and check in on us. Just looking out for you," he said.

"Well, don't. When I said I was off this project, I meant it. It's all yours. I have every faith in you. I'll be too busy to check in on anyone. You'll just need to rise to the occasion, okay?"

"Yes, you got it."

I can feel the security guard's eyes on me. I wish every bit of my tie-dyed bikini wasn't visible beneath this black crocheted beach cover-up. I spot a patch of sand on my thigh and brush it off. There was no time to change. I only have a short window to talk to René.

When I was in the cab, I dug up the schedule in an email I was copied on a few weeks ago. He should be in the middle of his sound check right now. After that, it's a tight schedule before the concert. He's doing interviews in his dressing room, meet-and-greets with contest winners, and a live interview with a local station. Just as I was arriving, my boss and Meri tried calling but I declined them both. I can't have any distractions. I'm finally putting my own needs first. And what I *need* to do now is let René know I finally heard the song he wrote about me. *Really* heard it this time. The fishermen, it turns out, were listening to "Take It Off." Which was a little surprising because I had no idea we were releasing it as the next single.

I can't lose my nerve now. I mean, I *am* losing it the longer I pretend to dig through my bag. But I really don't want to. I need to talk to René. Tomorrow, he's flying to New York for an album release event, then it will be a storm of promotions, and a three-month tour.

It's clear the guard isn't going to suddenly decide he feels sorry for me and let me in, so I pull my phone out and make the call.

Moments later, the large metal door clunks open and Camila steps outside, looking more tousled the ever. She looks me up and down and, after an unsettlingly long pause, approaches the security guard. "She's okay. She's with me." There's a sparkle in her eye. "She's one of our backup dancers."

The guard pulls an iPad out from under his armpit. "What's the name again?"

"She was a last-minute addition," Camila bursts out, enjoying herself. "But really, who needs to be on the list with moves like these? Show him, Dani."

This *would* explain what I'm wearing and I did start taking dance lessons, but two introductory reggaeton lessons do not a backup dancer make.

"Come on, Camila. I need to save it for the stage." My whole body's slackened. I'm squinting and scratching my hair, making it messier. My poor impersonation of a backup dancer is someone who's drunk and has poor vision. And possibly lice.

Camila stifles a laugh. Two roadies arrive wielding a bulky case on wheels and I take the opportunity to mouth the words "Help me" to Camila.

"Here"—Camila taps into her cell—"I've just sent a text to

the venue manager to add her to the list." In less than a minute, we're waved through.

We walk quickly inside, and when we get to another set of doors, I stop to thank her.

"It's fine," she says. "I should be thanking you." My face brightens at the thought. Camila, of all people, is rooting for me? "We need all the help we can get with this leak," she adds, and all I can fathom is a large pipe bursting somewhere near the stage.

"Leak?" I repeat.

Her eyes narrow. "Yeah." She sounds suspicious. Like I can't possibly *not* know what she's talking about. "Three hours ago, the whole album. Plus, a few other songs he wanted to release as a B-side in a few weeks. They're pretty sure Santiago's storage cloud was hacked because..."

The room has started to spin. All of the noise and activity coming from the other side of the closed doors suddenly seem menacing. "I didn't know."

Camila sizes my getup again. "Then, what are you doing here?" She positions her back to the door, waiting for my response. She's standing guard between René and me, using her body to block me from coming any farther.

"I... I need to talk to him."

"I thought I heard you weren't working on René's album anymore."

"I'm not," I admit. And something about her trying to protect René reminds me of how I've been with my mom and Meri. Camila told me she'd moved on, but I can see she's still very much stuck like I was believing we know what's best.

"Camila." I pause, knowing that what I'm about to say could make me end up back outside. "I know you said you're only styling René now, but do you think, maybe, it's time to step out on your own?" Camila registers this but doesn't budge. "For example, what about your handbags?" I ask abruptly.

She tilts her head, surprised I'm bringing them up. "What do you mean?"

"Are you still making them?" I feel caught. Like I wasn't supposed to notice what she was doing all the time. "I just think they're really nice."

"Yeah, I am. Would you like one?"

"Yes," I say wholeheartedly but quickly.

"Are you still taking pictures?" she asks, repeating my intention.

"Yeah."

"So, I'll make you a camera strap instead," she declares, sure of herself.

"That would be so cool," I respond even quicker, trying to speed things up. "You have so many talents of your own, you could do anything. Design handbags, rugs, any textile really. Your work is beautiful." I speed through my speech, hoping I'm not offending her. "Believe me, I know what it's like to get sucked into someone's orbit. In my case, it was very much by choice. I was stuck, possibly hiding, in that orbit, because it was easier than striking out on my own."

Camila adjusts her hair self-consciously and scrunches up her mouth. "I appreciate you saying that," she says at last.

I nod, relieved. Though the clock is ticking and she's still blocking me.

"And that's why I'm here," I add, worried I'm running out of time, "because I'm done hiding."

My voice quivers a little. Camila doesn't respond. "Do you think you could get me a few minutes alone with him?"

"I have a job to do, Dani. I can't be sucked into your orbit."

"Really?" I ask, aghast. "I have two words for you, projectile vomiting."

Camila grimaces, remembering how sick she felt the night I took care of her. "Ugh. Okay, fine."

The door opens to complete chaos. Half of the hallway is stuffed with people, the other with an endless row of road cases. I don't see Gabriel, the new marketing coordinator anywhere. He really should be here trying to wrangle this situation. This hallway is a fire hazard.

Camila takes my hand and guides me through the crowd. We pass a news reporter speaking loudly in Spanish into her microphone as she records a news piece to the camera. There are men and women with wide catering carts trying to get down the hall. We reach a door with a large group of people lingering nearby. Reporters and a group of mostly young women dolled up in slinky outfits. One girl is holding an enormous teddy bear wearing sunglasses. Camila nods at the security guard, and he opens the door for us.

She stays out in the hall and I step inside, my pulse racing. The room is set up for an interview. There are two cameras, lights on stands, and a boom microphone all aimed at a black leather chair. I take a seat in the leather chair and try my phone again. I need to talk to Mo; I want to help. I need to know how they're managing the leak. I see two missed calls from her, but no messages. I pull up my emails and find one she sent a few hours ago, with the subject heading all in caps. I click on it, but there isn't enough of a signal for it to load. Must every backstage at every arena be an impregnable bunker?

My already racing pulse picks up. All I can do now is think about what I want to say to René. I'm dreading the door opening yet simultaneously feel anxiously giddy about seeing him again.

Sitting in this chair, these huge cameras facing me, I feel like *I'm* the one about to be interviewed. It's my turn to open up and be completely real about my feelings. And I'm ready—I just have no idea where to start.

Ten minutes later, the door opens and Camila appears with René. He freezes when he sees me, like it's clear she did *not* tell him I was here. He opens his mouth to say something but Camila beats him to it. "You've got five minutes."

"I'm supposed to go first." A reporter in a skintight dress tries to push the door.

"Well, you're going second now," Camila says with a smile and shuts the door, leaving René and me alone inside.

"I'm so sorry about the leak," I say, rising. "How are you holding up?" He shakes his head. "It may end up helping you." I tug at my beach cover-up to try to make it longer and more presentable, but it bounces right back. "Some artists do this on purpose."

He rubs the back of his neck, his eyes on my outfit. "Yeah, that's what Maureen said."

"Can we sit?" I motion to the small chair positioned behind the camera.

He glances at it, then back at me. "I'm sorry—"

"No," I interrupt him, determined. "It's me that needs to apologize."

He stands there, considering this, then begrudgingly drops into the smaller chair. I sit in the leather chair, and watch as he takes off his baseball hat, sets it on his knee, and rubs his head anxiously. The look in his eyes makes me wish I could skip ahead to the part where we're all made up and I'm able to hold him and tell him everything's going to be all right.

There's so much I want to say. About my move to San Juan, for one. But that's not why I came here. "I found my father's dock," I blurt out, suddenly excited to share this with him. "It actually *is* sunken beneath the water."

He nods slowly, his face in a grimace. I thought he'd be happy for me, but this information only seems to make him more upset.

"Congratulations," I spit out nervously. "You've sold out tonight. Just you. And about *Billboard.*" The single hasn't budged from the top of the global charts the past two weeks. "Don't let the leak take away all the good things that have happened."

"Thanks," he utters. "Listen, I—"

"Please, let me get this out."

There's a loud knock at the door and Camila pops back in. It hasn't been five minutes. "Of course, Gabriel, I'll let him know," she says loud enough to be heard over the commotion in the hallway. There are two imposing security guards standing over her. "René, they need you to finish the rehearsal. But we have to clear out the hallway, so we're going to do the contest winners' photos first." Then switching back to a volume meant for Gabriel, "Oh, you need another minute, René? You got it." And then she's gone again.

René leans forward, preparing to stand.

"I heard the song," I say, determined.

He sits back. "I'm so sorry, I wanted to—"

"No, it's okay. I mean it."

His eyebrows rise, relieved. "Really?"

"Yes, truly. I still don't think you had to diss my blazers. They're a classic staple, nothing wrong with those," I say with a smile. "But I *really* heard it this time. Well, *most* of it. It was playing on a boat that was passing by when I was on the dock."

He bites his lower lip and there's something in his eyes that makes me unsteady.

"I finally understood." I'm impressed with myself, by how determined I feel to get through this. Even as René's eyes go from stressed out to disappointed. "You didn't want me to change, you just wanted to know all of me," I push on, even if it isn't what he wants to hear. "I just want you to know I've done a lot of crying over the past few weeks. Each time, it seems over something different. And, well"—I clear my throat, my drive waning—"I think they've cleared up my view of things, the tears. They've washed my windows, if you will." I'm rambling. "And then I heard the song again and I couldn't believe I'd been so blind. Or in this case, um, deaf."

René's frown deepens. "Dani, we do need to talk." His voice is somber and he hasn't had the faintest reaction to what I've just said. "But I need to go. The rehearsal was terrible and we had to cut it short for the call with the label about the leak."

I scratch at my thigh nervously and feel my palm wet with sweat. "Right, of course. Just let me say one more thing." He stills patiently. "That night by the statues, I . . . just want you to know I didn't mean what I said. I heard you talking to Camila, through your microphone, and I was just upset." I look at him again, feeling hopeless now. "I just never felt this much . . . for anyone. Or wanted this much for myself."

"Dani," he begs.

I tilt my chin up expectantly, but find a shameful look in his eyes. *We need to talk.* Something's happened since we've been together. Has he met someone else? Of course, why wouldn't he? It's been over two months. That's at least a decade in artist years.

"We're super behind." I can hear guilt in his voice.

"No, no. I get it. And you've got all this press to get through," I say at last, grabbing my bag and standing. "I'm the last person that should be asking you to make them wait." I'm out of breath somehow.

He stands hesitantly.

"Break a leg," I manage, though my throat's gone dry.

René nods, puts on his baseball hat, and walks out the door.

It's almost midnight when I get home. I left the arena and walked for hours. Then I had dinner at a bar with a lively crowd watching a baseball game on a large screen. And by dinner, I mean two glasses of wine and a plate of fried plantains.

Baseball. A cruel, cruel game when you think about it. The pitcher makes it damn-near impossible for the batters to hit the ball. And if they manage to make contact, they're chased down until they're sent back home. When you're playing at the pro level, it takes a miracle to reach first base. Why even bother?

We need to talk. No, it turns out we don't, because I've already filled in the blanks for him. By the time I get home, I know exactly what he would say. *We did have something. I'm glad you see it now, but I've moved on.*

That's why he was trying to stop me from making an even bigger fool of myself. I feel numb and whatever the emotional equivalent is of being run over. But as I get home, it's impossible to avoid my neighbor's party. It spills out of his apartment and onto the front lawn of our building.

"Try this," Pablo says, pouring me a cocktail. He's mixing drinks behind a round table near the front gate. Salsa music is blaring from a large speaker set up outside his front door, and people are dancing under his covered terrace. There are also folks hanging out on the lawn, sitting on the furniture normally set up under the terrace.

"What's in it?" I ask, but then don't bother to wait for a response. It's delicious and strong. *And exactly what I need.*

"Mostly vodka and pisco," he responds, his voice full of excitement. I can see he's glad I've finally arrived. He and Beatriz told me repeatedly how happy they are I'm their new neighbor. They think it's poetic I've moved from Miami to San Juan, when it's typically the other way around. Beatriz especially loves that I work for a record label.

I must look a disheveled mess, but I don't regret telling René how I felt. I'm proud of myself. I would have thought it'd make me feel weaker, but there's a certain sense of peace that comes from knowing I've given it my all. I feel broken, but not in the way I've felt the past few months. Sloughing along, trying to sleep it off, and counting the days until I moved here. Now my heart is broken but I feel alive. I can stand here and see the beauty in all of it. In having new friends, coming home to a party, and the scent of the ocean reaching me every time the breeze picks up.

A tall guy with thick, curly hair walks up to Pablo carrying a small cooler overflowing with ice. "I still don't think this is the best place for the bar. Never too late to move it." Something about his accent and the way he stretches his vowels reminds me of René. It hurts, but at the same time, I want him to keep talking.

Pablo ignores him and focuses instead on preparing another drink.

"I just think it would be better by the apartment so we can get ice and stuff from the fridge."

Pablo waves his cocktail shaker at him vigorously. "Dani, this is Miguel." Pablo pours the drink and hands it to his friend.

Miguel gives me a friendly kiss on the cheek, then sips his drink. "This one turned out better than last time."

Pablo takes a step back, pretending to be insulted. "It's perfect every time."

Miguel waves this off and walks away.

"How are you?" Pablo asks, turning his attention back to me.

"Terrible." I barely know him, but I already feel so comfortable around both Pablo and Beatriz. "I tried to win a guy back tonight, but it didn't work."

"He'll regret it." He winks, then walks off to greet someone who's arrived. His ability to say this to me with a straight face, without any knowledge of who I'm talking about, is so heartwarming, I'm momentarily soothed.

I'm surprised how easy it's been to make friends. I've been here three weeks, and between Pablo and Beatriz, work, and dance class, I've already made more friends than I have in longer than I care to admit. Even with the constant reminders of René, I feel, without a doubt, I'm where I'm supposed to be.

A new song comes on and I recognize René's moans immediately. It has a great, uplifting beat. "Do you know what song this is?" I ask Pablo, who winces as though I'm about to hit him.

"It's from El Rico's leaked album. Beatriz downloaded it. Please don't report us to your job."

I laugh. "The album will be out at midnight. If you promise to buy it in"—I look at my cell—"twenty-two minutes, then I guess it's okay."

"Yes, of course."

"*Mas te vale*," I warn with a smile.

The song revs up and I feel a dull pain in my chest at hearing René's gorgeous, raspy voice. I know all the songs on the album and this is *not* one of them. This must be what Camila was talking about. She mentioned other tracks they meant to release later for a B-side. As I start to sway to the music, I wonder if he wrote it on the island or after he left.

My arms are up over my head and my shoulders are moving. That's the funny thing about reggaeton. I absolutely love it now. I think if you're not willing to budge or let it in, then it's just noise grinding away, taunting you to move. But if you're open, you can step inside its repetitive beats and find a trance that gives you permission to express your sensuality.

I make my way across the lawn to the terrace and set my things down in a corner. It's a proper dance floor. They've cleared everything out except for the hanging plants and twinkle lights.

I shut my eyes, run my fingers through my hair, and let myself move. Feeling raw, I sense the music more than I hear it. When I open my eyes, Beatriz and Pablo and a few of their friends have surrounded me on the dance floor. While the sight is uplifting, there's no denying my sadness.

My heart aches, but I don't stop moving. Certain this will hurt for a while but also that my life will be better for having known René. If anyone ever asks, I will tell them it *is*, in fact, better to have loved and lost. The song ends and I'm out of breath. I wipe off the sweat and tears on my cheek.

You know when you're out on the dance floor and everyone's having a great time, but then another song comes on that makes everyone immediately wilder? That's what happens when "Take it Off," René's duet with Natalia comes on. *Not to me.* As soon as I hear the coqui frog sounds at the beginning of the track, I stop moving. But it's impossible not to savor the pure delirium the song causes in this group. When the dembow rhythm in a deep bass kicks in, I let go.

I decide to try out some of my new moves from dance class. Which aren't many, since so far we've focused mainly on *en pareja*, or couples dancing. And right now, my new friends and I are dancing in a circle and everyone's doing their own thing. I drop down low and come back up, feeling myself in this getup.

Pablo pulls back clumsily. The look on his face is hard to read. Scared? Confused? I mean, I get that I'm just starting out, but I'm not that bad a dancer, am I?

Beatriz is looking at me strangely, too. Miguel has practically stopped dancing. It takes me a moment to realize they're not looking at me. They're looking *behind* me. I turn around and my breath is sucked right out. René is on the dance floor. Lip-syncing to his own song. Looking as though he's supposed to be here and has danced beneath this covered terrace a hundred times. He smiles and reaches for my hand.

Chapter 48

HERE'S WHAT I'VE LEARNED IN DANCE CLASS SO FAR. WHEN you dance *en pareja*, the first thing you need to do is connect with your partner. You do this by matching their pressure. Wherever you and your partner touch as you dance—hands, shoulders, waist, or back—you're meant to push into ever so gently. This is true with salsa and bachata as well. You connect with just enough pressure, so you're both giving. This way you can transmit and receive messages clearly. Everything the teacher said sounded like she was referring to real-life relationships. *Unbreakable bond, open communication, trust.*

I give René my hand and something clicks. In the lapse of time it takes for him to place his free hand on my lower back, and for us to start moving, I have a zillion quick-fire thoughts. *His hair is wet. He must have had a shower at the arena after the concert. Camila must have told him where I lived.*

My moves are instinctive. I'm booty shaking, chest snapping, and body snaking. But everything is close to him. Tight and slow. Romantic, rhythmic reggaeton. His hands are tight on my waist, and up my back, along the holes of my open-knit dress. The feel of his fingertips on my skin sets every part of me on fire. Turns every switch. Heightens all of my senses. Everything rises to the surface like a volcano with multiple heat sources.

I can't stop smiling. Because he's here, of course. But also because I've never danced like this before. This makes me emotional for some reason, but not in a way that stops me from smiling.

After a twirl, he ends up behind me and I lean back, curving my body so it fits into his. My free hands reach for the back of his neck. His hands find my hips and we sway to the music. I don't know why René's here, but I'm not letting myself hope. I am, however, letting him know, without a doubt, how he makes me feel. Whatever I didn't get across with words earlier, I'm saying now.

I press back harder against him and drop my arms down by my sides. I don't need them to stay connected to his body. The song ends with him behind me, wrapped in his arms, his cheek on mine.

"Thank you," he whispers.

"You're welcome."

"So, can we talk?" he asks, pulling away.

It takes a few minutes to get him upstairs. First there are introductions and posing for selfies. All of which René agrees to happily.

"*Que lindo,*" he says, once we're inside my apartment.

"Thanks." Feeling a swell of pride, I give him a quick tour. He stops to admire a photograph I've hung in the kitchen. It's a picture I took of a chicken on the beach who appears to be admiring the sunset in Culebra. I offer him a beer and find myself lingering in front of the open door of the fridge. I'm stalling. After that dance, I don't know if I can handle hearing whatever terrible news he has for me. I may have been able to manage it before, but not now. Now, I need a minute.

Downstairs, the tone of the party has shifted. A mellower song by an Argentine singer I love is playing. As I open the beers, I notice the time on the clock above the stove: 11:55 p.m.

"Shouldn't you be at a launch party? Or outside, avoiding it with someone?"

He smiles but his eyes are sober. "What do you think I'm doing here?"

"I have no idea." I let out a nervous laugh and raise my glass. "To the success of your album."

"To your new life," he says at the same time.

We clink our glasses, and just as they touch, the lights go out. All of them. The kitchen, downstairs, the whole neighborhood. The music has also gone away, leaving only a steady flow of complaints coming from the courtyard below. Enough moonlight comes in through the kitchen window for me to see René's got an eyebrow raised, impressed our glasses tapping may have caused it.

"Do you have any candles?"

"Yeah, I think so." I check the drawers, and find a pack of tea lights. René uses the gas stove to carefully light each one. Together, we place them on small red plates and set them around the kitchen and the rest of the apartment. I try to maintain a safe distance, as though we weren't just all over each other on the dance floor. I meet his gaze a few times, and the tender look in his eyes makes me unsteady. He seems so content to be here, performing each task with the utmost care. Still, I refuse to get swept away. I feel I'm in a hot air balloon, with the blaze blasting, threatening to take off, but still firmly

tied to the ground. René's here being all helpful and looking at me like he wants to light *my* candle, but I know there's
something big he needs to tell me, something he seemed rather
ashamed of back at the arena.

"Are you there?" he calls from the kitchen.

"Yeah." The floor creaks as I walk back into the kitchen. The
room looks otherworldly now. Moonlight through my window-
panes casts a dark green light show on the floor, and the can-
dlelight bouncing off the red plates pours a soft pink glow on
everything. Including René. Who's leaning against the kitchen
counter, watching me. I can feel my resistance weakening. Even
in the dimly lit room, his dark eyes have the power to warm
up my whole body. I stop across from him and press my hip
against the small wooden dining table to steady myself.

"What happened out there? I thought you couldn't dance."
He seems poised to move toward me.

I huff, brushing off the compliment. I want so much to let
myself float off in this moment, but my hot air balloon has got
a few pesky ropes still binding it to the ground. "Look, I know
you have something you want to say, and believe me, it's okay.
Just tell me what it is. I'll be fine."

"Right." His face drops. "The thing is, Dani—"

The music comes back on outside, bringing the party to life
again. But when René hears the song that's playing, he lets out
a disgruntled sigh.

I turn away and try the kitchen light switch a few times,
but it doesn't work. "They must have speakers with batteries or
something," I grumble as I turn back to face him.

"That"—René drops his chin and points out the window—
"is what I needed to talk to you about."

I look out the window, confused. "What is?"

"That song."

I step toward him, closer to the window, and tune in. There's a lone acoustic guitar playing amid the sounds of waves crashing. I've never heard it before, but something about the melody sounds familiar. "Is this another one you're including on the B-side?"

"Yes. Well, I want to." He seems pained.

"I'm sorry about that. My neighbors told me they ripped off the album before we pulled it down, but they promised to—"

"No, no, I'm the one that's sorry, Dani. I meant to ask for your permission, and for your mother's, of course. But I kept going back and forth about including it. I thought you didn't want to talk to me." He speaks with urgency.

"What are you—" Then all of my muscles loosen. The sound of tapping. The distinct rhythm. Metal on wood. My dad rapping his ring on the side of his conga drum. Then, René's raspy, sexy voice comes through the window.

I've been around the world, but home's never felt this far away
I want to hear your voice and ask you
why I couldn't make you stay
I want to write you a love song, an old-style,
make you dance in the kitchen love song
Because I want good things to happen for you,
but it's killing me I can't be one

My vision's gone blurry with tears, but I can feel René watching me, desperate for a reaction.

I know I've been hiding, but now I'm done
You've been hiding too, takes one to know one

Can we meet away from the shadows
Where I've come to write you a love song

When it's time for the pre-chorus, it's my father's deep, comforting voice that merges the song into something more folkloric and traditional.

Meet me at the dock under the sea
Dancing bomba on the beach
The way you were meant to be
Wild and free

I'm doubly struck—to be hearing his voice at all, and by how crisp and clear it sounds. Like they've run the old cassette recording through some revolutionary refining tools.

"I thought I'd add one more collaboration to the album." René sounds contrite.

"I love it." The tears spill over and wet my cheeks. "I can't believe you did this..." I trail off, yearning to listen to the chorus.

Look what you've done, you made El Rico write a love song
Say things like I'm lost without you, you're the only one
But if the road ever leads me back to you
I'll never leave, 'cause wherever you are is my country
Wherever we are is home

I reach for him just as he steps forward to wipe away my tears, and we end up wrapped in a tight embrace, swaying to the song.

It's a deeply sweet, pull-at-your-heartstrings love song. My dad missing home, René missing me. At times, their voices are accompanied only by René's acoustic guitar and my father's conga.

"Look what you've done," René whispers in my ear when the chorus repeats. "You made El Rico write a love song." I can't help but hold him closer. "It was hard to write. The toughest one for me ever."

"Really?" I look up at him, basking in the heat of our bodies.

He nods. "Turns out admitting you miss someone is harder than writing about having foursomes with people you've never met."

"Go figure," I say as I laugh. "You know, Radiohead puts some of their best stuff on the B-sides."

"Oh, do they?" he mocks, pretending to be jealous. The song ends and we're left looking at each other. "I wanted..." He trails off. "This just isn't how I wanted you to find out."

"I'm glad it was like this."

"And we *did* get to dance in the kitchen."

"Yeah." I note the coincidence and feel a tingle up and down my arms. I think back to all the happy accidents that had to happen to bring us here.

The person on my father's dock becoming visible only when I printed the image large enough.

The fishing boat passing by just as that part of the song played when I was ready to hear it.

The guy whose position I took over, deciding it was time to open a yoga shop.

Camila walking by just as I was returning with groceries, and then telling René where I lived.

Do I suddenly believe in magic? I guess I don't *not* believe. Maybe I'm one of those magic agnostics. Let's just say I won't be turning down an egg cleansing the next time someone offers.

"There's something else I wanted to ask you." He pulls his phone out of his back pocket. "But that's another song," he says, tapping quickly into his cell.

Having found what he was looking for, he places the phone on the kitchen counter and hits play.

The punk rock guitars throw me. I squint, trying to identify the song. Then the lyrics begin and René doesn't lip sync or sing along. He barely moves.

The Ramones' "I Wanna Be Your Boyfriend" is the type of song that leaves little room for misinterpretation.

A smile spreads across my face as I approach him. He pushes forward and kisses me just as Joey Ramone asks for an answer. "Yes," I respond, my lips pressed to his. A rush of excitement shoots through me. "You know"—I pull away—"eventually you'll have to actually say something. You can't *always* let a song speak for you."

He grins and slips his fingers through the loops in my dress, pulling me closer. Resolutely, he lifts me up and sets me on the table, positioning his body between my legs.

"We'll see." He lifts his chin cockily.

My fingers slide slowly down his arms. He takes my hands, our fingers intertwining, and kisses me again. Whatever was still holding me to the ground comes undone.

Acknowledgments

Picture me standing on a rooftop giving this shout-out to the entire team at Forever, especially my editor, Sabrina Flemming. Your feedback was so spot on. Writing this book has given me so many gifts, and having the chance to collaborate with you was one of the best. I loved every single moment of it.

I am so grateful to my agent and guardian angel, Liz Nealon at Great Dog Literary. Thank you for reading and rereading this book, for your steady guidance, and for your confidence in me.

I am so lucky to have another career that I love. A million "thank you"s to Tom Cappello and Keely Walker Muse at Crazy Legs Productions. It's thanks to your support and flexibility that I was able to continue working while also having the time to write this book.

I'd be a nervous, shapeless pile of moosh without my beta readers. Jose Antonio Hernandez, thank you for being such a great reader and for sharing your extensive music business expertise. *And for laughing at all my jokes.* Luisa Varona, I'd be lost without your directness and experience with reggaeton artists. Kathleen Rajsp, your support and cheerleading on this one will forever hold a special place in my heart. Grettel Jimenez Singer, thank you for being there for me on the days I was losing steam. I am so grateful to have best friends that also happen to be writers. We get to commiserate, talk craft, and go on writing trips together. I think all of this proves I did good things in a past life.

For me, writing is a solitary, time-consuming passion. The importance of having a family that respects my goals and gives me an understanding nod and a smile every time I say "I can't, I need to write" cannot be overstated. I love you, Gabby, Grey, Ralph, Tommy, Barbie, Maytee, and Mel.

I want to send a heartfelt "thank you" to my readers and devoted bookstagrammers who connected with my first book and have been anticipating this one. I have also been moved beyond words by the many Puerto Rican readers who have reached out to me, excitedly awaiting representation in rom. com form.

And the biggest "thank you" goes to my Papito. Thank you for helping me with this book. I'm immensely grateful for the opportunity it gave me to learn more about your life in Puerto Rico and how you grew up. Thanks to you, I will forever be half Puerto Rican in my heart.

About the Author

Lissette Decos is a Cuban-American executive television producer with over twenty years' experience in reality TV formats of the love-wedding-relationship-disaster variety. Shows such as TLC's *Say Yes to the Dress*, *90 Day Fiancé*, and Bravo's *Summer House* have been molded by Decos's expertise in telling an engaging and oftentimes unconventional love story. In addition to her stint in the "unreal" world of reality TV, Lissette also spent a decade in New York as a staff producer for MTV, which helped her hone her expertise in all things pop culture, while searching for love in the big city. You might say she's got the story and the soundtrack for romantic angst down.

Find out more at:
LissetteDecos.com
Instagram @LissetteDecos